NOT AN ORDINARY DEATH

SHARON SCARBOROUGH

PUBLISHERS NOTE

All rights reserved under International and Pan American Copyright Conventions. Published in the United States by Enchanted Indie Press, LLC. No part of these pages, either text or image may be used for any purpose other than personal use. Therefore, reproduction, modification, storage in a retrieval system or retransmission, in any form or by any means, electronic, mechanical or otherwise, for reasons other than personal use, is strictly prohibited without prior written permission.

Copyright © 2019 Sharon Scarborough

**Cover design and interior formatting
for print and digital editions:**
Tosh McIntosh

Front cover background photo:
Zack Frank via shutterstock

**Published in the
United States of America by
Enchanted Indie Press**

Digital Edition (v1.0)
ISBN-13: 978-1-938749-41-4
ISBN-10: 1-938749-41-3

Print Edition (v1.0)
ISBN-13: 978-1-938749-40-7
ISBN-10: 1-938749-40-5

To
Steve and Larry,
cowboys who rescued me

AUTHOR'S NOTES

About the Subject

It is presumptuous of a writer to think he or she can teach the reader anything. I try and entertain a reader and hope I present enough of a mystery to make a reader pause to figure out who dunit?

That being said, any novel has something at the core and family has been on my mind. Therefore, much of this is about family.

About the Setting

This is a work of fiction and Broken Rock and Obsidian do not exist. The people, too, do not exist but are products of my own imaginings.

A SPECIAL NOTE ABOUT TEXAS RANGER BADGES AND THE COVER

Larger than the Lone Star State itself, Texas history reflects a combination of fact, fantasy, and legend, especially with regard to the story of the Texas Rangers and the wide variety of badges they wore from their beginning in 1823 until 1935, when the first official badge arrived on the scene, and continuing to the present day with a new badge used from 1938 thru 1957, and changed again in 1962.

Cover design for *A Promise of Water* symbolically reflects the four most important elements of the story: drought, murder, a *promise* of water that hasn't yet arrived, and, of course, our hero, retired Texas Ranger Oswald Nightingale. No other symbol can so effectively characterize Nightingale's role in the story, so it seemed to be a simple matter of finding a suitable image of a badge. The variety of possibilities that appeared within milliseconds of initiating a search, however, made the task of choosing one anything but simple.

The Texas Ranger Hall of fame and Museum website offers a fascinating article titled, "A Short Course on Fantasy, Replica, and Toy Texas Ranger Badges," directed specifically at folks who would like to own an authentic badge from the legendary law enforcement agency. But the fact is that there are very few genuine Texas Ranger badges, and unfortunately, a brisk and fraudulent market exists in which scam artists offer badges with fake certificates of authenticity.

The badge image chosen for the cover is clearly labeled as an

"Old West Obsolete Texas Rangers Company B" replica, with detailed information about how the badges are manufactured. And while no one can claim that the seller is offering it as genuine, the word "replica" would indicate that it is a duplicate of a real badge. According to the Museum article, however, this is one variation on what is known as an "1890's flag badge," and the wreaths are from a design found after 1961. This badge is no more authentic than the ones made from five or ten peso coins (as early authentic badges often were) and sold online with claims of being the real thing, in spite of the clearly visible evidence on the rear of the badge that it was made from a coin minted in 1947 or '48. The caution, "Buyer beware!" apparently is too often ignored.

For the purposes of cover design, the image need not reflect a genuine badge to carry the message that *A Promise of Water* is about a Texas Ranger. He's not a real Texas Ranger, of course, and it seems appropriately respectful of those who are for our hero to wear a fictional version representative of this unique law enforcement agency.

PRAISE FOR *A PROMISE OF WATER*

A great success for a debut novel, *A Promise of Water* by Sharon Scarborough is a character-driven Western that follows the life and the scuffles of a small town in Texas, a beautiful meld of a gritty investigation and political conflict.

Christian Sia, Reader's Favorite

Nightingale is a terrific character and with Garrick, the combination is dynamic. An excellent story that leaves you hoping Scarborough will write more!

Melinda Hills, Reader's Favorite

I really enjoy a good mystery story without the use of excessive violence, sex or strong language. If you prefer good, simple mysteries, then this book is for you.

Paul F Johnson, Reader's Favorite

1

At sunup, Oswald Nightingale stood on the cold prairie ground, taking in the area where millions of years ago a glacier had skidded and bucked to scoop out a basin of twenty-five rolling acres in the Texas flatlands. Misshapen mesquite trees tried to be impressive, standing on the brown dirt with hummocks of bunch grasses their only companions. The trees were scraggly and the grasses only waist high, so it was easy to see the skeletons of six new houses that dotted the acres and looked like orphans. When he cocked his head a little, the land undulated so that the pending subdivision offered small hills and valleys to the future residents, a piece of real estate that other people would envy.

Whoever dreamed up Mesa Heights deserved some credit. They had found a piece of ground that was different in these flattened plains.

A cold November wind whipped across the newly paved roads, encouraging him to pull his leather jacket tighter. By noon the temperature would be toasty; it wasn't there yet.

A turtle dove cooed in the distance. Nightingale liked it out here. Almost couldn't hear the interstate thirty miles away. Small dust clouds puffed around his boots as he plodded back to the truck, where he climbed back in and began the slow drive through the subdivision. Hopeful, he glanced in the rear-view mirror. Still no sign of his cousins.

His phone rang. Imogene didn't wait for a hello. Even in a hurry, her words were rounded and slow in coming. "Sorry we're running late, Oswald. Did I tell you which house it was? Take several rights and you'll see it. It's the one at the end of Wagon Wheel Drive. See you soon." She hung up.

He shook his head in exasperation. They wanted him here but couldn't be on time themselves. He'd gotten up early to be on time so Portia wouldn't be angry with him. It figured. Thank goodness the soft-spoken Imogene stood between them.

Some enterprising person had hand-lettered a sign at the intersection. Wagon Wheel Drive was the right-hand turn. About 100 yards straight ahead, on a cul-de-sac, was Portia and Imogene's new home.

Nightingale parked and stepped out of the truck. Somehow this wasn't what he had thought he'd see. The one-story house seemed to hug the ground and looked more modern than he'd expected. Tall windows faced him. The front door hung open. White siding covered one end of the house. The hip roof had decking but no shingles on the front. He stared for a moment. Squinting his eyes to clear his vision, he tried to assess what he had expected, tried to tamp down his frugal nature. How could these women afford such a house?

A buzzing noise and then the sharp screech of a hawk caught his attention. Looking behind, he thought he saw the shadow of the hawk as it flew over, before he turned back to stare at the roof.

A flash of light at the peak of the roof caught his eye. Was it a spark or a reflection? Whatever he had seen, it was over the southwest end of the roof.

He leaned forward and blinked. Nothing. Had to be a floater. Too high for anything else. God, how he hated aging. Not fifty yet but maybe time to get the eyes checked.

When he walked to the opposite end of the house, he saw a 1957 red and white Ford truck with no front plates had pulled up close, almost behind the house. He'd seen no other vehicles, but he wondered why he heard no hammer or clink of tools. Maybe the truck had been left overnight. Certainly would be safe enough out here with only rabbits and rattlesnakes.

Retracing his steps, he walked to the front door, which had swung shut, gave it three hard knocks, and yelled, "Hey, anybody home?"

He heard nothing, so he stepped inside. The living area had a vaulted ceiling and flowed into the dining room and kitchen. No drywall. Electrical and plumbing connections showed as raw pipes and wiring in the walls. A hall just off the kitchen led to a large bedroom with a huge bathroom and closet. Then another bath in the hall. He took his time, imagining the finished rooms. The house was built on a slab, so the floor walked hard. His boots tapped lightly on the subfloor, causing an echo in the spacious rooms. At the end of the hall was another huge bedroom and bath.

French doors led off this bedroom. As he opened the door and stepped out, he saw a tennis shoe that looked like it still had a foot inside it. Another step, and he stopped. A man's body lay on the concrete slab that would become a patio off the bedroom. His torso twisted unnaturally; he was not asleep.

Nightingale drew in a breath and felt his heart quicken. He'd seen dozens of bodies, but he never got over the shock of seeing a corpse for the first time. And that was when the body was expected. This was totally unexpected. He squatted and tried to find a pulse. Nothing. But the body was still warm.

He stood, backed away half a step, and began to take in details, assess what had happened. A safety rope swung against the roof, attached at the ridge. A tall ladder leaned against the house. Apparently, the man had been on the roof. He was young, probably in his late twenties or early thirties. He wore blue jeans, a long-sleeved blue shirt. A tiny trickle of blood came from his mouth. A pool of blood had formed under his head. Nightingale reached for his phone, then hesitated.

How long had the man been here, and had he fallen when Nightingale was in front of the house? Surely there would have been a noise.

Nightingale continued to look for evidence to clarify what had happened. He scanned the area for a hard hat. Nothing. He looked for a cell phone. Again, nothing. A wide belt with assorted tools wrapped around the man, but the safety harness Nightingale had expected was nowhere in sight. Maybe the fellow was just starting the day and hadn't gotten all his gear on.

As he stood, Nightingale turned and looked to the south, then to the north, scanning the horizon. His eye caught movement on the northern edge of the horizon. A lone horseman rode along the ridge slowly, and despite the distance, Nightingale felt the rider's gaze fixed on the land where he stood, exactly on the spot that he and the dead man shared.

He was unable to see the rider clearly. He turned to the house to fix in his mind where he was standing, and when he turned back, the rider had disappeared.

"Oswald, where are you?" Portia stuck her head out the back door. "What are—" She stopped midsentence and held her hand against the door frame so Imogene couldn't pass. Then they both pushed forward.

The women stood, shocked and silent for a moment, taking

in the contorted body and twisted neck of the man on the ground.

"Oh, Joshua," Portia said. Tears began to trickle down her face, bothering Nightingale more than he wanted to admit. Before he could stop the women, they pushed him aside and hovered over the body. They looked like sisters, instead of cousins, there to care. At five-foot six, Imogene was taller and thinner than Portia, who was three inches shorter, her frame well-padded, solid.

Imogene had on her nurse's scrubs. Her green eyes darted along the length of the body, gathering data, Nightingale guessed. She knelt, placed fingers against the dead man's neck, picked up his wrist. She shook her head. "No pulse, but he's still warm." She stared at the body. "I want to close his eyes, but I know I shouldn't."

"No, even though it's an accident, the sheriff will want to see things as they are now. Looks like he fell," Nightingale said. "Can you tell anything about how long he's been dead?" At his side, he heard Portia shudder and sob.

Imogene touched one of the man's fingers lightly and said, "I'd guess less than three hours." She stood and patted Portia's shoulder.

"You knew him?" Nightingale asked.

"Yes," Portia said. "We do not live under a bushel basket, Oswald." Her words were short, aggravated. "We had met him. As young as he is, why didn't he survive a fall from there?" Her hands shook, and she waved a hand toward the roof, glaring at Nightingale as if he should know why the man was dead.

Imogene slid her arm tighter around Portia, who drew in another shuddering breath.

"I'm sure Oz is acting as a law officer should," Imogene said to her cousin. Then she looked at Nightingale. "We've watched Joshua work. He was good, cautious. Strange that he was out this early." She gave voice to what Nightingale had been thinking.

They stood at the body even after he urged them to go inside. All he could do was keep them away from the body, so he stood with them and called Emergency Services. He had punched in the number for the sheriff's office when Portia took off her jacket and started to lay it over the man.

"Portia, please, don't do that," Nightingale said.

She said nothing, but the look she turned on him was venomous.

"This was not an ordinary death," he said. "I know you care about the man, but believe me, the sheriff will want everything as we found it."

Imogene had stepped aside. She shook her head and shrugged. "Portia, let me help you put your jacket back on. We can't afford for you or me to be sick. Let's go inside."

"I feel so sorry for him. He was just a child at heart, don't you agree?" Portia asked. She glanced at Imogene, who said nothing.

When the women went in the rear entrance, Nightingale hurried around the house to his truck and, working quickly, pulled on latex gloves, then went to the red and white truck that he'd seen earlier. The vehicle was not locked, and the keys were still in the ignition. One of them opened the glove box, where he found a variety of screwdrivers, new paintbrushes, and tattered gloves.

The only thing that showed any promise was a folded and yellowed piece of paper with a phone number on it. He scribbled the number on his palm and returned everything to the glove box. A quick peek under the seat showed nothing else, so he put the keys back and shut the door. He'd hurried with the search, so his walk back to his cousins was slow and measured with several deep breaths.

When he opened the front door, the women stood on one

side of the living room, close to what would be their kitchen. Nightingale went to them. "The sheriff may want to talk to you, since you knew the man, or you can tell me what you know about him, and I'll relay the information." He looked at both women, trying to avoid conflict with Portia.

To his surprise, Portia snuffled and started talking. This time she was soft-spoken, not angry. "We didn't know him really well. I met him just after we'd picked the lot and selected the floor plan. I left school early one day and swung by here. We were so happy about buying a new house…"

She looked at Imogene, who gave a tiny smile and took over the story. "I was standing at the street the first time I saw it, and I'm sure I looked dumbfounded. To me it was a worksite with a trench around it." She drew in a ragged breath before continuing. "This horrible old truck—the one parked out there—pulled up, and a young man got out and introduced himself. It was Joshua. He explained what footings were, and I said it would be handy to have him around to explain the building process."

As the sound of an ambulance siren grew louder, they walked to the front door and then out to their car. At their car, Nightingale said, "I'll tell the sheriff what you said about Joshua. Did you know his last name?"

"Tallman," Imogene said. "He thought that was funny. He wasn't that tall."

After promising his cousins he would update them later, he walked over to meet the sheriff and EMTs who had parked their vehicles behind his truck. The sheriff, he saw, was Dan Brewster from Lubbock. He and Brewster had been acquaintances, almost friends, but had worked together on only one case.

As they started around the house to the back, Brewster got right to business. "What are you doing here, Oswald?"

"I found the dead man. This is my cousins' house, and he seems to have fallen off their roof. They were here—just left—

and told me they had met him. Said his name was Joshua Tallman, according to what he told them."

They'd reached the body and stood over it. "Didn't look like he had safety gear," Brewster said. "Must have been an accident. What do you think?"

"Seems odd," Nightingale said. "Will you get a coroner's report?" So far, they were just two men discussing work. Nightingale wondered if Brewster knew he still had a position with the Texas Rangers. Probably. Rangers were like other people, and gossip about job status was high on the list of topics for conversation.

"Let's get back to my truck." Brewster moseyed around the house and toward his vehicle, chewing a cigar butt, contemplating something, but not sharing the subject. After a bit, he said, "This little enclave of houses has caused a bit of a stir. It straddles two counties and made a few headaches because of zoning. Anyway, I'm pretty busy right now. What's your work status?"

"I have some time." Nightingale decided that Brewster knew about his resignation from the Rangers, but he didn't know how much more the sheriff had been told. The detective business had mustered up one client, and then the governor called him to be a Special Ranger. He traveled to east Texas to work for the governor, and he had purpose. It was so simple—all he'd needed was a job.

"We'll take the body in with us. I'll let you know what we find on him. Keep in touch," Brewster said. He got into his truck and drove off, leaving his men to finish.

Nightingale walked back toward the house. Never hurt to get a second look.

As Brewster's men taped off the area, he heard the words "must have slipped" and "poor guy." They, like their boss, thought they were studying an accident, but something about the scene didn't ring true to Nightingale. Might be getting too sympathetic in his old age. Might also be that he needed work, something to keep busy. But the dead man had crystal clear blue eyes, the Paul Newman eyes that you couldn't forget, and even in death, he looked perplexed.

Everyone died with a different look, and this young man was certainly surprised—expected, of course, if he slipped and fell. But there was more here, a sense of confusion. That first thought had been good: perplexed. And that made the whole business strange. Again Nightingale wondered, was he just trying to find excuses to be busy?

He looked to the edge of the land where he had seen the man on horseback. Nothing.

He walked to the end of the house he had been facing when he saw the flash of light. The dry dirt and tufts of weeds didn't look thick enough to hide anything, but Nightingale walked back and forth, moving aside the Indiangrass and tall prairie dropseed with his foot, trying to find anything unusual. He hadn't mentioned the light to the sheriff because he wasn't sure that he really saw something. Now he was glad he'd said nothing. He moved to the outer edges of the lot while the sheriff's men looked and mumbled. If they had an enlightened theory of what went wrong, he figured Brewster would tell him.

An assistant to the coroner had shown up after the other emergency personnel. That meant he'd have to wait on the Medical Examiner's report for anything definitive.

After the last person had left, Nightingale returned to the rear of the house, squatted and looked at the small pool of blood. Joshua Tallman had landed on concrete, and his head had cracked enough for blood to seep out.

Nightingale stood and looked again toward the mesa. If the rider saw the fall, maybe he could shed some light on the circumstances. But there was no horseman.

It was almost noon. He walked through the house to the outside, wondering about bloodstains in concrete. As he approached the truck, his phone rang. He expected Portia to be inquiring about details on the dead man, but another female voice said, "Hello, Mr. Nightingale. Can you talk?"

2

"Good morning, Governor. Good to hear from you." He got in the truck and talked as he settled in. "I have some questions for you."

"I'll be glad to listen," Governor Patricia Daniels said. "But, first, I hope you haven't found new employment. I have another job for you."

Nightingale didn't immediately answer. He had a bad taste from his last encounter with the governor. She owed him explanations. But he also needed a job.

"I thought I had a job, but it looks like no one told the Ranger office here. I called the chief, and he said no one had contacted him. I'm still a Special Ranger to him, but I need you to verify that."

"I'm sorry," she said. "I hope it hasn't been unpleasant for you. I didn't know, quite honestly, what you wanted to do, so I haven't pushed about your rank. And if you can help me now, your status as a Special Ranger will be fine."

Nightingale doubted that the governor could empathize with his concerns, but he had never been comfortable arguing with a woman, so he listened.

"There is a man out your way who has bought a large acreage and built a house, which he has surrounded with fences and wild animals." The governor paused, and Nightingale heard a murmur in the background. "The man's name is Edgar Post. You may have heard of him. He's quite wealthy, deals in the stock market. A Yankee, but a good man nevertheless." She gave an artificial laugh.

"Don't think I've heard of him," Nightingale said.

"I'm told he tries to stay out of the public eye. However, he has offered his services as an investment counselor to the state for our retirement system. I want to know what you can find out about him. Public corruption is a subject bandied about easily, especially when it comes to state finances and friends of those in charge. I don't want charges of any sort of illegality to sully my time in office."

"How do you propose I do this?" Nightingale asked, trying to sound reasonable while seeing the challenge. "I'm sure you can get his tax returns quicker than I can."

"It will take more than tax returns. Just go talk to him for the time being. Why did he decide to settle out there in a near-desert? What does he want at this stage of his life? I've heard one thing, but I wonder what he would tell a man."

"Hm. Do I tell him you sent me?"

"We'll see. I told him we had to have background checks. He'll probably figure out your role. If he asks, then you may tell him."

"Is there anything you're not telling me?" Such a loaded question, but not telling was what the governor was good at.

"If you get into Austin we'll talk more. Will you help me out?"

"How about I call you tomorrow?"

"I see." The lady's voice changed a bit. In two words, she

became less cordial, less the friend, and probably more genuine. She usually got her way, but in this case, she would wait.

"I'll call tomorrow," Nightingale said. "Afternoon, ma'am." With that, he pushed the red button, but the governor had already ended the call.

He had a lot of thinking to do, and he needed to talk to Stanley Stockbridge.

∽

Broken Rock, Texas, reminded Nightingale of a movie set out of an oater. The town consisted of a Main Street and several short streets leading off into smaller paved paths with a few houses, or, if the street was long enough, into a state-owned highway. Most of the population of Broken Rock and Obsidian, next door, worked in Lubbock. Obsidian actually was more of a thought, a dream, a bump in the road, since the post office had closed and the population had to get their mail and groceries from Broken Rock.

Main Street had a couple of antique stores, a drug store, a feed store for animal supplies, a Dollar General, a doctor's office (which the doctor attended three days a week), and the office of the weekly newspaper, *The Broken Rock Intelligencer*. In the opposite direction at the end of the street stood a Catholic church, the oldest building in the county, surrounded by several twisted mesquite trees. Trying not to be outdone, Baptist and Methodist churches sat on side streets.

When Nightingale walked into Stanley Stockbridge's office, the publisher grunted, "I'll be done in a minute. Pull up a chair." Stockbridge claimed to be seventy years old. Nightingale didn't know if he believed that. The man had salt-and-pepper hair, a pudgy tummy from his desk job, and the slow voice of a true

Texan. He was engrossed in his two-finger method of getting out an editorial. The ancient Underwood typewriter clicked along, sometimes breaking into a clatter of ticks as thoughts flowed faster. Finally, he turned to Nightingale, who had taken his suggestion and sat. "Any luck on that story for me?"

Nightingale felt the heat of embarrassment rise. He smiled sheepishly, thinking of his school days standing before a favorite teacher. After he had resigned as a Ranger, he had questioned Stockbridge about what it took to be a writer. Stockbridge had suggested he write a feature for the paper, any subject, but of interest to Broken Rock readers.

Nightingale shifted in his chair. "It's harder than I thought, but I'll do it. I'm not here about that. I need to know about a man who moved in north of here. Edgar Post. Ever heard of him?"

Stockbridge raised bushy eyebrows and smiled. "Why do you want to know?"

"That's not much of an answer," Nightingale said, "but I'm curious about a man who has the money to move here and buy acres and acres of dry dirt and build a mansion on it. I haven't heard if he has ties with oil."

Stockbridge pushed back from his desk and went to a filing cabinet, from which he pulled a thin folder. "Don't forget: his mansion is surrounded with a fence that makes the border wall look shabby, and there's going to be a whole herd of exotic animals. It's hard to get information on Mr. Post, but I, too, was curious. This is off the internet, so I don't know if any of it is true."

Nightingale scooted his chair closer, took the folder, and opened it. The first article was from the *Baltimore Review* and was a general piece on a day in the life of a hedge fund manager, a list of best and worst of the species, and a tongue-in-cheek assessment of how much money one had to have to start dealing in hedge funds.

The second article was a short interview in *Business World Today* asking for Post's prediction for the future of hedge funds.

Neither article had photos. Stockbridge had a Wikipedia printout that reported Post was in his second marriage, had three children, and was a reluctant source for interviews but a firm star in the financial world.

"Looks like his biggest sin is making a butt-load of money," Nightingale said.

Stockbridge leaned back in his chair. "I have a friend on the Chicago stock exchange. I'd be interested to see what he says. But before I call him, I'm asking you again, why do you want to know?"

"Stanley, don't call anyone on my account. I was just curious. My cousins are buying a house in the Mesa Heights subdivision. I heard from some folks that someone with money had landed in that area north of Obsidian, and we all wondered."

"Yeah, building a house that covers almost an acre gets attention even without the fence. Seems like humans never get tired of ogling other humans with money."

"Any excuse for some questions and the possibility of gossip." Nightingale stood and pushed his chair back. "Thanks again. Gotta be going. By the way, do you know anything about the developer who's building those houses in Mesa Heights?"

"I think he built in Lubbock and maybe Sedona before starting here," Stockbridge said.

Nightingale left the folder on Stockbridge's desk. He'd check the internet when he got home. And, he didn't want to seem too curious to Stockbridge. That was why he threw in the question about the builder. One reason Stanley was a good editor was his curiosity. No need to feed his habit.

In the front office, a woman in her thirties was talking to the young man who covered sports for the paper. Both of them looked at him expectantly as he left the editor's office.

Nightingale heard the phrase, "You can go in now," and wondered who the attractive stranger was.

3

After he left the newspaper, Nightingale went to the corner gas station that had everything from toilet paper to motor oil and ordered a chicken leg and potato wedge for lunch. He walked to his truck, placed the brown paper bag, already dotted with grease spots, on a napkin on the seat beside him, and headed home.

The truck almost drove itself while he thought of the dead man and the governor's request. At the stop sign where he usually turned toward Sutton Garrick's house, he paused longer than necessary but decided to tell Garrick about the dead man and the governor's new assignment after he knew more. They had worked as partners for several years; now, after Nightingale had quit the Rangers, they still worked together and under the wing of the law enforcement agency because of the governor's various requests.

At his house, Bandit, the puppy he'd found in east Texas a few months earlier, smelled the chicken but got a single treat. After his own quick lunch, Nightingale told Bandit to go play and went to his office and turned on his computer. The machine was slow, and he had never felt comfortable with it. It was out of date, but it would help if he invested in a better internet connection. This was not the time to learn a new PC. Later, he promised himself.

His next step was to see what he could find on Edgar Post. Apparently, the name was not popular. He'd have to get access to the Ranger database. He called the office to check with Bob Gilbert regarding access to the information. Gilbert was out. Nightingale would have to call back.

Next, he plugged in the name Joshua Tallman. This posed the opposite problem. So many men were named Joshua that he quit looking for similarities.

He had shifted his attention to emails when the phone rang, and Imogene asked him to join them for supper. He had put them off too long. Feeling only slightly guilty—he had hoped he'd find out more about the dead man—he said, "I'd love to have supper with you. It'll take me a minute to get ready."

Imogene laughed. "Just come as you are and bring Bandit. I won't guarantee hot biscuits, but you'll get some fresh vegetables."

Nightingale didn't tell her how cold biscuits would be fine. In the back of his mind, he was glad to hear his cousin's voice, which sounded more upbeat than he had anticipated.

He wanted to ask about Portia but didn't. In the last few weeks, Portia had become increasingly barbed in her comments to him. 'Course they didn't see each other that much, so he didn't know when she had changed. He couldn't remember anything he'd done to deserve her ire.

Portia tended to worry, and he could tell from the encounter at the new house that she cared for the dead man, whether she would admit it or not and in spite of the fact that she said she barely knew him.

He changed jeans and shirt, fed Bandit, and they were soon on their way. He took the long way 'round to finally wind up at Portia and Imogene's house in Obsidian just as darkness was settling. After Bandit licked and wagged his way through the house, Nightingale put him outside to play in the backyard and went back into the kitchen.

Earlier, the women had opened the doors and windows to the warmth of the November afternoon. By now that warmth had dissipated to around sixty degrees and required closing windows. After he'd done that, Nightingale took the lemonade and whiskey drink that Imogene handed him and watched his cousins in a nervous, uncoordinated display of food prep.

He stood to the side while Imogene put plates and silverware down, and Portia took a stewer off the stove and poured black-eyed peas from it into a bowl. She set a bowl of creamed potatoes on the table, and from somewhere Imogene brought out a plate filled with pieces of chicken-fried steak. Imogene poured three glasses of wine, and she and Portia sat down. They sighed, and Nightingale did the same.

Nightingale waited for the serenity he usually felt when visiting to replace the tension in the air. Peace did not come. He decided they were all still bothered by the young man's death.

Portia handed him the platter of steak, followed by gravy, and they began passing bowls, filling their plates. When her hand touched his she said, "I'm sorry about my rudeness at the house."

Nightingale didn't want a big discussion. "It was a bad thing you saw. Try to forget it if you can." He went on to compliment potatoes, Jell-O salad, peas, and meat. He ate a few bites before he noticed that his cousins were not eating much. Portia was stabbing peas, taking a bite, and a drink of wine. She looked at Imogene and quickly glanced away. Imogene favored tasting the potatoes and then a sip of wine, with an exaggerated use of her napkin against a lack of lipstick.

Nightingale was determined not to ask what was wrong. Instead, he said, "I may need seconds on the peas and potatoes." Imogene almost sprang from her chair. He slowly looked at each woman, neither of whom would look at him. He was surprised that Imogene's hands were not shaking, with all the tension in the room.

Imogene took his plate. The bowl of peas had wound up close to her, so she started spooning up peas and talking. "Did you get any information on the dead man we found this morning?"

"Not yet," Nightingale said. He took the plate, now refilled with vegetables, but his appetite had waned. "Do you have any peach preserves? I think I'd like that and a biscuit."

Portia stood and went to the refrigerator, where she pulled out a Mason jar of glistening yellow peach preserves. "The biscuits are cold. Do you want one microwaved?" She placed the jar on the table.

"No, this is fine," he said.

Imogene placed a salad plate in front of him for the biscuit and sweets. She took his plate of vegetables to the counter by the sink, where she began filling small Tupperware bowls with leftover vegetables, while Portia dished out peach preserves on a saucer. No one said anything, and Nightingale felt a pre-storm tension building.

After she'd finished putting food in containers, Imogene backed up against the sink, crossed her arms, and stared at Portia as if her words would give strength to her female cousin. "Portia has something to tell you."

Portia had sat back down and now stared at her folded hands on the oilcloth-covered table. Nightingale turned to her, not knowing what he expected. She didn't speak immediately. She still had on her school-teacher's uniform, a navy shirtwaist dress, but she'd removed any jewelry and wore tennis shoes.

She looked Nightingale straight in the eye in teacher-mode. "I think the young man you found today had what you call foul play done to him. I think he was murdered."

Nightingale carefully put the remainder of the biscuit on the plate and pushed his drink aside. "Could I have some coffee, please?"

Apparently, Imogene had anticipated his request. He heard a switch flip, then water bubbling into the grounds. He folded his napkin, trying to think through what he would say. He didn't want to dismiss Portia's words immediately, but his first inclination was that her heart was ruling her head. So he returned her direct stare. "What makes you think that?"

At his words, her cheeks got pink. Her forehead wrinkled.

"The sheriff seemed convinced that it was an accident," he said.

Still standing at the sink, Imogene threw one hand in the air. "Portia, you must be specific. He can't read your mind."

"All right." Portia sighed, switched the fold of her hands. "He talked to me, Oswald. A lot. I felt like I might be the mother he never had."

"Start at the beginning. You met him up at the building site? Do I remember that right?"

"Yes," she said. "We decided that he could guide us through the building of the house."

"Do you think he gave you his real name?" Nightingale encouraged her.

Portia nodded, then threw her wadded napkin on the table. "Oh, I hate this. You think I'm crazy and gullible. Real name indeed."

"I think no such thing," Nightingale said. "But you have to give me some specific reasons as to why you think someone would hurt him."

Portia stood and turned around at her chair, then sat back down. "Okay, I was just wandering around outside the space where our new house would be, trying to figure out where each room would be. He walked up and introduced himself. We talked a bit, and he said he was almost done working on a big job and would be working on our house soon."

Nightingale looked at Imogene, who gave an encouraging smile and nod of her head.

"Did you see him after that?" Nightingale heard a groan from Portia, and this time when he glanced at Imogene, she rolled her eyes.

"You were agreeable." Portia raised her voice and turned in her seat to point a finger at Imogene. When she looked back at Nightingale, she said, "We had him over for supper several times. We wanted to learn about building a house."

Imogene shrugged. "Yes, I was agreeable. He educated us on construction as the house was going up." She pivoted back to the sink and began scrubbing a pot, obviously distancing herself.

"You were fond of him?" Nightingale asked.

"It wasn't just that. He'd had a streak of bad luck," Portia said. "He needed someone who cared. I see your raised eyebrows, Oz. He never asked for money, if that's what you're thinking. He was working on the construction of that huge house north of here. When he was done there, he came to work in our subdivision."

"Wonder how he landed the job on that huge house."

Imogene interrupted, drying her hands while she spoke. "He was good at what he did—building. And he insinuated that he knew the owner of the mansion. I don't mind admitting it. Your daddy would have said, 'You girls are acting foolish.'"

"Why would he know a rich man? Never mind. Did you believe him?" Nightingale asked.

Portia squinted at Nightingale and pursed her lips just a bit. He could see that she was tired of his questions. Her next words were terse. "We didn't ask details. Yes, we felt we could believe him."

He tried to be casual, sipped the coffee. "I went into Broken Rock today, and someone asked me if I knew the rich people who lived in the new house. People are curious when anybody buys all those acres, fences it in, and builds a huge home. People ask questions. They're curious. Made me wonder, too."

That seemed to satisfy her. "Joshua said the man managed other people's money. Said he was a billionaire and weird. But that was all."

"I still don't know why you think Joshua might have been the victim of a crime." He sounded skeptical, even to his own ears.

Portia didn't seem to notice. "He was too careful to have fallen," she said, quick-tempered and sure. Then she looked at him, straight on like his mother used to do. "I just have this feeling." She put a tight fist at her gut.

Nightingale was familiar with the gut reaction. He couldn't remember when his gut had misled him, but he didn't share that fact.

"All right, Oswald, here's the real answer to your question." Portia's voice quivered with emotion. "Joshua *said* someone wanted him dead. He tried to make a joke of it, but he looked troubled. That was the last time I saw him alive."

"When was that?"

"A few days before you found him," Portia said.

Nightingale could offer no immediate response, and he hated to use flimsy words, but he fell back on things he had said before. "I'll do the best I can, and I'll let you know what the sheriff tells me. This is his case. But don't expect anything soon. I wish I could promise more, but I'd be lying, and you don't need that. Right now, Bandit and I are going home."

They went through the usual ritual of goodbyes, and Nightingale walked out with a recycled brown bag filled with leftovers for the next day. Imogene walked with him to the truck. She reached inside the truck and petted Bandit.

Nightingale turned to Imogene. "Do you have any idea why Portia is so angry with me? What have I done? This last few minutes was the first time I've been out of the doghouse with her in weeks."

"I've noticed that she's more nervous, you know, on the surface nervous. Usually she hides it. And she's been a little cross with me."

"Am I just imagining that she doesn't like me?"

Imogene laughed and touched his arm. "We both love you. You're our kin. Yes, I've noticed it. But this will pass."

"If you say so," he said. "But I'm gonna keep you between us. And we'll get this other sorted out."

He pulled the truck out of the driveway, blowing out a breath of frustration. Portia would have to rise above her anger. Or, better yet, tell him why she was mad.

His thoughts went to the dead man and the governor's call. The body showed up before the governor called and the two things weren't related—thank goodness. Or were they?

Now he was channeling Garrick. Somehow Garrick would be able to find a correlation between the governor calling for Nightingale's help and dead bodies showing up. He always seemed to be able to connect the least likely subjects. The good thing about this one was that it had nothing to do with the governor's latest phone call. Garrick would still point out the timing; however, there were more important questions between the old man and Nightingale.

Along with the governor, Sutton Garrick owed him some explanations. Nightingale had heard someone in the Ranger office imply that Garrick might be his father. He was outraged, and the words had twisted and simmered until he could not forget the insinuation. His mother, Mary, was an angel, and he'd be damned if he'd let some rumor ruin her memory. He and Garrick would have to have a serious talk soon.

The thing was, he didn't like such rumors floating around. The implications ate at him, and he wanted them gone or cleared up. But Garrick and he needed to work together. So discussions would have to come after this case. For now, he shifted his thinking to what he needed to do next.

Tomorrow he would call Governor Daniels and ask what specifics she needed about Edgar Post. Better yet, he'd drive into Austin and get answers face to face. She was still a politician. He wanted to see her reaction when she answered his question.

4

Portia Shoemaker sat in the porch swing and considered her cousin, Oswald, as he and Imogene walked to his truck. Oswald was a gifted law officer. Undoubtedly, he wondered about her observations about Joshua Tallman's death. Portia figured Oswald thought that she reacted too much with her heart and not her head. He wondered if Joshua knew the man in the mansion and "was Joshua really who he said he was." Oswald probably wondered if the dead man reminded her of the young fiancé she had lost in the car accident so many years ago.

She wondered to herself if her concern was her soul trying to fill the space in her heart for the baby she had given up for adoption, which Oswald did not know about.

Portia watched his truck disappear into the night. Her mind continued to run in circles, so she waited for Imogene, the most level-headed person she knew, to talk through her misgivings. Otherwise, she knew she faced a sleepless night.

Imogene came up the walk, onto the porch, and over to the swing.

"You didn't tell him anything else that Joshua said, did you?" Portia asked.

"No. I did not tell him that Joshua said the man was his father. I thought you should do that, since he told you," Imogene said.

"I need to talk this out with you," Portia said. "Let's do the dishes. I hope you didn't wash all of them."

They walked silently to the kitchen. They had cleared dishes so often the action was almost like a dance. Each woman moved with her own chores in mind, and tonight they were more deliberate than usual. Portia figured that, like her, Imogene was lost in her thoughts.

Portia finally spoke, though not about current events. "Do you remember when you came here from Tennessee?"

Imogene stopped wiping the table, and a smile grew across her face. "Yes. You were a lifesaver. You will always be my best friend as well as my cousin. But why do you bring that up?"

Portia dried a plate, placing it on the table as she spoke. She felt the need to gather scenes from the past into her heart. She shut her eyes tight, thinking about the first night Oswald had come to visit after Imogene had moved in. Oswald hadn't known that Imogene was there. "Do you remember the look on Oswald's face when he saw you? He had called me the week before and told me that you were missing. Cyrus had called him asking about you."

Imogene gave a short humph, not dismissively, but not serious. "Fear is a great motivator for disappearing. I thought Cyrus might kill me if he found me. I knew I'd be safe here."

"That's true. I would have killed Cyrus if he'd showed up."

Imogene's green eyes grew big. She stopped washing dishes and stared at her cousin. "You would have killed him?" Her voice seeped down to a whisper. "I've never heard you say such a thing."

Portia returned the stare, fearless. "Some people just don't need to be on this earth." She spoke her belief, and such a thing had obviously never crossed Imogene's mind. Apparently, Imogene had not been prepared for this. Strange, in all their years together, they had not talked about those days of Imogene's arrival. Then, too, Imogene hadn't commented on the .410 shotgun that Portia kept over the mantle. Nor the small Ruger that Portia kept in her purse. For all her common sense, Imogene didn't notice some things.

Portia pushed the dishes to one end of the kitchen table and sat at the end where she had cleared a space. "Let's sit and talk about Joshua. And Oswald."

Imogene put steaming cups of coffee down on the oilcloth. "This is decaf," she said. "Would you rather have wine?"

"No," Portia said. She was trying to act normal, unworried, while her mind ran like some hamster in a cage. The only way to surface from the burden she carried was to talk and listen to new ideas. "Do you remember how serious Oswald was as a child?"

"You forget that I didn't see him that often as a child. He's younger than us. How old is he?"

Portia nodded. "I think he's about forty-eight. He's four years younger than me. But I remember when he was little. As a child he was very serious. He seemed to have no sense of fun. I don't know why that was the case, but when they visited, and that was rare because none of us had the money for traveling, he held back and wanted to stay with his momma and daddy. The last time they visited, he was six or seven, so I guess he was shy."

"Still is, except when he's being a Ranger," Imogene said.

"I know, but humor me," Portia said. "We joked that he acted like he was born in a three-piece suit; he was so stiff." She looked into her coffee cup, as if she could see someone in it. "I don't know that he has changed that much. I hate to add to his worries."

"My dear cousin"—Imogene let out a breath that Portia recognized as her wiser-than-thou sigh—"even though he's a bit younger than us, he is certainly wise in the ways of the world. He has been in law enforcement for how many years? Thirty or something. I'd bet his ideals are a bit tarnished. I'm sure he has seen people killed in various bloody ways, and he has seen enough heartbreaking situations to be almost immune to anything we might tell him, including anything about Joshua.

"I remember my mother saying he was too honest for his own good. His father would write to us and tell how he would ask if they could go by the Ranger office when they went into town. He's always been like a policeman. He doesn't need your protection. Is that why you're so worried?"

Portia felt a blush move up her neck as she half-way smiled. "I hesitate to tell Oswald everything because it sounds preposterous. I think Joshua got into trouble for gambling or stealing, and he didn't want to tell us that. I know he had a good heart, but he was troubled. What do you think?"

Imogene leaned forward and squeezed Portia's hand. "I agree. The boy couldn't sit still through a meal. He may have been killed by someone who hated him, although I find it hard to imagine anyone who could hate him. But I have great confidence in Oswald, even though he's always been a bit distant. You, we, told him the important things that we knew. We'll stay in touch with him and see how this goes."

Portia drew in a long breath and exhaled. "You constantly make me see the common-sense side of everything. I'm going to read and go to bed."

"I'm going to bed now. I got a call from the hospital, so I'm going to work at 6 a.m. I'm glad Oz didn't stay later."

Portia nodded agreement and went to her room. She didn't read but pulled out a diary. The pages were yellowed after so many years, and she could see the damage that her tears had done. She'd come home after Paul's funeral and knew she had to leave her mother and father.

Paul had been the love of her life. Now, years had diminished the sting of his death, but not the heartache she'd felt after she'd left home. She closed her eyes and smelled the cloying fragrance of roses and gardenias from his funeral. Her mother went with her to see him buried, but her father had claimed he had to work. She never knew whether her father was religious or not, but that night he'd come by her room and said, "Maybe this is best. Maybe God has something else in mind for you."

Portia had been unable to speak, but she knew that she had to leave. She didn't have to ask to know her father would not abide her having Paul's baby. So that night after her parents were asleep, she packed a small bag.

The Tennessee night was cool. It was spring and windows were open, the perfect time to drop the bag of belongings outside of her window. The next morning she tried to act normal by having oats and milk but could hardly finish before saying goodbye to her mother, acting like she was on her way to school.

Outside of the house, she grabbed the bag and walked toward the road. Jasmine lived close, and as her friend walked to the bus, Portia whispered from the side of the road. "Jasmine, Jasmine."

The girl jerked around. "Portia, you like to have scared me to death. What are you doing out here?"

Portia remembered the gravel road, rough and uneven against the soles of her shoes as she stood, too embarrassed to look her friend in the face. "I guess you know Paul is dead," she said.

Jasmine nodded. "Yes, I'm sorry."

"Well, we were going to be married, but I'm pregnant and I need to go away to have the baby. I thought maybe you knew someplace I could go." She felt the heat of the shame on her face.

"It's not that bad," Jasmine said. She touched her arm, and for some reason, Portia felt soothed.

Jasmine looked around to be sure they were alone, then went on in a low voice. "I know several girls who have 'gone away.'

Look, I can't miss this bus, but this is not the end of the world. Go to Slate City, Indiana. There's a place called Clark House. They'll put you up until you have the baby and they'll get him or her adopted. They're kind. I've visited with our church."

Jasmine had said the last few things in a hurry. She was running, backwards, in order to make it to the bus. "Write to me and let me know how it goes," she said and turned, sprinting away from Portia.

Portia had a little money from a part-time job. She'd been working to help her mother clean houses. That was enough to get her a bus ticket to Indiana. On the bus, she looked out the window and never cried. Her own actions had caused this, and she had to do the right thing. She had herself and soon her child to look out for.

Only once did she think about keeping the baby—when she first felt movement. She was mopping a floor, and when she felt the flutter, she straightened, put her hand on her stomach, wondered about this miracle inside of her.

She dared to dream that someone might want her and her baby. But even then, without the benefit of Imogene's level head, she knew she could not raise a child. She was young, had barely finished high school, and had no income. She had no idea what she would do after the baby was born. Then one day she saw a policeman's patrol car and remembered Oswald's love of the Rangers when he was young. Her mother had said he'd gone to work for the state police as quick as he could to prep for becoming a Ranger.

Strait-laced Oswald might lecture. He might turn her away, but he had been a quiet, listening child, and he might help her because they were family. She wrote to him in Broken Rock, Texas. She had no post office box or route number, but she sent him a letter saying her fiancé had died. Could she visit him? She also asked him not to contact her parents. She gave her address as a small diner next door to Clark House, where she sometimes washed dishes and knew the owner.

In a few weeks, she received a letter from Oswald. "I would be glad to see you. If you decide to come, please go by bus to Lubbock, and I will pick you up." The note was as stiff as he was. He had given her a phone number to call him.

In her rocking chair, thinking back to that time, Portia didn't know how she had come to her current irritation with Nightingale. After he and Garrick returned from their last job, she'd noticed Imogene and Garrick talking on the phone almost every day, then meeting for coffee, if Portia overheard correctly.

Was her irritation more accurately aimed at Garrick? No, lately Nightingale wanted to know everything about their lives. Or did she just imagine his nosiness? Did he resent her independence? He knew answers to questions before she asked them. Had he changed or had she changed? Why was he such an aggravation to her?

Oswald had been a great help when she first arrived. She stayed with him for a few months, and he never asked for details of why she showed up in west Texas. He didn't ask about her family in Tennessee. She appreciated that. He had to know she had problems, that she'd run away from home, but he never pushed her for explanations. He'd helped her find a room to rent in Lubbock. More than a few times he paid the rent. He called and checked on her. She'd worked two jobs and finished college and begun teaching school. He'd helped with the down payment on the house she now owned. In his brusque way, he gave her a support system.

But she'd never told him about the baby. No one in her family knew about the baby, but she remembered the sadness that had become the underpinning of her life. She remembered hearing him cry and wanting to see him. She did raise her head enough to see a tuft of dark hair in a blanket. She had done the right thing, only to be haunted every day. And if she told Nightingale about the baby, she knew he would be judgmental and think she was tainted. That's what people back home always thought of unwed mothers.

Now she wondered if her baby boy would have been like Joshua. Would he be kind to older women? Would he wonder who was his real mother? Would he hate her for giving him up?

5

The next morning at 6:00, Nightingale called the governor on the private cell phone number that she had given him. Her "hello" did not sound chipper.

"You're a man of your word, but you didn't have to call this early," she said. "Are you working for me?"

"I thought I'd drive in and talk to you this afternoon, if you're available." Nightingale was standing in his backyard, looking at his roof, thinking it was steeper than his cousin's new house, but he didn't know if he would die from a fall off it. Broken bones, yes, there'd be a lot of those, but...

"I'm leaving this morning for a speech in the Rio Grande Valley," the governor said. "Maybe next week?"

During a sleepless night, Nightingale had thought about what he wanted to know from the governor. He had decided to lay out his questions, no matter the worry about bugged phones. He looked out past the fence of his back yard onto the flat prairie that was such a part of his life. "I guess we'd better talk now, then. I have two questions. One: Is Broken Rock still part of the state water plan?"

The governor cleared her throat. "Yes. I told you that already.

These things do not move quickly." Her tense tone conveyed her exacerbation at his question.

She was a woman of her word, so he went to the next question. "Do you still want me to check out Mr. Post?"

A noise of papers rustling, muffled voices—could it be bed sheets pushed aside—all of it came through the phone, and Nightingale imagined the scene.

"Yes." She sounded aggravated. "Please talk to him and see what kind of impression you gather. I want to know what makes him tick. Why did he settle in such a barren part of the state? What are his ambitions?" After a long pause, she said, "Is he honest?"

"And if he asks if you sent me?"

"If he asks, tell him the truth. I did send you. And, Mr. Nightingale, don't question me again. If I trust you, you should trust me."

"Yes, ma'am." The governor quit the call before he could. She was angry, but she had always emphasized that he should give her the truth and speak his mind. She simply reacted badly when she heard it. He smiled to himself. Like Portia, the governor stayed mad at him much of the time. Maybe he would learn from one or the other of them about why they were so angry and what he could do to alleviate such anger.

Probably not.

Coffee cup in hand, he watched Bandit run a circle in the yard and went back into the house to re-read his clippings on Edgar Post. The dog didn't know how lucky he was.

6

Portia didn't sleep well after thinking so long about her diary. Deep inside, she didn't like Oswald much these days, and it was probably due to his ego. She pushed aside the fact that she might have an ego that interfered. Whatever the problem was, she needed to stay at home for the day. She called Principal Sullivan and told him she needed the day off. She offered to call a substitute, which pleased him, and after she had the position filled, she climbed back into bed to think.

Her mind went first to the new home that she and Imogene had decided to buy. But the buying of the house had been fraught with worry. She knew they could make payments on a mortgage, but she could hear the doubt in Nightingale's voice anytime the house was mentioned.

She had thought he would be flattered when they asked him to come and look at the house, but he seemed put off by the request. She wanted him to be glad for their accomplishment. They were buying a house—on their own. But she didn't see or hear anything from their cousin that might show his happiness for them.

Over the years, Portia and Imogene had discussed their

extended family. It was an odd mixture of people that neither woman understood. After a year or so, they both admitted to missing some of the family but not enough to call or go back to Tennessee in search of anyone. They never said it directly, but Portia knew that, subconsciously, they were trying to build a family here, with Nightingale, in Texas. All they wanted was someone to care.

She and Imogene regularly asked Nightingale over for a meal. She had asked him to attend school events or church. Imogene had done the same, but Oz rarely attended anything except a meal, and he had never invited her and Imogene over to his house. She hated to think of his decor. Lord knows he probably still needed a woman's touch. She remembered, from her short time living with him, a house just suited to a man and his dog, barren of furniture except for a La-Z-Boy for the master and an occasional chair with worn upholstery for the dog.

She and Imogene tried to be a part of his life, but it was an uphill battle with Oz. And now this new problem entered the picture: the dead young man.

When she heard movement downstairs, Portia got up. "The coffee always smells so good when I don't make it," she said as she entered the kitchen.

Imogene smiled but raised her eyebrows at her cousin. "You're not dressed?"

"I'm staying home. I woke up at three, so I plan on getting a nap sometime today."

"Good luck with that nap," Imogene said. "I should be home by seven."

"I'll have supper ready."

"Great." Imogene stood and stretched, then left the kitchen, and Portia listened as the stairs creaked under her footsteps.

Portia expected sadness after Joshua's death, but there was a heavy gloominess, too. She could tell that Imogene cared for him like she did, just to a different degree. She pulled a carton of eggs from the fridge and stared at them, finally selecting one to boil, while she thought about her last encounters with him. He had seemed uneasy the last time they talked, but she had told Oswald about that.

She put the egg in some water, laid out frozen ground beef to thaw for soup later, and made toast. It was useless to go back to bed. She was still puttering in the kitchen when Imogene stuck her head in and said goodbye.

She started a to-do list for the day and went upstairs to get the number of the builder for the new house like Oswald had asked her to do. Most likely John Chavez already knew about what had happened on the site, but if he didn't, as the construction supervisor, he should. While she made her bed, she decided to go to the house to see if yellow tape was around the site stopping everything, like she saw on television. She expected the sheriff to call the builder and tell him about the dead man. She had no idea how Joshua's death would hinder construction, and she was not going to ponder the dilemma. Finally, with a sense of purpose, she put on slacks and a sweater and called Chavez. She was not surprised when he didn't answer the phone

∼

AT MESA HEIGHTS, ONLY A REMNANT OF YELLOW TAPE remained attached to the back of the house. But the good side was that while they might not be in the new house before Christmas, she thought they would have a new house by the spring.

No one was working on the house today. She roamed from one room to the next, thinking about colors and furniture placement. She avoided the back bedroom. She didn't want to see Joshua's blood outside her door, and when that vision hit her, she hurried out of the house.

After she left the site, she stopped at a house on another street. The men who she had seen working on the houses so often were there. "Excuse me," she said to one who looked familiar. "We've spoken before, and you've worked on my house—over there. Are you still working on it? Do you work for Mr. Chavez?"

"Yes, we remember you, Miss Portia, but we do not build on your house unless Mr. Chavez tells us. We will work there next week."

She almost asked about Joshua but stopped herself out of respect for Oswald's involvement. He would not like her nosy intrusion. She looked at her watch. She'd spent two hours just walking and thinking.

Back at home, she was going upstairs as her phone rang.

Jack Sullivan, the principal of her school, started the conversation by asking about her health. He was such a gentleman; she smiled as she assured him she'd be back at work the next day.

Sullivan joked that her class was too quiet when she was gone.

"Is everything all right?" she asked.

"Fine here at school. We've had a request for a tutor. A homeschool student needs help with English, primarily literature and writing. I thought you might be interested. The youngster is new to this area. His sister came with him. His family or a driver will bring him to your house, and they've offered twice the usual fee for your help."

"He doesn't want to be a pupil at Obsidian?" Portia asked, and even as she said it, she realized that the majority of people who had oil money, or other means, chose to not have their children attend the local schools.

Portia admired Principal Sullivan. He rarely faulted a child. He showed that talent again. "His sister said he's doing math and science on the internet. I'll call his former school to see if there were problems. The family obviously likes having private teachers. Do you want to give me a decision after I talk to the other school?"

"Yes, please," Portia said. "I'll probably do it."

They quit the call, and while she waited, Portia poured out her cold coffee from the morning, added the vegetables to the meat in the crock pot, and went upstairs. She was changing the bed linens when Principal Sullivan called again.

"The school had nothing but praise for the boy," the principal said. "Frankly, that makes me a little suspicious, but it's your call. Do you want to tutor him?"

"Yes, I'll give it a go. Give them my phone number, please. We'll coordinate a time and he can come meet me. Is this another child from the riches of oil?"

"I don't know, but the boy's sister is very affable. You can ask her if she comes with him."

"Good idea," Portia said.

Twenty minutes later, she had a call from a number she didn't recognize. It was Carolyn Post, who turned out to be the sister of Portia's potential student. By the end of the call Carolyn and her brother, Adam, were scheduled to be at Portia's house for introductions and planning at four that afternoon.

After Portia hung up, she made a list of questions for Adam. Those answers would help her know what reading she'd ask him to do. She would also ask about his writing skills, maybe a short test later. She always felt a tenderness for the children from wealth. They had so much but still needed so much.

7

After talking with the governor, Nightingale had called Sutton Garrick. When no one answered the phone, he decided to swing by the older man's ranch. Garrick had hired help who lived on the ranch, but they might be on vacation, and Nightingale had visions of the old man falling off his horse out there and no one finding him until he was dead. Except for the fact that he ate antacids like candy, Garrick was a healthy man. And Nightingale was fond of the old coot, so he headed for Garrick's ranch.

At his destination, Nightingale noted the time—8 a.m.—and got out of his truck and approached the house, admiring Garrick's low-maintenance rock-and-cactus landscaping. The house, the shiny blue truck, the grounds, everything had the fastidious look of Sutton Garrick.

A young man and his wife, Billy and Sophie Bonilla, helped Garrick with the tough work of keeping a ranch going. The work included some cooking, housekeeping. As Nightingale was wondering who got the credit for the healthy plants, Garrick himself opened the front door. "Do you always skulk around before you knock, or do you just skulk and leave?" Garrick gave a toothy smile and stuck out a hand to shake in greeting.

"I'm considering stealing some of these cacti for my own yard. Will they live through our winters?"

"Sophie assures me we can cover this stuff with burlap and it'll come back next spring. But you didn't come to look at my plants. Talk to the governor lately?"

As they walked inside, Nightingale saw no changes in the house, but the smell of pot roast with bay leaves was new. He took a long, deep inhale of the aroma.

Garrick seemed amused. "I'm telling you, Nightingale, you need a woman. But you're not here for a lecture. Why *are* you here?"

Nightingale felt the prickle of stubbornness. "Thought I'd come by after our foray into east Texas. Can't I be neighborly?" He sat in a big leather chair and watched Garrick's back as he started toward the dining room and took a left toward the kitchen.

"I'm getting coffee. You want a cup?"

Nightingale stood and walked into the dining room, where he leaned against the door-facing and watched Garrick. "No coffee, thanks. Have you come across any information on this rich fellow who bought a big spread north of here and built a huge house? That's my new assignment from the governor."

Garrick squinted over a large mug of coffee. "Ah, the reason comes out. I was in Broken Rock yesterday, and O'Riley at the hardware store caught me up on the gossip. You'd have better luck staying in the know if you were friendlier."

"If it's gossip, it's probably a lie. I was up at that new subdivision yesterday with Portia and Imogene, and I noticed construction of a new house and a water tower when I drove north. But the main thing about the subdivision was a dead man." He waited for Garrick to face him, eyes wide. "Looked like a young man fell off of Portia and Imogene's new house."

Garrick visibly perked up at the idea of a death. "How far did he fall? Was it an accident? Just off of a house doesn't seem like enough to kill a man."

"Garrick, the man fell. He looked like his neck was broken. The sheriff is getting an autopsy. I've got to go." Nightingale was already frustrated. The man was over sixty years old and the idea of a suspicious death was like a Christmas gift to him.

Garrick turned back to the coffee pot. "I talked with Imogene last night and she mentioned the body. You don't sound convinced that he fell."

"I'm waiting on the medical examiner before I decide, but it didn't look right" Nightingale took a step toward leaving.

"You don't have to hurry," Garrick said. "O'Riley had more to say about Post. That's the man's name, Post—in that huge new mansion. He told a real estate person from Lubbock that he wanted to buy seven hundred to a thousand acres. The Craigs didn't mind selling, so they carved out a thousand acres, closed on a proposed survey, and within a week Post had started construction on the house. He paid cash."

"Why here? Isn't he from the east coast?"

"Don't know about that. Got a lot of the house built while you and I were in east Texas working on the water deal. Construction started before we left town, but they were low key, so not much was said. And people around here have been focused on trying to survive a drought," Garrick said. "This fool's got his own water supply, like a town. Now, that is some money. Did your cousins mention him?"

"No, they didn't. But you know how gossip is. I'm going to meet the man. I'll let you know how it goes."

Nightingale waved as he walked out the front door, afraid if he waited Garrick would invite himself along. For this first encounter, he wanted to meet Edgar Post by himself.

Nightingale knew Garrick well enough to know that he had tried mightily to control his questions about the body. In the last two years, he and Garrick had revived a friendship from several years earlier. Nightingale enjoyed the old man's company. Garrick was pushy, egotistical, and didn't mind playing outside of the law when necessary. He also had a sixth sense when it came to catching criminals. But there was also this question of the rumor floating around the Ranger office. Nightingale let that go for the moment.

Nightingale sat in the truck a minute, thinking. He had resigned from the Rangers six or so months ago and regretted the move. To him the organization was the best law enforcement agency in existence. The men who ran it were a different matter. Garrick was also a former Ranger but didn't have the organization on a pedestal. They often discussed their differences. Nightingale told himself that he was usually right. He had learned a lot from Garrick, sometimes gaining a different perspective, but the man had flaws.

Through the flaws, Nightingale wondered what his mother had found fascinating about Sutton Garrick.

8

Nightingale smiled to himself as he buckled up and then made a quick turnaround out of Garrick's drive, heading toward the Post ranch. It was barely nine in the morning. Post might still be in bed.

Nightingale didn't have a script, so he went over what he knew about the man as he drove. Garrick had told him nothing new. The information that he'd found on the internet stuck with him. The odd bits were about Post's friends. One of them collected his own urine and had done so for several years because he believed the government was conspiring against him. He hadn't sent the samples in for analysis, just hung on to them.

Another man by the name of Hartford had been in Post's company for several years. The man had been good at choosing winning stocks until technology came into such prominence. According to the articles, he couldn't predict with the certainty of computers. Nothing in the written material said he was fired. Rather, Post kept him on as a consultant, and the opinion of the article was that this subsidizing of a loser, loyalty to friends, seemed totally out of character for Post.

Another friend, also male, was known for the number of women he had dated. He'd married once, divorced once, and, according to stories, had so many strange desires regarding sex he scared off most of the women he dated.

Nightingale wondered how, or if, any journalist ever confirmed such gossip. He didn't expect to run into such problems, but if he did, it would be a first for Broken Rock.

As he drove past brown, beaten fields where cotton had grown only a few weeks ago, he wondered if Edgar Post knew how hard Texas winters could be. Nightingale looked forward to cold weather but not the barren fields of the winter, even though he knew it was part of the natural growth cycle. Post probably never noticed the fields, and if he did, Nightingale suspected that any difficult time of extreme cold or heat could be made tolerable with enough money.

The wrought iron gate that blocked the road into the Post enclave didn't budge as Nightingale drove closer. After staring at it a bit, he rolled down the window and pushed the button at the call box.

After the third push, he got a disembodied voice clearer than the McDonald's drive-through. "Yes, sir?"

"My name's Oswald Nightingale. I'm a Texas Ranger, and I wanted to welcome Mr. Post and his family to the area. Just a friendly visit. Thought we might talk a bit." He sat in the truck, giving the voice time to decide.

Without a word, the gate clicked and began to open. Nightingale expected the screeching of metal, but he heard nothing of the sort. The gate opened silently. He drove through.

Inside the fence, the road was cobblestone, unlike the paved entry, curving slightly before making a great loop in front of the Post mansion. A uniformed bald man, whom Nightingale assumed to be a butler, came out and waited for him to get out and come to the front door. Once he was there, the man said, "This way, sir."

"And you would be who?" Nightingale asked.

"I'm Reeves, sir. The butler, sir."

The house was modern with a touch of English royalty. In the entryway, Nightingale admired the marble floor. The stairs were wood with a transparent glass guardrail and handrail of sleek metal in a neutral chrome. He would be hard-pressed to name the style of the house. He didn't have long to ponder the question. The butler made a tiny bow and said, "This way sir."

He followed the man down a black-and-white marble tiled hallway to a room that he assumed was a study or library. The walls were lined with books, like something out of a movie. But again the styles were mixed, this time mahogany with steel and glass.

A man of about five-foot-eight stood in a corner. The man took a step forward. "Welcome, sir. I believe at the gate you said your name was Nightingale, like the bird." He offered a hand to shake.

Nightingale accepted the outstretched hand. "I must assume you are"—he waited, letting the air fill with anticipation, but his host waited also—"Edgar Post."

The man nodded, the condescending nod of one who is better than his guest, his eyes briefly closing in agreement. "Would you like a beverage? Tea, coffee, cola, alcohol?" Edgar Post waved toward a chair. "Please, sit."

Nightingale's first thought had been to leave as soon as possible. This small man standing in front of him gave off the air of a king. But leaving would be too easy and would answer none of the governor's questions. "I'd like coffee, please, black." Nightingale chose a large leather recliner and sat back with a sigh. "You've built a beautiful place here."

Post's mouth made only the slightest pout of discontent. He

nodded to the butler, mumbled about coffee, and sat on the edge of the couch across from the Ranger.

"I wish you had called earlier, Mr. Nightingale. I'm sure we could have a productive conversation if we had the time. As it is, I'm leaving soon for a meeting in New York."

"I understand, Mr. Post. I only stopped by to say welcome. I have to admit I'm curious about why you chose this barren part of the country to settle in, especially when you still have business in New York." Nightingale sat deeper into the chair and accepted the coffee that the butler brought. He hoped Post's ego was big enough that he would need to explain his choice for the acreage and house.

Post's lips moved slightly upward. The morning sunshine through one window on the back wall drifted through his black hair, which had delicate grey at the temples and the beginning of more salt than pepper. Probably colored it. The man had to be in his sixties and looked at least ten years younger. "I selected this area because it is quiet, undisturbed, not burdened with zoning laws, and very close to the center of the United States. It is in a state that could use my financial advice, and I have offered my services free of charge to your governor. I want to 'give back' because of my good fortune."

"I imagine the state will be grateful for any help you can give." Nightingale set his coffee on the table beside his chair and started to stand. "I'd love to continue this conversation, but I know you need to leave."

Post stood as well and gave a slight bow of his head.

"If you don't mind me having your phone number," Nightingale said, "I'll call before I show up. And next time I'll bring some of my cousin's homemade peach preserves."

Suddenly, a door to the side that Nightingale had not seen burst open, and a young woman rushed in. She had strawberry blonde hair, and her whole face was red from some emotion that Nightingale couldn't interpret.

"Dad, Billy is hurt."

Post frowned but looked confused, like he had no idea what the woman was talking about.

"Carolyn, what do you mean? What are you talking about? Billy who?"

She walked toward him, tears streaming down her face. "Billy, your son and my brother. He's hurt. He may be dead." Her sobs were quiet. Then, suddenly the color left her face. She grabbed the back of the couch. Her eyes closed, and Nightingale thought she might faint.

"Carolyn, are you okay?" Post walked quickly to her and guided her around to sit on the couch. He grabbed a cover and wrapped it around her. Then, as she leaned back, he went to stand behind her and began to massage her shoulders. She immediately sat up, and his hands dropped away.

Nightingale said, "She's had a shock. I suggest you call a doctor, an ambulance."

The butler materialized and Post nodded to him, "Reeves, do as he says. Get a doctor."

Nightingale heard him dial 911. But there was some confusion about where to send the ambulance, so he took the phone, explained who he was, and gave them the location and his phone number. He was not deeply worried, but the girl did look sick.

Post bent toward the girl's ear and whispered. She made no move to acknowledge his comment. Every sound in the room echoed, the girl's hiccups, the grandfather clock's extra loud tick-tock.

Post looked cool. As a matter of fact, he seemed annoyed about this problem. He checked his watch. He paced behind the couch where the girl sat. He said nothing, but his face was flushed, his forehead wrinkled. Then he signaled the butler, and the two of them had a private conversation. The butler left.

"You may leave, Mr. Nightingale," Post said. "We can take care of this now."

"That's all right," Nightingale said. "I want to see that she's okay."

"I appreciate your concern," Post said, but his words sounded more sarcastic than sincere. Obviously, he was accustomed to directing events on his terms.

Nightingale walked to the library door and opened it, hoping to hear a siren. When there was nothing, he turned back toward the couch.

"You'll be fine," Post said to his daughter. He looked at Nightingale and explained. "She's always been nervous. She fainted the day we left New York to come here. The doctor blamed dehydration."

"Medics should be here in a few minutes," Nightingale said. The sound of the siren came then, and soon the butler guided medics into the study.

The conversation with the medics was tame. Post again told about the other fainting episode, and the medics said they suspected dehydration. Post insisted they take her to the hospital. He would follow in his car.

Nightingale watched, but he stayed back on the edge of the group. He heard the medics' assessment and wished he knew more.

As the medics carried the girl out on a gurney, Post and Nightingale followed. When they got outside, a black SUV drove around behind the ambulance, and Nightingale watched as Post talked to the driver and then climbed inside the black car. The window went down and Post said, "Thank you for your help. I'll be in touch."

As Nightingale said, "I'll come by the hospital," the window on the SUV went up, cutting off his words, and both vehicles drove away.

Nightingale walked to his truck. The sun had not hit noon yet, but the day was already shaping up to be over seventy degrees, hot for early November.

And, as the radio voice predicted a pleasant fifty degrees for the night, he drove out of the place slowly, looking for exotic animals on the flat plains and seeing nothing.

On the way to the hospital, Nightingale reviewed the strange scene he'd just witnessed. Who was this Billy? Was he dead? Did Post have a son he didn't acknowledge? He certainly acted like he had no idea what the girl was talking about.

The girl's voice kept coming at him, an abrasion, irritating and needing more information. Who was Billy? Apparently, she thought she had a brother, and equally apparently, at least on first observation, Post had no idea who she was talking about. If she stayed in the hospital, Nightingale intended to talk to her. And if not, he still intended to talk to her, but first he would try to shake some trees and get more information on Post.

~

He drove toward Lubbock, planning to go by the sheriff's office and then the hospital. That would allow time for some progress on the state of the girl's health. Once he hit the city limits, he grabbed a quick drive-through sandwich and headed for the sheriff's office on Broadway. He hoped for information on the man who fell from the house, but he thought he needed to tell Sheriff Brewster about what had just happened at the Post house.

Nightingale parked at a meter across from the sheriff's office and told the officer at the admitting desk who he was and that he needed to talk to the sheriff. He waited for a civilian to leave the sheriff before he went in.

Dan Brewster welcomed him but wasted no time. He seemed frustrated. "Glad to see you, Oz." Brewster motioned one hand toward a chair, and Nightingale sat down. "This job has gotten too big. I bet you're wondering about the man that fell off the house."

"Yes. Have you heard anything yet?"

Brewster shook his head. "Sorry. I have to stay on them if we need a rush. We've been covered up. As a matter of fact, I was gonna ask if you could take care of the man you found for me. It looked pretty routine and you were first on the scene . . ." He stopped midsentence and seemed to consider his words. "You're still a Ranger, right?"

Nightingale's first thought was to ask Brewster what was bothering him. The man seemed agitated beyond what the situation called for. "Yeah, I'm a Special Ranger, according to my papers." He tried to sound light, like a title didn't mean that much. "I'll contact the medical examiner, if that's okay with you. Or were you getting an autopsy? Maybe I just need the coroner."

"I requested an autopsy because one of the EMTs thought he had a wound on his neck. The paperwork is done to transfer the body to you."

"A wound on his neck?" Nightingale asked. "I'll ask the medical examiner about that."

"Good idea," Brewster said. "Sad situation when there's no family." He stood as if to emphasize his hurry to get Nightingale out of the office.

"I think you need to know about something that happened this morning," Nightingale said. He explained about visiting Edgar Post and the daughter's words.

When he finished, Brewster cocked his head to one side. "What were you doing out there?" Brewster had lost part of his friendly smile. Everything about him slowed down as he sat back down at his desk.

Nightingale used part of what he had told Post as his reasoning for visiting the man. "I was being friendly. My cousins and people from Obsidian had asked me about that big house. Then some folks at Broken Rock asked, too. I was curious. Now I'm even more curious. Why does it matter, Dan?"

Brewster left his desk and walked to a window that had a view of Lubbock. He took a deep breath. "The man came up here. Made an appointment to see me." Brewster turned from the window, his mouth pinched in distaste. "He came here to tell me he is a friend of the governor and his house is valuable. He wanted"—here Brewster stepped closer, both fists clinched—"to make me aware that I might need to have my guys make some special trips to be sure of security. Can you believe the audacity? I don't think I've been so angry in a long time."

Nightingale knew Dan Brewster as a man of long patience, but no man liked to be pushed. "I'm sure he's out of his element here. I'm thinking this daughter may bring him down a notch or two. Do you know if he had a son named Billy?"

Brewster sat down, now flipping a pen on his desk. "I haven't researched further than what's in the file, the man or his family. I appreciate you telling me what happened." He looked up at Nightingale, his face now devoid of emotion. "I'll let you know if I hear anything. Thanks for coming by."

Nightingale took the heavy hint and left. He didn't like the feeling of unease that he had during the conversation. Brewster had more on his mind than a questionable death, and his reaction from Post's visit could have been brushed off, but Brewster saw it as cause for extreme anger. Post was the type of man to rile people easily. He was an outsider here, and that made Brewster and Nightingale colleagues. Even with those caveats, Nightingale didn't feel like he and Brewster were together on Post events. Brewster knew something that he wasn't sharing.

But even more than his concern about Brewster, Nightingale thought about the offhand remark that an EMT had found an injury on the dead man's neck. In Nightingale's experience, the EMTs were thorough, maybe too detail-oriented, but he definitely wanted to talk to the M.E. as soon as possible.

9

As he drove to the medical examiner's office, Nightingale mentally replayed the conversation with the sheriff, but the only conclusion he came to was that they both had the same experience in their meetings with Edgar Post. The man thought his wealth gave him special privileges and protections. West Texas would be a good place to learn different.

Nightingale knew the medical examiner in a professional capacity. The man, Mac Belschner, had been a friend of Garrick's for several years. As the county and city grew, Belschner had become more of an administrator, supervising but keeping a hand on each case and still performing autopsies.

In the M.E.'s office, Nightingale explained that Brewster was so busy he had asked Nightingale to take over the case since, on the surface, it looked simple. Also, Nightingale explained the victim's name was possibly wrong. "It may not be Tallman. May be Post."

Belschner barely blinked. "We're running behind, short-staffed. I'll send the report when it is done."

"Did you happen to notice if there is a mark on the man's neck, like a needle injection?" Nightingale asked.

Belschner looked over his glasses. "I'll send the report when it is finished. Good day."

~

Nightingale decided the next stop would be the hospital and then the Ranger office before he drove home.

At the hospital, he found Carolyn Post's room, but she was asleep when he looked in. He was leaving as Edgar Post walked down the hall.

"What are you doing here?" Post asked. He didn't bother to lower his voice or hide his displeasure.

Nightingale looked back into the room, but Carolyn Post didn't wake. "I was concerned. Just wanted to see that she's okay."

"Mr. Nightingale, please, be honest with me. You are here to question my daughter about her wild accusations."

Edgar Post had walked to the side of his daughter's bed, so he was between Nightingale and the girl. A window on the opposite wall let in enough sunshine that the blood vessel at Post's temple had an odd reflection, showing his rising pulse rate along with his temper.

A hospital would be the place to have a stroke. "No, sir, you're wrong, but I'll leave." At Post's back, his daughter's eyelids fluttered.

Outside the room, Nightingale knew he'd get no details of her condition, but he asked the nurse at the desk the generic "How's she doing?" and received the generic "She'll be fine."

"Sorry about the commotion," he said.

The nurse held up a hand to stop him. "Don't worry," she said. "He's already told us where his kingdom is." She smiled, and Nightingale was glad she seemed to be on his side. He quietly left, heading to the Ranger office.

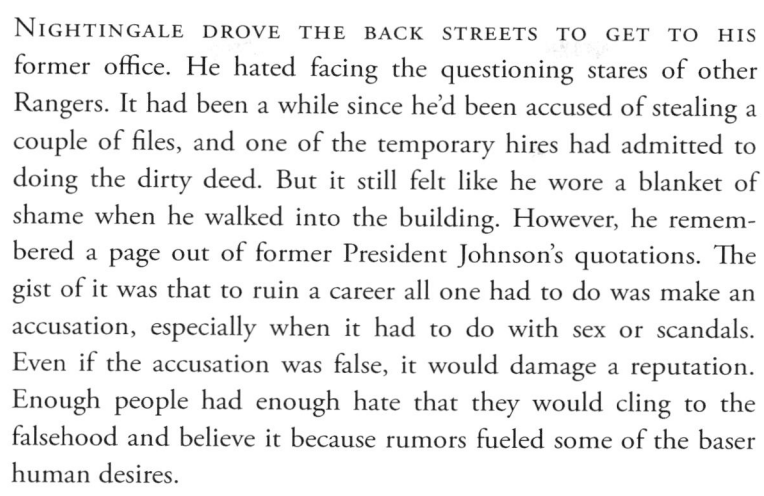

NIGHTINGALE DROVE THE BACK STREETS TO GET TO HIS former office. He hated facing the questioning stares of other Rangers. It had been a while since he'd been accused of stealing a couple of files, and one of the temporary hires had admitted to doing the dirty deed. But it still felt like he wore a blanket of shame when he walked into the building. However, he remembered a page out of former President Johnson's quotations. The gist of it was that to ruin a career all one had to do was make an accusation, especially when it had to do with sex or scandals. Even if the accusation was false, it would damage a reputation. Enough people had enough hate that they would cling to the falsehood and believe it because rumors fueled some of the baser human desires.

To Nightingale's way of thinking, every man and woman usually had something of which they were ashamed. A person accused of affairs or bribery, or anything salacious, made it possible to shift guilt into anger and believe that the rich and famous, or one's neighbor's or family, were just as bad as oneself. Therefore, people liked to find sinners amongst themselves. And if they weren't great at forgiveness, it made life much more tolerable.

Nightingale had worked his way up in the system to head up several successful investigations. He had men who liked him and a few who hated him. Two officers in the department despised him. He tried to avoid them.

But this day, when he walked into the office, he had the feeling that a thaw had taken place. He walked back and found Bob Gilbert staring at a computer screen. Gilbert didn't look at him. "What are you creeping around about, Oz? I've always been better at that sneaky stuff than you."

Nightingale grinned and stepped into the room. "Still watching porn after all the help leaves?"

Gilbert stood and they shook hands.

"Thanks for the information I needed when I was out of town," Nightingale said.

Gilbert shushed the thanks and picked up his hat. "Let's get outta here. The wife is out of town, and I need a drink. You look like you could use one."

Gilbert told his admin that he was gone for the day. They each took their own vehicle and drove to a small restaurant on the east side of town. The place was built around an Irish theme. It was expensive and never frequented by people Nightingale knew. The tables were spaced far enough apart that no one could hear other conversations.

Once they settled at a table, Nightingale gave Gilbert a highlighted version of his trip to east Texas, including the fact that Sutton Garrick had been there.

Gilbert raised his small glass of Bushmill's Black Bush as a toast. "To Sutton, who is a stellar Ranger. I miss him every day." After a good-sized swallow, Gilbert continued, "What's next?"

Nightingale went on to tell Gilbert about the man who fell off his cousins' unfinished house. "Brewster is convinced it was an accident and asked me to take over the investigation. I told the coroner to send the autopsy results to me at your office. I know there are some bad feelings still in the office. If you'll just watch the mail, I won't have to come by much. And if I still have access to the database, that would help."

Gilbert nodded. "I think you're still under the white hat category, but I'll make sure. Just keep me in the loop."

"But I haven't told you about my morning."

Gilbert smiled. "I can't remember when you've talked so much."

He gave a shortened version of his morning at the Post residence. When he finished, Gilbert said, "You're not doing Welcome Wagon, so I'm guessing this has to do with the governor."

Nightingale didn't confirm or deny. He didn't have to. Gilbert knew about his various jobs for the governor, senators, and other people in upper-level positions, and that was enough. "What do you know about Edgar Post?"

"Nothing. He called me. I've got to tell you, Oz, he was just a very nice citizen on the phone, cordial. Course he let me know that he was well-off, but he wanted to be low-key. I kinda liked the guy, but I have a reliable source from the sheriff's office who told me about Post's visit to the sheriff, and that was not cordial. Has Garrick met him?"

"No," Nightingale said. "Why do you ask?"

Gilbert stared at him like he'd had a brain fart. "Because—and I think you know this—Garrick has the best internal bullshit indicator of any white man I've ever met."

"Coming from an Indian, that's quite a compliment. I'll be sure and never tell Garrick you said that. He wouldn't let me forget it."

They ordered food and talked about other things until dark. Nightingale didn't realize how much he had enjoyed talking to Bob Gilbert until he was driving home.

The drinks had made him mellow, but he realized that Gilbert was a good friend. As he pulled his truck into the driveway, he figured he could count his friends on one hand. Surely he and Garrick were friends, but Nightingale knew there was more bothering him than friendship. People talked. People had insinuated that he and Sutton might be kin.

Nightingale had tried to ignore the idea, but lately it was like a festering wound. He wanted to forget it and could not. Sutton Garrick had trained him as a Ranger. Nightingale didn't know when he'd first heard about the rumor. He tried to get the memory to the front of his brain and knew it was like a sleeping monster—it should be left to draw up into a knot and die.

In the house, his phone rang. He picked it up and walked to the back porch where Bandit waited for him. With a practiced move, he simultaneously opened the back door and said, "Hello."

Mac Belschner's Texas drawl didn't start immediately. "Nightingale, you'll need to come by my office tomorrow morning. Got some strange findings on this body of yours."

Nightingale looked at the clock. Ten o'clock. He didn't know the M.E. worked so late. "Can you give me any information now?"

"Not over the phone. I'd rather show you. Don't come before nine."

10

The next morning, Nightingale waited for the second alarm before he put his feet on the floor. Sleep had been troubled with small "what ifs" running around in his head. What if the dead man was high on drugs? What if he was part of a gang? What if he had been killed after he hit the ground? And, to be honest with himself, Nightingale hoped for an ordinary death because his cousins were imaginative individuals, and he didn't want to deal with the amateur detective thoughts and machinations that they might concoct.

Barefooted, in jeans and a shirt, he made a pot of coffee and went to the back porch, where he lifted weights while Bandit ran around the yard. Nightingale had chosen the house for the tree in the back yard and, at the time, for its lush green grass. Since that time, he'd found out that the owner had watered the lawn—a lot. After he bought the place, the rains had also decreased. He tried to keep some green in the back yard, but the latest drought had killed most of his efforts. Last year had offered no relief. He suspected the next war would be over lack of drinking water but couldn't worry for the world.

His closest neighbors were a mile away, but their house was

visible. They had joked that if either household ever needed help, they'd send up a flare. With this drought, though, a flare might not solve as many problems as it would create.

Exercise was never a favorite pastime, but he enjoyed running and had a treadmill where he often got some of his best insights. Today he did the minimum with weights and sat on the back step watching the dog before heading inside for a shower. Once again, he was happy with the six-foot-tall chain link fence that kept Bandit in and other critters out. He'd chosen the fence so he and his first dog could see out onto the prairie. He knew his hidden claustrophobia would kick in if he put up a wood fence.

Back inside, he had a cup of coffee and halfway listened to the local market report on the radio even though he didn't understand much about pork bellies. Somehow, if corn futures were up, he felt better.

When Garrick didn't answer his cell phone, Nightingale decided that he had probably gone into Broken Rock to spend time with Constable Robinson, as he often did in times of boredom. Both the constable and Deputy Hall admired Rangers, and Garrick had a built-in audience for tales of his exploits when he went to their office for a few hours of bullshit. At seven thirty, Nightingale made sure Bandit had access to the house through his dog door and headed for Broken Rock to see the local constable.

Nightingale thought of Broken Rock as a set out of an old western. Most buildings were two stories with shared walls. Other structures had several feet of space between them. The jail, made of concrete blocks, shared walls with a vacant building to the right and the newspaper offices to the left. Several antiques stores were scattered up and down the street. He had rarely seen customers in any of them, however, he guessed the desks in the constable's office came from some store along the way. A staircase in the office led to a living space in the second story.

He didn't know how often Robinson slept there, but it struck him as a handy addition. And he seriously doubted that Robinson or Hall made an excellent salary. Both of them had second jobs, when anything was available. Parking on the street was free, and one of the vehicles was Garrick's navy-blue truck. He parked beside it. A glance at the newspaper office showed it to be open, and the young man who covered sports was leaving with a camera in his hand. Nightingale waved. He wondered if the attractive woman was still around and why she had needed to see Stockbridge. With no reason himself to see the editor, he scanned the street for other cars and, seeing none, moseyed down the street to the constable's office.

Sure enough, Garrick occupied a cane-bottom chair in front of Constable Robinson, whose feet were resting comfortably on his desk. Deputy Hall nursed a cup of coffee at his desk.

The constable's office was plain and functional. Down a short hall, visible to anyone walking in, were the old-fashioned barred enclosures that served as a jail when needed. The cigars that Robinson favored had left a pungent, fake-cherry smell that couldn't cover the chemical tang of bleach from the commodes.

Everyone said hello and Deputy Hall offered coffee. Nightingale stood around for a few minutes listening to the men talk in short syllables about the weather before he interrupted them. "Garrick, need to talk to you. See you fellas later."

Garrick followed him out of the office.

"I'm headed to the M.E.'s office. You were so interested in the dead man, I thought you'd want to go along."

"I definitely do, but how about you following me to the ranch, or vice versa, and we take one vehicle?"

Nightingale followed the blue truck. When Garrick joined him, Nightingale said, "Might as well drive by the place where we found him, since you haven't seen it."

"Well, about that," Garrick said. "After what you told me

yesterday, I drove up to the subdivision, but I didn't want to get my DNA on what might be a crime scene. Tape was blowing in the wind. I know Imogene won't take to that if it stays around."

"Yeah, they're both looking forward to getting into the house before winter." Nightingale had picked up on Garrick's observation about Imogene, but he let it go. "Let's go look things over at the new house, anyway," he said and drove on.

"What are they gonna do with their old house after they move out?" Garrick asked.

"Try to sell, I guess. Haven't told me."

Nightingale enjoyed having Garrick along. The old man might be a problem with his outspoken ways, but he had a keen sense about people. Another thing was that Garrick didn't mind working for free. They could exchange insults about no pay and Garrick would threaten to quit, but it was all talk. For the moment, Nightingale was happy with his decision, and he knew the way to be fair to Garrick was to tell him everything. He recounted his day with Post.

"Will that be something you tell the governor?" Garrick asked.

"Not the specifics. She usually trusts my senses, and if she asks for why, I'll tell her how I came to my conclusions. I don't know enough yet for a solid decision, but Mr. Post likes himself. Everybody will know his proclivities because he'll tell them."

"And the body showed up when?"

Nightingale could help the small smile. "I know what you're getting at, but this dead person has nothing to do with the governor, so don't try to bring in that tarot card, crystal ball-predicting voodoo stuff that you drag out when I work for her."

Garrick held up his hands in mock surrender. "Just wanted to point out the coincidence."

Nightingale had no time for it. "So, if you didn't go into the house, what did you do?"

"Guys were working on other houses. I talked to some of them. Not much luck. You know my Spanish."

"Did you mention the dead man?"

"No. Seemed out of line."

Nightingale slowed the truck to look at Garrick. "That never stopped you before. You sick?"

"No, smart ass. I just didn't feel like giving those guys a hard time."

As they drove into the Mesa Heights subdivision, they could see the progress that had been made on several houses. The streets were paved, and a few additional sites had signs of new construction starting. Nightingale pulled the truck up to the curb in front of his cousins' new house. "Let's see if anything has changed."

The day had warmed to high fifties, so they left their jackets in the truck before crossing the brown ground. Tufts of sandy bluestem grass waved in the wind, and buffalo grass still clumped in big knots of dirt leading to the front door.

"This is gonna be a hell of a lot of mowing," Garrick said.

"They'll probably surprise me with something like a yard of river rock or plastic turf, but I haven't asked yet," Nightingale said. He stopped and looked at the house for a minute. The long windows reminded him of his cousins' current house. However, the house had a contemporary air that grew on him and seemed different for his cousins. It would eventually look like the dream home both women wanted. But now it was a skeleton with a sad beginning.

Garrick continued on around the house, and Nightingale caught up with him at the bloodstained concrete. "The roof looks steep," Garrick said. "You didn't see safety gear?"

"I saw a rope attached to the anchor on the roof. And there was a ladder. There are two anchors if you look up there. The rope was swinging loose, but he didn't have a harness on. He was splayed out like he'd slipped or tripped backwards. His neck was twisted, and Brewster mentioned a possible scratch or injury on his neck that was hidden from us. I read up on some safety rules from OSHA last night, and I've got to talk to the supervisor, but I wanted to talk to the medical examiner first."

"Sounds like a good plan. Let's go see Belschner," Garrick said.

As they drove out of the subdivision, Nightingale looked for some sign of men at work. A parked truck at the entrance was the only thing he saw, and it had no one in it. Granted, it was early, but he felt like a pall had come over the entire area.

~

ON THE OTHER HAND, THE CITY OF LUBBOCK SEEMED vibrant for nine in the morning. Nightingale parked in the lot attached to the county office building that housed the M.E.'s office. Several cars and trucks indicated a busy start to the day. The office had an administrative assistant, but she had other duties as well as taking care of the M.E.'s visitors and was not at her desk. Nightingale and Garrick looked around and, by unstated agreement, headed down the hall to Belschner's office. Nightingale knocked on the open door, and they walked in.

Mac Belschner had always been a studious doctor. Nightingale figured he probably read medical journals for entertainment and wrote books about anatomy as a hobby. Belschner was sitting at his computer, and when he turned to face them, his eyes were glazed, his mind obviously still on his computer subject. It took a few seconds, but he finally smiled and greeted both of them by name.

"Interesting article," he said. He stood and waved to the two Rangers. "Follow me. It's about the time of death determined by insect matter in a…" He stopped mid-stride. "I'm sorry. I get caught up in my work. You want to know about the man that you found. I understand that you have a name for him, but I'm waiting on a confirmation."

He pushed open double doors, and the smell of formaldehyde and antiseptics filled the air.

"Whew," Garrick said. "How do you work here all the time, Mac?"

Belschner ignored the question and walked to a corpse under a sheet. He gave the sheet a dramatic flip. "I wanted to show you what I found," he said. "I can't give you an official conclusion right now. His neck was broken, but there was another factor." He waited a long minute.

Nightingale and Garrick looked at each other. "His neck was broken? Give me some clues, here, Mac. Was he murdered?" Nightingale asked.

Belschner smiled, obviously enjoying his role. "There are several peculiar things to note. He had some odd drugs in his system, a Rompun/xylazine mix. Ranchers use it to sedate horses and sometimes cattle. The injection of the drug mix was administered in the neck."

"How and when?" Nightingale asked.

"The injection looked to be at an angle above and behind the man, so I would guess someone taller than he was," Belschner said.

"Were there signs of him struggling against an injection? I guess I don't know what to ask," Nightingale said.

"I think you need to know how quickly the drugs would act," Belschner said. "The answer is within seconds, and no, I saw no sign of a struggle against an instrument or person. He was turned, probably away from the person, and was injected."

"Did the drugs kill him?" Nightingale asked.

"I don't know for sure. I'm still waiting on some of the lab results. Right now, I can't tell you positively what killed him. With the right dose, he didn't feel anything when he fell. The strange thing is he had no other broken bones. I'm guessing he was limber, like an intoxicated person in a wreck who has broken bones."

"I guess those drugs are common around here," Garrick said.

"Common in a veterinarian's office. I don't know how ordinary it would be for our ranchers."

"Earlier you implied that you didn't think he died from falling off a roof," Nightingale said. "So when did his neck get broken?"

"I must recant that opinion, Mr. Nightingale. Both the broken neck *and* the drugs raced to end his life. Either one could have killed him." Belschner's tone was terse.

Nightingale realized he'd become accusatory with his last speculation. "Sorry, doctor. I'm just trying to get my facts straight. Give me a hint."

"Mr. Nightingale, the human body is not a game. Sometimes the greatest jolt from a car wreck causes no damage, but sometimes the slightest jostle breaks a victim's neck. I will call you when I have new information." With those words, he covered the corpse and turned away from them.

The air conditioning clicked, and frigid air blasted the room. Already cold, it would soon be icy. "Thanks, doctor," Nightingale said and motioned with his head toward the door as he and Garrick walked out.

11

Silence filled the truck as they drove away from the medical examiner's office an hour before noon. Nightingale felt a buzz of questions inside his head. He was surprised by Belschner's finding, even though he had thought the man's death looked odd. Then, too, Portia's intuition nagged at him. She had mentioned that knot in her stomach when he was having supper with them. She also said Joshua's death was not an accident. She thought he'd had 'foul play done to him.'

She'd admitted that she'd kept some things secret in her own past. The same might go for the things she knew about Joshua. Maybe there were bits and pieces that she or Imogene didn't think were important but might be information that would help an investigation. He would have to talk to her again, and it wouldn't be easy, knowing how hostile she had been of late.

"I don't think Belschner was happy with his findings," Garrick said.

"I don't know about that. I think he likes the challenge, but the question remains: was it murder and is it really Joshua Tallman? Belschner is precise. We can wait for the final analysis. But we need to find out who the man is. Portia says his name is

Joshua Tallman, but I don't know what to think. Can you check missing persons? I'm going to the subdivision to find the man who hired him. That's no flimsy operation. They've got to have payrolls, background checks." He stopped to let Garrick out at his house. "If all else fails, I'll drive into Austin."

∽

AFTER LEAVING GARRICK, NIGHTINGALE CALLED PORTIA'S cell but got no answer, so he left a mundane will-call-later message, then drove to Broken Rock and stopped at the *Intelligencer*. Stanley Stockbridge was in the paste-up room with the woman Nightingale had seen in the offices earlier in the week.

Stockbridge saw him through the big double doors and raised his voice as he waved an invitation. "Come on in. Nightingale, this is Ms. Evelyn Hartley, who is considering buying this newspaper. She knows all of this stuff is useless"—he waved at the room of light tables, waxers, pica poles, and assorted chemicals —"but there's a museum in Lubbock interested in taking it off my hands. Or the high school might want it."

Nightingale took off his hat and shook hands with Evelyn Hartley. She was not as beautiful as he'd thought at first, but she was attractive in a way he couldn't describe. Exotic, maybe? No. He'd think about it. Her narrow face was framed by shoulder-length auburn hair that she had pulled back into a clip at her neck. Curls escaped at the side. She was thin, and Nightingale suspected that she might have too much nervous energy. However, her grip was warm and strong, and she grinned, smiling straight at him, almost daring him to categorize her. Her huge brown eyes twinkled at some inward joke, making him wonder if she was serious about buying the newspaper.

"You look skeptical, Mr. Nightingale," she said. "I grew up around newspapers. 'Course it was in the east. I'm looking forward to living in Broken Rock and getting a southern accent as soon as possible."

Nightingale returned the smile. People usually didn't read him that well. "Didn't mean to look anything but friendly," he said. "Welcome. I was going to ask Stanley if he'd join me for lunch at the Amish restaurant. Maybe we could all go."

Stockbridge asked for a raincheck. "We've got some business details to clear up. And after we get everything taken care of here, Evelyn has to find a place to stay, something to rent. Evelyn, excuse us a minute."

Stockbridge took Nightingale by the elbow, and they walked to his office. "Thought I'd tell you that the new man in town called me and told me that he was going to buy the newspaper. He asked my price and said he'd come by in a day or so and pay me cash." Stockbridge had been speaking almost in a whisper. Then he began pacing. He pushed the door shut before facing Nightingale. "That man would ruin this paper. I won't let him have it."

"That's a mighty bold statement, Stanley," Nightingale said.

"I know. If this woman doesn't come through, well. . . I don't know, but I'm worried, and I wanted you to know. I guess we need to get back to her."

They returned to Hartley with smiles on their faces. Nightingale nodded and said, "Hope to see you soon," as he walked out. He needed time to think. He felt like a rude youth, like the ones his mother had warned him against. But Evelyn Hartley's smile stayed with him. He hoped she would buy the *Intelligencer*.

Nightingale walked toward the restaurant and stared at his reflection in the door while he mused over what else he could do to find out the true identity of the dead man. Somehow, the phrasing that his cousins used, "he called himself Tallman, but he thought that was funny because he wasn't really tall," made Nightingale think they didn't really know the man's name and that's why they never gave him a straight answer about it. If he was Post's son, he might have changed his name after leaving home. Nightingale needed DNA.

The door opened and John Miller, owner of the restaurant, stood there, looking at him quizzically. "Would you like to come in?"

Nightingale felt foolish. He'd been caught thinking of something else. He mumbled something as Miller showed him to a table, making no comments. John Miller looked like he always did, starched light-blue shirt matching his eyes, and suspenders for his dark pants, like many of his Amish brethren. He had an air of peace about him. Nightingale wished he knew the man better.

No one else was in the restaurant. They rarely had huge crowds, but the business was steady, and Nightingale always saw people in there enjoying the food.

Sarah Miller brought cutlery to the table. Nightingale guessed Sarah to be anywhere from fifteen to twenty-two. She wore no makeup but had a sprinkle of freckles across her nose, and her skin showed no signs of ever being in the sun. Nightingale found Amish folk, even the men, to be beautiful in a fresh, natural way. She laid a one-page menu in front of him and said nothing.

"Water, please. And I'll think about what I want to eat."

She nodded and walked away. Nightingale stared at the menu and realized again that the quiet in the restaurant caught his attention. Every restaurant he'd ever visited had some sort of music thudding under and through and over the noise of customer voices. As a matter of fact, most restaurants were too noisy. John Miller's establishment was eerily quiet. Nightingale heard muffled voices from the kitchen and the rattle of silverware. The squeaks of the wooden floor led him to look up at Sarah's Miller's blushing face. Nightingale remembered her blushing every time he saw her.

She placed the water on the table. "What would you like to order?"

Nightingale's experience had been that the vegetables were good and the burgers delicious. He gave himself a star for healthy eating and ordered a vegetable plate, knowing the green beans would be homegrown, the potatoes loaded with butter, and the corn from their freezer, but all of that seemed satisfying. "I'd like cornbread, too, if you have it, and if your father doesn't mind, I'd like to talk with him."

Sarah blushed a hot pink and hurried to the back.

In a few minutes, a somber-looking John Miller came through the kitchen door and stood at Nightingale's table. "Is anything wrong? Sarah said you wanted to talk to me."

Nightingale tried to lighten the man's obvious concern. "Nothing, John. I just wondered if you've met your new neighbor?"

A slight smile came onto Miller's mouth. "Oh, yes, you mean Mr. Post and that big house of his next door to me. He came to the school one day. He was kind, but"—Miller hesitated as if searching for a word—"unusual. He offered money to me to update the school." Miller smiled as big as Nightingale had ever seen and became transformed into a light-hearted man. "I explained that we are self-sufficient, but I asked him to talk to his drivers to give our buggies some consideration on the road. Then he left."

"Anything else?"

"Yes. He had a young boy with him. A child I would guess was twelve or thirteen. He introduced him as his son, Adam."

"I wonder about the fence. I see it in front of the property. Does your property abut Mr. Post's?"

"In parts," Miller said. His gaze wandered to the door where a couple of ranchers were coming inside. Miller excused himself and seated the two men on the far side of the establishment.

John Miller was a leader in the Amish fellowship, and Nightingale wanted to keep a good relationship with that body. John had called him once about locals driving too fast around their buggies, but he'd been low-key, never pressing charges. The Amish made a good, no-nonsense community. The information about Post was interesting—he certainly seemed ready to throw his money around—but now, Nightingale had to get to the real reason for his visit.

When Miller returned to the table, Nightingale continued. "John, I'm curious about anyone moving here and putting up a tall fence. I've not been around the entire property. Has Mr. Post put the fence all the way around his land?" Nightingale saw no use in pretending that he had only concern for the Amish people. He was tempted to tell Miller the real reason for his questions but thought better of it.

Miller gave the slightest nod. "As far as I can tell it goes all the way around." He smiled. "My land only abuts his for a few miles, but the children had great fun watching the equipment and workers as the fence went up."

"So, have the traffic issues resolved?"

"Yes, and I think the noise will be less as they settle in."

"Noise?" Nightingale asked. "What noise?"

"He put his airport on the back side of the property. His helicopter and airplanes." Miller's smile stretched as he turned one finger around to mimic the rotors. "But we know we must adjust to some things, too."

His food was on the table, and he needed to let Miller get back to his work, but Nightingale had one more question. "What do you think of the new subdivision outside of Obsidian?"

"I need more customers. I wish them well. Enjoy your meal."

Nightingale said thank you and began eating, enjoying the vegetables and looking forward to custard pie.

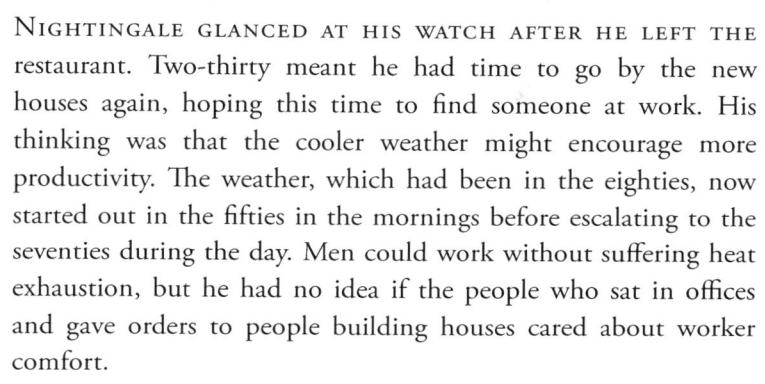

Nightingale glanced at his watch after he left the restaurant. Two-thirty meant he had time to go by the new houses again, hoping this time to find someone at work. His thinking was that the cooler weather might encourage more productivity. The weather, which had been in the eighties, now started out in the fifties in the mornings before escalating to the seventies during the day. Men could work without suffering heat exhaustion, but he had no idea if the people who sat in offices and gave orders to people building houses cared about worker comfort.

He guessed jobs were subcontracted by the primary subdivision owner, but he had to research to find out how this particular subdivision operated. The streets were paved and some electricity set, but he didn't know what the plans were for water. Lake Alan Henry and the Ogallala aquifer supplied most of the water in the area. He was guessing septic tanks would provide sewage service. Then again, how much minutiae did he need to find the name of the dead man?

He still had questions for his cousins, but he didn't want to wait any longer. At the subdivision, activity was back. Two trucks were lined up on the curb of the main entrance. He drove into the street where he remembered his cousins' house was going up. A few houses from there he saw men. He parked the truck and walked quickly to them. Their unease was palpable, but so was the fact that they were three men to his one. Two men were on the roof, and one was handing lumber up to them.

They were Mexican; the Mexicans he knew were usually friendly and caring. He walked closer to the man on the ground and said, "I need your help."

The man on the ground relayed the message to his friends on the roof. They said nothing in return.

Nightingale said, "My cousins are buying one of these houses. A man died a few days ago at their house on the other street. I'm trying to find out who he was. He was a roofer. If you could tell me who hired you, where is the office? I could ask them."

The man standing in front of him said, "My name is Arnoldo. I think you are talking about Joshua. We only met him once. We begin the houses. We told him we could help with the roof." He turned to look to the men on the roof.

"You know John Chavez?" Nightingale said to the man's back.

A long pause filled with Arnoldo saying something in Spanish to his friends on the roof. No one replied.

"That was the man who hired me," Arnoldo said. He didn't face Nightingale when he spoke but kept handing boards up to his coworkers.

Nightingale saw that he would only cause ill will if he continued. "Thanks anyway," he said. He walked to his truck and drove back to the small mobile office that he'd seen every time he'd driven into Mesa Heights. He'd seen the sign saying, "Heavenly Homes at down-to-earth prices," in a poster covering one window. He scribbled the Lubbock address and phone number on a piece of paper.

He drove out of the subdivision determined to find out something concrete about the dead man. Maybe Lubbock would give up some secrets.

Sitting in his truck at the strip center where Heavenly Homes had an office, Nightingale pulled out his phone and dialed the number he'd written in his palm. A recorded voice told him he had reached a number that was disconnected or no longer in service. Disappointed but not surprised, he walked to the front of the shopping center where he saw a directory.

The office was closed and looked deserted. A map on the front door showed many of the lots at Mesa Heights sold. A phone number was printed on the door, and as Nightingale stood there, he tried it. It was disconnected. He worried that his cousins had put a down payment on a house that might never be completed. Scams like that were usually perpetrated on Mexicans who didn't have a good grasp of English, but for all their education, he felt like Portia and Imogene were too trusting. Still, there could be a couple thousand dollars at stake.

The afternoon had disappeared, so he drove home, thinking that he still needed to talk with his cousins. A silver truck with New York plates sat in his driveway. He stopped behind the truck and walked to the driver's side.

Carolyn Post had her window down. "All right if I exit the vehicle?"

Nightingale appreciated the attempt at humor. "I'm hoping you have no weapon."

When she slipped down out of the truck, the girl looked more like a woman than he remembered from their first encounter. He guessed she had deliberately found the tightest blue jeans she could get into. And she'd left the top button to her shirt undone. For a moment he wished for a cab camera. But several years of wisdom clicked into place; he stood back, keeping his face impassive.

"When did you get out of the hospital?"

"Last night," she said.

"I'm surprised your father let you come over here."

"He doesn't know I'm here," she said. "I want to tell you why I--why I was so upset the other day." She stood by her truck, one hand still on the door handle, like she might decide to jump in and drive away at any minute.

"My father is not married to my mother," she said. "I know that sounds pretty ordinary, but I had an older brother that my father denies."

Nightingale tried to sound casual. "Really?" The situation was not that odd to him. However, as she rolled her eyes in frustration, he guessed she was trying to preface her words and explain some of her earlier actions.

"No, you don't understand. My father denies that Billy is alive. He plays with words and often lies, so now I think he's right. I think my brother really is dead."

She looked and sounded so sad, Nightingale almost believed her. She was like a child, hurt because something had gone wrong in her family. This girl was different from the one who had broken into the discussion between her father and Nightingale. At that time, Nightingale thought she sounded like a shrew, spoiled and argumentative. Now she seemed softer, more understanding.

"I don't know why you're telling me," he said.

"Because"—she looked away, over his shoulder— "I think the man who died in the new subdivision was my brother."

"How did you hear about that? And why do you think he might be your brother?" Nightingale asked.

She ignored the first question. "My brother called me a while back, when we were still living in New York. I was mad at him, but he said he'd see me when I got to Texas and we could talk."

"You were mad at him?"

This time she looked directly at him, her eyes angry with him or her brother, but full of venom. "Because he escaped and told me he would rescue me when we were older, but he never did."

"I still don't know why you think the dead man is your brother," Nightingale said.

"He called me again, four days ago," she said. The sadness crept back into her voice. "He told me that he had worked on the house that I now live in. He said he saw our father. He told me he was working for a construction company and that some people were mad at him. He was worried because he owed money. He'd never asked me for money." She looked away again, a guilty droop to her eyes. "He didn't ask for money then, but now he doesn't answer his phone and I'm worried." She glanced at her watch. "I've got to get home."

She turned abruptly and was back in the truck in seconds.

"Wait a minute. What else did he say?" Nightingale asked. For some reason, the image of the person on the horse the day he discovered Joshua's body came to him. He wondered if it could have been her but had no time to ask.

She started the engine and didn't look at him again. Nightingale shook his head and stepped away from the truck, wondering if she was telling the truth. Truth lately seemed to be a commodity no one had a grip on.

12

Nightingale watched the girl drive away and started toward his house. She acted odd, but the whole situation seemed odd. He was halfway to the front porch when his phone rang. It was Governor Daniels. Nightingale stood on the porch and admired the sunset while he listened.

"Mr. Nightingale, do you have any news for me on Edgar Post? I'm scheduled to meet with him in a couple of hours."

Nightingale closed his eyes to try to better hear every nuance in her words. He wished he could see the governor. He relied on body language in conversations. She sounded frustrated.

"I've met with him, more than once," he said. "I'm not his favorite person, Governor. I'm worried about him, his character. I can't describe it. His daughter became ill while I visited him, and he acted put off that she dared to be ill. But he did go to the hospital with her."

He didn't add the degree of Post's frustration at his daughter's illness. There was no way to explain that to the governor because it came from Nightingale's assessment when he watched Post waiting.

A half minute of silence filled the phone. Nightingale thought through how much he could safely add.

"That's interesting but not a character flaw. Do you have anything specific? I need facts," the governor said.

Nightingale took a deep breath. "His daughter, who was sick, thinks he may have something to do with the death of a man who she says is her long-lost brother. We are checking on the identity of the man, but I have nothing concrete for you. I've had a couple of encounters with Mr. Post, but it would take an hour to tell you all of it and you'd still have no conclusion."

Another long pause. "I see." She drew in a long breath and exhaled. "All right, I won't decide anything definite tonight. So, what is your opinion? Truthfully."

"If you're considering putting a large sum of money in the hands of Mr. Post, waiting would be my advice."

"Thank you. Keep working on it. I'll call later." She hung up before Nightingale could say goodbye, but where he started the conversation wondering about her mood, now he knew. She *was* as frustrated as she'd sounded. She was also very unhappy.

Nightingale had worked for different male governors, a couple of state senators, and a judge. This was the second time he'd worked for Governor Daniels. Part of his job for any of these people had always involved a subconscious assessment of why some people committed crimes. And it also involved an assessment of his clients, such as the governor. Why were they a senator, governor, or judge? And why did they need him?

He liked and respected the lady governor. Deep down, and he didn't tell many people, he thought women were better doctors than men because of empathy. He'd decided Governor Daniels was a good governor for a somewhat similar reason. She really seemed concerned about the people of her state. She had said, "Watch what I do, not what I say in speeches."

He thought she was probably lonely, and that accounted for

some of his concern about her and Edgar Post. He wondered about her family, so he went to his computer. He'd read some articles about her when he first worked for her, but he wanted a refresher.

She had children, an ex-husband, and a gift for leadership. The flavor of what he read led Nightingale to solidify some of his prior thinking. She was tough, but she was a woman who had been very involved with family, and now she was in an arena of tough people, most of them ready to throw her aside with the slightest charge.

She had no confidant after her previous chief of staff, who had proven to be a criminal. Even through that trouble, she'd been tough, but he feared she was emotionally vulnerable. He hoped that her pushiness about Edgar Post was not because she hoped to find a good friend in the man. But, no, Nightingale shook off the thought, almost laughing. Post couldn't be a friend to Mary Poppins.

He went to the kitchen to find food for himself, and Bandit came inside when he heard movement in the house. Nightingale wanted to talk to one or both of his cousins, so he called them while he waited for a microwaved pot pie.

Portia sounded tired when she answered.

"Hard day?" he asked.

She sighed, and he heard the ding of her microwave. "I'm having hot chocolate. I'll fix you a cup if you'll come over."

"I'll come by tomorrow. I need more information on the company you bought your house from by tomorrow."

After a pause Portia said, "Okay. Have you heard anything else about Joshua's death?"

"No." He told himself he was not lying but would tell her everything when he knew more facts. "About the company, Portia, did you give them money?"

Those words were all she needed to pounce. "Why are you

prying into my business? Yes, we gave earnest money, and I'm sure they're reputable. The principal of our school is buying out there."

Nightingale moved the phone away from his ear. This was the reason he didn't like getting tangled up with Portia. She didn't know how to get along with kinfolk who asked questions.

"I'm not doubting you. But I need contact information so I can get some answers. The Lubbock office of the builder is closed."

"They told us that would happen. I have the builder's Austin number." He heard the rustle of fabric and the click of keys and then she read a number to him. "The foreman's name is John Chavez. He's met with us once. Seemed nice enough but hurried."

The number she gave him was the number he'd gotten at the subdivision and at the shuttered office in Lubbock. He didn't mention that. "Anything else?" he asked.

"No." She paused. "But we're supposed to meet with him at the house tomorrow."

"Great," Nightingale said. "Do you mind if I meet with you?"

Silence filled the phone, but finally, Portia spoke. "Be there at nine tomorrow morning. Imogene and I will drive our own cars and go to work from there." She didn't say good-bye, just quit the call. She was thoroughly irritated, but Nightingale chose to ignore it. As usual, he didn't understand her anger. If he didn't ask questions, he couldn't help. Maybe he should talk to Imogene.

He called Garrick. "You have any luck with the missing persons?"

"Yeah, the man was my long-lost cousin."

Nightingale ignored the smart remark. He heard a series of long breaths and exaggerated sighs, Garrick's venting without words.

"It's too soon and you know it," Garrick said. "I put the

information from the M.E. into the system, so we'll wait. Why are you calling at this hour?"

"We're going to the subdivision tomorrow morning. I'll pick you up at eight."

"Yes, sir, I'd love to go with you. Can you see my smile?"

"Sorry," he said and hung up, not waiting for Garrick's further answer, and it occurred to him that he might be taking his frustration with Portia out on the other Ranger. He'd apologize in the morning.

13

Nightingale woke at 4:30. Bandit looked up at him from his bed on the floor, put his head back down on his paws, and closed his eyes. "You have no sense of adventure," he said to the dissembling dog.

He started coffee while considering the reason for waking early. He had dreamed about the dead man and Carolyn Post, but in his dream, they were lovers and not brother and sister. He didn't like the thought, wondered where his subconscious came up with such an idea, and figured it must have been those tight britches she was wearing.

That took care of introspection, so he went back to thinking about Joshua. The medical examiner had said he was injected by someone taller than him, standing behind him. He'd read on line that the drug mix Belschner mentioned acted quickly, and no one could have climbed to the roof after that kind of injection. But someone could have gone up on the roof to him, after he was there. That still left the injection a mystery because a man would not have stood still on the roof and waited for an injection in his neck.

Nightingale continued imagining what might have happened

while he did some warm-ups and then lifted weights. When he saw the first rays of the sun, he went inside and showered. He made sure Bandit could get in and out through his dog door and then headed to Garrick's place. He was barely in the drive when Garrick came out in full Ranger dress: coat, tie, and starched slacks.

Garrick got in the truck, pulled the seat belt snug, and placed his coffee cup in the holder between them. "You think I don't notice what's going on, but you need to be civil to me, and barking out orders like you did last night is not civilized."

Garrick turned slightly to look at Nightingale. "I know you resent those years I was in charge and called the shots and ordered you around, but, hell, Oz, I've changed. I was wrong to be such a pain in the ass, but you were eternally late and needed to be jacked up."

Nightingale took a small pleasure in recognizing that Garrick had got the point he'd been subtly making last night, but he didn't like the older man correcting him. He dropped the idea of an apology. "Good morning to you, too," he said.

He waited a few minutes before saying more. "The man in charge of the construction site is meeting Imogene and Portia at the house. I hope he can tell us who the dead man is."

Garrick nodded. "We may be getting some cold rain soon. Will they be in the house before Christmas?"

"Not unless there's a miracle."

Neither of them spoke again until they got to the site. The women were already there. They came out of the house smiling and greeting their guests like it was already Christmas and they had settled in their new home, barren and cold though it was.

Imogene spoke to both of them but looked at Garrick. "Come inside. It's chilly inside but there's no wind in there. It's already charming. I want to show you around."

Inside, the house showed some progress with construction.

Nightingale was surprised. "They've been working in here. You have walls. Did anyone get permission to do this?"

Portia stepped to Nightingale's side and gripped his arm. He was surprised at the strength in her hand. "Don't you dare say anything. We don't want trouble for those men. Imogene and I asked them to do what they could to hurry things along. Oswald, they worked inside the house. Joshua fell onto the concrete pad outside the house, where the patio will be. Please don't cause problems."

Nightingale looked at Garrick, who was trying mightily not to smile. "Where is this man who was going to meet us?"

Portia let up on the pressure on Nightingale's arm. "He's been late the two times we've met him."

"Whether or not he shows up, I want his phone number—a working number," Nightingale said. As the words left his lips there was a knock at the front and a man walked in.

Imogene and Portia said in unison, "Mr. Chavez."

The man came directly at Nightingale, his shoulders back, his gaze steady and friendly. He wore a shirt and red tie with a blazer that looked like it had some cashmere in it. He had on ostrich boots.

Nightingale introduced himself and Garrick. Chavez turned to the women. "We can discuss your house after I talk with these men."

Nightingale assumed that Chavez had talked with Portia and knew everything, so he explained that he had found the man who fell from the roof and that he was working with the sheriff. "I need to know the man's name and all the background information you have for him. His death may not have been an accident."

"I will gladly give you the information, except it is in Austin. I will call you with his identification number. He told me he had worked construction before and gave a reference. I admit I did not check the reference. If men do not work, they are fired, so I thought there would be no problem." The man's accent was mild, making his speech sound a bit formal.

He continued, his eyes still on Nightingale. "His name was Jeremy or Johnson or Joshua. I don't remember his last name. I asked him some technical questions about roofing and about safety, and he gave the right answers." Chavez shrugged. "We hire a man for his skills and his legal status. I hope you understand that."

"It seems strange to me that your company doesn't have an office here or in Lubbock," Nightingale said. "By the way, the man who died didn't have on safety equipment."

John Chavez's eyes narrowed. He looked like he might be sweating despite the cold air surrounding them in the house. "My company found they had"—he paused, looking around the room like he was searching for words—"overreached. Managing a building project from a distance is difficult, if you want to keep a good reputation. We decided to sell the lots to individuals, and they will follow the subdivision rules for building. We have filed the subdivision rules with the state. The house for these ladies, and two others, are the only ones my company will build. And now, I must ask you for some identification. You have to understand that I was not here to witness this terrible accident."

Nightingale pulled out his identification, and Chavez took a minute to look at the badge and business card.

"I have never heard of a Special Ranger," Chavez said. "I need your address and phone number."

"I work for the governor," Nightingale said. He gave the man the address of the Ranger office and his cell phone number and got Chavez's phone number in return. "One more thing—" he began.

"Excuse me," Portia interrupted. "We have to get to work, and we need to talk with Mr. Chavez about the construction of the house. We *will* be able to have our house finished?" Frowning, she turned first to Chavez and then to Nightingale. "Won't we, Oswald?"

Imogene stepped between them. "Of course, we will, but Oswald has to follow the laws, and I'm sure Mr. Chavez's company must, also." Imogene's eyes held Nightingale's. Her look was one of exaggerated pleading.

Nightingale took the hint. "Sure. Glad to meet you. We can talk on the phone or I can come to Austin, if I need more details." He walked toward the door.

Garrick exchanged goodbyes with the women and followed Nightingale outside.

Inside the truck and headed into town, Garrick said, "Were you trying to piss them off, or are you just gifted that way?"

"I wasn't trying to do anything. Portia is just really touchy lately. Ever since she told me that Joshua was murdered, she's been cross with me. Really, she's acted like she's mad at me since we got back from east Texas. But what is so bad is that one minute she's nice and the next she's biting my head off."

"Does she object to you asking questions? Maybe it's a woman's lib attitude, and she wants them to take care of themselves and their business. She doesn't want you horning in."

Nightingale shook his head. "I don't know. I thought she wanted my help, and now I've got to pursue it. The heck of it is, you can't investigate a murder without asking questions."

"What now?"

"I had a visit from Edgar Post's daughter. She said the dead man is Post's son, so I'm going to ask Post for a DNA sample. See if he'll cooperate by giving us something to check out against the dead man."

"Right, and if you believe he'll cooperate," Garrick said, "I have a bridge on my ranch with a pot of gold under it that I want to sell you."

14

Nightingale glanced at the clock on the dash, hoping that Post would still be at the house at ten in the morning. Garrick said nothing, which for the moment was fine.

Nightingale tried to shift his thoughts off his cousin and back to Post. He wondered again why a rich man from the city came to the flatlands. Couldn't be for the landscape.

To his right, a field that last week had been full of cotton ready for harvest now looked like an avenging army had burnt the space. A brown swath of empty stalks was the only indication that something had grown there. On the other side of the road, a crop of sunflowers had been harvested. The acres and acres of sunflowers had been a good crop to watch. Plants grew to be over six feet tall and made an amazing picture of bright yellow right before harvest. After the crop was combined, the field lay flat, like the cotton, any sign of life beaten out of it.

"Why do you think Edgar Post came here? Why come to this barren land?" Nightingale asked.

"I've wondered," Garrick said. "You and me didn't have much choice. We were born here, but you remember that woman, Casey, who visited from Tennessee?" Garrick said. He was referring to an investigating officer whom Nightingale had worked successfully with a few years earlier. "She seemed to think that we all are reflections of our environment. Maybe Post didn't like reflecting where he came from and thought he'd look better, maybe more rugged, coming from a place like this.

"I'd say he's got some motive we don't know about that only this land can answer. Maybe he came here to find his son. Maybe he's got a business that will thrive in this open space."

Nightingale grunted skeptically. "We'll see."

"I'm looking forward to meeting him," Garrick said. "Hope I can meet his daughter, too."

In spite of Garrick's cheery tone, Nightingale had his doubts. "Where's your usual skepticism? You only talk that baloney when you're playing poker."

"Is he expecting us?" Garrick asked.

"No, I didn't call."

The gate was open, so Nightingale drove through and parked on the circular drive in front of the house. The butler came to greet them and asked them inside. Nightingale explained they needed to see Post.

"Mr. Post had business in town. He was not expecting you."

"I'd like to talk with Carolyn Post, if he's not here."

The butler bowed and asked them to wait. He disappeared for a minute and was frosty when he came back.

"This way, please," he said and led them down a hall to the familiar room Nightingale thought of as a library. Garrick began reading book titles on the shelves; Nightingale stared out the window.

"Gentlemen." It wasn't Carolyn but rather Post himself who entered, throwing open the French doors they had entered, reminding Nightingale of what his mother called a whirling dervish.

Post glared, and his reddened face let everyone in sight know that he was angry. Dressed in a sweatshirt and blue jeans, he didn't look like he was going to a meeting, and Nightingale understood the butler's frostiness. Post's hair was the color of dark mahogany, sprayed, or something, so it did not move. The dead man's hair was the same color.

Post ignored Garrick's outstretched hand and self-introduction. Instead, he zeroed in on Nightingale, his anger betrayed as much by the vein protruding at his temple as his words. "After our encounter at the hospital, I didn't expect to see you here—in my home without an invitation."

"A murder investigation has a different set of parameters," Nightingale said. "We needed to talk to you, so we came to you. We could always have you come to us, if you prefer a subpoena."

Post turned away from the two men and walked to stand behind a couch. When he turned back to Nightingale, his anger seemed to be in check, although his flushed face denied his cool words. "What murder? I assumed you were here to see my daughter."

Nightingale had noticed this quick change in Post before. He had an overbearing personality and lightning-quick mood changes that made discussion difficult. Nightingale found himself deliberately slowing his words as a counterbalance. "Maybe later. You may have heard that a man died at the new subdivision that's outside of Obsidian."

Post gave a shallow shake of his head his head. He remained stiff, uncaring, but he listened.

"A man fell—or was pushed—off a house that was under construction in the new Mesa Heights subdivision. The coroner believes the man was murdered. Some of the men who worked with the dead man said he claimed to be related to you. Just wondered if you knew him. And would you mind giving us some saliva for a DNA test to rule you out?"

Post stared, looking incredulous. He blinked and shook his head.

Nightingale's face remained friendly, neighborly.

"Mr. Nightingale, I am guessing that this request of yours is because of some wild accusation from my daughter. She is under psychiatric care. My daughter said she talked with you, and there were questions, so I will answer. No, I have no older son who has been a nomad for many years and is now dead. You cannot have a DNA sample from me. If you pursue that ridiculous idea, you will meet my attorney. Now, you and your sidekick need to leave."

He walked to the library doors where the Rangers had entered and held one of them open, so angry now he was visibly shaking. "Stay away from my family." Almost as an afterthought, he growled, "And next time—call before you show up, or better yet, don't come a next time."

∼

NIGHTINGALE AND GARRICK WALKED ALONG THE MARBLE-tiled hall toward the outer door of Edgar Post's house. The butler had hurried ahead of them. But they took their time, admiring art on the walls, not saying sentences as much as muttering syllables that would mean nothing on any device that might be, and surely was, listening to them. At the front door, they put on their hats and went to the truck, which was waiting just where they had left it.

They took their time here, too, buckling seat belts and leaving. Once out of the enclave, Nightingale turned to Garrick. "So, you wanted to meet him. What do you think?"

"The man is dangerous."

Nightingale didn't try to hide his surprise. "How can you say that after one meeting? I don't like him, but dangerous?"

"Oz, you asked me." Garrick shrugged, tugged at his hat, and said nothing else. He looked out the window at the fence they were passing on one side of the road.

Nightingale wanted more out of him. "I think his anger is a bit uncalled for." He looked sideways at Garrick, checking for a reaction.

"It's a wonder he hasn't had a stroke," Garrick said. "Everything is bottled up in him, and he's angry at everyone. I'd guess he has no friends—I mean real friends. I'd guess he has a wife he lies to and a beautiful mistress stashed someplace."

Nightingale listened for a subtext to Garrick's comment and heard none. Basically, Garrick confirmed some of his, Nightingale's, own conclusions that Post was ego-driven and had anger issues that could be dangerous. He probably wouldn't mention his speculation to the governor yet, but it was not a good picture for Edgar Post.

When he got to Garrick's house, Nightingale turned into the drive and waited for him to get out.

Garrick pulled the door handle and looked away from Nightingale toward the field across from his house. It, like most of the surrounding land, was flattened prairie, barren and ugly under the November skies.

Nightingale waited for him to step away from the truck, wondering about his thoughts.

"You know, Nightingale, I had a speech prepared. I was gonna quit working with you after you've been ordering me around so much lately. But seeing that man... I've come to consider that none of us knows what goes on in another person's mind. I've always enjoyed working with you, but if you still want to work together you need to respect me. And if you want to order me around, then you can find yourself another man. I don't have to have this job." He closed the door quietly and walked away.

Nightingale watched him go. Then he pulled onto the road. Garrick and he had argued before; Garrick had cussed and raved at him, but he had never been like this. His words stung, causing bitterness that fed doubts. And Nightingale had no idea what had happened to elicit such an ultimatum. As a matter of fact, he had more reason than Garrick to be angry.

They had to talk, more than just assertions and mean words. They had to talk about truth.

15

Garrick walked into his house feeling the brief stab of loneliness for his wife. "Nancy, if you were here, I'd quit gallivanting across this prairie. Miss you, girl." Didn't do any good, except to make the hurt a bit less. The thoughts of his wife made the conflict with Nightingale seem small. They needed to talk, like they used to do, but not now, not in the middle of an investigation.

Inside the house, he smelled onion and bay leaf, the makings of beef stew. He placed his hat on a side table and shook his head, trying to physically get rid of the sadness. Never worked, but he tried just the same.

He saw no sign of Sophie, the woman who cooked for him, just the beefy aroma of the stew. No speck of dust showed. She had dusted and cleaned, too, while he was gone.

He glanced toward the kitchen, then he headed down the hall and into his office. Edgar Post bothered him. The man had enough pent-up rage to start his own nuclear war. He had no criminal record or Nightingale would have mentioned it, but he had the look and the eyes of a killer. And somehow— Garrick had been with Nightingale long enough to know this—Nightingale expected a crystal-ball assessment from him. Garrick had been his own worst enemy by talking to his former partner so often about gut reactions.

Actually, for the first ten years as a Ranger, Garrick had followed the book. He wrote up every detail and consulted superiors when in doubt. Gradually, he backed off and observed, holding his instincts to himself but keeping count of when they were right. That proved to be most of the time.

But when Nancy was killed by an escaped prisoner who hated him, Garrick realized he could not rely on his senses because when people close to him were in trouble, his senses shut down. Emotions took over.

He sat at the computer and typed in Post's name. There was little information. A few business articles in the publications, but nothing on his family, not even a Facebook account. Garrick had a grudging admiration for the lack of social media entangling Post.

Soon, though, the meager findings let his brain wander. For some reason, his thoughts went to Imogene. She was always smiling. At least, whenever he saw her.

In the last few years, he had hoped for a companion—a woman to love, even though no one could replace Nancy. Imogene would never try to replace Nancy. But he feared he was far too gloomy and uneducated for a woman like Imogene.

Lack of education bothered him. He'd finished high school, but that and courses to keep up with Ranger rules and regulations were all he had. Imogene didn't flaunt her training as a nurse, and he appreciated that. He enjoyed talking to her. 'Course he enjoyed talking to most women. Fact of the matter was, he just enjoyed women more than men. Women generally had more empathy with people than men. And they didn't mind talking about emotions like love and hate. He enjoyed thinking about other people's emotions. He liked trying to figure out other people, just not himself. He gave himself a half smile at his self-awareness. So why was he uneasy? He couldn't sit still. He decided to drive into Broken Rock.

He quit the computer and went to his truck. He would find nothing new, but he could talk to people, have a beer, and escape this web of darkness that had covered him since he got home. He drove the back roads.

He'd left home when he was fourteen. After working on farms and in oil fields, he decided he needed more income to live like he wanted. He'd seen early on that the most respected men in the west were often law men, Rangers.

Rangers were not perfect. He'd heard about the forced confessions, the arrests and convictions of innocent people. He'd seen some of it, but the men he knew were basically good men who now and then got carried away with their duty. Time had taught him that living through a crime made a person's perspective change.

When Broderick had killed Nancy, Garrick went numb. He quit being a Ranger that day and became an animal after his prey. He went through the house and picked out a rifle and pistol and lots of ammunition. He saddled a horse and rode out thinking of nothing except how much pain he could inflict on the man who had killed his wife. When he found Broderick, he shot him, in his knee first, then two more times before he finished him off. He made sure the man suffered before he brought his body back and handed in his badge. Then he went home and climbed into a bottle.

After Nancy died, he was surprised at the way his thoughts circled in on themselves, tearing at him with atavistic savagery, making him dissect his mind, his heart, his love and hate. He questioned every case he had handled, every human he could remember, all the way back to his childhood.

Somewhere in the middle of his rage, Nightingale's mother,

Mary, had reached him and helped him see that Nancy's death was not a punishment because of him or the way he lived. But he was not proud of his life.

As he tore through memories, he tore through events. Mary Nightingale had rescued him. And he was ashamed of his love for her, both early and late in his life. He owed her, and her son, more than he could ever repay. He'd always wanted Nightingale to be his son; in fact, he usually thought of him that way.

The thing was: why had this meeting with Edgar Post triggered his memories of the past which he thought he had put to rest? Was it Post's mannerisms, his ego and pride? Something hung there behind this wavering screen of memories, scritching at him but just far away enough to be unknowable.

Edgar Post cared for no one but himself. But it had to be Post's lack of care for family that cut to the quick. Something about Post pulled up dead memories and, eventually, Garrick would know what about the man connected with his own melancholy and made him know that Edgar Post was dangerous.

Garrick had been driving a back road, not noticing his surroundings, and the first building he saw was Josephine Holly's Bed and Breakfast. His watch read noon, so he wasn't surprised that he'd wound up here.

In the last few weeks, he had admitted to himself that he didn't understand Josephine, but he still loved her pies. He considered Josephine a good friend and someone who continually educated him on women. Garrick smiled at the sight of the big Victorian house and pulled his truck into a parking space, hoping Josephine had something baked.

Nightingale's past relationship with Josephine had complicated Garrick's vision about her and Oz and love in general. He sat in the truck a minute, gathering his thoughts. This was the first time he'd seen Josephine since returning from east Texas. He had wanted her and Oswald to marry because he thought they needed each other. He had been wrong on many counts. He'd meddled and now regretted it. Well, he'd pretend that everything was fine. It really wasn't his business.

He let himself through the white picket fence, admiring the roses that had been added after water became more available.

He didn't see Josephine until she pushed the screen door open. "Sutton Garrick, it is so good to see you." She hugged him, drew him into the house. "I just got a peach cobbler out of the oven. Come in and meet my new lodger, Evelyn Hartley."

Garrick pushed aside his recriminations and headed into the dining room. A good-looking woman—auburn hair streaked with copper, eyes that made him think of Nancy—laid her phone down on the table when Josephine began the introductions. Her eyes sparkled with fun, a touch of humor. He'd bet she was really smart, always a trait he admired in a woman.

"Evelyn is hoping to buy the newspaper, the *Intelligencer*. But it seems that when her back was turned that carpetbagger Mr. Post also expressed a desire to purchase the paper," Josephine said. "And on that note, I'm getting us some cobbler."

"How'd you find that out?" Garrick turned to Evelyn as soon as he heard Josephine's words.

"Mr. Stockbridge told me," Evelyn said. "We have a contract, but I told him I wouldn't fuss if he sold to a higher bidder."

"And?" Garrick asked.

The woman smiled like she had a tremendous secret that she was about to share. "Mr. Stockbridge said, 'It will be a cold day in hell when I sell to a man with the moral compass of an alley cat.'"

"Sounds about right," Garrick said.

Josephine came in with peach cobbler and ice cream at that moment. "I haven't seen Oz since y'all got back in town." She glanced at Hartley and continued. "Oswald and Garrick work together on Ranger issues. Oz and I dated a little bit. We decided we were just good friends."

Then she looked at Garrick. "Isn't that what he told you, Garrick?"

"Right." Garrick nodded, following Josephine's clues, which explained a lot that he didn't know.

As he anticipated the food to come, he ruminated on this new information. He couldn't imagine mentioning Josephine's comment to Nightingale. That would stir up too many old feelings. But he might want to know about Post's interest in the newspaper. For a man like Post, a newspaper would not be all he wanted.

16

After leaving Garrick, Nightingale drove home. Bandit welcomed him by getting off the couch and following him into his office. His stomach told him it was lunchtime, so he made a sandwich while Bandit watched.

He bribed Bandit to sit and stay for a treat, then sent him outside and called Bob Gilbert at Ranger headquarters to stress his need for information on Edgar Post. "I'll see what I can find out," Gilbert said. "Don't get your hopes up. You know as well as I do that men with that much money seal files, hide lawsuits, hide their lives."

Nightingale thanked Gilbert, pitched the ball to Bandit, and checked email. In a few minutes, he and Bandit were in the truck for the trip into Broken Rock.

The day had gotten unseasonably warm and, as the afternoon approached, so did a few dark and ominous clouds. A shiny black Mercedes was parked in front of the newspaper office. No one that Nightingale knew owned a car like that. It had to belong to the newest rich guy, but why would Edgar Post be at the *Intelligencer* office? He parked at the end of the street and walked up to get the answer.

The young man who covered sports and the girl who answered the phone were in the front office. The girl had wide eyes and the vacant smile of one who was listening to the back room. The man, who Nightingale admired as an excellent photographer, shook his head and put a finger to his lips to shush Nightingale. The voices were loud. Apparently Stockbridge disagreed with something that Post had said.

"Mr. Post, I have given my word. I have a buyer for the newspaper, and I have given her my word and a contract agreeing to sell it to her." For a few words, Nightingale couldn't hear and then Stockbridge's voice grew louder. "I will not break my word, no matter how much money you offer me."

Nightingale was leaning against the back door when Post and a boy emerged from the hall leading to Stockbridge's office. Post had a frown on his brow, an angry sneer on his lips, and one hand on the youngster's shoulder. When he saw the Ranger, he stopped. His fingers dug into the boy's shoulder.

The boy winced and pulled away.

"I might have known you'd show up," Post said. "Bidding on a paper that is for sale is not a crime, you know."

Bandit was standing next to Nightingale, and when Post continued talking and walking toward Nightingale, the dog began a low growl. He was only fifty pounds, but he was pure muscle and anyone who threatened Nightingale had to go through the dog.

The boy inched away from Post, toward the front door. His face was white, and his eyes had not left the dog. Sweat glistened on his forehead and above his lips. His fear was almost tangible.

Post was so enthralled with his own performance he didn't notice his frightened son. He stopped speaking. The room was eerily quiet—except for the low rumble from the dog.

Nightingale touched Bandit's harness. "No, sit." He touched

the dog lightly to check the harness, hoping the leash would hold.

Edgar Post glanced at his son, the dog, then Nightingale, and back to his son. He nodded. The boy sucked in a quick breath, then ran. He hit the door and raced to the car, where he pounded on the car window until the driver came 'round and opened the door.

Nightingale felt Bandit's body tense against the harness, ready to run after the prey, but he stayed.

Post turned to Stockbridge. "Call me if you change your mind." He went out the door and got in the back seat of the car with his son.

Nightingale walked over to Stanley Stockbridge. "Did you know he was going to offer to buy the paper today?"

"I told you about his call talking about bringing me money for the paper. He called again, just a little while ago, and said he was interested in buying. I said I already had a buyer. Then about thirty minutes ago he called. Said he was parked out front. He wanted to make an offer on the paper and had his son with him.

"He came inside. He wanted to show the boy the place, educate him, teach him how to buy real estate. I said I'd already sold it. He was cordial to begin with. But once I said that, he started offering to beat Evelyn's offer." Stockbridge made a gesture toward the hall back to his office, and Nightingale fell into step beside him.

"How'd he know what she offered?"

"He didn't," Stockbridge said. "He knew what I was asking and added two hundred thousand to that. Cash."

"Why aren't you taking his offer?"

Stockbridge had walked behind his desk, but he didn't sit down. He stared at Nightingale, and his upper lip arched like he smelled something bad. "I don't like him."

Nightingale looked at Bandit and grinned. "That makes two of you."

17

Nightingale left Stockbridge, deciding to call the medical examiner as soon as he got home. He pulled into the drive and had one foot out of the truck when Carolyn Post whipped her truck in behind his and slammed on the brakes. She threw the truck into park and hopped out holding a plastic Ziploc bag with something inside it. Bandit jumped across Nightingale's lap, barked once and ran, tail wagging, to Carolyn.

She stiffened and backed against her truck, apparently scared of the dog, who continued to sniff at her tennis shoes laced with red ribbons.

Nightingale called to Bandit and put him back in the cab of the truck.

The girl seemed to relax and held the plastic bag out. "I overheard your conversation with my father. This hairbrush has only his hair, dandruff, cells, the whole bit."

Nightingale didn't speak immediately. This offer from a daughter to help determine her father's guilt didn't make sense. He didn't know how to phrase his questions. After a bit, he said, "Are you sure?"

"I guess it looks odd. He's my father, and I can't explain it, except to say I loved my brother, and my father will never consent to a DNA sample," Carolyn said.

Nightingale took the bag. "I may have a hard time using this legally. There are nuances in the law, and he should be notified, but--"

Her eyebrows shot up. Anger contorted her mouth. "Then give it back."

She grabbed at his hand, but he pulled his arm away. "Wait, I'll try to get a court order. I'm grateful for the help, but it isn't as easy as it seems on television."

"You don't want to help. Are you like the rest of mankind—you can be bought?"

"I'll ignore your rudeness for the moment. While you're here, tell me when you last saw your brother. Why are you so certain he *was* your brother?" He wondered if she would see the weakness in her argument.

She stiffened at the questions. Her eyes looked everywhere, as if for a quick escape. Her gaze found the horizon, beyond them. She was skinny and tired, her eyes huge and dark-circled. When she finally spoke, her voice was rough with emotion, her eyes glistening with tears. "I knew he was my brother because we had a blood pact. We were the only ones who knew what it was. And he wrote to me off and on, not often. Sometimes he called. He never asked for anything."

"Did the man you knew mention the blood pact to confirm his identity? Do you know anything about his work, his friends?"

She shook her head, rubbed the back of her neck. "Yes, he brought it up. I don't know anything. I was so angry at him. For years, I wished I could beat him up, but then when he got here, I wanted to see him and talk to him like we used to do." She swiped a tear off her cheek, averting her face as if Nightingale wouldn't see. "I wanted him to tell me everything would be okay."

"Did you ever get to see him face to face in the last few weeks, since he was here?"

She frowned. "No, I didn't. And I needed to." She looked at Nightingale, and he saw a realization hit her. "I wanted him to put his arms around me like he did when we were little. I just wanted his comfort. If he had just touched me, I would have been okay. With him dead, I may never be okay again."

Nightingale waited a minute. He knew what she meant, but he had not credited her with such mature thoughtfulness. "Maybe, if we get all of this sorted out, you'll feel better about everything." He felt sorry for her.

She looked at him and again shook her head. "I don't think so." Then, as quick as she had come, she turned on her heel. "I've got to get home."

Nightingale watched her walk to her truck. He wanted to help her, to help the dead man, and to help Portia and Imogene, but there was no way to help any of them when he knew so little.

He looked down at the bag in his hand. This was something he had not expected. He'd have to see what he could make happen with the hairbrush. And at the same time, he wondered about Carolyn Post's motives. Did she truly love this long-lost brother so much she would betray her father? On the other hand, maybe the question to ask was, why did she hate her father so much that she would betray him?

∽

NIGHTINGALE TOOK BANDIT INSIDE AND THEN CALLED Belschner's office to see if he was still there. The M.E. was brusque but not unpleasant. "Come ahead. I usually do my best work after everyone else has gone."

When he got there and handed the bag to Belschner, the latter was cooperative, unsurprised. But when Nightingale explained his need to see if the man whose DNA was in the hairbrush might be related to the dead man, Belschner paused for a minute. "Well, this is kind of a strange request. I'm sure you have a good reason?"

Nightingale didn't answer directly. "This case is more sensitive than most. You find out any more on the death?"

"As I told you at the outset, his neck was broken. I now believe it was broken in the fall, but I was not convinced of that earlier. However, had that not happened he would have died from the drugs."

"That makes it murder. We need to find out for certain who he is. How long will the DNA check take?"

"It could be weeks. I'll call tomorrow and explain our need for haste."

Driving home again, Nightingale noticed that the night seemed to have dropped suddenly from the sky. In reality, the clock sat on 8 p.m., and clouds covered the moon. As he pulled into his driveway, he wondered who used the word 'haste' in conversation. And more importantly, who was parked in his spot in the driveway?

An outside light at the back corner of the house lit the far side, but the lack of moonlight convinced Nightingale that he'd be getting a new light at the driveway after tonight. The vehicle, a small Ford, was not familiar. As he squinted into the darkness, his eyes adjusted, and he reached under the newspaper lying in the passenger seat to pull his gun out of its holster.

The door of the small car flew open, and Josephine Holly got out, waving both hands. "Don't shoot," she said, laughing. She put her hands in the air and walked toward his truck.

Nightingale heard his heart thud. He let go of the weapon, opened his door, and planted both feet on the ground as she neared him. He had to act normal and told his arms and legs to quit moving like robots. His mouth was dry. He had to speak and could not. Thank God for the dark.

Josephine was quicker than he and grasped both his hands, attempting to pull him to her. He knew he was a prude, but affection was not in his plans for this woman. He didn't know exactly how to act, so he stood, not speaking but not feeling sorry for the closeness either.

As if on cue, the timer on the porch light flipped that light on, revealing the side of her face. "You are a beautiful woman," he said.

Josephine shook her head and laughed. "You have never said that. You must be in shock at me visiting."

Nightingale smiled. She knew him too well. On their own, his hands returned her hold, and he noticed the lightness in his chest caused by being near her. "You want to come in? It'll get chilly out here pretty quick."

"I've brought a peach cobbler for you." She returned to her car and brought out a cloth bag that Nightingale recognized as one she'd made to carry casseroles and desserts to picnics and potluck suppers. She handed the bag to him and draped her coat over her arm as they walked to the house. "Garrick came by today and had some cobbler. I needed to talk to you, so that seemed like a good excuse to come visit."

His heart had quit thudding so loudly. As she spoke, he tried to figure out why she felt a need to talk to him. Inside the house, they went to the kitchen. Josephine petted Bandit while Nightingale made coffee and got out dishes for the cobbler. He cast around for something to say, realizing that he used to talk to her about his work. That didn't seem right now, so he leaned against the counter while the coffee perked. Josephine walked to the back door and let Bandit outside.

She seemed comfortable in his house, even though she'd only

been there once before. He was not comfortable and drew in a long breath, hoping to get more relaxed.

She came back to the table and patted the chair next to her. "Please sit down, Oz. I won't bite. And I'm not angry. I hope you aren't angry either."

"No," he said. He had thought he was angry but couldn't conjure up bad feelings at the moment. "I'm surprised that you're here."

"I had to come. I knew you'd never come to see me."

Nightingale didn't bother to argue; she was right. "How about we both just tell the truth," he said. "I was relieved, but that didn't make my heart quit hurting."

"I'm glad to hear that. My heart hurt, too. You want to hear my theory?" Grinning, she looked at him, and he smiled back.

He picked up spoons out of his mix of silverware, handed her one, and dug into the cobbler. "It doesn't count that I'm weaker after I've had peach cobbler."

Josephine sipped her coffee and took a deep breath. "All right. Here it is. I think we both care for each other, but when marriage was brought into the equation—well, I think we both knew that marriage would have ruined that for us." She reached over and touched his hand. "Our love is not tough enough for a good marriage."

Anger that he thought he had put aside came on him. He put the spoon down, feeling his face harden as he tried not to grit his teeth. "You don't know that much about my love. You were scared of marriage." He looked over at her and quickly away. "And you still are."

"You're right," she said. She pulled her hand back. "I've been married, and I never want that again."

Nightingale looked at the cobbler and then at Josephine. He took a deep breath. "I'm glad you've been honest with me. And I'm glad to see you."

"I miss our talks," she said. She walked to the back door and let Bandit back inside.

Nightingale realized that he, too, missed the talks, but things had changed. Now he couldn't share his thoughts about work and crimes and criminals. He thought the void that her presence left was what he missed. But really, he thought that Josephine wanted a good friendship. Rather than take the risk that he wanted more, she simply didn't get involved. He thought maybe he was just understanding that about her.

"What are you working on now?" she asked. She had changed the subject easily, as she always did.

He sighed, glad he finally understood. "Not much."

She put up one hand as a stop sign. "Sorry, you can't tell me anything, right? Don't bother. Garrick asked me about the rich man who moved in north of here. I don't know a thing except Evelyn Hartley, who's at The Morning Glory, doesn't like him. She said he was trying to buy the newspaper out from under her, and she was afraid he would succeed."

Nightingale went back to his cobbler, as he had done on other occasions, but this time to keep himself from talking. They exchanged general questions, finally coming around to the man who fell off the house; he filled her in as much as he could.

With his dessert gone, he felt that the momentum of the evening had slowed, too. "Did Garrick mention anything else?" he asked.

"No, Evelyn was sitting there with us, and we talked about the town mostly."

"I wonder how she found out about Post bidding against her," Nightingale said.

"Stockbridge told her. I think he called her." Josephine stood to leave.

Nightingale stood, too, thanked her again for the cobbler, and walked with her to the car. He stepped back a bit to avoid the temptation of a kiss. Josephine liked kisses, as did he, but he could not be casual about kissing. He breathed deeply, realizing that his bitterness was gone, and he needed good friends. And he'd be glad to work at it to maintain this friendship.

Nightingale watched as her car lights got smaller and smaller. Bandit rubbed against his leg. "Dog, I swear you are part cat. This cold weather makes you feel good, but I'm going inside to get a hot shower and go to bed."

He went up the porch stairs and into the house, walking through to the back door to let the dog out. Bandit was growling low and walking across Nightingale's path, back and forth, back and forth, like he wanted out quickly.

"What are you so worried about?" Nightingale asked.

As he neared the back door, Nightingale saw the glow of a light beyond his backyard fence. When he pulled the back door open, the light went out. As soon as the door was open a crack, Bandit pushed through it and almost flew into the yard, running and barking until he had to stop at the fence. A figure jogged across the back of the land, a silhouette that disappeared.

He heard an engine, a motorcycle maybe, but couldn't be sure because of Bandit's barking. He couldn't be sure of anything except someone had been watching his house, and he didn't like it.

18

It was late at night when Patricia Daniels arrived back in Austin from the Rio Grande Valley. She'd given a speech and walked a fine line to avoid pissing off anyone. Politics in the Valley was always a dicey matter.

She called Nightingale. He didn't answer, so she left a message. "What have you found out about Post?"

Mike Haywood, her driver, seemed to make the time pass faster. She trusted him implicitly, especially since he had been a policeman in the Valley. The Rio Grande Valley always made her uneasy because she didn't understand it. The chasm between rich and poor wasn't just a chasm; it was a massive crater. Most of the people she met were simple good souls who worked hard and often died without a whimper.

But on the other side of that crater were the rich. They were generally very rich and very careful with their money. They, too, worked hard, but they knew that, if they wanted to, they could leave. She could do little to help the situation, so she pulled her thoughts back to the present.

Now, almost at the governor's mansion, she felt jittery. She thought the Good Lord was a better friend than anyone human and sometimes she talked quite frankly to Him. She believed that God had sent Nightingale her way. But she didn't want him, or anyone, to know how she depended on him.

Once they had reached Austin city limits she felt better, and now, on Guadalupe, she felt almost home. The big car turned right and moved slowly inside the gates. A guard opened her door, and she raised her voice, "Thanks for a good trip, y'all."

She heard several "yes, ma'ams" and "have a good nights" as she walked into the house. She turned off the glaring lights as soon as she reached the panel and went directly upstairs to her bedroom, where she shut the door and continued thinking while she took off her jewelry, shoes, and hose. She sat on the side of the bed and reached for a pad and pen.

Jittery was not good. God was giving her a message, and she'd better not screw up. Daniels had grown up as a Baptist and, at one time or other, had also been Methodist and Catholic. The mixture had been a problem when she was campaigning because her opponent, a tall, well-heeled gent from Abilene, said she was flaky, couldn't make up her mind.

She shot back that she'd found the Good Lord in each of those denominations. She and Jesus were on a first-name basis, and she would pray for him.

Her opponent was stiff on camera, and it showed. When a black senator tried to hug him and he lurched backward, the failed-hug moment went viral. Social media said he was a hypocrite. From that point on, Daniels never mentioned her opponent's name, pretty much taking the high road. The man became almost frenzied, and eventually raved too much. To her advisers, she had said, "I gave him the rope. He did the hanging himself."

Now, here she was in a situation, and she needed some big-time help from somewhere. She'd said nothing to her advisers about her consternation regarding Edgar Post. They'd had dinner one time in Austin, with her people seated at the next table. But they had been alone enough that she wanted to know more about this man, who was so sure of himself and so charming. The trip to the Valley had given her time alone to think about him. Now, more than ever, she wanted to hear what Nightingale had found out about him.

During their dinner together, Post and Daniels had talked about music and sports, budgets and her children, and his children. She remembered him saying, "You are an intelligent, beautiful woman. Why aren't you a CEO of a major company instead of a governor of a state?" The dinner ended, and she went back to the governor's mansion. Before she got into bed that night, she received a formal text request from Post for an appointment the next day in her office. She wrote back that her secretary would call him.

And then, the next day, he walked in at two o'clock, told security that he had to see her, stood before her desk all stiff and proper, and said, "Mrs. Daniels, I am totally smitten with you. Could you meet me for dinner in New York the day after tomorrow? Other governors will be in town for a gathering, so you can truthfully say the trip is work-related. I promise I will be a total gentleman." She broke into laughter and met him in New York as requested.

They only had lunch, but she felt an attraction that made her blush. And Edgar talked, whispering crazy, tempting things that only she could hear about what he wanted. She was never alone with him, and for some unfathomable reason, she was glad of that. And then he had presented this idea of becoming an advisor for the state retirement fund.

Driving back from the event in the Valley, Daniels had stayed submerged in her own head. And suddenly, it became simple.

She would ask two state senators and two representatives, a small committee, for their advice on Post's offer to advise her. So here she was, much like after their dinner together in New York. She could not get the man off her mind. She didn't like that in herself, that lack of control and decisiveness. However, she didn't want to recommend a man who was a risk to the state.

She was not surprised when she had a text from Edgar Post. "Any word on my offer?"

Immediately, her anger went to Oswald Nightingale. If she recommended a shill, her enemies in the other party would crucify her in the press.

She had a state to run and people to meet. She picked up the phone. Nightingale would answer or there would be hell to pay.

"Hello, Governor. How are you, ma'am?"

"It's late, Mr. Nightingale. Do you have any news for me on Edgar Post? I'm scheduled to meet with him, possibly tomorrow."

A pause followed, and she guessed Nightingale had closed his eyes to zero in on the subtext in her words. She'd worked with him enough to know he was like a sponge in soaking up an opponent's thinking. One more reason why he was so good at his job.

Governor, I'm worried about him, his character. Did you know he's trying to buy a weekly paper out here?"

In the space that followed he heard coffee or a drink being poured. "That's interesting. Do you have anything specific?" She didn't like being pushy, but a quiet anger drove her. "Mr. Nightingale, I need information. I need facts."

She heard Nightingale's deep breath. "The only thing I have is the death of the man I told you about earlier, who may be a son Post denies having. We're checking on the identity and it involves DNA, so it takes time. I've had several encounters with Mr. Post, none of them pleasant."

He heard classical music in the background. "I see. A son he denies having." She drew in a long breath. When she spoke again, her voice sounded disappointed, but at least there was no hint of anger. "All right, I'm going to wait."

"That's the wisest thing to do right now, ma'am. I would not give Mr. Post a position of power with state revenue, not even advisory."

"Keep working on it. We'll talk later." She hung up before Nightingale could say goodbye.

The governor placed the phone on her bedside table and stood alone in her bedroom. She seemed to be paranoid a lot these days. She hadn't always been that way.

She remembered a time when she did not stand in her bedroom thinking about how she used to be. At one time she had trusted most of humanity. She had three children. She baked cookies and was involved in the children's school activities. She had a husband who loved her.

She became involved in PTA, the City Service Club, and too many more organizations to count. Then came city council. And then mayor. Her husband began to tease, "Reckon you'll ever cook again?" At first that was funny, but somewhere along the way, her husband's sense of humor had vanished—and so did he, deciding to live with another woman, taking Daniels's children and her trust with him.

She shook her head and reached for a cigarette, breaking the spell. Sometime in those years she had broken her own heart, but she was quick to take the blame. She gained more titles, more offices, and in the process, she began to like herself even less. She'd always been smart and attractive. As a candidate, no one told her she was still smart and good-looking, but she got applause when she spoke, so she plowed forward. It had been too late to stop the damage.

During her times with Post, she had alluded to myths that women could not be both smart and good-looking. Post had protested.

Now, in her bedroom, she walked to a window and looked out, seeing nothing. After all these years, she didn't trust very many people. She still trusted Nightingale, though she wasn't sure how much she liked him as a person. She didn't trust Edgar Post, but she liked him. She liked him far too much.

So why did she feel like she was a wicked woman when she admitted such things to herself? Because she knew she had come close to the edge with the man. She had to know more about him. She needed to meet his children, to spend more time with him. Yet, at the same time, she held back a part of herself. She had no close friends, no close relatives, and longed for connection to someone.

Here was a man who said he had the same longing, and when she was with him, she felt like he that was true, except when she saw the look behind his look. His eyes were deep, but she saw no feeling, no emotion. His touch was gentle and electric. So why did she still rely on a Texas Ranger for a final decision?

19

Someone was in the room. Nightingale was on his side, facing the door. He'd heard nothing. The dog would have barked if anyone came in the house. Hot, stinky air pushed at his nostrils, and he opened his eyes. Soulful eyes looked at him. The dog moved in for a lick, and Nightingale rolled away.

He laughed and came out of the bed quickly. "Your breath is terrible," he said. "You're getting teeth brushed today, even if you fuss."

He pulled on slacks and went to the back door to let Bandit out, then walked straight to the coffee pot. As the pot began to bubble, he picked up the phone to call Imogene.

"I know Portia is teaching but I need to talk to both of you today." He expected resistance—at least a comment about early birds. "Sorry about the time, but I don't usually sleep till seven o'clock."

Imogene cleared her throat, avoiding an answer for a moment. "Portia hasn't felt well, so she planned to take the day off," Imogene said. "Come on over. We'll both be here."

He took care of breakfast and Bandit and headed for his cousins' house. As he drove, Nightingale tried, yet again, to figure out what might be the reason for Portia's recent short temper. She had been testy when she first came to Texas. She needed his help and was grateful to receive it, but she had seemed put off by his kindness. Lately, though, she seemed fine—unless he asked a question that she considered too personal. Then she would cut him off with something like, "I don't believe you need to know that, Oswald."

She needed help but wanted to be independent. The first year that she had taught school, she sent him small checks to repay him for his help with rent and groceries. Nightingale never cashed the checks, and one day when she had asked him over to her apartment for dinner, she let him know of her displeasure.

He didn't go that often to eat with her because he knew she was on a tight budget. When she had first arrived in Lubbock, she went to the local dry goods store and got a part time job. She worked at another job as well and soon was self-sufficient, although he noticed she lost weight. After she had been there three months, she told him she was going to college. "Do you need help with tuition? he asked.

"No thank you," she said. "I've been to the bank. The vice-president said he knew you and they would loan me some of the tuition in a few more months. I'll just wait and build up some more savings."

She called him to come over for supper soon after that.

He should have been prepared because he could tell Portia was tense during the meal. She was a good cook, but she didn't eat much, just pushed green beans and corn around on her plate. At the end of the meal, she stood and started to talk.

"I appreciate your financial help, Oswald, but I am trying to maintain some modicum of dignity by paying you back what I owe you. I will never be able to go back to Tennessee. This is my home now, and you have been a force in helping me to belong here. But I need you to cash those checks."

Nightingale didn't know how to take her words, not sure why he was getting lectured. "But we're family, Portia. You don't have to pay me back."

Her face reddened, and he knew he had his foot in his mouth.

She spoke slowly, enunciating every word. "Yes, I have to pay you back. I have to prove that I am capable of taking care of myself. You don't understand what I went through back home. You will accept this or I…I will never speak to you again."

Even though he didn't know how to handle her, Nightingale knew more about her than she could guess because of his ties with law enforcement. He knew about her dead fiancé and he knew about the baby, but he never told Portia that he knew. Her family, heartbroken, searched for her, but he never told them that she was safe. Even though, to Nightingale, that seemed like cruelty.

Portia acted like a gunshot victim. She was afraid every dark corner held someone to hurt her, and she was determined that she would avoid ever being hurt again. So, he agreed with her. "If that's what you want me to do," he said, "I'll do it."

He put the checks into a savings account, and when Portia wanted to buy the house in Obsidian, he had the money for her to "borrow" as a down payment. That, too, she paid back, but by then Imogene had joined her and had a job, so he had felt like the payment was not hurting them financially.

He felt like there was more to Portia's story, but he never asked. And he never told her that the money she kept using was what he had saved for her. She thought that the money he loaned her was from an inheritance left to him by his parents. His income had been so little at that time that he would never have had the money to help with the house down payment out of his salary. And he had used the little that he inherited on the purchase of his own house. But she didn't know that.

Nightingale knew his cousin was smart, a great teacher. Students loved her, everybody loved her, so he didn't know what was causing this particular case of angst. He hoped Imogene would help him to not push a stick into the hornet's nest that was Portia these days.

He hated arguing with Portia. She had been extra thorny of late. Conversely, he tried to remember any cross words he'd ever had with Imogene. There were none.

While he drove, he decided to tell them that he was still waiting on the Rangers database to help him with identifying Joshua, and he could truthfully say that the man had been poisoned but they didn't know by whom. He wouldn't stay long. More time with them simply translated to more arguments with Portia.

His phone rang. It was Garrick, but Nightingale didn't answer. He'd talk after seeing his cousins.

When he stopped the truck, Imogene came out on the porch to meet him. The wind had picked up, and clouds had moved over the sun. The temperature had dropped, too. Winter seemed to be teasing them. Soon, bitter cold would surround them day and night.

Imogene smiled at him.

Portia opened the screen door, looking more rested. She took his arm, and they walked into the living room together. "I haven't been very good to you of late." She smelled like his mother.

"You're wearing Momma's perfume."

"You're right. Years ago, I asked her what it was, and I bought it."

Nightingale said nothing. His throat felt raw. He swallowed and remembered his mother telling him, "You have little use for kinfolk now. Later on, you will need them."

"Do you want coffee?" Imogene asked.

They drifted toward the kitchen, and Imogene started coffee

without his yes or no. Portia put sugar and milk on the table while Imogene placed cups. She also put out a tin of blueberry muffins and some dessert plates.

Nightingale smiled. They still treated him like a youngster led by desserts.

Portia noticed his smile. She sat down beside him and covered his hand with hers. "I haven't been good to you, and I apologize. I also want to tell you both some things you may not know." Her hands covered Nightingale's, but her eyes were locked on Imogene's. She began by telling them both about the baby.

"Paul and I were engaged. I loved him more than anything. After he died in that car accident, I had to leave, especially after Daddy said Paul's death might be a message that I needed to do something else with my life. So a good friend helped me leave." Portia glanced at Imogene and then Nightingale. Her voice was strong, but her face was blotched, her eyes drooped at the corners.

Imogene's face reflected her empathy for her cousin. Portia stopped for a minute, cleared her throat, and said "Imogene, let's have that coffee, and I'll continue." She seemed to need a break.

Imogene's eyebrows raised. "Sure."

Portia turned to Nightingale. "No questions, Oz?"

"Not now." He cut the muffin on his plate in half but wasn't hungry.

As soon as Imogene sat down, Portia continued.

"So. I couldn't keep the baby, but I dreamed about it. For an hour or so. I went to one of the sisters, and she just asked me questions. She was very sympathetic, but she continued with those questions and waited for my answers. She never said I was right or wrong, but then sanity returned, and I realized the best thing for a child was to give it a good home. I wrote to you, Oz, before the baby was born. You may remember that?" She looked at Nightingale, who nodded.

"You were brave," he said.

Her answer was a shrug. "I had a baby boy. They took him away, but he had dark hair, like Joshua. Then I came out here. And Imogene came later."

Portia took a deep breath and straightened her back. She poured cream and sugar into her coffee. "I've thought of that baby every day of my life. I worry that I felt sorry for Joshua—or maybe a kinship for him—because of my baby. My son would be close to Joshua's age. I'm hoping, now that you know, you'll understand that and forgive me a bit."

"There's nothing for me to forgive, Portia," Nightingale said. "You were doing what you thought was right."

She blushed, sipped her coffee, and sniffed. "Well, I left out that Joshua told me the rich man who built the huge house with the fence was his father."

Nightingale took a large drink of coffee and placed his cup onto the saucer with barely a clatter. "When did he tell you that?" He schooled his features to not relay his elation at her statement because, after all, it might not be true.

"About a week before he fell off the house."

"Did you believe him?" Nightingale tried to keep his voice low. He refolded his napkin.

"No. He had asked me for a small bit of money a few days prior, and I told Imogene about that. We decided to loan him one hundred dollars, agreeing that we would probably never see it again."

"Did he give you any background as to why he thought that man was his father?"

Portia's eyes darted toward Imogene. She primly clasped her hands in a different configuration on the table and clamped her mouth shut.

Nightingale noted the move and picked up his coffee. "I

mean," he said, "I thought he might really be who he said he was."

"I'm afraid the boy was delusional, Oz," Portia said. "I wanted to believe him, but he told me story after story about where he had been and what he had done. He said he'd worked on houses in Las Vegas and then worked as a guard in one of the clubs. He said he gambled and got into debt. That's why he needed the money."

Imogene nodded along with Portia's narrative. "He told us he lived for a while in New York, but that life was too hard. He said he lived there a while after running away from his father. He told us that story one night when he had supper here. Everything was a fantasy."

"So, you didn't believe him?" Nightingale asked.

They looked at each other and shook their heads. "We wanted to. But it just seemed so. . . strange," Portia said. "Do you believe it?"

Nightingale had a hard time with his next words. Maybe *he* needed the man to be Edgar Post's son. Only DNA would tell. "Yes, I think he may have been telling the truth."

20

As he walked out of his cousins' house, Nightingale was grateful that Portia had talked openly. She was almost back to the Portia of years ago. He'd never tell her that he'd known about the baby. Some things were better left alone. He drew in a long breath and headed to Garrick's house. At a little after ten o'clock there was more than enough time left in the day to accomplish several things.

Garrick answered the front door with a ruffled apron around his waist. Nightingale grinned as he slowly looked the older man over from head to toe.

"The way you're looking at me, with that lust in your eyes, makes me think I should never wear an apron around you," Garrick said.

"If this is what you have in mind when you mention me needing a woman in my life, then I'll never have one 'cause I won't be caught dead in an apron."

"Wouldn't look as good on you," Garrick said. He pulled the corner of the apron out and, waving the meat fork in his hand like a wand, did a semi-curtsy. "What are you doing here besides criticizing my sense of fashion?"

"I want us to go visit Mr. Post's first wife. Her name is Cordelia Comet."

"You got this from downtown?"

"Yeah, Gilbert found a few things. She lives in Vidalia, so we can drive over there in about an hour. Also, in the Ranger files, which no one needs to know I have access to, I found a man who has the name of Post's weird friend. He's about an hour north of the woman, so we may talk to him, too. You want to go or too busy cooking?"

Nightingale didn't say anything about the tense parting between the two men the day before. He would apologize at some point, but at the moment keeping the conversation light let him read his partner better. And partner was what Garrick was. They had worked together for over twenty years. They had each saved the other's life more times than he could count. Nightingale pushed aside his thoughts, catching on to Garrick's optimism.

"You know I wouldn't miss it. I've been piddling here in the kitchen. Started some beans, but the girl can cook better than I can." Garrick continued to talk while he pulled a piece of paper and a pen from a kitchen drawer. "I'll leave her a note." He scribbled something on the paper and put it on the counter on top of his folded apron. "Let me get some coffee in my thermos, and I'm ready."

Once they were on the road, Nightingale filled in the details of his visit to Portia and his call from Gilbert.

"So, is this dead man's claim all you've got?" Garrick asked.

"No, Post's daughter is hanging on to that accusation she made earlier. She brought me a hairbrush that she says has Post's hair follicles in it. I took it to the medical examiner for DNA testing."

"Good thinking," Garrick said.

"I don't know if we'll be able to use it in any way, but it will make my argument stronger in my head. I can always get her DNA, but I didn't think of it 'til after she left. I guess I thought this would be easier, but it's all getting more complicated. The thing is, why is his own daughter so set against him?"

"Maybe her father's money has her attention," Garrick said.

"Money is always an issue, isn't it? But she seems to really care about this brother. Maybe she thinks her father killed her brother, and she wants revenge."

"Seems like she'd give you more information than what you've got. We still don't know if the dead man is her brother, do we?" Garrick asked. "What do you know about her?"

"Nothing really. She came here with the family when they moved into the house. I doubt she's ever had a job. Guess I'll ask Gilbert to see what he can find on her, too."

"What about this so-called friend? What's his name, Hartford? Danny Hartford? Why do we need to see him?" Garrick asked.

"That's part of the information for the governor, but it may help us, too. I read about him in two articles. One writer thought that he and Post started the hedge fund together. That was never mentioned except for the one time. The other article said he fell out of favor because his predictions began to be full of errors."

"Predictions about what?" Garrick asked.

"I'm not sure," Nightingale admitted. "But from what I've read, hedge funds are some of the riskier investments. One fund can include several different companies, plus real estate, and shares in companies. Men like Post's friend, Danny Hartford, could predict the best times to buy and sell. Computers have put those guys out of business. Some companies make buying and selling decisions based purely on what the computer tells them. Apparently, Hartford and Post were friends for years before Post set up his company. Something happened; none of the things I read nailed down what it was, but Hartford was golden for several years, and suddenly everything he predicted turned to sand. Post kept him around for a few years and then he simply disappeared."

Garrick looked over at Nightingale. "And? You can't just stop the story there. You have an address, I take it?"

"Yes, Gilbert's sources said he wound up out in this direction. He bought a little ranch and stays put."

"Reckon this Hartford guy is part of the reason Post came out here?" Garrick asked. "A man who's that rich wouldn't move out here to be closer to the ex-wife or buddy, would he?"

"That's why we're going to talk to them. Vidalia is to the east. According to my GPS, Cordelia Comet Post lives up here on our right, just off the interstate. The town is small." A sign next to a mile marker led the way to Vidalia.

"That building with the picture painted on it is hers," Garrick said.

"Yeah. Somebody thought they'd paint... What is that? A creek with frogs around it? Weird. Guess they're like all of Texas and would be glad to have a creek with water."

Nightingale parked the truck, cut the engine, and looked around. The street was paved, and the town reminded him of Broken Rock. The building in front of them was red brick with a glass front, probably built in the '50s. Two stores sat on either side of it, one brick and one wood-shingled, but neither of them looked inhabited. Unlike the buildings in Broken Rock, which shared common walls, these stood alone, the width of a man's shoulders separating them. Farther down the street were more storefronts in similar brick buildings, but it was impossible from where he sat to see if the buildings were home to viable businesses. Nightingale slid out from under the steering wheel as Garrick exited the passenger side.

"This is really odd," Nightingale said. The street was deserted. He'd parked beside a white Ford Taurus, and next to that was another white vehicle. When he stood still, he could hear the distant noise of the interstate highway—and nothing else.

Garrick pulled his hat down. "I think I'm gonna walk down this way a bit and see what I can see."

Nightingale nodded. "This may take a while. Wait in the truck if you get back before me." He pitched the keys to Garrick.

"Comet Art," with a star shooting from the A, was printed on a heavy wooden door. Underneath "Comet Art" was printed, "Cordelia Comet, Owner." It seemed appropriate that this building had the mural on the side, too. The door, dark, rich, carved, looked like it came from an old building and was probably more expensive than the building to which it was attached.

A sign marked "Open" hung loosely on a brass door knocker on the front door, so Nightingale pushed the door and walked inside. Music, a Yo-Yo Ma and Chris Thile recording, played softly in a sparsely furnished art gallery. The place was spacious and set up for art. Hardwood floors reflected recessed lights. Nightingale counted a dozen paintings. He began looking for a room at the back of the building when a woman walked in by way of a side door.

"May I help you?" she asked.

Nightingale took off his hat and smiled as he walked to her. She was a small woman, wearing a large man's shirt that had liberal spots of paint all over it and hung over a pair of blue jeans. Her thin hand was cold when she reached out and shook his. Her eyes were the same hazel color, with gold flecks, and her face was the same oval shape as Carolyn Post's. When he looked at her, she seemed familiar. "Ma'am, I hope it was all right to come inside. I'm looking for Cordelia Comet."

"And you are?" she asked.

"I'm Oswald Nightingale. I'm a Ranger."

"In that case I guess it's safe to admit that I'm Cordelia Comet."

"If you have a place that's more private, I'd like to tell you why I'm here," he said.

She smiled. "Mr. Nightingale, I wish we needed to worry that this place might become overwhelmed with customers, but unless things change greatly, we will have all the privacy you want right here. What can I help you with?"

"I need to know if you were once married to Edgar Post, and if so, do you have a son?"

Cordelia Comet looked down and drew in a long breath. "Maybe we should go to my studio." She didn't wait for an answer but walked to the front door, removed the "Open" sign, and flipped a lock. Nightingale followed her through the door at the rear of the room.

21

Through the rear door, the building stretched to the size of a warehouse. To his right a room about twelve feet by twelve feet had been partitioned off with studs and wallboard, designating where more-permanent walls might eventually stand inside the larger room. As he followed her into that unfinished area, he noticed that the ceiling seemed to be finished, but if the coming winter proved to be like the past, he figured a lower ceiling and insulation would need to be added. Daylight through a skylight made the place feel airy.

An easel and paints, along with brushes and canvases, sat around the wall. Two canvases seemed to be in current use. The smell of paint and turpentine lingered, despite a large fan roaring at a window on the far wall.

"Welcome to my home." She waved an arm around the small room. "I try to paint," she said, "but commissions on name-brand artists pay the bills. I still have contacts in New York and some artists like having their work sold out here. A few people with oil wells will keep me in business, if I'm frugal."

She sat on a red leather couch that sagged in the middle and motioned to several chairs for Nightingale. "Take your pick," she said.

He settled in an upholstered chair across from the couch.

"Good choice," his hostess said. "I just had that one refurbished. It's sturdy."

She looked around the room, and in the bright light, Nightingale saw lines around her eyes that aged her. Her mouth trembled like she might cry.

She drew in a long breath and looked at him. "You asked if I had a son. Yes, I did. And I was married to Edgar Post. I left the marriage when the boy was eleven. I had a daughter who was seven. I am not now, and was not then, a good mother. Their father had the money to take care of them, so I left."

"Have you seen your son recently?" Nightingale watched the woman, who seemed determined not to look at him. The answer was slow in coming. He wondered if this was a pattern that would help her hide information about her son—or whatever else she might be reluctant to talk about. Maybe she was hesitant in speaking with law enforcement folks. He'd seen such reactions more times than he could count. Or maybe she was just thorough.

"No. We talked on the phone a few weeks ago. Why are you asking about Joshua?" Here she did look at him, scared, a mother's fright and a mother's suspicion.

"We've had a death in Obsidian." Nightingale watched Cordelia Comet's reserve begin to crumble. She closed her eyes. "We don't know who the dead man is, but. . . . "

She seemed to rally, grasping at threads of hope. "It can't be Josh. I would know if he's dead. I would feel it, here." She knotted one fist in front of her chest. "Why have you come to me?"

"Before he died, the man told one of my cousins that his

father was Edgar Post. Your name came up when we researched Mr. Post. Are you aware that in the last year your ex-husband purchased almost a thousand acres and built a large house between Lubbock and Obsidian?"

She sprang up from the couch. "Then why aren't you asking *him* if he knows the dead man?" Anger and fear mixed together in her face. The composure that she'd shown at first was dropping away with each fact that came out. "Josh's father was Edgar Post. I will guarantee that."

"Mr. Post denies that he has an older son."

Color drained from the woman's face. Her eyes glistened with tears. "Oh, the poor kid. I thought, hoped, that Edgar would show him and Carolyn some affection, you know, love them." She walked to the big fan and turned it off. In the sudden silence, her next words seemed too loud. "So, *have* you talked to Edgar? Is Carolyn there?"

He nodded. "Have you been in touch with Carolyn?"

Again, she paused. "I've called her every year on her birthday. She hates me."

Nightingale stood. He felt sorry for her. She appeared to be alone and to be having a hard time accepting that the dead man might be her son. "Ma'am, if you can give me something to check your DNA, I'd be much obliged."

She continued to stand by the window fan and didn't respond at first. Her back was to him and she seemed to be peering between the blinds which covered the top part of the window that held the fan. She snuffled, pulled the hem of her shirt to her eyes, and faced Nightingale. "I'm sorry, what did you say?"

He repeated the request.

She shook her head, smiling ruefully, and walked into a tiny area where he could see a coffee pot and microwave. "I'll be happy to prove you wrong," she said. "I'll spit in a plastic bag."

She returned from the kitchenette, shoulders back, trying to smile, but the bravado had disappeared. She handed him a sealed plastic bag and went with him to the front door, which she unlocked. "Here." She handed him a business card. "In case you need to get in touch." On the back she had printed a cell phone number.

When he got outside the front door, Nightingale looked at his watch and then at the truck. Five till two and they still had a person to track down. As he closed in on the truck, he saw that Garrick was there, his hat pulled down over his eyes as he napped. A few raps on the window, and the locks snapped open. Nightingale slid under the steering wheel. "I found Joshua Post's mother. DNA is in the bag. What'd you do?"

"Walked around town a bit. Went to the barber shop." Garrick leaned toward the windshield and pointed down the street to a storefront that looked closed. "Yep, the barber does a brisk trade in gossip. I told him we were visiting Ms. Comet, and they, his hangers-on, filled me in on how her business is doing. The men in the shop don't know how she stays alive, and nobody can figure out who buys painted pictures. They said she had a young man visit a couple weeks ago. That might have been her son."

"Wouldn't surprise me," Nightingale said. "She denied she'd seen him, but she's eaten up with guilt. We're going to try to see Danny Hartford. His ranch has a Brewster address, but the only thing I know about him is in that file."

Garrick thumbed through the two sheets of paper, taking the time to read. "So, he and Post were buddies for a while and when he could no longer predict the future, Post cut him loose."

"That's what the papers say. His story reads strange. We may not get within spittin' distance before he shoots at us. Then, again, maybe I'm being paranoid," Nightingale said.

"Sounds odd." Garrick looked up from the pages in his hand. "Sounds like somebody out of a Pete Dexter novel." He put the papers down, looking serious. "If that's what he's like, you're not being paranoid. But maybe this guy is different."

"Did the gossip include a description of the man who visited her?" Nightingale asked.

"Nope," Garrick said. "You said she had guilt problems. What exactly?"

"She admits to leaving the marriage when the boy and girl were young. Seemed to think that Post had lots of money and he would take care of them. Now she acts like she regrets it, but still says she's not a good parent."

"Makes you appreciate a good momma and daddy, don't it?" Garrick asked.

Nightingale felt Garrick's stare, and the question came to him, but this was not the time. "I had the best parents in the world. I won't ever understand families like Edgar Post's." He let the words sink in before continuing. "Why didn't you ever have kids, Garrick?"

Garrick turned to look out at the flatlands, but not before Nightingale saw him squint and put on sunglasses. "Don't know. Me and Nancy married kinda late, and then she died. It just never happened." He cleared his throat and swallowed hard. "You gonna get gas anytime soon?"

"I'm stopping if I see a pump. I don't see anything that resembles a restaurant, but we need to get some kind of food."

"Yeah, I could use some fried chicken, if it hadn't been setting around since this morning," Garrick said. "I'll buy for both of us if it's fresh cooked."

"We're in luck. There's a station. Did you hear anything else at the barber shop about Ms. Comet?"

Garrick shook his head. "Forget the chicken. This place is too small. Let's just grab and go." After pumping the gas, Nightingale purchased a Baby Ruth and bottle of tea for himself, while Garrick got peanuts and a cola. An hour after stopping at the gas station, what they assumed to be the house they were looking for came into sight. A tall brick building, it stood alone, the solitary house for miles. A gate crossed the road that led to the structure, but it wasn't locked, so Nightingale got out and pushed it open, then drove through.

When he got back in the truck he said, "I'm gonna drive real slow so he can see us."

Garrick nodded and pushed his jacket away from his weapon.

The two-story house looked like some mighty hand had slammed the front flat. No shutters, no porch, nothing except a plain brick structure. As they drove closer, the property's disrepair became more evident. Paint cracked and peeled from windows and trim. Brick on the house suffered from a dark growth of something, probably mold, creeping up around the concrete block that formed the foundation. About fifty yards away, a detached garage housed a rusty John Deere tractor and a small black Mazda truck. Grass had not been cut during the last summer, possibly ever.

Nightingale pushed the gear into park and continued to stare at the house. He unlocked his seat belt. "I thought I saw a curtain move upstairs. You stay here and watch as best you can. I'm gonna knock on the door."

"I'll stay close to the truck," Garrick said. "If he starts shootin' you jump in the passenger side, I'll drive, and we'll go hell bent for leather out of here."

"Did you see the curtain move?" Nightingale asked.

"No," Garrick said.

Nightingale slid out of the truck. As he walked, he glanced at every window for signs of a weapon. He'd never been afraid of a fight, but he didn't like an ambush. The house needed a porch.

Instead it had a small stoop with two steps up. He knocked on the front door and stepped back, waiting. No sound came from inside, but the door creaked open a small crack.

"What do you want?" The voice had no body attached to it. Nightingale didn't think a gun was pointed at him. The voice croaked with the dryness that comes from not talking. It sounded tired, not dangerous.

"I'm looking for Danny Hartford. I'm Ranger Oswald Nightingale, and I'd like to talk with Mr. Hartford about Edgar Post." Using the respectful "Mr." title might help in getting inside.

The door opened a bit more, revealing a six-foot-two beanpole of a man in overalls. He wore a faded red- and blue-checked flannel shirt under the overalls, and the tips of scuffed boots stuck out at the bottom.

"I'm Daniel Hartford, and I have nothing to say about Post."

The wind had gotten colder. Nightingale shivered. "Sir, Mr. Garrick and I came from Broken Rock hoping you could tell us something about Edgar Post. All I have is an article that's several years old that mentions at one time you were partners. Could we come in and talk?"

Garrick walked up from the truck.

Hartford opened the door wider and pushed his rimless glasses up on his nose. "Do I know you?" He took a step closer, straining toward this new figure at his front door.

"Don't think so," Garrick said. He stepped closer and introduced himself.

"You're as old as I am," Hartford said. Garrick made something like a sour half-smile. Suddenly, Hartford's shoulders relaxed. His eyes crinkled in a squint as he pushed the door so the opening was smaller. "Y'all come around to the back. We can talk in the sunroom."

Nightingale looked at Garrick, and they both hesitated.

Keys rattled, and a sound of knuckles against wood got their attention as Hartford stepped back into the shadows. "I'm not a housekeeper, and I don't have a wife. You can come to the back or you can leave." With that, he firmly shut the door.

22

Nightingale and Garrick started back toward the truck. "What do you think?" Nightingale asked.

Side by side they stood in the tall grass. Garrick pulled open the driver's door. "Could be an ambush," he said.

"I'll go back there to meet him first," Nightingale said. "You can act like you're looking for something in the truck. Then you seem to find it. If I motion you in, it's okay."

Garrick nodded. "Be careful."

Nightingale walked around the corner of the house, glad that it was too cold for rattlers. In the knee-high grass, he was wide open for bites. As it was, he moved slowly, taking in the house that was too big for a single man and watching windows that looked to be covered with towels and sheets. The house looked like someone had dropped it out of the sky. It had no personality. He thought he'd never seen such a plain structure.

He was surprised when he rounded the corner. A sunroom had been attached to a back door. Otherwise, the rear of the house was a carbon copy of the front, with one door as the main access.

Hartford had walked through the sunroom and stopped at

the open door. "Is he coming?" He waved one hand toward the front of the house, apparently including the truck.

"He's getting a coat or something," Nightingale said. He stood back, looking at the addition to the house, admiring it. Inside the glassed room he saw a glass-topped table and wicker chairs. Thoughts of an ambush dissolved. "Did you add this? Good idea."

Hartford seemed pleased at his reaction. He stepped outside and walked with Nightingale around the glass room. Hartford pointed at the places where the addition joined his house. "It's rough. I only did part of it."

The addition was rough, but it was something the house needed. And it added some flavor to Hartford. He was not as ordinary and tough as he seemed. He had some artfulness, maybe some humanness, that the front of the house denied.

"I needed some sunshine, so I ordered a kit. But you don't need to lie to me to get information about Edgar Post."

At that moment Garrick came around the house. He had put on a jacket.

Nightingale ignored the remark about lying. The sun was getting low, and a chill had filled the late afternoon air. "Can we go inside?"

"In the sunroom, not in the house. Nobody goes in my house. We'll be out of the wind," Hartford said.

Garrick made the appropriate grunt of satisfaction and opened the door for the other two men.

Inside was cozier than Nightingale thought possible. Very little wind seeped through and the area was soundless, almost like the inside of a spaceship.

Hartford didn't invite them to sit down. "What do you want to know about Edgar Post?"

They had no script, so Nightingale started. "How long did you know him?"

"We grew up together," Hartford said.

"Where was that?" Nightingale stood at the back of a wicker chair and watched Garrick as he moved to the side in order to view Hartford's face.

"Oklahoma." Hartford looked at Nightingale. "You can sit down, if you want to, but I don't want you here when it gets dark. Why're you asking me about Edgar Post? I haven't laid eyes on him in ten, fifteen years."

Nightingale pulled out a chair and sat down. Garrick kept his stance at the windowed wall, though he had turned and was staring out at the horizon and Hartford's bleak backyard. Hartford had not wasted money on sod or grass seed. Little bluestem, windmill grass, and switchgrass grew up to Hartford's steps. Then near Hartford's truck, a black-jack oak twisted in the wind.

"He's applied for a job with the governor, so we were asked to talk to people who knew him," Nightingale said.

Garrick's eyebrows made a quick arch and settled back into bushy levelness.

"Humm. That's interesting." Hartford took a step and sat across from Nightingale. "What does he want to do? Edgar Post doesn't do anything out of the goodness of his heart." Hartford made a small half-smile, showing a few missing teeth. "Don't tell me, it has to do with money and how much he can make for the state."

Nightingale smiled with Hartford. "How long did you work with him?"

Hartford leaned back in his chair and gazed upward, mumbling and counting. "Let's see, I guess it was ten, eleven, I lost count when it got to be miserable. I guess it was ten good years and two or three of hell. The thing is"—he put his hands on the table, leaned forward, and shrugged— "when the stakes are that high, it doesn't take many losses to gut you—or Edgar Post. At least that was what he thought."

"Sounds insecure. How does a person live like that?" Nightingale asked.

Hartford's sarcastic smile relayed more bitterness. "People cope in different ways. Some turn to drugs, some to drinking. I think Post did a little of both, but he didn't let them control him. And he never was at fault. He became mean—to me." Again, Hartford shrugged, as if meanness was expected.

"But you stayed with him. Right?" Nightingale asked.

"I stayed for two years after the losses started." Hartford stared at his hands, clasping them tighter.

"But why," Garrick said. "Could you see that things were going to be bad?"

"The first year wasn't too bad. You've got to remember that the fees will keep a large fund afloat if the investments are judicious. Going into the second year, Post started on me hard. He had a Ph.D. in math, and my expertise was analytics. He should have known as much as I did."

"But he blamed you, right?" Nightingale asked.

A frown of anger engulfed Hartford's face. The clasped hands became fists. His eyes squinted tight. His lip sneered. "He told me that I needed to retire."

In the huge silence, Garrick said, "Surely, you objected."

Hartford didn't hear. He simply continued his story. "That's after all the years I made him a fortune with my predictions. He relies totally on computers now."

"Did he fire you?" Nightingale asked.

"I told you. I retired. Look"—Hartford opened his hands like he was teaching a class— "hedge funds are tough. I think they're getting less popular because we've had a market that's harder to predict. The fees in a fund are astronomical. Two percent of ten billion dollars as a management fee is hard for some folks to imagine. Then they also get twenty percent of the profit. Can you imagine that? Playing with other people's millions? Hoping to make billions?"

"Sounds like a lot of stress," Nightingale said.

"It is if you care about the people involved, which never was Edgar's strong suit. He's a narcissistic bastard who would sell his mother to the highest bidder. His children don't have a chance."

"Did you know his family?"

"I met his first wife once. He had a boy, a toddler at that time," Hartford said. "In a few years, he had another kid—a girl, I think—and then his wife left. I felt sorry for him." He looked at each man. "Can you believe that?" He shook his head, giving a fake laugh.

"Do you know of anything questionable that Mr. Post did in his business ventures?"

"I know of some, sure. But I won't tell you names or details. And I don't have paper evidence."

Garrick interrupted. "Why should we believe you then? Maybe you're bitter because he cut you off."

Hartford turned on him, his face twisted in anger, his fists clenched. "You're damned right I'm bitter. I helped him start that business. He couldn't have done it without me. He cares for no one. I've known him for a long time. He shows no emotions, no feelings, and will destroy anyone in his way."

He flattened both hands on the table and hoisted himself to stand. "And now, gentlemen, I want you to go. I've told you all I know, and I doubt I'll sleep well tonight. Old memories are not pleasant." He walked to the door and stood by it. Outside was dusky. In a few minutes, a curtain of darkness would fall around the glass enclosure.

Nightingale stood. There had to be more that the man was not giving up. He thanked Hartford as he walked out. "Do you mind giving me your phone number if I have more questions?"

"Don't have a phone. I'll call you if I get one." With that he closed the door, and they watched him as he went through the sunroom and inside through the back door of the house.

The two men walked carefully through the tall grass back to the truck. Neither one said anything until they were in the truck and had some distance from Danny Hartford.

Garrick started. "If I ever get that bitter, please just shoot me."

"He doesn't need to be here stewing over his past," Nightingale said. "I guess he just wants to be left alone. And he sure doesn't have a good feeling for Post."

"He'll die in that house, by himself, and no one will find him until rot has started in his body. And he condemned Post for not caring about people. Well, he's not the poster child for caring for humanity." Garrick was fuming, and Nightingale didn't know why. "And why did you mention the governor asking about him?"

"It just seemed like a plausible excuse for us to be asking questions. What are you so pissed about?"

Garrick sighed, a sad sound. "I hate to see old people alone, like him. He's so confused he thought he knew me. He's stupid and arrogant, and he'll die with no one caring." He turned to look at the empty prairie outside the window. "Everybody needs a person who cares."

He sounded so frustrated. Nightingale didn't reply.

"So, has the governor checked in? What did you tell her? Or what will you tell her?" Garrick asked.

Nightingale's phone rang. He slowed the vehicle and pulled off the road before he answered. After asking, "Was anybody hurt?" he listened and put the phone down. "That was Constable Robinson. We're going to Broken Rock. Somebody threw a bottle of kerosene into the back windows of the newspaper."

The return trip was no longer a quiet meander. Nightingale hit the accelerator.

"Was anyone hurt?" Garrick repeated Nightingale's question to the caller.

"Scared bad, but no one hurt. Robinson and Deputy Hall are trying to keep the peace."

"Did anyone see or hear anything? If someone lobbed a bottle though the windows, wouldn't they be seen making their escape? I guess I never thought about what was behind the newspaper offices," Garrick said.

Nightingale had turned on emergency vehicle lights, thankful for the flat road in front of him. "From what I remember, there's a wide alley, then the street, actually a gravel road, then the backyards of a few houses. And the yards are better called pastures. Last time I looked, one house back there had a horse and another one had a couple of cows. There aren't lights. No use looking tonight."

Darkness was heavy when they drove into Broken Rock. However, the small town had lights on in almost every store. The newspaper office was brightly lit, and the number of vehicles outside promised a circus inside. Nightingale parked, and they went in.

Constable Robinson was talking to Stanley Stockbridge. Evelyn Hartley sat at one of the desks. Her cheeks were a bright pink. Her fingers tapped the desk. Nightingale had decided when he first met her that she didn't sit still very often. Now she looked like she was barely containing her rage—or was it fear?

Constable Robinson walked over to Nightingale. "Hall and I are going to the office to get evidence tape to put up in the back. It will keep anybody out tonight. I think anybody who was in town when it happened is still here. Nobody's gone home."

"Thanks." Nightingale turned to Stockbridge. "Can we go to your office? Maybe Miss Hartley, too?"

To Garrick he said, "Go help Robinson and Hall. Y'all can seal off the alley, but no heroics. Leave lights on in the buildings.

Ask them if they saw anyone or heard anything. Be sure and carry a weapon and a lot of light. Don't do a search. We'll do that tomorrow."

In his office, Stockbridge said, "I was scared to death. After the bottle of kerosene flew in, we got under the light table. It smelled horrible—worse than now, if that's possible. I expected a fire. Then when nothing else happened, we ran to the office and called Constable Robinson."

"Did you hear or see anybody?" Nightingale asked.

"I thought I heard an engine or chain saw—some kind of noise. I had started to the window to see what it was when the bottle with kerosene in it came flying in. I'm sorry, but I didn't try to look after that."

"I can't believe the bottle didn't break," Nightingale said. "It's a wine bottle. I'll take it with me. Maybe we can get prints off it. We'll need you to write down everything that happened. Any ideas about who might do such a thing?" Nightingale was assessing the scene as he asked questions. Some kind of unease pushed him to move quickly. The answers coming into his head centered on why he had this burning worry about his home, his belongings, his dog.

Stockbridge and the woman looked at each other. "The only person who might be really mad at me is the new guy, Post. But I don't think he's that uncivilized."

"Do you both have places to stay?"

"I'm going home," Stockbridge said. He looked at Evelyn Hartley.

"I'm staying at the B & B," she said. "Stanley, would you mind dropping me off?"

Nightingale walked with them toward the front entrance, where he met Garrick, the constable, and the deputy. The acrid smell of the kerosene penetrated the air in the building, and everyone seemed glad to get to the outside.

The windows had been opened, but some of the kerosene was on the floor. The edge of a piece of cloth that was in the bag with the bottle looked like it had scorched but not actually flamed.

"We'll be checking in early tomorrow," Nightingale said over his shoulder to Stockbridge and then turned to the three officers. Some unspoken worry clouded his thinking, even as he asked obvious questions. "Did you get some tape up?"

"Yes," Garrick said. "Robinson offered to stay at the jail and check on this place during the rest of the night."

A sense of relief came over Nightingale. "That'll be good, Constable. I don't think whoever did this will return, but don't take chances." He wanted to get home—he felt a heavy unease and needed to leave—so he talked as he walked away. "We'll be here early tomorrow morning to walk the alley behind the newspaper and see what's there."

Nightingale turned away from the others and picked up the pace to his truck. "This makes no sense. We need to get home. I don't like leaving my house and Bandit alone when this kind of meanness is happening."

23

Nightingale couldn't account for his discomfort, but he drove faster than normal, telling himself that everything was fine. He remembered the flicker of light behind his house. Someone had been watching his house when he was there, and it was likely they were watching it when he was gone. He was so focused on his empty house and friendly dog that Garrick's voice startled him.

"I think they're scared enough that whoever threw that bottle will stay away," Garrick said, "and there are enough men at the bar ready to kick ass that anybody who knows the town will go back wherever they came from."

"That's all we need. Vigilante justice. I'll feel better after I get home."

"Yeah, the pup always cheers me up," Garrick said. "Any ideas about who did the damage tonight?"

"First idea would be Post, but I agree with Stockbridge: I don't think he'd be that crude. And, personally, I don't think he's that brave."

He slowed the truck to make a turn on the shortcut to his house. "If anyone saw or heard something, that will help. We'll have to wait till tomorrow, though, for that." The night seemed very dark. The solitude that Nightingale usually enjoyed tonight seemed a threat.

"I went to school with one of the men who lives back there. I can talk to him, or do whatever is necessary," Garrick said.

"One of us can go to the homes behind the offices tomorrow and ask folks if they heard or saw anything," Nightingale said.

He tried to remember if he had left on any light in the house; sometimes he did, but now he wasn't sure. Garrick quit talking. They'd be at the house soon.

"You're worried about Bandit, aren't you?" Garrick asked.

Nightingale ignored the remark, not wanting to say what he feared. "There was so much commotion in town, I think if anyone had even an inkling of who threw that bottle, they might have come and talked to us tonight."

"Good point," Garrick said.

"Or, the commotion might have a backfire effect. Some people might have stayed away from us because of the uproar," Nightingale said.

"In times past, those people would be organizing for a riot, and they'd have no idea what they'd be yelling about," Garrick said.

"Stockbridge may have more enemies than we know about—or than he does. For that matter, Evelyn Hartley may have hidden detractors." Nightingale pushed the accelerator harder and neither man said anything else.

When he pulled into his driveway, his seatbelt was already undone. He was out of the truck and running up the steps to the porch when he stopped. "Listen," he said.

Garrick was a few steps behind him. He stopped on the last step. "I don't hear anything."

"Yeah, we should be hearing Bandit. He always barks when

he hears the truck." He unlocked the door as thoughts of why the dog was silent gnawed at him. "Bandit, here boy." Silence.

He flipped on lights as he ran through the house.

On the back porch Garrick called, "Bandit, hey boy, come on out." Silence. "Would he dig under the fence and get out?"

"No. And he would never go with anyone." Nightingale's throat burned. "Somebody was out back last night. Bandit barked, and they ran off."

He grabbed a flashlight from a kitchen drawer, and the two men stepped into the back yard. "My eyes will adjust in a minute," Garrick said.

"Surely nobody would harm a dog," Nightingale said. He cast the light around the fence, knowing what people would do. People killed each other. There was no reason for them not to hurt an animal.

He swept the light around the yard and a few feet from the back fence he saw a pile of brown and white fur. His eyes stung, and he ran. "Bandit, hey boy. You're okay. Garrick, hold the light on him." He looked for blood and, seeing none, he put his head onto Bandit's chest. A heartbeat, faint, but there.

"Over there," Garrick said. He pointed the light at a pile of ground beef and a bone. "Looks like he threw some of it up."

"We're heading to the vet." Nightingale scooped the limp body up and held it close. "Get in front of me." Garrick caught on and went ahead, throwing open doors, grabbing an afghan off a chair, and running to the truck. He didn't bother with locks.

He ran to the passenger side, waiting as Nightingale placed Bandit in his lap. Nightingale got in and called the Ranger office as he turned the truck around on the lawn and hit pavement. Trying to sound calm and knowing that was impossible, he identified himself to the nighttime duty Ranger. "I'm bringing my dog to the emergency vet. The dog's been poisoned. I don't have the number of the vet. You'll have to call for me. Down the street from your office—it's life or death. I'll be there in fifteen—no, ten—minutes." He turned on the emergency lights and drove like hell.

Garrick held the dog close, all the time talking to him. When the dog's body jerked and stiffened, Garrick's voice grew grainy with tears, "You're gonna be fine, Bandit. We both need to quit eating everything in sight. Can't you talk to me?"

At the clinic, Nightingale stopped in a screech of tires and ran around to the side, taking the dog from Garrick. The older man just managed to get to the door of the clinic in time to pull it open.

Inside, Nightingale half-ran toward a door that obviously led to a doctor. A young woman came around the desk, putting her hand out to stop him. "This is a veterinarian clinic. Are you prepared to pay—"

Nightingale ignored her and shoved open the door to the back. He stood in the open doorway and raised his voice. "I am a Texas Ranger. My office called you that my dog has been poisoned. Now you get me a doctor before I haul this entire clinic in for obstruction of a criminal case."

A young man in scrubs hurried down the hall.

"Doctor?" Nightingale said. "My dog has been poisoned. We need help."

"Sure, bring him back here. Put him on the table." The doctor flipped on the light, talking to the young woman while he looked in Bandit's eyes. Other people came in. They began tying masks on. "What did he eat? Do you know?"

Nightingale gently laid the suffering Bandit on the table. "Something in some meat that someone threw over a fence. He's been convulsing."

The doctor stepped in front of Nightingale. "Sir, you've got to leave. Nurse, we need the stomach pump and some carbon." He pushed Nightingale aside and told the nurse, "Get MacDonald. We need help—now." Another man came in.

The girl that Nightingale had threatened put her arms out to encompass Garrick and Nightingale. "Please, you need to get out."

Nightingale couldn't remember feeling so useless. He and Garrick did as she said and walked to the waiting room.

Nightingale's bones were quivering, and his hands shook. Garrick turned away and walked to the end of the room, which was glass and looked out on the street. He pulled both hands down across his face before he turned around.

"Sorry," Garrick said. His rugged face looked even older. "I'm really attached to the little dog."

Nightingale swallowed hard. "Guess we both are. I won't be satisfied until I find the sick person who did this." Thoughts were flying from one subject to the next. "I'm calling the Rodriquez family tomorrow. They're still the best trackers in the state, right?"

"Yeah, Reuben or Cruz, either one. I guess Reuben has more experience cause he's older, but I'd take either one of 'em."

Nightingale listened for noise from the rear of the building. Trying to keep his mind off what was going on back there, he forced himself to think about what needed to be done tomorrow, about who might have thrown that bottle of kerosene. He paced around the vet's outer office as he thought. Out of the muddle of those thoughts, he began to see connections, a kind of dark plan behind what had happened. Maybe whoever threw the kerosene used that as the Judas goat to keep Nightingale's attention away from his house. It worked.

Garrick stood, looking out the large windows into the dark night that was punctuated with a few streetlights and some businesses with neon signs that seemed grotesque in their sadness.

Nightingale came up beside him and said, "Gilbert is probably still up. It's not close to midnight. He'll have some men to help us." He went back to pacing as he pulled out his phone, dialing Gilbert's home number. When the man answered, Nightingale gave him a brief rundown on what had happened.

"Is somebody with you?" Gilbert asked. When Nightingale told him it was Garrick, Gilbert sounded reassured and said he would be in Broken Rock in the morning.

He walked back to Garrick. "Gilbert said he'd like to help. He'll probably bring some men. He should be at the newspaper by eight tomorrow. One of us can be there."

Garrick looked at his watch. "Since it's not that late, you want me to call Imogene and Portia while you call Rodriquez?" Garrick asked.

Nightingale hesitated. The women loved Bandit, and suddenly he didn't care if Portia was mad at him. "Good idea," he said.

He stared at the phone a minute, remembering how he'd first heard of Reuben Rodriquez's tracking abilities. "Call one of the Rodriquez family," Gilbert had once told him. "They can find a rattler in a desert and tell you who it bit and why." Nightingale had come to see Reuben—or his son, Cruz—as the best trackers he'd worked with during his time as a Ranger.

He called the number he had for Reuben, apologized for the late hour, and explained what he needed.

"I or my son will be at your house at sunrise," Reuben said. "These dogs are our friends, and we love them, do we not?"

For some reason, Nightingale felt better after Reuben's words.

Garrick had gone outside to make the call to the women. He was gone so long that Nightingale began to wonder what was taking the time. He watched through the windows as Garrick walked back and forth as he talked. Finally, he came inside.

"Imogene said they'd put Bandit in their prayers," Garrick said, his eyes glistening.

These words, too. eased Nightingale. The Lord always seemed to be looking out for Imogene and Portia, so their focus on Bandit could only help. Actually, Nightingale's mother, Mary, would have been quick to tell him that the good Lord had his hands full when he took care of both women in their younger days. The thought of his mother brought a wash of sadness over him. His mother wouldn't appreciate his melancholy. "Get up and do something," she'd say.

He turned away so Garrick couldn't hear him. "That's what I plan on doing, Momma. I'm gonna find who did this."

24

At midnight, the doctor came into the waiting area. "We've done all we can," he said. "If he lives until morning, he's got a good chance. He's healthy and young, which is in his favor. I'll be honest—I don't know right now what will happen."

"Can we see him?" Garrick asked. He shrugged and held his hat close to his chest. "I know it sounds silly. I'm an old man, and the pup means a lot to me. If talking to humans helps, then why not talk to a dog?"

The veterinarian smiled. "I totally agree. Say something to him. He's knocked out right now and he still has tubes in, but encouragement never hurt anybody."

He led the way to the place where Bandit was. The dog looked dead, but he was no longer convulsing. Nightingale, watching Bandit's chest move as he breathed, felt an awkwardness come over him. Finally, clearing his throat, he spoke. "We're here for you, Bandit. Get well, and we'll—ahm, we'll get you some new treats." He patted the pup's shoulder and stepped back. He walked toward the doctor as Garrick bent down to the pup's ear.

"You might as well go home," the doctor said. "I'll call if there's a change."

Garrick walked out in time to hear the last sentence. He smiled, like he was in on a secret. Outside of the vet's office, he gave Nightingale a nod and a half-way wink and said, "He's gonna be okay."

They walked out to the truck silently. Something seemed to have come over Garrick in the last few minutes. The old man had never been religious, though at times he seemed to have a second insight into understanding the human heart. But he certainly seemed to be pretty sure about Bandit's recovery. Nightingale, too, wanted to believe that Bandit would be okay, but he was not going to get his hopes up only to have them dashed to the ground later.

He glanced over at the older man. He was walking easier, his shoulders no longer moving stiffly. It was, well, it was odd. Finally, he could stand it no longer. He stopped abruptly. "Okay, I give. What has brought on this hippy dippy shit and you pulling Bandit's recovery out of thin air? Do you suddenly have religion? Has some angel told you about a miracle?"

"No, no." Garrick looked a little embarrassed. "I just feel sure that the pup is gonna be okay. I guess I am acting odd. I was scared while we were driving up here. I said some things—not out loud—but I feel calmer now. I don't even know that I was asking anyone specific for help. I feel better. Guess it shows."

Nightingale dared not make fun of him, but he was a man of facts. Standing in the dark streets of Lubbock with the dim streetlamps, Nightingale squinted, trying to see if Garrick showed signs of a stroke. He didn't have slurred speech. He made a quick decision to let it go. "I'm glad one of us feels better. Let's get home."

Once they were on the way out of Lubbock, Garrick said, "Why don't I sleep on your couch, and we can come back up here early tomorrow morning, or you can decide how you want the investigations to go and I'll be there, ready to take orders."

"You can have the couch or the spare bedroom. Bedroom is probably more comfortable," Nightingale said.

He didn't want to plan the next day, but he knew he had to. He also knew he had to quit worrying about Bandit, and the only way to do that was to go on with work. "Okay, we need to talk about what happened tonight, or last night now that we're into a new day."

Garrick nodded in agreement. "I figure you must have some ideas."

"Call me paranoid when I say this, but I think tonight was aimed at me. The damage at the newspaper was handy—maybe someone wants to stop the sale. Post is the only person who's mad about that. I'm friends with Stockbridge, and I've been a burr under Post's saddle, so he struck out at the dog. Which makes the episode at the paper just a delaying tactic to get to Bandit. We need to visit Post at home early tomorrow."

"I agree."

"Do you buy the idea that this is aimed at me?" Nightingale asked.

"I can see why you would think the attack was aimed at you, but it's a stretch to say somebody threw a bottle bomb into the newspaper to get at you," Garrick said.

"You think I'm too focused on Post as the culprit?"

"Right now, we're both too tired to think straight about it. Neither one of us likes the man and I kinda hope we can nail him, but we don't know enough yet, and we're bushed."

Nightingale said nothing else. Soon he pulled into the drive of his house.

As he turned to release his seatbelt, a sliver of light bounced beyond the backyard fence. "Did you see that?"

He shoved open the truck door and ran around the corner of the house. The light flickered—gone. His service revolver was in his hand. He aimed and fired.

25

Portia stood up, pushing her chair so it scooted away from her, and began pacing as she waited for Imogene to join her. They often spent time in the living room, listening to music and discussing their workday. However, this was different. Imogene was talking to Garrick on the phone, but something was wrong. It was late, almost midnight, and Imogene's voice from the other room had that vibrato that signaled tears.

Portia heard her say "good-bye" and rushed to her chair, trying to avoid the obvious—she had been snooping.

"Portia, someone has tried to kill Bandit," Imogene said as soon as she crossed the threshold. "That was Garrick. They're at the veterinarian's office in Lubbock." She walked to the other rocking chair and dropped into it.

Muted sounds of a symphony filled the room for a minute. Imogene seemed gobsmacked. She stared at the fireplace where there was no fire. Before another movement started, Imogene said, "I know there are bad people in this world, but I've never understood why they pick on animals and children to make them suffer."

"Don't forget old ladies like us," Portia said. "We don't know for sure how Bandit acts around other people, but I'll bet Nightingale has made someone mad and they took out their gall on that poor puppy."

The sounds of a piano swelled and intruded into their musings. "*The Children's Corner Suite* is not comforting me tonight," Imogene said.

"Nor me," Portia said. "It was kind of Garrick to call us." Portia looked to her cousin to say more. She wanted to hear about Bandit, but she had other worries, as well.

Hopefully, Imogene would say something to elaborate on her relationship with Garrick. Portia was troubled. In the last month, Garrick had called Imogene almost every day. When he came by the house, he never stayed long. He always had a reason—a recipe to share, a cutting off a rosebush, something trivial—and he always included her in the small chats, but she wanted to know more. She and Imogene usually shared everything, but that was not so in this case.

Imogene walked to the record player and stopped the recording. "I don't know that kindness was the motivation. He needed to talk to someone, anyone. He kept clearing his throat. Bandit was poisoned, and Sutton held him as they drove into town. I think he was fighting off tears."

"I am going to be honest here." Portia looked at Imogene and drew in a deep breath. "Why is Garrick calling you so often? What is up? Has he asked you out? All of a sudden I am worried about you, and I'm worried about Nightingale, and poor, dead Joshua." She clasped her hands together to force a stillness she did not own.

"Worried about me?" Imogene asked. "Why?"

"I don't want you to be hurt," Portia said. "And don't roll your eyes and make fun of me."

For several minutes neither woman spoke. The hum of the

heating unit droned on as if everything was fine. Portia was almost holding her breath.

"How would I be hurt? If you mean by Sutton Garrick, we've had lunch once. We're friends," Imogene said.

"Lunch?" Portia said. "When did you have lunch? You haven't said a word about it to me. You don't know him. He's been married before. I mean, I know you don't have to. . ." Portia's voice trailed off, and she realized she sounded like a parent. "I'm sorry. I interrupted," she said.

Imogene bit her lip and continued. "We've talked on the phone several times. That's true, but I like his company." Imogene had a tiny Mona Lisa smile that raised more unease in Portia. Imogene stopped the rocking chair and leaned toward Portia, resting her arms on her legs. She spoke softly, trying to coax Portia to reveal her true feelings. "Is there anything wrong with that? I can quit taking his calls if you think I should."

"No, that's not what I mean." Portia felt heat rise in her face. She was probably beet red. "Face it, Imogene. We are not spring chickens. Neither one of us has been on a date for more years than I know. We're buying a house and will be obligated for over two hundred thousand dollars. Then we had a dead person, who died at our new house, and now we have a poisoned dog, whom we love. Events are stacking up on me, and I feel overwhelmed." Portia was into the strength of her speech. She got up and paced, walking from her chair to the front door and back.

Imogene didn't interrupt.

"The man who I see now is not the Sutton Garrick I used to know," Portia said. "I must admit that he seems to have changed. I don't think he had a heart when I first met him. He and Nightingale worked together then, despite the 'one Ranger is enough' motto. And the change I'm seeing is so," she paused while she searched for words, "so drastic that I am doubting myself. Worse, I'm doubting him."

Portia stopped mid-step and faced her cousin. "You know I have lived a lot by my wits. I go by my gut feel. But so much has happened, and I am so deep into my caring for everyone involved, that I'm totally confused. Have I done anything that might have caused any of this?" She threw her arms out in supplication, and Imogene stood and went to her.

They hugged briefly. Imogene led Portia to her chair and then pulled her own rocking chair closer. "Have you got everything out now?"

Portia nodded, took a deep breath, and sank back against the pillow in her chair. "It all sounds so silly and hyperactive when I say it out loud, but in my head, I have these huge worries swarming at me. I apologize that I've made the last few days miserable."

"The days have been...stressful, yes that's the word, not miserable. But we've had a lot of different things happening lately," Imogene said. "And, as far as Sutton is concerned, we just enjoy each other's company. It's fun having a man's perspective. But listen, Portia, is buying a new house bothering you? Are you worried about the finances?"

"I guess that's part of it. I had no idea there were so many things to select for the house. And what do we plan to do with *this* home? We've talked of selling it, but we have no idea how much money we could make. Or what about renting it? Do you want that headache?" Portia stopped. She realized she'd begun talking faster and louder as she voiced her worries. She also felt like she was lying and avoiding part of her worry, but she was ashamed of that. Ashamed that she was scared of Imogene leaving.

"I thought we'd decided to sell. We should call a realtor in and get a price in order to be sure of our cash. And if it doesn't sell, maybe the fates are telling us something and we should keep it for a better real estate market," Imogene said.

Portia sat up straighter. "I had no idea you knew about real estate. I was going along until you started talking about 'fates.' Really, Imogene, you can't believe, well, anyway. . ."

"Portia, you've always known I'm a little strange in my thinking," Imogene said. She grinned broadly, and Portia laughed when she caught on.

"You're teasing me," Portia said.

"Only a little bit," Imogene said. "Are you feeling better?"

Portia nodded.

"I'm going to bed," Imogene said. "Come to my room if you want to talk more. I won't tease. We need rest so we can help tomorrow if Oswald needs us."

Portia felt Imogene's hand give her hand a reassuring squeeze on her way to the stairs. Portia nodded her head and kept her eyes closed. If she opened her eyes, Imogene would see the lie and demand more. But she had faith in Imogene's pointblank way of dealing with everything. Imogene saw the best in everyone, even in Sutton Garrick.

In all probability, Joshua had lied when he told her he'd talked to his sister and she was ill. He never clarified if his sister had a cold or a life-threatening disease. That was a different conversation, and here Portia tightened her eyes shut, trying to see where they had been standing that day, trying to get the details straight. He'd been talking nonsense as far as she could discern, so there was no reason to mention it to Imogene or Nightingale—considering how the latter already wondered about her mental capacities—without adding more to the confusion.

And for all her trying to include Nightingale as family, Imogene was all Portia had. Nightingale was like trying to be family to a cactus. He was alone. He didn't even realize how he would be a better person if he let family in, let some love in.

When it came to bare facts, she was jealous of Garrick's attention to Imogene. She thought of him as a paper cutout of a cowboy who really liked himself. What if Imogene thought she loved him? He might take Imogene away, and Portia would have no one. And now? Now she was unsure about every person she thought of as family.

She used to trust her senses, her gut. She'd finally seen that she couldn't solve Nightingale's problems or hers and Imogene's. She'd certainly not helped Joshua. Better to stay out of everyone's life.

26

In the darkness behind his house, Nightingale glanced around and saw Garrick, but no figure attached itself to the light he had spied beyond his fence. He blinked, squeezing his eyes shut and open, giving himself time to see what was before him.

"What did you see?" Garrick's voice came from behind.

"I saw a light. Didn't you see it?"

Nightingale stood rooted to the spot. Garrick didn't answer, and he figured the old man just shook his head and went inside. The temperature had dropped to freezing, and in his light coat he would normally shiver, but anger and heartache fired an unnatural heat. Seeing no more movement in the distance, he walked around to the gate at the side of the house and onto the back porch.

Garrick was already in the kitchen. "You want some decaf coffee?"

"Yeah, I'll put some milk in it to help me sleep." Nightingale's phone buzzed with a text. He tapped the note, relieved to see Portia's name show on the screen. Her text was all caps, CALL ME.

Leaving the coffee making to Garrick, he dialed her number.

"How's Bandit?" she asked.

Nightingale started to retell what had happened, but Portia interrupted. "I know what happened, but I wanted to tell you that Imogene and I will take care of him while he convalesces."

Nightingale couldn't stop his smile. "You make me feel really good knowing that. We'll have to see how he is overnight."

"He's going to be fine," Portia said. "But you have to work, and we've decided he can stay here and one of us will be with him at all times. So don't tell me no. Just call before you bring him. Now get some sleep. Good night."

He heard the space of an empty phone line and stared out the kitchen window. He sighed. Somehow, her to-the-point words, herding him into agreement, relieved him. His shoulders softened. He turned around to watch Garrick, who had been with him since early morning of the day before. Garrick poured a cup of coffee with the assurance of a butler. For the first time since his parents' death, Nightingale felt like family was near him. And in that comfort, he knew he could rest for the night.

He relayed Portia's offer as he and Garrick had their coffee. They sat for a minute, silent, too tired to move. Nightingale thought about Cordelia Comet, Danny Hartford, the kerosene bomb at the newspaper, but something else nagged at him. "Is there anything you'd like to tell me about you and Imogene?"

Garrick's face melted a little. He smiled but didn't look at Nightingale. "Well, we enjoy each other's company sometimes."

"My God, I've got to turn up the lights. You're blushing." Nightingale felt his face might split from the smile he had. Relief from the grief he felt for Bandit flooded into him. "I must be the densest son of a gun in this territory. Have you had honest-to-goodness dates?"

"No. We just enjoy talking to each other. She's special to me, and I guess she doesn't know it, so don't tease her. I like to talk to her." Garrick acted a little put upon, maybe embarrassed, so Nightingale didn't push further.

"Imogene has had some really hard times," Garrick said. "She reminds me of your mother some." He stared into his coffee cup like he was a hundred years away from the current time. "She's sweet and wise, but nobody is going to take advantage of her."

Nightingale again heard the opening for his question, but he let it go. The night had been filled with too much emotion.

∽

NIGHTINGALE SLEPT BETTER THAN HE HAD THOUGHT HE would. At 5 a.m., he called the animal hospital. The technician who answered told him she had peeked in on Bandit. "He's sleeping good, hasn't torn out his tubes or anything. I'll have the doctor call you."

When he came out of the shower, he smelled coffee brewing. Garrick was in the kitchen looking at a newspaper. "Could I borrow a shirt after I shower?" he asked. "I can get one more day out of these jeans."

The jeans still had traces of the creases that Garrick paid the dry cleaners to put in them. He freely admitted that he told the cleaners he wanted the jeans so stiff with starch they could stand alone.

"Sure, in my closet. Use anything you need," Nightingale said. "Talked with the clinic. Vet is supposed to call. I'm taking the phone with me while I walk the inside of the fence. Cruz Rodriquez will be here soon. I told Gilbert you would meet the Rangers at the newspaper at 8 a.m. Did I forget anything?"

"Not that I can think of. You want me to parcel out the orders in town?"

"You're in charge down there. I can't be at both places.

Gilbert left everything up to me, so I'm passing the newspaper bottle-bomb investigation to you."

Garrick smiled, folded the newspaper, and stood. "I'm gonna cook some eggs and toast. You want any?" He turned to the refrigerator.

"If you're making them scrambled with milk gravy, yes."

"I'll do it. I'm gonna crumble that sausage that I saw in the fridge into the gravy," Garrick said. "If I'm not back here when you go see Bandit, I'll go later."

Nightingale looked out at his backyard, sobered by the thoughts of the night before. "Sure. We'll meet up when we can."

He walked out into the cold morning air. The night had hit freezing, but the day would likely warm. He started at the northwest side of his house.

The sun was barely up and the night had deposited a heavy frost, but Nightingale was determined to walk the inside of the fence that surrounded his backyard. He dared not walk the outside of the fence. The tracker would do that.

He'd worked with Reuben and Cruz Rodriquez before. They could read signs like no one he'd ever seen, but they couldn't read anything that had been trampled over. He didn't think the poisoner came inside the fence, but he'd be careful. He carried a flashlight and walked slowly, straining to see anything out of the usual that would give him a clue about the person who had hurt Bandit.

As he walked, he considered the people who had been touched by the mutt he had brought home from east Texas. Bandit went with him on most errands into Broken Rock. The only places the dog didn't go inside were the grocery and restaurants. Portia and Imogene loved the puppy.

He'd been surprised by Garrick's reaction more than anyone. Though he denied it, tears had shone on Garrick's face as they drove the dog to the veterinarian.

Under the oak tree, Nightingale aimed the flashlight at the fence and back to some of the beef still laying on the ground. He went inside for a baggie to put the meat in and was back outside when his phone rang.

It was the vet. "Bandit's vital signs have improved. He's still sleeping and may sleep until noon. His sensitive stomach, which made him throw up, probably saved his life by getting part of the poison out, but he's still a puppy. I'd like to keep him here, with IV fluids, for a day. You can pick him up tomorrow if he continues to improve."

"That's great news," Nightingale said. "Is it okay for me to come and visit?"

The doctor's voice had a smile in it. "Sure. We'll look forward to seeing you."

He quit the call and glanced again to the spot where he found Bandit, under the huge oak tree. His stomach knotted in anger. Somehow, he heard his mother telling him to get over the anger, so he whispered thank you and added, "So help me, God, I will get whoever did this and they will pay."

27

After dropping Garrick at his house, Nightingale returned home. The time was 7:45, and Cruz Rodriquez was waiting in the driveway for him. Nightingale and Rodriquez went back a few years, and neither sought the other's company. Still, there was respect between them, which was all that was needed, at least on Nightingale's part, to get the job done.

Nightingale invited him in and explained the events of the last evening. He finished the conversation with, "I've promised myself to get whoever did this. I'm hoping you'll find something along the fence line." They walked through the house and stood looking out onto the back yard.

"Who's your closest neighbor?" Cruz asked.

"Michael Brown and his wife Eloise. Brown had renovated this house before I bought it. An older couple had owned the house and several thousand acres. He was buying their land. I told him I'd like to buy the house if he would carve out five acres, including the oak tree, and sell it to me. That was several years ago. Once we get outside, you can see the distance for yourself." He pointed in the direction of his neighbor's brick house. "We don't see each other, generally. He works in Lubbock. I don't know if his wife works outside the home, too."

"So his fence attaches to yours." Rodriquez waved toward the entire back acreage. "But where, out there, would a person start from to get to the back of your house?"

"The land beyond the fence is mine for a piece, and then it's Brown's. The only fence between us is at the side. The barbed wire attaches to the white wood fence on the side of the property between us. Brown grazes a few cattle when there's enough grass for the animals to eat. I have two or three acres behind my chain-link fence, and I told him to let the cattle on it if they want it. You can see it's rough in the back and doesn't grow much of anything. A couple of nights ago I saw a light out there. Thought I heard a motorbike, or something with an engine. It'd take a daredevil to ride it in the dark because of the bunch grass and clods of dirt. It's funny how you can look and see level land, but the land you walk on is coarse and unforgiving. It's several miles to a road, but Brown's land meets the Craig property at some place. Craig sold some of his land to Edgar Post. I don't know how it all ties up back there."

Nightingale watched Rodriquez as he looked over the land in every direction. About two acres lay between Nightingale's patch and the Brown house to the southwest. A person would be visible, though not in detail during the day, even at that distance, but the side was not where he'd seen the light.

"We'll start at the north-east end of your house. We can go along the fence and walk further out if we need to. You have paper and pen in case we need to write measurements? I've brought my camera for photos, but I'd like you to take some shots with your phone as well," Cruz said.

"Yeah, I'll do back-up photos." Nightingale held up his phone as evidence.

"I'm guessing you didn't find any tracks inside the fence, is that right?" Cruz asked.

"Right," Nightingale said. "I think whoever did this just pitched the meat over and ran. Anyone who has watched my house at night knows that Bandit runs out if he hears or sees anything back there."

Cruz had slowed, waiting for Nightingale to catch up. He half turned, waiting for something more from Nightingale, but when he said nothing further, Cruz headed back toward the fence. "I know this is important. Let's get started." They walked to the gate which opened onto the land under discussion. Cruz pushed his hat back and stepped out slowly, carefully looking over the ground in front of him before moving his feet.

The frost of the night before had started melting on the border of green turf. Sunshine sparkled off the droplets of water. "Buffalo grass?" Rodriquez asked.

"Yeah, I had the sod brought in after I put up the fence, way before I had Bandit."

"But you had a dog before this one." Rodriquez was talking as he walked, and the man was a good tracker, but Nightingale wanted to concentrate, not talk.

"He died a few years ago."

Rodriquez stopped and squatted at some invisible clue. "Here's part of a print of a shoe," he said. "If you get down here, you can see it better." He took shots with his camera and then asked for Nightingale's phone.

He held the phone at several different angles, snapped pictures, and handed the phone back. When Nightingale looked at the items on the phone, he clearly saw a footprint. He looked again at the grass and then knelt to look at the print closer to eye level. Rodriquez walked ahead.

Nightingale caught up as Rodriquez stopped and turned to

look at the house, which now sat directly in front of them. The tree was just inside the fence.

"That's a good-looking tree. We don't have many live oaks around here," Rodriquez said.

"Yeah, me and Bandit both love the tree. Sometimes, I just stand inside and stare at it. In the summer, I go out and stand in the shade and take a few steps into the sunlight. The temperature difference is several degrees. The next drought may get it, but not if I can help it. This bunch grass and field looks about like your ranch, doesn't it? Flat and brown from November 'til spring. The tree will probably outlive me."

Rodriquez walked a few feet along the fence and pointed to the area at his feet. "Here's where the person pitched the food over. The grass is trampled." He squatted and, even though the morning sun was up, pointed a flashlight onto the crushed grass. "Your culprit is five foot five or less. The shoe size doesn't match a tall person. And it's not someone with a lot of meat on his bones."

"Speaking of that, why two kinds of meat? I mean steak and ground beef, what's the reasoning?" Nightingale asked.

"I don't know," Rodriquez said. "I'm guessing that if he didn't eat one kind, the other was a backup. But most folks out here couldn't afford both."

"We're going to have a new type of training when I get Bandit home. It's going to be 'leave it' no matter how good it smells. No matter if I'm here or not," Nightingale said.

"Okay, I'm going to walk the rest of the fence and the area behind us, where there's no grass. You coming?" Rodriquez asked.

"Sure. Wouldn't miss it. I always learn something from you."

Slowly, they crisscrossed the area behind the fence. Nothing else became apparent near the fence. But fifty feet away, in the clumps of grass, Nightingale spied a small spot of oil. The ground was rough with clods of roots from the grass, but some kind of vehicle had been stopped. "I see some tire tracks," Nightingale said.

"You're right. It's a motorcycle. Can you get a mold of those tire treads?"

"I hope so. This is good information." Nightingale called Gilbert, explained his situation, and requested some scene-of-crime lab work after Gilbert and Garrick finished their search in Broken Rock.

They walked for another half hour and then went back to the house, where Nightingale tried to pay Rodriquez for his work. "We've been walking out there for almost two hours," Nightingale said.

"Please, don't insult me," Rodriquez said. "You are a friend. Call me anytime."

Together they walked to Rodriquez's truck. "You must bring this Bandit to see me when he comes home," Cruz said. They shook hands, and he was gone before Nightingale could say more.

In his kitchen, Nightingale looked out toward the oak tree and the fence. Whatever the reasoning for the attack on the newspaper and Bandit, it might be a coincidence that both events occurred as they did. In the cool morning air, he found his assumption of the night before to be like fairy dust. Why would anyone throw a bottle filled with kerosene into the newspaper to get at him?

He wanted to call Garrick to check on his progress. Instead, he walked out to the oak tree. The light he had seen had to be farther away than he had imagined. On this level terrain, whatever light he saw could have been a mirage, but he hadn't fantasized two sightings.

While he waited to hear from Garrick, he decided to make more phone calls. He would call the newspaper first. Maybe one of Stanley Stockbridge's firebrand editorials had elicited a bottle bomb from an angry reader. Stanley was a liberal surrounded by conservatives, and sometimes he forgot that fact. Also, no one had delved into Evelyn Hartley's background. For all he knew, she had an ex-husband lurking in the alley, ready to commit various kinds of mayhem.

None of those ideas accounted for the attack on Bandit, but he felt like he and Rodriquez had a good start on those culprits. He went into his office.

He punched in the newspaper phone number, surprised by the voice that answered. "Stanley, how you doing?"

"I'm counting my blessings that there was so little damage done last night. I heard about Bandit. How is he?" Genuine concern came through in his voice.

"I think he's going to be all right, but I'd rather nobody else know that just yet. I don't know if you've talked with Garrick yet, but can you think of anyone who might be mad as hell at you?"

"I've been asking myself the same thing, and I can't think of anybody. Post was pissed at me, but I'm small potatoes for him. I've even asked Evelyn if she had anybody following her." Nightingale heard the smile in his words and heard the chair creak as he swiveled around. "Since she's not here I'll tell you I paid a professional outfit for a background check on her."

"Why would you do that?"

"Because I care about this town and the people, and I wanted a good person to buy the paper. I'm going to still be living here, you know."

"Well, what did they tell you?"

"She's got a lily-white background, not even a traffic ticket. She's got a boyfriend, but not the kind to throw bottle rockets. Been a freelance writer and worked at newspapers all over the U.S. Grandfather left her money to buy me out. There you have it."

A minute of silence followed. "Are you still there?" Stockbridge asked.

"Yeah, sorry," Nightingale said. "Just thinking. Everything was okay at your house?"

"Yes. I've tried to think of who all is mad enough to hurt me. I even looked back at past editorials. I've aggravated just about every rancher in all of west Texas at one time or another—even the chicken rancher. But for them to pick now to destroy me seems not only odd but psychopathic. And nobody out here is a psychopath. They're all too busy making a living or getting rich. You know these people as well as, or better than, I do."

"You make sense, but someone out there... Never mind. If you think of anything—I don't care how strange it may seem to you—you call me. Thanks, Stanley."

Nightingale refilled his coffee cup and thought about Governor Daniels. A short update was all he could offer, but sometimes just staying in touch was good.

He had never lied to the woman, and he didn't know exactly what he would say. But he didn't want to practice a dialog. She said they should trust each other. This would be a good test.

She answered the phone in that canned way that made him know she had company. "Do you have new information?" she asked.

"Yes, ma'am. I can't tell you the details just yet, but I wanted to confirm a few things that were not definite when we talked before. We think the dead person is related to Mr. Post."

"Just a minute," she said. When she came back, the background noise had ceased. "Surely you don't think he killed someone."

"No, it's not like that. We don't know who killed the man, but I really have to get more things confirmed before I can tell you anything else, and I stick by my earlier recommendation. Don't hire him yet."

"That's good enough for me. Call me as soon as you have something concrete." She hung up the phone, and Nightingale shook his head. A person's priorities depended on whose ox was gored. He wondered if their sense of justice had the same malleability.

His concern went back to Garrick. If there was a clue about who threw the kerosene bottle, Garrick would find it. However, Nightingale's obsession was about Garrick's past and how their lives were tangled together. While they were demanding honesty in the investigation, now would be the perfect time for honesty with each other.

28

After Nightingale dropped him off, Garrick hurried into his house, thinking a mile a minute. He left a note for the couple who ran his ranch, looked in the mirror once, and with a lighter step, walked to his truck. This would be like the old days. He'd be in charge. He sat in the truck for a moment, going over the plan to meet the Rangers who would be in Broken Rock. He'd give Constable August Robinson and Deputy Hall a thrill and let them be a part of the search.

Once he was on the road, the drive seemed quicker than normal. He parked the truck in front of the newspaper and went in to talk to the editor. Stanley Stockbridge was not in the office, so he went next door to the constable's office.

Two Rangers were with the constable in the cramped office. Charles Foster, standing next to the coffee pot, was one of the men who'd given Nightingale problems when he was a regular member of the force. The other man was Bob Gilbert. Garrick could think of no reason for Foster to be a part of this investigation, but as acting head of the Lubbock office, Gilbert could do whatever he pleased.

Gilbert smiled, shook hands with Garrick, and leaning closer said, "Let's go outside a minute."

Standing in front of the constable's office, Gilbert started the conversation. "I wanted to be a part of this as soon as Nightingale called me. He said you'd be in charge of the search. Do you know Foster?"

"I know of him," Garrick said. "In Nightingale's version, the man is a trouble-maker."

"That about sums him up. He's been at odds with Nightingale, but I think he can be a decent officer. "

"Okay, he's your business. Might be good training. Let's go back inside," Garrick said.

Back in the office, Garrick shared the plan with Robinson, Hall, Gilbert, Foster. "We'll start the search in the alley in back of the newspaper offices. When we finish there, we'll get statements from anyone who was around last night. It was late when it happened. The drugstore stays open until eight, but I'll bet everyone else was gone before that. We'll need to go door to door to check with everyone."

The newspaper offices were sandwiched between an antiques store and the jail, euphemistically called the constable's office. The jail had tiny barred windows and a single skinny door to the alley. After that was a vacant shotgun-style building and then the Amish restaurant. The gas station was the last business at the other end of the street before crossing to the church. Garrick had checked the back door to the constable's office and decided to walk around the gas station to start the search.

Garrick had not been on a search in a long time, and now he remembered why. It was a boring but valuable chore. He looked down the alley. Someone had brought a mattress and leaned it next to the dumpster. Several black plastic bags sat on top of and at the side of the dumpster that served as the catchall for the antiques store, jail, gas station, and restaurant.

At the far end of the space, the Amish restaurant had a remarkably clean-looking container. A narrow strip of pavement ran next to the buildings. It was broken and pock-marked with potholes but served the purpose of looking a little bit better than gravel. The pathway next to the alley was about eight feet wide and "dirt path" was an accurate description. As a matter of fact, the path and alley might as well be one. Garrick guessed the refuse truck for the county had to drive on both pavement and dirt path to get to the dumpsters.

The saving grace was a fence that the Temple family had erected. The family had owned the land next to the alley as long as Garrick could remember. Their house was visible in the distance, but he would visit them later.

Standing in the alley with the group of men, he said, "I want us to walk at a slow pace and space ourselves to walk the width of the alley and path." He gestured to indicate the width of the alley and pointed to the trash container and a few loose boxes. "We'll have to walk around the dumpster and whatever else is in our path."

The men lined up with Constable Robinson closest to the buildings, then Deputy Hall, Garrick, Foster, and Gilbert on the outside, next to the fence that marked the land owned by the Temple family.

As the officer-in-charge, Garrick had given Robinson and Hall evidence bags in case they found something, and they all had plastic gloves. With the number of bags limited, any clue anyone found would have to be described so that each man heard and agreed. He didn't want a dozen bags of junk floating around with no officer claiming to have found what they held.

"You want to brief us on what we're looking for?" Gilbert asked.

Garrick raised his hat and ran his hand back over his hair before adjusting the hat to his head. "This won't be easy. The smell alone is horrible. There's years of debris here. Look for anything that looks out of place or new. Anything that might be used if a person wanted to throw a bottle of kerosene through a window." Garrick looked at each man and zeroed in on Foster, who didn't seem to be paying attention. "Is that clear, Ranger Foster?"

Foster snapped his body straight as a soldier. "Yes, sir."

Garrick continued with his advice. "Pretend you're the person about to fling a bottle of kerosene through a window, wanting to hurt somebody or make a statement. What would you need? How would you do it?" He glanced around at the men one last time. "Okay, let's go."

The sun was brightening the area, magnifying the smell of the trash bins. Garrick walked slowly, looking at his companions as well as the area in front of him. A refuse container sat directly in his path.

Foster drifted toward the dumpster. "Should we go through this stuff?" Foster asked.

Garrick didn't see pawing through garbage as an answer to their quest, but maybe something might come of it. "How about you pull a couple of those bags down? No need to go through everything, but we can see if there's anything worth pulling out."

To Garrick's surprise, Foster began taking bags out, showing them to him, and waiting for instructions.

"I figured a body had to be moving quick and probably didn't leave much behind, just guessing," Foster said.

"I'm thinking it might be kids," Garrick said. "They'd be more likely to be sloppy and leave clues. But anyone going to the trouble of a bottle bomb might throw an extra bottle or a box of matches in there. Though probably not in bags."

The other men gathered around the dumpster, and when nothing became obvious, they put the bags back into the trash container and continued their trek down the alley.

"Walk slow," Garrick reminded them.

When they reached the end of the alley, they all looked to Garrick.

"Okay, dry run," he said. "Let's walk back up."

Each man turned and walked back.

At the end of the exercise, Bob Gilbert said, "Wait a minute, there's something hanging on the barbed wire over here." He walked to the fence, and on the lowest strand of wire, a piece of red ribbon fluttered from one of the barbs. "Looks like it was used as a shoelace. Has an aglet on one end and the other end is unraveling." He carefully pulled the ribbon off and, grinning at Garrick, dropped it in an evidence bag.

"Good job. Let's split up and get some statements," Garrick said. "I'll talk to the Temple family. Y'all decide who'll talk to who. Have a partner and one of you take notes while the other asks questions. We'll meet back at the constable's office when we finish."

Garrick walked back to his truck and drove to the street that ran by the gas station. He'd known the Temple family as long as he could remember. Robert Temple had been a classmate when they were in elementary school. Robert had married Jane Cherry and took over the ranch that his father had inherited.

Garrick stopped his truck at the corner of the fence where Gilbert had spotted the ribbon. He stared across the field at the low-slung brick house that Robert had inherited. Garrick had attended Robert and Jane's wedding reception at that house. Garrick hadn't been married then. Hadn't gotten serious about anything but being a Ranger. But life at that time was already serious for Robert. Garrick shook his head and put the truck into gear. He didn't like this reminiscing. Reminded him how short life was. For some reason, that got him to thinking of Imogene.

Hell, yes, life was short. He really enjoyed that woman's company. "Comfortable" was the word he thought of when he thought of Imogene. And he smiled. Like some old fool, he kept smiling. He could talk to her about anything. She didn't insist he quit cussing. 'Course, they hadn't had a real date yet, but that was going to change. Yep, just as soon as he finished talking with Robert Temple that was going to change. Garrick goosed the accelerator. Time to get this thing done.

At the end of the road, Garrick turned right and soon eased the truck into Temple's driveway.

Nothing moved around the house. The place seemed deserted, but he knew Robert and Jane lived there, so he parked and walked to the front door. The house had an ominous quiet. No animal noise. Even the wind chime was still. Garrick knocked, and a young man who favored Robert opened the door.

Garrick introduced himself and asked for Robert Temple, explaining that he hoped to find out if anyone in the house had heard or seen anything out of the ordinary late the day before or during the night.

"Dad's not here. I'm Larry Temple. No one was here yesterday. Mom had surgery. We got home about midnight." The young man didn't speak forcefully, but like a strong wind, the words seemed to push Garrick backward.

"I'm so sorry," Garrick said. "I knew your parents when we were in high school. I hope your mother will be okay. Tell your folks that I'm thinking about them." He turned and caught onto one of the support posts as he stepped off the porch. He steadied himself for a minute to be sure of his next move.

On solid ground, he wondered why this news had affected him so deeply. But he knew. The job was not as glamorous as he remembered; nothing exciting happened. The job no longer completed him. He wished he had gotten smart sooner. Damn the wasted years chasing criminals and hoping for a quick adrenaline rush from confrontation. It was hard to admit he'd been so wrong. Life was more than just a job.

And now priorities had changed.

He wanted a long life—a healthy life. Maybe a life with Imogene. But if she didn't want to be with him, he still wanted a different life. He hoped he'd realized that soon enough to take action and make his life worthwhile. He stared toward the town, his mind veering from his personal goals to what he was trying to find out from this family.

Anyone in the Temples' backyard or patio, even in the rooms at the rear of the house, could see and hear a lot of what went on in the alley behind the newspaper. Probability was someone had seen or heard something in the time frame he was interested in. He'd ask each family member personally when they returned.

He moved automatically, walking to his truck, driving to the end of the road, back into Broken Rock, stymied for the moment by the wall he'd just hit. Maybe the idea of a sick woman reminded him of Nancy dying. Maybe he should be paying closer attention to small moments. Maybe. Maybe what? He didn't know.

After the short drive into town, he parked on the street and sat in the truck a few minutes. Strange as it seemed, he wanted to talk to Imogene right then. But that was impossible. He picked up his phone and put it back down. She was probably at work. She did important work as a nurse. She was needed. She never told him that, but he knew she was good at being a nurse because she was so kind. She probably knew Mrs. Temple. He'd bet Imogene could tell him how Jane Temple faired after her surgery.

He'd go to the hospital today when they went to check on Bandit. He'd find Imogene or Mrs. Temple, or both, and get some answers. But for now, he was gonna quit this gol-darned worrying about getting old.

Finally, he picked his hat up off the seat, blew out a frustrated breath, and walked into the constable's office.

29

Portia didn't sleep well after the news about Bandit. The next morning when she woke at 5 a.m., she wanted to stay home. She called Annie Hernandez. She told Annie what she had planned for her classes, and when the call ended, she knew she would go back to students who barely noticed her absence. Then she sent an email to her principal at the school that she would not be in for the day and she had already called a substitute. When she heard Imogene in the hall, she went downstairs to the kitchen.

"I hope our new house is as warm and cozy as this one." Portia walked to the counter and poured herself some coffee. "My student comes for a lesson today. Oh, and I'm not going in today. Didn't sleep well."

Imogene looked up from her crossword. "I think that's wise. Why don't you go back to bed for a few hours? I'm leaving soon; the house will be quiet. Your student doesn't come until the afternoon, right?"

"Yes, but I always feel too guilty to sleep late."

Imogene laughed. "Yes, your parents and mine made sure we worked every second of every day. I don't like to think about it."

She stood and put her coffee cup in the sink. Then she placed one hand on Portia's shoulder and gave it a light squeeze. "I can stay home. Are you sure you're okay?"

"Don't be foolish," Portia said. "I'll be fine. I'll read until I'm sleepy. Then a short nap and I'll cook some supper. Soup sound all right?"

"Yummy." Imogene nodded and went upstairs.

Portia sat with the day-old newspaper, staring at the words but not really reading. It was useless to go back to bed. She got out a small pan, added water, and when it boiled, poured in steel-cut oats. She stared at the gray mix of grain and water. The porridge looked like her life at the moment, bubbling and gray. How would it be to be in the house, alone, with no Imogene to talk to? Hell, that's how.

Imogene padded down the stairs, her nurse's shoes barely eliciting a creak on the steps. She stopped at the kitchen door. "Bye. Call me if you get to feeling worse."

"I'll be fine. Have a good day," Portia said. She waved one hand, gave an exaggerated smile, and walked to the front of the house. Imogene drove away without a backward glance.

As she walked back to the kitchen, she continued to worry with the blues that had attached themselves to her psyche. She and Imogene had lived together for almost twenty years. And in that time, they had been like sisters. Portia had kept some things in her life secret. She was certain Imogene had kept some secrets to herself, but Imogene was her best friend and confidant. They talked about their differences before they became problems. Anything she had not told Imogene was best left unsaid.

And now that she was worried about Imogene leaving, she was trying even harder to be pleasant. Not that they ever quarreled.

In the time they had lived together, each had learned how to get along with the other. Portia loved having Imogene with her.

Portia looked out the window at the frosty lawn and smiled at remembering Imogene telling her that the dress she'd decided to purchase for her awards dinner made her look like a "too-ripe pumpkin." She walked back to the kitchen, still remembering.

They rarely discussed men. They kidded sometimes about the scarcity of single men their age, and Portia sometimes said, "Can you imagine living with that man?" Now that she thought about it, she was always the one with the acerbic remark, but she had thought it was because Imogene was simply a gentler soul. Imogene probably hadn't commented because she really considered the question.

Portia felt confident that she was reading her cousin's new friendship with Sutton Garrick as more than a passing whimsy. Imogene thought she was a sphinx about her emotions and most of her life, but Portia could see that she enjoyed Sutton Garrick's attention. Imogene moved differently; her step was lighter in the last few days. And more importantly than anything, she seemed happier since Garrick had been calling.

Portia stirred the oats and pulled the box of brown sugar out of the cabinet. Almost immediately, she remembered herself and Imogene as children eating cold oatmeal. No one else in the world loved cold oats as they did. Her mind went back to the problem she'd been considering at bedtime as she poured the oatmeal into the bowl and added two heaping spoonfuls of sugar on top. She set the stewer of oatmeal dregs on the counter and sat down to think. She always liked to go over the worst part of a problem first. What if Imogene and Garrick fell in love? Or what if Imogene fell into infatuation and Garrick didn't?

If she mentioned either of these ideas to Imogene, she would protest, but Portia had to consider what was possible, and love was possible. At least it was for Imogene. And as much as Portia had disliked Garrick over the years, she was honest in her assessment of him earlier. He had changed. Maybe he was older and more aware of how short life could be. Or maybe he was leading Imogene into a world of unhappiness. It wasn't like Imogene was a child, but Portia hated to see her hurt.

Of course, in one way, she envied Imogene's courage. She was ready to take a chance on getting hurt, whereas Portia had long ago decided she would never take a chance again. If one never loved, one would not be hurt. She thought that she and Nightingale probably shared that philosophy. So whatever happened, she would be there for Imogene, and together they would be fine.

Having solved that problem, Portia dug into her oats, tasted too much brown sugar, and reached for the pan of oats to add more to her bowl and temper the sweetness.

She didn't enjoy eating alone, so she finished quickly and went into the living room to complete her plan for what she and Adam would cover in the lesson.

At noon, she called Nightingale. She was surprised when he answered.

"I'm checking on Bandit," she said. "I'm at home today in case you need to bring him here."

"That's very kind," he said, "but I don't know if they'll let me bring him home yet. If they do, I may stay home for a day or so to make sure he's okay. I do plan on taking up your offer to keep him during the day until I get this case resolved."

"Good. Have you found out anything else about Joshua?" A long, almost tangible, pause came over the phone, and in it, Portia heard Nightingale's hesitation. "Oswald, don't tell me anything." She disrupted the subject before he spoke. "Forget that I asked. You'll let me know when you have news. Goodbye." She hit the end button before he could reply. Elated at her own generosity, she walked out to get the mail.

30

The day had gotten cloudy but was still a warm sixty degrees. Nightingale walked onto the back porch, and after the brief call from Portia, he called the animal hospital.

The vet was encouraging. "He's still weak, but he's young and very healthy otherwise. He came very close."

"I'd like to leave him one more night, if you think he'd benefit, but I sure do miss him."

"Yes, another night would be good. But it'll do him good to see you for a while tonight. Bring a favorite toy or blanket for him, and we'll let him rest here one more day," the doctor said.

Nightingale got the favorite blanket and a chew toy and put them in the truck. He was going back into the house when Garrick turned into the driveway. Nightingale waited for Garrick, and they walked into the house.

"How's Bandit?"

"Doctor thought it would be good for us to visit. I want him to stay another twenty-four hours out of harm's way. I'd just as soon whoever tried to kill him think that they succeeded. We can grab something to eat at a drive-through and compare notes on our way into town. Does that work for you?"

"Sure. I want to go by the hospital. I'll explain while we drive. And we need to leave this with the lab." Garrick held up the evidence bag with the ribbon in it. "And I've got a tire track they made a mold of, but the picture is on my phone. Gilbert took the mold with him. Looks to me like it's from one of those little sporty motorcycles, and I don't know anyone around here who has one. I've seen them in Lubbock, usually with a student riding them."

Nightingale asked where they found the ribbon. By the time they reached the Ranger office, they had each covered the day's events, but Garrick, distracted and unusually short on words, had left large spaces between thoughts.

Nightingale figured something outside of the investigation was bothering Garrick, but he didn't think the time was right to ask. On the other hand, Garrick usually had no qualms when it came to probing into Nightingale's life, but maybe he'd decided tonight was not the right time.

They left the ribbon at the medical examiner's office. Belschner was not in the office, so Garrick planned to call him in the morning to explain the ribbon.

The streets were dark when they stopped by the hospital. Nightingale waited in the lobby while Garrick went to Jane Temple's room. Normally, Garrick told any and all if he had been treated poorly or if anyone had insulted him. But tonight, he seemed distracted. Nightingale didn't know how close Garrick had been to Robert and Jane Temple, but he hoped the hospital visit would solve whatever was clouding Garrick's usual prickly personality.

Garrick walked out of the elevator smiling. "She's good," he said. "Robert said what they found was benign. And guess what? Jane said she saw a little motorcycle drive through the alley behind the newspaper twice during the last few days. She wasn't sure what days, but she was outside and heard a low put-put, like a motorbike. The second time, she had Robert's binoculars around her neck. The bike was red. Couldn't tell who was driving."

"Not even male or female?" Nightingale asked.

"Oz, she's still groggy from the surgery, and I didn't feel like being a jerk and pushing for more. I'll go see her again later and see if she can tell me more."

The visit to see Bandit was sad. Though he weighed fifty pounds, the puppy was weak and wobbled when he tried to stand. A technician lifted him out of his crate and onto a blanket on the floor. Nightingale and Garrick sat down beside him, and he climbed into Nightingale's lap, nosing his head under Nightingale's hand for a rub.

"He looks peaked," Garrick said.

At the words, Bandit climbed over to Garrick's lap and laid down, his tail beating a happy thud-thud. He closed his eyes. They sat there for a while, the dog seeming content to doze.

If Nightingale was betting, he'd say Garrick had the look of a new father. After about twenty minutes, they transferred Bandit to Nightingale's lap.

"I'll go get us two coffees for the drive back," Garrick said.

Nightingale leaned back and closed his eyes while he rubbed the puppy. When he felt the touch on his shoulder and looked up, the tech was grinning.

"You dozed off," he said.

The wall clock pointed to nine. The tech helped Nightingale return Bandit to the crate and promised that he was doing very well. "He's an active dog, so we'll take him out tomorrow for a walk. He'll sleep all day, and that will help him recover. We may give him more fluids, but you can probably pick him up tomorrow."

Nightingale thanked him and went into the waiting room.

Garrick handed him a cup of coffee, and they walked out into the crisp, cold night.

Once they were in the truck, they sat for a minute. Garrick was the first to speak. "I didn't know I was so fond of the little critter." Neither one looked at the other. They busied themselves with seat belts.

Nightingale's phone vibrated in his pocket before it rang. An unidentified number showed on the screen. He drew in a long breath, said "Hello," and waited.

"This is Belschner. I received the DNA crossmatches. The hair that you brought to me is a 99.9% positive match with our young John Doe. It undoubtedly belongs to the dead man's father, and I'd be willing to testify to that. The office called to tell me that Garrick came by and left some ribbon."

Nightingale explained the piece of ribbon, thanked the man, and put the phone in his pocket. He relayed the information to Garrick.

"I'm in a fog with all this good news," Nightingale said. "We should be happy." He leaned forward to look up through the windshield at the sky. The moon shone bright, and stars looked like Christmas lights.

"Maybe. You look at the stars, and I look at the darkness around us." Garrick leaned forward to stretch his lower back. "My tenderloin is hurting, and that's a sure sign that a shit storm is coming."

31

Nightingale drove slowly on the way back home. "Don't know about you," he said, "but I'm tired."

"Yeah, me too," Garrick said. "We both drive like little old ladies--slow and weaving over the line when we're tired."

Nightingale gave a half-laugh and pushed the accelerator to sixty miles per hour. "I've got to plan what to do next. We'll have to wait for lab results on the ribbon you found behind the newspaper. We'll need alibis from the people at Post's house for the morning that Joshua died. We've also got some tire-track molds that need analysis. I keep going back to the M.E. saying the chemical was injected in the man's neck. How in the hell?" Then facetiously: "Maybe he did it himself before he went to the roof?"

"I'll check with Gilbert tomorrow morning about the motor scooter. He might find something red on the college campus." Garrick had pushed his door open almost as soon as Nightingale pulled into his driveway. "You want to come by my house or me to meet you at the Post mansion?"

"I can come by your house. You want to come in for a minute? Maybe have some coffee?"

"No, thanks. After your guest bed, I'm ready for a good night's sleep."

"Wait a minute," Nightingale said. "Something's bothering you. Ever since you went to Robert and Jane Temple's house, and at the hospital, you've been off your feed. It's more than just worries about Bandit. Or Imogene. What else is bothering you?"

Garrick pulled the door shut and glanced at Nightingale before returning his gaze to the fields and flatlands surrounding Nightingale's house. "This is not gonna be a long philosophical discussion," he said. "I met the Temples' son, who told me about Jane's tumor. I've known them a long time, and they're good people. In the hospital, I watched them, and they still love each other like the day they married—or more. I'm not religious, and you know that, but I got to wondering what I've done with my life that's worth a hill of beans." He drew in a long breath. "I'm healthy, I think, and I'm enjoying life, but I could die any minute."

He held up one hand, stopping any comment that Nightingale might make. "We've talked about all this stuff—or talked around it—before. But I want my time to be better spent. Life is short, and I really think a lot of Imogene. I think a lot of you and that dog, too. Now, I don't want to talk anymore. Goodnight."

He pushed open the truck door and was on his way to his vehicle before Nightingale said a goodnight that only he heard.

After his quick departure, Nightingale sat in the truck, wondering if Garrick would call Imogene after he got home. That seemed like a teenage kind of thing to do, but caring about a woman made for odd doings in a man. Those odd doings included what Garrick had just said because, for Garrick, those few words amounted to a speech before a roomful of people.

Nightingale walked into his silent house, noticing the emptiness. A cold gloominess had sunk into the walls. He missed Bandit. He missed humans. Even though he wanted to be a hermit, he knew he could never cut himself off from humanity. A new structure would not solve his loneliness. And, as he had realized before, a wife was not the answer either.

He went to his computer. Bob Gilbert maintained a strict policy that only the trustworthy few could get into the database that he was privileged to see. Nightingale had had access until he left the organization, but maybe when Gilbert said, "white-hat category," he was letting Nightingale back in for this case. Sure enough, the cursor asked for name and password. Even this part was different because the system asked for a code. Nightingale took a guess, used the old name and password, and the system opened.

He tried to work quickly. A touch of arthritis had enlarged and stiffened a few finger joints. That, along with the lack of practice, made him need to look at the keys for accuracy. A trail of his visit would be embedded in the site, but if he didn't work too long or ask crazy questions, maybe no flags would go up. He put in Cordelia Comet's name. Everything he found was a repeat of what Gilbert had told him. After he typed in Danny Hartford's name, he sat back and waited.

His computer was slow, and not for the first time, he saw that he should get an upgraded Internet connection and a newer machine. He wrote down "new computer" at the top of the paper he was using for notes on the case. When he looked back at the screen, a list of published articles filled the page. He looked first at the lines marked classified.

When he clicked on one, the system asked for another pass code. He didn't have one. He knew Gilbert's wedding anniversary date and tried that. It worked.

He found less than a dozen articles. One said Hartford and Post grew up together. The writer had birth certificates to show that Hartford and Post had the same mother. When the mother died, the boys struck out on their own. Danny Hartford hadn't indicated anything about knowing Post's family, but he did mention two children—a boy and a girl—that Post had. The information left Nightingale still at loose ends.

He printed the shortest articles and skimmed through the longer ones. When he got to the end of them, the time was close to 1 a.m. He was sweating. He was tired. But he had found an interesting note on a truck registration. He printed it. A full day lay ahead, so he backed out of the program, closed it, and shut down his computer.

∽

Nightingale woke the next morning at ten 'til five. He congratulated his inner clock for waking him. He'd dreamed that he'd searched for Edgar Post all night and never found him. Now he looked forward to confronting the man. He was soon headed to Garrick's place.

Wired on coffee, Nightingale started talking as soon as Garrick was in the truck. "I checked the internet last night for things we might have missed. No one has delved into Danny Hartford's past. I checked on the license plate on the truck that we saw parked behind his house. The truck is registered to Saul Hartford, middle name Daniel. Saul Hartford has a long history in the investment world."

"Let me guess," Garrick said. "He's kin to Post."

"How did you know?"

"Just guessed. He was too forgiving, maybe. He acted like he wanted to tell us more but just couldn't," Garrick said. "What's the whole story?"

"I don't know that we'll ever be sure of it, but I think he's Post's half-brother. But even if he is, I don't think he's significant to us. He doesn't know enough about Post to cause any change for us in this investigation."

Nightingale turned to go by the Mesa Heights subdivision. "I want to go to the back of the house again," he said.

No one was in the subdivision. A few "Sold" signs graced some lots, but there was no sign of new construction. The cousins' house looked no different from the outside. Both men peeked in the side windows on their way to the back. "They're making progress," Garrick said.

"Yes, I wonder if Portia and Imogene have been up here to see how it's going," Nightingale said. "Has Imogene said anything about their plans?"

Garrick stared at Nightingale, a half-way smile on his face. "You're not good at being subtle, are you? But to answer your question, no, Imogene has not said anything to me about building this house or selling the other one. And I don't plan on asking her."

"Okay, okay." Nightingale held his hand up in surrender. "Just wondered." As they walked on, he said, "I think we can eliminate Danny Hartford as a suspected killer. If he is related, he probably still holds a grudge about being pushed out of the business. But I don't think he's strong enough and agile enough to have killed Joshua."

"I agree," Garrick said. "More than that, I don't think he would have recognized Joshua as Post's son. So that puts Hartford way down the list as a suspect."

At the rear of the house, they stumbled over rough ground full of dirt clods and pieces of rock and broken concrete. Yellow crime ribbon flapped in the wind, still stapled to one corner of the house. The blood from the dead man's head still stained the concrete that would eventually be a deck or patio.

"They'll probably tear that up, don't you think?" Garrick nodded toward the blood stain.

"I'd bet on it," Nightingale said. He looked up to the roof. "We haven't had anyone say they saw the man on the roof. I'm wondering, could someone have brought his body here right before I arrived? If so, then maybe he didn't fall off the roof but was killed someplace else."

"That sounds better to me than the notion that he fell. That would account for no climbing gear, too," Garrick said. "It's good, but I'm not excited about it. We still have no motive for anyone killing him, whether he's on the roof or on the ground."

Nightingale saw his new theory as easier to believe until he examined it. "From what I've read he didn't need a lot of climbing gear for roof work, so we can forget that part of it. He had the ropes to attach to the anchors. And the ladder was there. The thing that bothers me is we still have no motive. I keep thinking, 'Surely, his father wouldn't kill him,' and if he did, why?"

"Surely not," Garrick said. "I've seen some mean and wicked things as a lawman, but I've never seen a man kill his own flesh and blood. It's not natural."

32

Nightingale and Garrick didn't talk as they picked their way through the construction debris. November mornings now maintained a crisp chill until about noon, but the sunshine made the fields and grass glisten as the frost melted. A dark mood hung over Nightingale despite the sparkly day all around him. He was grateful that Garrick was not talking, but the silence didn't fit the day, so he said, "I've wondered all night about why anyone would kill Joshua. We need motive."

"Right, but we haven't talked this out and written it down like we usually do," Garrick said. "Too many things going on. Usually, we knock around enough ideas between us that we know what's possible and what's not."

"You're right. We'll do that after we see Post. Make a list and see what fits. I think it's all connected."

"I worry when we agree, but I can see that possibility. What about Danny Hartford?"

"We can discuss him, but to me he's out of the picture. And I'm going to ask Portia and Imogene if they have anything more to tell me."

"You think they're leaving something out?" A sense of unease edged Garrick's words.

Nightingale tried to explain. "You know as well as I do, sometimes the details mean a lot. They're almost confessional in their truthfulness. Maybe they left out a tiny thing that would mean something to you or me."

He walked away from the house and turned around so he was looking at the rear. "If he was up there at the peak when I came up to the front of the house, he could have lost his balance, thrown up his hands…"

"And you could have seen a reflection off of his watch or ring when he fell," Garrick said.

They stood side-by-side, peering up at the roof. "I like the premise," Nightingale said, "but he wasn't wearing a watch or ring. Come on, let's go visit the Post mansion. Maybe we'll have better luck there."

They went to the truck, and while he drove, Nightingale caught Garrick up on his talk with the governor.

"I made some phone calls while you searched the alley. I called the governor and told her I had some doubts about Post. Told her to hold off on giving him a job that controlled a lot of money," Nightingale said.

"Yeah, a dab of that money is my retirement," Garrick said. "I'm curious about what the governor is really after, but that can wait. Do you think that body we're calling Joshua is Post's son?"

"Yes, don't you, after what Belschner told us?"

"I do, but I don't think Post killed the boy. Mind you, I don't like the man. He's a weenie and a liar, but not someone who would kill his son."

"That's really scientific," Nightingale said. "I'll be sure and tell her your observation."

"I knew you'd appreciate that. But why do you think…"

Garrick turned in his seat so he could look at Nightingale. "Why do you think this is so important to her?"

"I try to not think about any of the 'chores' I do for her. I've worked for two other governors and all of them have politics at their core, so everything I do ultimately has political implications. She's run hot and cold on information about Post. One time she calls and wants something immediately, and the next she's decided to be patient. I've got a theory about what's happening, but I don't want to offer it yet. There's our next stop."

He was glad to see the gates of the destination ahead. He introduced himself to the speaker, and the gates swung open. He looked sideways at Garrick. "That's too easy."

Garrick smiled. "I told you last night--a shit storm."

Nightingale parked in the curved drive in front of the house, and Reeves, the butler, emerged as he and Garrick headed to the door. "Sir, may I help you?"

"We're here to see Edgar Post," Nightingale said.

"He is out of town on business. Can I be of assistance?"

Nightingale had not called ahead. He'd wanted to surprise Post, hoping for an advantage. His pride had caused this wasted trip. "I'd like to speak to Carolyn Post, then. And may we come in?"

The man tipped his head and stepped aside.

Garrick went in, and Nightingale followed suit. The entry to the house was a massive foyer, with a black-and-white marble floor. A broad staircase cascaded gracefully down to the marble floor, and sashaying down the stairs like royalty was Carolyn Post. She wore blue jeans and a silk blouse, but it might as well have been a swimsuit. She was beautiful and knew it. For the first time since he had met her, she had on makeup and looked older. Warning flares went off in Nightingale's head and not because he was attracted to her, but because in his estimation, beautiful women at her age often caused heartache for themselves and their families.

When she saw him, a smile broke across her face, and she missed a step, almost tumbling down the remainder of the stairs. "Mr. Nightingale, it's so good to see you."

Nightingale introduced Garrick, who said, "Nice to meet you, ma'am."

Carolyn's eyes grew huge. She turned to Nightingale and whispered. "Is he for real?" Then she did a follow-me gesture with her hand and seemed to be striving for composure as she walked down the hall.

She led them to the room Nightingale had been in during his first visit. The butler murmured something, and Carolyn ordered coffee and tea. When he left the room, she went to a writing desk, scribbled on a notepad, and said, "What can I help you with? My father isn't here."

"I need to see him as soon as he returns," Nightingale said.

"I'll tell him as soon as I see him. He doesn't like for me to call when he's in the middle of business. Why don't you have coffee before you go?"

When Nightingale had seen her before, he thought she had a certain gracefulness. Now, however, she seemed agitated and her movements were too hurried.

From the side door, the butler came in with the tea and coffee. The boy Nightingale had seen with Post a day earlier in Stockbridge's office was walking in behind Reeves.

Carolyn became even more hurried. She muttered to herself as she spilled both tea and coffee while trying to pour the hot liquids. When she brought coffee to Nightingale, the cup had a piece of paper under it. The paper was soaked in coffee because the cup and saucer shook in the girl's hand. "I know you want to get back to work, quickly. Adam, please give Mr. Garrick a coffee."

Adam let out a huge, put-upon sigh. He moved slowly, almost daring the liquid to slosh as he took a cup of coffee to Garrick.

When Garrick said, "Thank you," the boy stood and looked at him for a moment. "Do you like his dog?" he asked. He nodded his head toward Nightingale.

A small, sad smile touched Garrick's mouth. "Yes, I do. He's a smart dog, and he likes me, in spite of myself. He's taught me a lot." His smile faded. "Someone poisoned him night before last and he may die."

"He's a dog—how could he teach you?" The question came with the verbal attitude of a smart-aleck teen. Nightingale watched the boy because he remembered his reaction from their encounter at the newspaper. He was scared of Bandit, and Nightingale guessed that the boy had knowledge about Bandit's poisoner.

Garrick looked at the boy for a long minute, his face serious. He carefully placed his cup on the table by the chair. "The puppy will fetch the ball with me anytime day or night. He always welcomes me when I visit Nightingale. He's patient, will wait on me or Nightingale to do our chores before he has to go out and do his business." He glanced at Nightingale. "He's a good friend no matter if I yell at him or feed him. Humans could learn a lot from dogs."

While Garrick had an audience, Nightingale had removed the note and slid the sopping paper into his jacket pocket.

"He was going to bite me when I saw him in town," Adam said. "My father said he should be taught some manners."

"At the newspaper, right?" Nightingale asked.

Adam nodded and blushed.

"When will you know if he's okay?" Carolyn asked.

"Two days," Nightingale said. "The vet and the Ranger lab are running some tests. We found a few clues. We'll find who poisoned him."

Carolyn Post had perched on the arm of the couch. She seemed as engrossed as Adam in the talk about Bandit.

Nightingale was getting nowhere, so he put aside the coffee, stood, and picked up his hat.

Garrick followed his lead.

"We'll be going now," Nightingale said.

"I'll walk you to your truck," Carolyn said.

Once they were outside, Carolyn looked toward the ground and said, "I couldn't talk inside. Our father has put in cameras, so he sees everything, and the butler tells him everything else. Have you tested the hair in the brush?"

Ignoring her question, Nightingale said, "Do you know of anyone in this complex that has a motor scooter or a small motorcycle?"

The girl looked up at him. "I thought you were going to help me. No, we don't have a motorcycle, and anyway, we wouldn't be allowed to drive it. Especially not my brother. He might hurt himself," she said, the sarcasm evident in her voice. She turned and quickly walked away.

Before she reached the door, Nightingale raised his voice to her back. "I need to talk with your father. Tell him to call me when he gets home."

They got in the truck and drove away. The gate was already open when they got to it. "I don't know what makes me sadder," Nightingale said, "knowing that boy probably poisoned my dog, or knowing those two are captives in that place."

"What makes you think him, not her?" Garrick asked.

"The boy is a product of his father. He said his father said, 'somebody should teach him some manners.' I think Post's young son saw that as an okay to poison Bandit." After a minute, he added, "And you're right, maybe both of them did it."

33

Nightingale set his foot on the accelerator as soon as they cleared the gates of the Post mansion. "I don't understand most of what we've seen in the Post household the past few days."

"I noticed you didn't use the word 'family' in reference to them," Garrick said. "Where is the boy's mother?"

"His mother and Post live separately. I don't know what the arrangement is between them." They drove for a few miles in silence before Nightingale continued. "We need to get started on the work list. Is my house okay with you?" Nightingale asked.

"You have coffee?"

"Yes, and some left over peach cobbler," Nightingale said.

"That's all I need," Garrick said.

"I need more, but I think a sandwich will be enough. It's close to noon." Nightingale turned the truck onto the paved road that led to his house. "Do you remember the first time we started making a list to go over details of a case?" he asked.

"Actually, I do," Garrick said. "Must'a been the second case we worked on—the kidnapping. That little girl who everybody thought had been kidnapped, and actually she'd run off with a cowboy. We had so many suspects we decided to make a list."

It had proved to be a valid way to examine a case. In complicated cases, the information became a spaghetti bowl of mixed messages that, considered separately, didn't make sense and led to a dead end. But sometimes when several separate incidents were laid side by side and considered for all elements, the separate incidents began to coalesce as parts of a whole.

But there was another factor that was necessary for success: It took two people considering all those elements to ultimately solve the case. When one person looked at the facts, he often went over the same issues and circled back to the same conclusions because his mind had already been made up. However, two people, especially two competitive people, often came up with bizarre but correct ideas. Garrick was one of the best Nightingale had seen at this type of reasoning because he didn't mind making strange, off-the-wall guesses about anything that had happened or anyone who might be affected.

When he stopped the truck, he noted the truck odometer. "Get this," he said, "it's less than ten miles between my house and Post's."

"So, as the crow flies, it's about five miles. Right?" Garrick asked.

"No, more than that, but close."

Inside the house, Nightingale gathered two steno pads and pens from his office and put them on the kitchen table. While Garrick started the coffee, Nightingale made a list:

1. Joshua Tallman (Post?), murdered.

2. Edgar Post, father. Did he know Tallman? Did he know he was his son?

3. Bandit, poisoned.

4. Danny Hartford, reclusive former associate (partner? half-brother) to Post. He helped Post establish his reputation in the financial world. Left—or was discarded—by Post. How bitter is he?

5. Bottle bomb at newspaper

6. Governor and Edgar Post? Does this have a bearing on the murder investigation? Refer to Garrick's question: What is really bugging the governor?

As the coffee brewed, Garrick leaned against the counter. "What's on your list?" He picked up one of the steno pads and put it on the counter, writing as Nightingale read his list. "What about the ex-Mrs. Post? She needs to be on the list, too."

"Right," Nightingale said. "Her name is Cordelia Comet. After what your friends from the barber shop said, I'm wondering if any of them would be able to recognize Joshua in a picture."

"We'd have to ask. You know people are funny. They kinda made sport of her, like any bunch of guys, but I could tell they were proud of having an art gallery in their washed-out town. They might get protective if we push the wrong way."

"Maybe she'll tell you the truth after she hears that her son is dead." Nightingale watched Garrick as he tried the idea on him.

"She doesn't know me. She met you." Eyebrows raised to reflect a question, Garrick looked sideways at Nightingale..

"I want to get your read on her. It's too odd that her son was this near and she claims to have not seen him. And why did Joshua not mention her to Portia since he told Portia that he knew his father owned the big house? I'd be willing to bet they saw each other before he died. Maybe if you go see her, she might tell you what she wouldn't tell me."

Garrick sipped his coffee and looked out toward the back yard. "Okay. I'll call tomorrow. I guess you've considered the idea that Joshua and the mother, or maybe just him alone, could have been trying to blackmail Post."

"I've thought about it. What about how Joshua was killed? New ideas?"

"If we go with what Belschner said, somebody taller than the man had to be on the roof to administer an injection, push the man off, and hope he broke his neck. Or we go with your other theory, that he never fell off the roof, that he was killed someplace else and the body dropped off at the house. Have you asked Belschner about a time frame for something like that?"

"No. I don't think it's possible because nobody saw anyone out at the building site, and the body was still warm when I got to it. I'll call Belschner right now and see what he thinks."

Nightingale made the call and put the phone on speaker so Garrick could hear his side of the conversation. He posed his question to the M.E., whose answer came through loud and clear:

"No. Impossible. Even if he was killed at the gates to the subdivision, the time of rigor would be later because of the cool weather. If you had arrived later, maybe, but rigor starts in two to six hours after death. And when the body got to me, rigor mortis still was not fully in effect. Also, there was blood flow from the head wound. Corpses don't bleed. Besides that, you told me that you saw no one. Sorry, Ranger, that's the way I see it."

Nightingale laid his phone on the table. "Guess you could hear," he said.

Garrick nodded.

"He's convinced the man fell off the roof."

"Next on the list," Nightingale said, "is Bandit. I think his poisoning and the bottle bomb at the newspaper are tied together. I think Post's son, Adam, did it." He glanced at Garrick.

"Agreed. But it makes the thrown bottle seem petty," Garrick said.

"It was petty. He's a child, trying to do what his father says should be done, as he interprets it. It was an elaborate plan for a child to think through. He was buying time, assuming I'd go into town to check on the newspaper while he poisoned Bandit. It's scary. What if Daddy doesn't like a human, and the child acts on that?"

"What do we do till we get something concrete?"

"We wait and work on the death of Joshua," Nightingale said.

"That doesn't seem promising," Garrick said. "What about Danny Hartford? Can we get anything out of him? He's tall enough that he could have been the culprit who gave the injection, but I don't think he could have gotten on the roof and left without being seen. He doesn't move that fast." Garrick almost stopped but his face lit up with a new thought. "That presents the same problem as the other method of killing him. How did someone get away without being seen?"

"That's been my problem from the start," Nightingale said. "I got there early, I didn't see anyone at the site, and I didn't meet anyone driving out of the subdivision. So, I don't see how anyone was there before me." He stood and began to pace the floor. "Did you ever read the Sherlock Holmes short story about the snake that was a pet and bit the owner because it was angry after Sherlock hit it?"

"No, missed that one," Garrick said.

"What I'm saying is, we're not thinking of how this *could* have been done. We keep going over how it *couldn't* be done." He was getting angry and knew there was no reason for it except for frustration. "Let's go to a different subject. This time-of-death thing is getting in the way."

Nightingale's phone rang. When he answered, he was surprised to hear the Amish restaurant owner say, "Hello, Mr. Nightingale. John Miller here. From the restaurant?"

"Hello, Mr. Miller. Yes, I remember you. How can I help you?"

"Mr. August said I could use his phone," he said. "I am calling because last night the noise from our new neighbors kept us awake. They have usually complied when we make a request. But last night it was more noise, around midnight, and lights. It continued for several hours."

"I'll see what I can do," Nightingale said.

"You told me to call you. I hope our names will not be mentioned," Miller said.

"We'll try to avoid that. Thank you for calling."

Nightingale hung up the phone and leaned onto the table. "That was John Miller. He owns the Amish restaurant in Broken Rock and happens to be the neighbor of Edgar Post. He's got a complaint about noise from the Post place. That makes a pretty good reason for a search warrant, and while we're at it, we'll expand the search items to cover chemicals like the ones that poisoned Bandit and Joshua. We can mention party noises if we're asked."

"Shouldn't be hard," Garrick said.

"And I don't want Miller's name on this." Nightingale stood and started pacing. "I had hoped Post would get back here and we could talk to him. Do you agree that Adam Post is responsible for the bottle rocket?"

"The boy? I don't know." Garrick answered so quickly, Nightingale knew that, like him, Garrick had been going over the events of the last few days.

"What about killing Joshua?"

Garrick didn't answer for a long moment. "Anything is possible. Some men have no moral conscience and can use chemical bombs on babies and children. I don't think the boy killed Joshua. Maybe Edgar really didn't know he had a living son, other than Adam."

"In other words, maybe Edgar did it. I think he's capable, and that makes him a danger to the governor," Nightingale said. "As I mentioned earlier, just 'cause we can't imagine it, doesn't mean it didn't happen."

Another question haunted him like a six-hundred-pound gorilla on the table between them. This didn't seem like a good time, but there wasn't a good time to ask this question—and he'd put it off long enough. Maybe, just maybe, Garrick had an answer for him.

"Since we're on the subject of fathers, are you aware there was, possibly still is, a rumor that you are my father?" Nightingale tried to keep his voice low, his words even. His eyes didn't leave Garrick's face. And Garrick showed no shock at hearing the rumor now.

The older man pushed aside his coffee cup, clasped his hands on the table. "I don't know when I first heard it. Had to be at the Ranger office. Somebody made a remark that we looked alike, or acted alike." Garrick stood and got a glass and filled it with water. He set the glass on the counter and left it. This wasn't like him. Even in dangerous circumstances in the past years, Nightingale rarely saw him so uneasy, but he, too, felt his inward resolve shaking.

"I don't know about you," Garrick said, "but I got ragged some because we were the most successful guys working. Had to be envy. I never thought seriously about what men said, because I knew it wasn't true." Garrick paused and looked out the window over the sink.

Nightingale had promised himself that he wouldn't get personal if he ever got the chance to ask Garrick about this shared history. But how could he avoid it when everything in him said that this *was* personal. "How could you let that go? You said you cared about my mother, but you let some fool rumor ruin her reputation?"

"Nobody believed that you were my son. God knows I wouldn't have minded. And Nancy would have loved the idea."

"I doubt that," Nightingale said.

Garrick smiled and corrected himself, as he returned to the table and sat down. "You're right. She wouldn't have liked it. But anybody who ever saw you with your daddy would know whose kid you were."

"That's bullshit. You let it go and ruined my mother's name." He felt and heard the tremor in his own voice. Anger overtook good sense.

Garrick's face grew redder, and his expression showed his confusion. "You're totally out of the realm of reality. How long has this been festering?"

"A while. It's my mother we're talking about." Nightingale's frustration seemed like an echo in his head. He tried to lower his voice and couldn't. "For God's sake, how long have you known that some people thought I was your bastard child?"

"It wasn't like that. What was said was vindictive and meant to hurt. I heard it, like you, from mean little men and mean minds." Garrick looked like he'd aged twenty years in ten minutes. "I was proud of you. I told people it wasn't true." He put one hand up as if Nightingale might strike him. "Sit down a minute and listen to me. After Nancy was killed, I about lost my mind."

He couldn't sit. His head roared, and the years of working with Garrick came at him. Garrick, the hothead. Garrick, the risktaker. Garrick, the lucky one who never got shot.

He remembered the speculation when Garrick came riding into town on a horse, like an old western movie. Garrick rode up to the Ranger office and almost fell when he dismounted because he'd been shot in the leg. The convict who had killed Nancy Garrick was dead on a horse tethered behind Garrick's mount. Nightingale ran out to catch him and help him into the Ranger office.

Word in the office was that Garrick would be reprimanded and possibly kicked off the force. It didn't happen. But Garrick went home and disappeared in a fog of depression and Jack Daniels.

"I was drinking to try and forget. I wanted to be numb, not just physically, but mentally." Garrick's gaze was that of a man in another world. He sat across from Nightingale, his hands once again folded on the table.

"I don't know how long I drank and fought the loneliness after Broderick killed Nancy and I brought him in. Over a year, I guess." His voice cracked. He picked up the cold coffee and drank it. "So one night there was a knock, and when I stumbled to the door, it was your mother." Garrick laughed and tears started down his cheeks. "I thought I was seeing an angel. I told her, 'Girl, turn around so I can see your wings.'

"But she lit into me like a tiger. She said I was lazy and dishonoring Nancy's memory. I should be working, not drinking myself to death. She went on and on. Brewed me coffee, and when she left, I was stone cold sober with a headache from Hell. She said a lot more, but basically, she straightened my ass out. She said she'd told your father she had a mission she had to do. He knew where she was and didn't mind her rescuing me." Garrick looked at Nightingale, anguish cutting deeper lines in his weathered face.

"And you want to know the icing on this? The next morning, your momma and daddy came and dragged my ass out of bed at five o'clock and cooked breakfast, and we all ate together. They came every morning for a week like that. At the end of the week, they said goodbye, and I went back to work."

Nightingale felt an icicle run up his spine. "You didn't stop drinking."

"That wasn't the point. I cut way down, and I went back to living."

The air seemed to have gone out of the room. Garrick stood and put his coffee cup in the sink. "You're gonna have to drive me home," he said.

"You could stay," Nightingale said. His voice trailed off.

"Not tonight," Garrick said.

Neither man spoke during the drive to Garrick's house.

Garrick opened the truck door and turned to Nightingale. "What about tomorrow?"

Nightingale stared into the darkness and finally turned to Garrick. "I wanted you to know how hurt I was. My mother was an angel to me, too. She deserved my best and your best, not some stinking rumors from hate-filled people."

"You're right. I apologize. If she was here, I'd apologize to her. And to your father. I did that when they helped me. But I won't apologize for being proud of you, like you *were* my son. As it is, I hope we can remain friends."

"We've still got a case to solve," Nightingale said. "I'll call you —early."

In the low interior lights of the vehicle, Nightingale thought Garrick looked better; maybe some of the wrinkles had smoothed out. Didn't matter. The important stuff had been said, and they had a murder to solve.

34

When Nightingale woke the next morning, the first thing he saw was Bandit's empty crate. If the vet agreed, Bandit was coming home today. Nightingale had hoped to stay home when he brought the dog back, but he wanted to get a search warrant and see Edgar Post soon.

His talk with Garrick came whispering into his thoughts in bits and pieces. He felt better, a weight lifted. He didn't know how Garrick would be. He wanted to call the man, but he needed to think some more.

With that much in front of him, at 6 a.m. Nightingale picked up the phone and called his cousins. Imogene answered.

After a short discussion, Imogene said she would be home during the day and would "love to have Bandit visit as long as necessary."

"I want him home tonight, if possible," Nightingale said. "I must admit I probably need him more than vice versa."

Nightingale said he'd try to bring Bandit about mid-afternoon. He called the vet next and planned on picking up Bandit between 1:00 and 2:00.

Congratulating himself on progress, he called the judge to schedule a visit to get the search warrant.

Nightingale hung up realizing that he'd not lost sleep over the confab with Garrick. In fact, he felt better than he had in some time. The question and discussion about Garrick being his father had been bothering him for a long time. He had harbored a low-level anger that had picked at his consciousness, making him less effective in his job.

No matter what innocence Garrick claimed, Nightingale could tell that the issue had been haunting him, too. Garrick, for all his bluster was a man who valued family and Mary Nightingale's reputation. And he probably did wish that Nightingale was his son.

Thinking about Garrick's words gave Nightingale a strange frisson of unease. He loved and admired his father. Nathaniel Manley Nightingale would always be a hero to his son, and his mother was almost angelic in his thinking. The exchange had given him a peace he hadn't experienced in months. He'd gone to bed and gone to sleep.

But now, in the bright morning sunlight, Oswald faced the task of correcting rumors or letting them die. At the same time, he admitted to himself that he had a deep caring for Sutton Garrick. Eventually he and Garrick would talk again about their odd relationship. But all of that could wait. It would have to wait until what lay before them was solved.

Next, he called the Post house and found that Edgar Post was still away. The only thing left was to drive into Lubbock and get the warrant signed by the judge and then collect Bandit.

∽

AS HE DROVE INTO LUBBOCK, THE CONVERSATION WITH Garrick took over his mind again. But now he thought back over the last few years. He didn't know how to tell the older man that he cared about him. God knew he had enough of a problem when it came to telling a woman that he loved her. This was tantamount to parting the Red Sea. Like so many things in his life, he would have to think about it.

Maybe he was worried about something that was unnecessary. He once asked his father why he didn't give his mother jewelry. His father had said, "She knows I love her by the things I do for her. We don't have a lot of 'stuff,' but she makes me happy and I try every way I know to make her happy."

When Nightingale gave the matter some deep thought, he realized that the snarky comments had been from within the Ranger office. The timing had been right around when his mother had been ill. He never shared his worry for her with anyone except Gilbert and Garrick. He didn't remember the specific time, but Garrick was right: envy probably was at the bottom of the comments, and it was something he overheard, something meant to sting and hurt, and he reacted. Most likely, Garrick hadn't known that Nightingale had heard the insinuations, so there had never been a reason for him to bring the subject up.

They would continue to work together. Now the friction that Nightingale had felt because of somebody's mean-spirited speculation and Garrick's non-involvement was done. He was relieved.

At one o'clock, he walked into the vet's office. The receptionist remembered him and took him into the back. Bandit was out of his crate and, when he spied Nightingale, ran to him.

The vet walked into the room and led Nightingale and the dog to a smaller area to talk. "You'll need to watch what he eats for a while, and be careful around new people. I'm sending some soft, canned food home with him. He had a bad jolt. If he associates anyone with his experience, he may jump them, and you'll have to answer questions later."

"You think he may know who fed him the poison?" Nightingale didn't think that was possible.

"Definitely. If he smelled someone that pitched that meat to him and they come near him later, be careful. He's not a mean dog, but he's smart; he knows."

"I think I'll just keep him away from everybody except the people who love him." Nightingale thanked the doctor, bent down, and clipped Bandit's collar onto his leash. He threw the dog's blanket over his shoulder, picked up the cans of dog food, and they walked out.

When they got to the truck, Nightingale opened the truck door, but Bandit sat down on the sidewalk and looked up at him. "Sorry, Pup, you don't have the energy to jump and I didn't notice." Nightingale felt his throat tighten. "Let me help you inside." He picked the dog up and put him on the seat inside the truck, where Bandit lay down.

He drove to Imogene and Portia's house. There, he shared what the doctor had told him and explained how weak the dog still was. "I'll pick him up later this afternoon," he said, "and bring him back tomorrow morning."

"That sounds perfect," Portia said. She'd had a short day at school and was talkative. "By the way, the governor is going to be at a fundraiser tomorrow night. Our rich neighbor, Mr. Post, will be there, too. I'm attending and hope to meet the governor. You still work for her, right?" Portia's voice had just enough questioning and wonder to make him think she still thought he'd lied about the governor. Clearly, she found it difficult to believe that her very own cousin moved in the circles of important people.

Nightingale looked at Portia, knowing she was curious about more than his work with the governor. "Only part time. Where's the shindig?"

"A big ranch between Amarillo and Lubbock. I've got the

directions in my purse. I guess I'll have to donate to her campaign."

"You're driving up by yourself?" he asked, wondering if she would ask him to join her.

"Yes, shouldn't take too long. I want to meet her, up close and personal," Portia said. She turned her full gaze on him, her eyes squinted in meanness. "Also, construction on the house is going well. I know you've been covered up with other things, but Mr. Chavez said, depending on the weather, we might be able to move in February. Since this is November, that will give them December and January to finish the house. But I guess you already knew all of that since you've been keeping such a close eye on things for us. Right?" Her voice ended in an upward, sarcastic tone. She was not happy.

Nightingale glanced at Imogene, who rolled her eyes and shrugged an "I don't have a clue" movement, clearly trying mightily to stay out of any fray between him and Portia. He raised his eyebrows, trying to get across to her how he needed her to intercede or interpret, but she stayed silent.

"We needed your help on the house after—after finding the body, but I've heard nothing from you," Portia said. "After that one meeting with Chavez, what have you done? Nothing. You always want to be the hero, just like you used to want to know everything about my life when I first moved here."

Nightingale knew his mouth was hanging open and was sure he looked foolish.

Portia continued. "Well, I wanted you to be a part of our family. We are related, you know, but most of the time you refuse to darken our doorstep. So… so…" Her voice trailed away, and she drew in a deep breath. She had been looking at him, but now she turned away. Her head drooped. Suddenly she straightened, her voice stronger. "You need to go now. We love Bandit, and we'll take care of him. I simply wanted to clarify some things."

Nightingale felt like he'd been ambushed. He waited a bit before speaking. He wanted to tell Portia to get lost, but he'd regret that. Instead, in a stilted voice, he said, "I'm glad you have progress on the house. I'm sorry that I haven't been a bigger help with that." He paused to swallow and said, "We have no news about the dead man."

Portia stared at him. Imogene said nothing and turned away, obviously embarrassed and unwilling to offer any comment to either cousin. Nightingale walked out the front door and left it slightly open, afraid he would break the glass if he slammed it.

35

Garrick shivered and looked at the phone in his hand. The sunrise was beautiful, but why in hell was he barefooted and on his front porch? Had he heard the phone ring? No one was talking now. An irritating dial tone cut through the peaceful silence.

Still groggy from lack of sleep, he stared at the phone. Obeying his frigid feet he went inside and tried to piece together what had led him to the front porch. Gradually, it came to him. He'd been dreaming and Nightingale asked him about Mrs. Comet.

For a while, he had dreaded last night's confrontation with Nightingale, often hoping it would never happen, but now he was glad it was over. He hadn't slept well. That's where Mrs. Comet came in.

Women were creatures that Nightingale didn't understand and he had always assumed that Garrick did. Garrick had not tried to dissuade him of the idea, but if they got through this tough patch, Garrick would be more honest with the younger man. After all, he'd spent most of the night not sleeping and thinking of two women, but that did not mean he understood them.

Garrick felt himself smile as he thought of Mary and Nancy. He had loved them both. He had also wished that Nightingale had been his son. Why was it that men got so smart and saw what they needed for a fulfilled life—after they were old codgers?

He had on pajamas, and the top was unbuttoned. After putting the phone in the kitchen, he returned to the front porch to look at things as he remembered the night when Mary Nightingale came to his house. Yes, she had saved him, and he had followed through on changing his ways. He took a deep breath, felt clean and satisfied, and went inside. He started the coffee.

He had had a hard time getting to sleep last night and finally got up. He had walked the floor between the living room and bedroom and talked to both Mary and Nancy. They both told him that he deserved everything that had happened, but he was basically a tough old cuss who needed to get on with his life. However, he didn't need to become a soft-headed old geezer who cried and admitted his love of Nightingale as a son. He'd said what needed to be said last night, and that was the end of it.

He was embarrassed for himself. He knew that would pass. But it would take time. He would get over it. He was not comfortable with Nightingale last night. In the truck, he wished he could walk home instead of being in the same breathing space. Real men didn't talk about love for a woman or anyone else. For instance, he might say he'd like to marry Imogene, but saying he loved her? He was getting pretty soft-headed, but he had not come that unspooled, or had he?

His love for both Mary and Nancy was part of the problem, and he still loved both of them. However, things had changed overnight, and he was still alive and felt happy. Nightingale had called and not mentioned their words. He would do the same.

He and Nightingale would continue to work together. He had pretty much bared his soul last night to the man. Walking toward the shower, he noticed that he was smiling and staring out each window at the flatlands of his ranch with a lighter heart.

All he could do now was continue working with Nightingale to end this case and see what followed.

He would resurrect himself, and the way to do that was to continue to work as a Ranger and prove that he had the gumption to be better now than he used to be. He'd never had any luck in quitting the Rangers, but he'd never felt this wise before.

Out of the shower and dried, he pulled starched jeans and a fresh shirt out of the closet and thought of Imogene. He wanted to pursue a relationship with her. With new work and Imogene in his sights, how could he go wrong? He felt himself smile.

He walked into the kitchen, and his reverie stopped when he heard Billie and Sophie entering the back door. He told them he'd be out for the day and went to his office to call Cordelia Comet Post.

Luck was with him. She answered on the first ring. He introduced himself and explained his hope to speak with her and ask for her help.

He heard some words run together and a thickness in her speech. A bit after the fact he said, "Did I wake you?"

"No, I was awake but haven't spoken this morning, so my voice is croaky. You come on down, Mr. Sutton Garrick."

Garrick quit the call and considered the fact that the woman slurred her words at 7 a.m. He had been in such circumstances himself, and he didn't like to remember them. He wondered how much Cordelia Comet knew and how much she was trying to forget. Did she know more about her ex's business then she had let on to Nightingale earlier? Did she have an idea as to why Post had set up shop in this remote neck of the woods? Or was she trying to forget what she knew?

The drive was pleasant, and at a few minutes before eleven, Garrick parked his truck in front of the "Comet Art" sign. The "Closed" sign was out, as it had been when they'd visited before. Garrick walked to the barber shop and renewed his acquaintance with the proprietor. When he walked back to the truck, the "Closed" sign remained on the art door, but Garrick went up and knocked. A disheveled Cordelia Comet opened the door, coffee cup in hand. He didn't have to ask. She was definitely hungover.

She didn't ask who he was, just stepped aside and started talking. "Seems strange to me that a Ranger was out here asking questions a few days ago and now here's another lawman asking questions." The woman stopped in front of a print of three cowboys coming out of a snowy canyon. Garrick recognized the print as an Atkinson but said nothing.

"That was Nightingale," he said. "I was with him last week. We work together a bit. I visited the barber shop that day. Just went back and talked to the owner a few minutes ago. We found out a little more about the dead man, so I--" Garrick was talking and watching her expression. He caught her when her legs gave way before she melted onto the concrete floor.

He hoisted the woman over his shoulder and walked toward a door he saw in the rear wall. He didn't know if it was grief brought on by his words, or liquor, or low blood sugar that caused her to faint; could well have been all three.

Garrick laid her gently on the worn leather couch that he found in the back room. He looked for towels and dampened one in a sink in the bathroom.

She opened her eyes when the cold towel touched her head.

"I'm going to be sick," she said.

He grabbed the nearest trash can and held her head. When she had nothing left, she lay back against the cushions and turned her head away from him.

"Where's the coffee?" he asked.

"The little bitty room behind the door is my pretend kitchen. Everything I have is there."

Garrick walked into the area. "Not much here," he said, "but I think I can make us breakfast."

"I can't eat."

"Okay, but I need food, and when you smell toast and coffee and eggs, you'll want some. Just lie there and feel sorry for yourself. I'll leave the door open so you can holler at me if you need anything."

Garrick deliberately kept his back to the door, which wasn't hard since the hot plate, toaster, and coffee maker were in a row on the countertop. He hated that there was no bacon in the tiny dorm-sized refrigerator. The smell of good pork at breakfast was important. He'd have to make do with the aroma of coffee and toast and his famous milk-gravy scrambled eggs.

When everything was ready, he prepared two plates and placed hers on the coffee table that had been pushed to one end of the couch. When he came back with his plate and coffee she was sitting, wrapped in a blanket, staring at the food.

He pushed a newspaper off the coffee table and scooted his plate to the vacant spot. The woman watched him but didn't offer to help.

"I deserve to feel sorry for myself," she said.

"Let's eat, and then we'll talk," Garrick said. He pushed the plate closer. "Toast will feel good in your stomach. I've been there; I know."

"When were you last drunk? A week ago? But not in those starched jeans and shined boots—and not alone at home." She sat on the edge of the couch and picked up a piece of toast.

He mentioned a couple of bars he'd known and loved. When he got to The Laughing Cow "up in east Texas with a wood stove for heat and only four brands of whiskey," he saw she was having trouble focusing, so he got to the task at hand. "Why do you think you deserve to feel sorry for yourself?"

"Booze always depresses me."

"There's got to be more to it than that, but if you want me to, I can ask questions, like have you heard from your son?"

She looked at him, her eyes glistening with tears. "That's cruel, but no, I haven't heard from him and I won't again. His body is in Lubbock."

"How do you know?"

"I drove into Lubbock after the other Ranger was here. I saw Joshua's body. I went to high school with the sheriff. Don't give him hell. He got me into the coroner's office."

"You knew he was in this area when you talked to Nightingale, right?" Garrick asked.

She nodded. She was still teary, but she was upright and needing more coffee. "Yes." She watched Garrick refresh her coffee and sighed. "When I left New York and my children, I thought I was doing the right thing, but I'll never know for sure. I called them, often at first, and then less often." At his questioning glance, she finished. "Because I could tell they still expected me to return. They wanted me to come back to them. "

"How old were they?"

"Carolyn was nine. Josh was eleven," she said. "I thought they could handle it. I went to boarding school at seven."

"Good memories?" Garrick knew he sounded bitchy and didn't care.

"No, it was awful. But Edgar Post was awful. He didn't hit me, but mentally, he beat me down every day. He called me names, told me I was worthless—always out of the way of the children, of course. But I really thought that he would take care of them. He acted like he cared about them. He always put on this big display when he was around them, giving them money and telling them to buy toys, showing how much he loved them.

At least that was his idea of affection, and I wanted out so bad, I just let it pass."

She smiled and leaned back a little. "I hadn't thought about it for a while, but he didn't like to touch them. Never hugged and kissed. Me? I wanted lots of love and hugs, no matter how dirty and sweaty or sticky they were.

"After Josh turned twenty and had been on his own a few years, he called me. I could tell he wanted to ream me up one side and down the other, and I told him I was sorry, which was the truth. I don't know if he ever forgave me, but we kept in touch. I helped him with cash when I could, but he didn't ask often. I called Carolyn after he told me he had talked with her, but she clearly hated me. I think Josh tried to explain. And she may understand better now that she's lived with her father for several years."

Garrick flipped the record button on his small device. He wanted to remember everything. He looked at Cordelia and raised his eyebrows. "Do you mind?"

"No." She shrugged.

He quickly continued. "Why would anyone want to kill Joshua?"

She had quit crying and seemed to think about the question. "I don't know. Unless his gambling debts were worse than he told me. But he always wanted to pay up, and the debts were usually less than a thousand dollars."

By now he'd moved so they were sitting together on the couch. She looked at Garrick and smiled. "In one way, he was like his father. He didn't gamble a lot because he couldn't control it. He wanted control, but not the control of an egomaniac, like Edgar. Joshua just wanted control of his own life. He didn't care a lot for the frills and comforts that money can buy." She sipped her coffee, and Garrick waited. He heard his heartbeat and wanted her to say more, but she didn't need to be encouraged now.

"I can't imagine what Edgar thought when Joshua presented himself. Edgar has the ability to simply cut out a piece of his life and never miss it. It can be wife or child or mother or anyone who would matter to you or me. He closes himself off and never thinks another thing about it."

"Is he capable of killing his son?" Garrick asked.

It was the diffusion of light that transformed her. She looked at her hands and then at Garrick. She stared, unblinking, promising the truth. "He would kill anyone if he thought he could gain money or power."

They exhaled together, and it was only then that Garrick realized how tense the conversation had become. He waited a moment and took a drink of coffee.

"What do you know about Danny Hartford?"

A sly smile crept onto her mouth. "He's Edgar's half-brother."

Garrick raised his eyebrows, which made her smile.

"Glad to see that I can surprise you a little," she said. Then she slid closer to him and placed her hand on his jaw, guiding his face to hers. "I'll bet I could surprise you even more."

When she started to kiss him, Garrick thought of Imogene and the kiss became a light tap on his cheek when he turned his head. Cordelia Comet pulled back and quickly stood. "Sorry," she said. "Guess I again misjudged the end result."

36

Portia watched Nightingale walk out the front door with Bandit whining for him, while Imogene held his collar. Imogene had said nothing. The time was close to three, but the air that swept into the house before Nightingale pulled the door closed promised a cold night. She had filled the role of the wicked witch.

She'd been hurtful, but she couldn't stop the words from flowing out of her mouth. She turned on Imogene. "Don't you say a word. He always wants to be the one who saves everybody, the hero, but we need him, and he's showed up one time to talk to Chavez. He hasn't helped us a bit. And nothing has been done about poor Joshua." Her voice cracked as she rushed past Imogene to hide her tears.

In the kitchen, she drew deep breaths and put on water for tea. The squeak of the hardwood floors under Imogene's steps, along with the occasional click of Bandit's toenails, gave away their location as they came closer. Portia told herself she was righteously guilty. Maybe she expected too much from Nightingale, but she didn't think so. She'd been short, sarcastic, generally a witch to Oswald—and he deserved it.

"Bandit and I are going outside for a walk. We'll stay back here while your student is here. It's Adam today, right?"

"Yes," Portia said. "He's a strange child. I don't know if he'd cotton to Bandit or not." She walked over to the dog whose tail began wagging. She bent down and scratched his neck and ran her hands over his fur. "He doesn't know what loving he's missing, does he, Bandit?"

"I think I hear a car," Imogene said. She pulled on a coat as she walked toward the back door. "I'll take him out back." She clipped a leash on him, and they were gone, leaving Portia with her tea and thoughts.

Portia glanced out the back door, envious that Imogene didn't seem to be filled with bitterness like she did. Nightingale was the closest relative, except for Imogene, that Portia had. He had helped her since she came there but he was aloof in his kinship. Being a Ranger remained Oswald Nightingale's primary purpose in life. Yet didn't he see that he needed his cousins? Didn't everyone need family? Apparently not. She chafed at his lack of commitment to her and Imogene.

She was hurt that Nightingale showed so little caring for her and Imogene. When it got to the nitty gritty, she was feeling more alone every day and Imogene was at fault too, but she couldn't be angry at Imogene. They had lived together, had the flu together, made budgets, laughed and cried together—no, she couldn't be angry with Imogene, but she could be angry with that egotistical man, Nightingale.

She poured hot water over an Earl Grey tea bag. She heard a knock, and as she went to the front door, she saw the reddish-blond hair of Adam Post through the half glass. Her heart softened for him. She'd had the boy for four lessons, and he remained a puzzle. He was intelligent and soft-spoken but saw no need for reading extensively and hardly any need for training in writing. His assignment for today had been to write an essay on the value of reading. After their discussion of the lesson and what Adam thought of the subject, she planned on assigning *To Kill A Mockingbird* as his next lesson.

The boy came in quietly and stood watching her. As she brought her tea over to the table, she said, "How have you been, Adam? Are you ready to talk about the humanities?" She didn't expect an answer, but the boy mumbled something.

"I'm sorry," she said. "I didn't hear you."

"It doesn't matter. Here is my work. I'm sure you won't like it."

She smiled as they walked to the writing desk that helped form a perfect study area in the living room. Portia scanned the essay and saw what she expected. "You don't see much value in reading," she said. She kept her voice low and tried to be casual. "However, we should be able to discuss what we both think. I'll read closer but this seems to be well-written."

The boy gave a low, mocking laugh and sat at the desk with his hands folded. He possessed a self-discipline that Portia couldn't understand.

"Did you look up any of the books I suggested?" she asked.

"No, ma'am. I don't like to read."

"You've said that, but did you ask your parents, or any adult, if they ever learned anything from a novel?"

Adam looked at her and Portia knew from the scorn in his expression that this boy's parents had never mentioned reading. She didn't give him time to answer. Instead, she said, "Do you mind telling me what your father does and if your mother works outside the home?"

"My father has his own company. He owns and manages a hedge fund. He talks to me about making deals and money and buying and selling. My mother stays in New York. Sometimes she calls and asks me if I'm eating properly." Adam blushed and said the last sentence in a caustic tone.

"I apologize," Portia said hurriedly. "I should not be asking personal questions."

Adam shrugged and looked away. "I did read the list you gave me. One of the things on the list was how books"—here he broke into a sing-song memorized recitation—"'reveal how people have tried to make moral, spiritual, and intellectual sense of the world.'"

Portia hated to give up. "But shouldn't we consider other people's ideas?"

"I don't see how any book can help make sense of the world," Adam said.

Portia thought maybe she was being too stern. "Okay, let's talk about this later, after you've read something on my list. I'll loan you my copy of *To Kill A Mockingbird*, and we'll discuss some of it next week. Now, let's move on to structuring an essay."

Adam sighed, and Portia moved on to talk to him about organizing facts and data. Once in a while, Portia asked about applying their work to real life. Adam kept his answers to one line, sometimes one syllable. Eventually the hour ended, and they both stood up. As Portia handed Adam his jacket, she started to list again what she expected of him when he came for the next lesson.

From the back of the house she heard the door slam and the low words of Imogene to Bandit. Adam's glance flicked past her, across the room—and he froze, his face filled with horror. Portia turned to look behind her and heard a low growl of anger from the dog. Almost immediately, his nose lifted, his mouth opened, and he began howling.

The boy stood frozen for a long minute. Then he started sliding sideways toward the door, while his eyes stayed riveted on the dog. Portia turned to see Imogene, who had squatted by Bandit, softly talking, begging the dog to quiet down. Then

Adam jerked the front door open and tore off across the porch and out to the waiting car.

Portia stepped from behind the desk and noticed a trail of drops leading to the door. The boy had peed on himself as he ran away.

37

After Nightingale left Bandit with his cousins, he drove to the new house. The afternoon temperature was in the low fifties, perfect for the work he hoped to do at the subdivision. He had planned the stop even before Portia's sharp words but had kept his thoughts to himself and hadn't argued. Trying to defend his actions to Portia seemed useless. Something was bothering her besides his lack of action, but he had no clue as to the source. And right now, he wanted to concentrate on Joshua's death and the scene where it took place. He hoped to see Arnoldo and Miguel, the two men he'd met on the day Joshua died.

At Mesa Heights Estates there was little activity. No house had been finished, but he saw progress on several framed structures. More of the streets had been paved, and curbs added. Somehow those small things gave him hope that this would not turn into a desolate area with his cousins owning the first and possibly only finished house.

Despite the fact that nothing was totally finished, he could see the most progress on two houses on different streets from the cousins' house. Some form of solid sheets of insulation wrapped around the wall studs, giving the structures definition, but more important, it looked like roofs were done. So who was doing the roofing since Joshua Tallman was dead? He had to find those two men. Now he had a passel of questions for them.

He parked the truck along the curb and got out, standing for a minute, studying the place that would be Portia and Imogene's new home. It would eventually have personality, a warmth that came from the women, but now it looked stark and cold and naked under the cloudy November sky.

He faced the house and headed toward the right-hand side, walking slowly to take in every bit of surroundings.

The houses sat on acre lots, which he knew because he recalled Imogene saying she would have to start over with her orchard but that would be easy on an acre. In this case, their house would be the last one on the street, and no house was under construction next to them. A wide swath of land stretched from the rear of the house the distance of a football field to a newly erected fence.

The fence continued to wrap around the property like it had a sense of purpose and these people would be expected to stay inside that purpose. Nightingale thought the fence was more good news that the developers were living up to their end of the bargain. But then he began to wonder what property they bumped up against.

Nightingale had always thought his sense of direction was lacking, and now he looked again at the fence and suddenly realized that part of the sense of dread he'd been living with the last few days, the sense of something nagging at him, had come into focus in his mind. That fence not only marked the boundaries of the cousins' subdivision, it also served as the dividing line between Edgar Post and Mesa Heights.

One side of the subdivision butted up against Edgar Post's land, and the fence was the shared property line. How had he never realized that before? Of course, there had been a survey; but why had he never asked them to see it? He hoped his cousins never had to encounter Post, who no doubt loved the fence, if he knew it existed. But Post was also greedy, and how long would it be before he did notice the fence and wanted the property on the other side. So the property line had to be legal and documented for Nightingale to feel like Post would leave his cousins' land alone. If Post decided he wanted what was on the other side of the fence, he had to face a fight. His cousins needed to be prepared.

He had asked Miller about Post's fence and here was his answer. Post had not fenced this subdivision—the new owners had put up the fence. He hoped it was slightly inside the property line so Post could put his huge fence on his line, if he decided to. That would make two fences in the back of Portia and Imogene's new home, which Nightingale thought might be good. It looked like a litigation nightmare—or dream, depending on who won. However, his speculation would be his secret. No need to make more worries for the women.

When he considered it more, he realized that Edgar Post would probably never venture outside of his enclave unless someone dragged him out. As long as the people in the subdivision stayed on their own land, he would never know they existed. They were several miles away from his house, which had the taller fence around it. No one knew where Post had stopped that fence, but, hopefully, it would never matter. When Nightingale circled back to his first thought, he realized that he was reacting to a situation that hadn't happened because he didn't like Edgar Post. As a matter of fact, his dislike was intense and bitter, and that made it all the more critical that he leave his feelings outside of the case and try to be excruciatingly fair with Post.

He turned back to the house, and as he considered the roof line, someone said, "Mr. Ranger, you are back?"

He turned. "Miguel, Arnoldo, it's good to see you." He

stretched out a hand and strode to them. "I need to talk to you. Looks like you're staying busy." He swept one hand around the area to encompass the added construction. "Are there new workers?"

Arnoldo nodded. "More people wanted houses than John Chavez first thought. The company he works for is happy." The two men nodded in unison.

"Who puts on the roofs?" Nightingale asked.

"We have friends who could do it and needed the work," Arnoldo said. "We told them to be more careful than Joshua was. Have you found anything else about him?"

"Not much. Have you thought of anything more that you knew about him?"

"No, but we would like to know if there is a service for him. We might take off a few hours to pray."

A wave of something near to guilt came over Nightingale. He hadn't thought of a funeral. "You're right, of course. I'm sorry, but I don't have any information about a service. If I hear of anything, I will come and tell you." He nodded somberly, and they looked reassured. But he needed more from them, so he went on. "I know I've asked this before, but was there nothing odd or off-beat in his last days at work?"

Miguel grunted and touched his partner's arm.

"You think so?" Arnoldo asked.

Miguel nodded.

"He had a visitor on horseback a day or so before he died," Arnoldo said. "When we got here, his truck was here. He always came early. We didn't see when the visitor arrived, but we were putting on work gear when Joshua came up on the back of a horse with a beautiful lady. He got off and went to Miss Portia and Imogene's house, and soon we saw him on the roof. I do not know where the lady on the horse went. He did not look at us or say anything when he came up. We would have joked with him if we had the chance. We all worked through the day, and he left early. The next day, you found him."

"What did the woman look like?" Nightingale asked.

"She wore blue jeans and a shirt. I don't remember the color of the shirt, but Miguel says it was blue. We didn't see her hair. She had it up, under her hat."

Nightingale didn't hear Miguel say anything, but he had one more question. "What about the horse? Anything?"

"It was a bay with one white stocking. Small, about fifteen hands high and glad when the extra weight of Joshua got down." Miguel said. His voice was low, gritty and almost smiling when he described the horse's relief from the weight of the man.

Nightingale was slow at understanding what Miguel had said—in fact that he said anything at all was such a surprise—that the men were walking away before he refocused on them. "Wait a minute," he said. "I need to borrow a ladder, and would you help me get on the roof?"

A few minutes later, Nightingale had put on tennis shoes from his truck and followed Arnoldo up the ladder to the roof of the house. Arnoldo kept up a, "Be careful, watch your foot" chatter, which didn't help Nightingale's unease at being off the ground. When he felt sure his feet would not slip, he stood and walked a few steps up the sloped shingles.

"This is not good for your cousins' roof," Arnoldo said.

"I just wondered how far he could see up here," Nightingale said. He looked out across the land that spread out to the rear of the house beyond the fence. In the distance, he saw the roof of the two-story Post house. The fence that Post had erected encircled the house and outbuildings, stretching to the east, separating Post land from the house and barns of John Miller. The land that Post had purchased, outside of his enclave fence, had been fallow for a year and had a barbed wire fence. And the barbed wire fence, short and in disrepair, rested just on the other side of the fence around his cousins' property. Because it was so short, he had not seen it before standing on the roof of the house.

If Post brought in exotic animals, as he had said he was planning to do, the taller fence around his enclave would have to be taller and stronger. Currently, to Nightingale, this land and the brownish-green vegetation covering it looked like it needed rest. Mesquite and hackberry were the primary trees. A reddish-brown slash that had once been a ranch road cut through the brush, but it was a dead end. It did make a good boundary between fields if Post decided to run any game animals, but a fence would be necessary. Right now, Post seemed to have the enclosure where he wanted it.

By sitting down and inching across to the ladder, Nightingale made his way off the roof and back down to the ground. Miguel and Arnoldo waited, and with several thank yous and good-bye waves, they took the ladder away. Nightingale was glad to be walking on firm ground.

More important, he'd discovered the ridge that ran slightly up and away from the fence. He could see where he thought Joshua had met the mysterious woman and where he himself had seen a rider on a horse.

38

Outside of the art gallery, Garrick climbed into his truck and headed for Broken Rock. The time had passed quickly. It was three o'clock, and the cloudy day was darkening too soon. Once he settled into the drive, his thoughts crept up. He'd never been prone to examine his theories or reasons for his life and the choices he'd made, but suddenly he was examining every thought he had. His encounter with Cordelia Comet had made him sad. She had given up on love and emotion with her children and now could retrieve nothing.

Her sad life reflected his own broken years. Age was creeping —hell, running at a fast pace—up on him, and he saw the need for getting on with things, like his feelings for Imogene.

In his head, he saw the word "feelings" and wondered what that meant to him. He rolled the word around in his mouth and mind and knew he was avoiding the word "love." That word was a biggie. It meant commitment. It meant sharing your money with someone else. It meant standing in front of a truck to save someone's life.

In order to lessen his worries, he called Imogene. "I'm in the back yard with Bandit," she said. He could almost hear the smile in her face. "We were going into the house. It's getting cooler."

He became tongue-tied and cleared his throat so she would know he was still there. "I'm on my way back to Nightingale's, and I thought I'd swing by and visit a minute with you first, if y'all didn't mind."

"How long before you'll be here?" Imogene asked.

"Oh, probably be another hour or so." He swallowed hard and hurried on. "I don't have to come by. I just hadn't seen you in a day or so and..." His voice trailed off because he had no good reason to see her, except he wanted to be with her a few minutes and talk about things like they always could.

"I'd love to see you, and I'm sure Bandit would like to see you, too."

"Yes, I need to see the pup. I won't stay long. Reckon Portia will mind?"

"No, Portia would like to see you, too. She's with a student now, but I'll tell her after he leaves. She made muffins today, and I'm sure she'd like for you to have one or two."

"Great," Garrick said. He rushed his goodbye and quit the call before Imogene could change her mind. For the rest of the drive, every time he caught his reflection in the mirror, he saw himself smiling. "Silly old coot," he said, but he didn't care. Happiness, after all his sadness, was finally a possibility.

He was glad he had talked to Cordelia Comet. He was glad that the puppy was doing well. Suddenly, Joshua Tallman Post inserted himself into the truck. How had Joshua been given a hypodermic from above? Garrick still didn't believe it. The medical examiner liked to think he was always right, but everyone made mistakes, and this time he had to be wrong.

Or maybe someone came along after he fell and gave him the shot.

~

Nightingale thanked Arnoldo and Miguel for their help and information. After they walked away with their ladder, he moseyed around the house again, looking at the ground and then back to the roof. He wanted to get a better look at the big picture.

The acres of Mesa Heights had once been cattle pastures. Lush greenery had never taken root. This land harbored brownish-green sprigs of alfalfa, sorghum, and fescue leftover from years past. Most of the ground around the house was still broken clots of dirt. Driving into the subdivision, Nightingale had seen discarded water bottles and sandwich wrappers attesting to human occupation. The area around his cousins' house seemed exceptionally devoid of such items.

Then he saw a glint of metal and squinted at it. He stepped closer, and taking an ink pen from his pocket, knocked away the dirt. It looked like part of a syringe. He straightened up and went to the truck for gloves and an evidence bag.

Once he'd picked up the tube, he felt like he was done with exploring for the day. He wondered again why there was no mess around his cousins' house and tried to control his speculation while he drove to Lubbock to deliver the item to the medical examiner.

Belschner held the dirty bag up, almost snarling at it. "Is this all you found?"

"That's it," Nightingale said. "Is it part of a syringe?"

Belschner pulled on gloves and turned to Nightingale. "I'm going to need some time before I can give you any information about this. Call me tomorrow." He turned away, and Nightingale fumed.

"Should I go look for more pieces?"

"Not now," Belschner said. "I'll let you know tomorrow."

Nightingale blew out a breath of disgusted hope and walked out. He stopped for milk, eggs, and a bag of coffee before heading home, but he planned on getting onto the computer as soon as he got in the house. He wanted to find out what he could about syringes before he went back to talk with the medical examiner.

He gave his house a cursory glance as he turned into the driveway. The house was frame, with the porch he loved and the fence in the back that he intended to make taller and stronger to keep out intruders and bad meat. He stared a minute at the house, thinking he'd paint it next spring. Then he walked around the truck to get the groceries out of the front seat. His hands were full when he made the last step onto the porch, so he had to bend to set down the milk and get the key out of his pocket.

He didn't know if he heard the whine of the bullet, but he felt the flesh tear and growled a profanity as it ripped through his left shoulder, splattering parts of him on its way out of his body into the siding of the house. He rolled and used that movement to fall behind the shrubs that grew around the porch, which he hoped concealed some of his body from the shooter. Two other shots did not find him. However, he guessed a scope of some power had him in sight. He hunkered down on his knees, holding his service revolver close and sticking as near as he could to the house. He wasn't mortally wounded, but his shoulder hurt like hell. And he couldn't hold it to stop the bleeding and shoot at the same time. He heard a fourth shot and then heard no more. The shots that missed him were probably sunk into the siding.

He kept waiting for sounds. Where was this guy, and why was he shooting at him? As if in answer, his phone rang. He laid the weapon carefully on some dry leaves and pulled the phone from his shirt pocket. Garrick's name came up. Nightingale heard, "Hey, I'm back but not home."

Nightingale fumbled the phone, dropping it and cursing. Finally, he got it in hand. "I've been shot," he said.

"What? Where are you?"

"My house," Nightingale said.

"I can't get there soon. I'll call Lubbock and Broken Rock to get help. How bad?"

"I'm okay for the moment, but I'll probably need a doc," Nightingale said.

"Shooter still there?"

"I don't know. Maybe. I'm not standing up to find out," Nightingale said.

"Just hang on," Garrick said. "Help is on the way."

39

Garrick called the Broken Rock constabulary to explain Nightingale's dilemma, and the officers drove to Nightingale's house in one vehicle, siren blaring. Another vehicle, a Range Rover owned by a local oil baron, had loaded up with four men from the gas station and followed close behind the constable. At the driveway, Robinson and Hall came out of their vehicle, guns raised, calling out to Nightingale. The Range Rover backed into the drive and the men piled out, guns at the ready.

No shots sounded. The constable found Nightingale on his knees, leaning against his house.

"How bad?" Robinson asked.

"Thanks for coming. Not as bad as the blood looks," Nightingale said.

"We'll get you to a doc," Robinson said. "Do you think he's out there still? And what direction did the shots come from?"

"Across from the house, over yonder," Nightingale nodded across the road. "I'm guessing it was somebody in the field. That's a good piece. I imagine he had a scope, but I moved at the right time." One of the men who came to help mumbled a bit and told Robinson they were going to check out the field. Nightingale thanked them as they went to the vehicle, thinking they'd be lucky to find anything.

"Hall and me can take you to the hospital," Robinson said.

"I hate to be a problem, but I guess I'll need stitches and a tetanus shot." Nightingale thought pain meds might be a good idea, too. "It mainly tore through muscle, no bone. I was lucky."

Robinson helped him stand. The porch and shrubs spun a bit, and Nightingale wobbled, blaming his dizziness on the loss of blood. "Better get a towel out of the house so I don't get blood on your seats," he said. To the side, he heard Deputy Hall pick up the keys and the groceries he'd set down before the bullet hit him and go into the house while he and Robinson walked to the truck.

Robinson tilted the front seat back a bit and Nightingale sat down, careful to keep his shoulder away from the seat. Robinson walked away and talked a few minutes to the men in the other truck. They roared out of the drive, and Robinson came back as Hall arrived with a towel for the bloody shoulder.

"I told the men to see if they could find shell casings, tracks, or any signs of the man who shot you. It may be impossible. We're losing light," Robinson said.

Nightingale saw no good end in complaining about losing clues under the feet of well-meaning men looking to find someone shooting at him. They were trying to help. He leaned his head back against the dusty upholstery of Robinson's truck, clutching the towel against his throbbing arm.

Constable Robinson yielded the steering wheel to Deputy Hall for the drive to Lubbock. Robinson sat in the back.

Through barely opened eyelids, Nightingale watched the lights of the truck as they drove into the darkness. They had not gone far when he heard the snap of a seatbelt unbuckling and felt the slight tug as Robinson pulled on the seatback to scoot himself closer.

Sure enough, the constable's voice said,. "Any ideas about who shot at you?"

Nightingale had asked himself the same thing, so he told Robinson what he'd concluded. "When something like this happens, I usually guess it's somebody on the current case who's pissed at me. But the bad thing is, August, I have so many enemies, it could be somebody from years back."

"Sorry to hear that," Robinson said. "I always think of you as well-liked."

Nightingale closed his eyes, trying to think of who might want him dead. Several men he'd put in jail had wound up in prison and probably would enjoy seeing him dead. But most of those men, if they were out, wouldn't want to put in the work it would take to make that happen.

There was one woman who'd sold her child, and he'd gladly had testified against her. She, too, would like to see him dead, but he knew she was still in prison.

And there was always Edgar Post. A genuine hatred exuded from Post, but he'd most likely calculate the cost, and Nightingale thought he wouldn't want to waste good money on killing a Ranger. The risk would outweigh the odds. Then, again, Edgar Post had so much money he'd never miss what it took to kill a cowboy.

After that thought, Nightingale began to doze, waking when they pulled into the emergency entrance at the University Medical Center. A dark cloud came up the back of his neck when he stepped out of the truck. Robinson apparently had noticed his knees slightly buckle because he asked, "Are you okay to walk?"

"Sure, I'm fine. Don't tell Hall that I tripped." He smiled and swept his good arm over the constable's shoulder. This had never happened before, so he shook his head, gaining a bit of reality. "Let's wait for Hall," he said, and as soon as the deputy walked up, he said, too loud, "Okay let's go." He didn't tell them how grateful he was for their presence. He hoped if he squeezed an arm, they would understand.

Before they got inside, Nightingale told Hall to call Garrick and update him on where they were. "He's coming by the house," Nightingale said, "and he needs to wait if he gets there before us."

The woman at the night desk recognized Nightingale. "How bad are you hurt this time?" She came around from behind the glass screen and walked them back to the curtained cubicles. Looking at his shoulder, she said, "I'll help with the paperwork. Wait here for the doctor."

Nightingale sat on the exam table. A nurse came in and helped him take off his shirt. She cleaned the wound, making a few comments, and a doctor soon came in.

The doctor talked as he worked. "Guess you're used to this," he said. Then he looked at Nightingale's face. "Sorry, I'm sure you never get used to this."

"If I get used to it, I need to quit," Nightingale said. He didn't want a philosophical discussion, but sometimes even smart people said dumb things.

The doctor nodded. "I've got to write up a report when there's a shooting."

"I hope so." Nightingale tried to sound lighter.

The doctor picked at the raw tissue, which was finally numb, cleaning the wound, putting in some stitches, and applying a large pad of gauze. "You were really lucky. Must have been a large weapon, or ammunition, because you've lost a good-sized piece of flesh but no bone. I'm ordering an injection of antibiotic, and we can add some pain meds to that, if you wish. You'll still need prescriptions filled for home. Do you have anyone to stay with you?"

"Yes," Nightingale said. He didn't look at Robinson.

The doctor scribbled out a prescription for pain and one to ward off infection, patted Nightingale's uninjured shoulder, and told him to see his regular doctor in a few days to change the dressing and check on stitches. They all walked to the car, planning to go by a pharmacy and then back to Nightingale's house.

On the drive back, Robinson said he or Hall could stay the night.

Nightingale tried not to sound rude. "I appreciate the offer, but I don't need company. Besides, Garrick will be getting there later." He left the thought hanging, like Garrick might stay, all the time knowing he would never encourage that.

When they got to his house, they insisted on going inside with him. Nightingale could hear Hall walking through the bedrooms and onto the back porch. Doors slammed—closets, he guessed. At nine o'clock, Robinson and Hall faced Nightingale at the front door. "Are you taking those pain meds?" Robinson asked.

"Took one about fifteen minutes ago," Nightingale said. "Now you two go on home. I hate to run you off, but good night. And thanks for your help. You saved my hide."

He left the porch light on, then went around to each room turning off lights and checking locks on windows. After checking the locked front door—again—he spread a quilt on the big lounge chair and sank back into it. As he turned on the television, he heard a key in the lock. Without getting up, he grasped his service revolver and sat waiting. Bandit came bounding into the room and onto his owner. Nightingale tensed to catch the dog on his good side and let the revolver slide into the covers.

Garrick turned back from the door, talking to the dog. "Now, I told you to not be jumping. Come here."

The older man looked somber for a minute. "You okay?"

"Yeah." Nightingale tried to be lighthearted, but the pill had made him groggy. "I'd get up and dance, but my dancing arm is clipped."

"Well, while you're incapacitated I'm gonna stay all night. I'm plum tuckered out. You awake enough to talk?"

Nightingale looked at Garrick and saw two of him. He shook his head and clarity came for a moment. "Let's make some coffee. You sound like you've made progress."

He struggled out of the chair and followed Garrick into the kitchen, walking slowly, feeling the dizziness more than he wanted to admit, trying to ignore the look of concern he'd seen etched in Garrick's wrinkled face.

He sat at the table while Garrick started the coffee. "The ex-Mrs. Post went into Lubbock and used her feminine wiles to see her son's body. She said it was him, but she couldn't think of anyone who would want him dead." Garrick stood at the kitchen counter, a far-away look in his eyes. "I guess that's an ordinary thought for a mother. She was drunk when I got there, but she sobered up."

"She'll testify?" Nightingale asked.

"Yes, but I don't see how that will help. She also confirmed Danny Hartford is Post's half-brother."

"You hit a geyser of info," Nightingale said. "Give me some coffee so I can digest this."

"There's more," Garrick said, a troubled sound in his voice. He looked at Bandit, who was lying next to Nightingale's feet. When Bandit saw Garrick's gaze, he raised his head, and his tail began a happy thumping on the floor.

Nightingale reached down and patted the dog's head while Garrick told him what happened when Bandit saw the boy, Adam.

"He howled?" Nightingale asked.

"He literally cried, according to Imogene and Portia. Imogene teared up when she talked about it. And the boy's reaction." Garrick's voice had become a whisper. He paused and swallowed. "I have no doubt about who left that meat the other night." He reached into his pocket for treats and gave a couple to the dog, looking up surreptitiously at Nightingale.

Nightingale watched them through his drugged haze. He knew that when the drugs wore off, he would face a dilemma. What to do about the boy? But for now, he couldn't think that far ahead. "That leaves us with a juvenile who poisons animals. We still need to find a murderer, but we can't prove how he killed his victim." Nightingale shifted in his chair. His shoulder ached and stung like a thousand bees had attacked, which briefly broke through his haze. "I feel sorry for the kid, but then I want to paddle his ass."

"I don't think that's 'appropriate' nowadays," Garrick said, using air quotes.

"So do you agree that he probably threw the bottle bomb at the newspaper office and then high-tailed it up here to poison Bandit?" Nightingale was having a hard time keeping his thoughts on the subject. "And if we agree on that, where does that leave us with the killer of the man who fell off the house? Do we have any proof that the kid is guilty of poisoning my dog? No."

"So, where from here?" Garrick asked.

"We've got to get evidence or confessions, and the boy is walking around with a lot of guilt. About evidence, we've got to get something from those tire tracks—maybe tomorrow." He fought back a yawn. "I'm going to sleep now, and I plan to have an incredible recovery tomorrow morning. Let's get up at five or six tomorrow morning, and then we'll go to Mr. Post's palace and hope we find something."

Both men stood. Nightingale braced himself on the table before straightening.

"I need some time with Bandit," Garrick said. "I also need to shake the dew off the lily, as I'm sure our dog does. I'll bring him to your room when we get back in."

Nightingale was glad for the alone time. He started walking toward his bedroom, holding to the edge of the table and moving slowly. Adam Post, obnoxious as he was, went with him in his thoughts. No court would take the Bandit's howl as evidence against the boy. And he really got no satisfaction out of causing troubles for him. He sat on the edge of the bed, staring out a window. The child didn't have a chance with Post as a father. All the kid had learned was to get a deal from his fellow man by hook or crook. And Post had practically told his son that the dog needed to be taught some manners, which Adam must have interpreted to mean killing him.

What would his own father do? Nightingale smiled to himself, thinking about Nathaniel Nightingale offering a proverb or story of some sort to get across what he needed to say. In this case, he'd say, "If it feels wrong to you, if it feels wrong in your gut, then you probably don't want to do it, 'cause it's wrong morally."

He heard Garrick and Bandit coming in the back door. He raised his voice to call to Garrick and when the man stood at the door, he said, "You told me that my father said my mother was on a mission when she rescued you. How did she know you needed rescuing?"

Garrick looked embarrassed and knelt to pet Bandit. "I don't know," he said. "I heard your dad say one time that Mary was led by something he couldn't get a hold of. Far as I could tell, he was right. It was something that I never understood. It was her intuition, her senses, I guess." He almost smiled. "Is that all you needed?"

"Yeah, I was thinking about Adam and wondering how to explain to him about knowing right from wrong."

"Good luck," Garrick said. "That child is following his father. You know the old saying: 'A fish rots from the head down?' Children follow their parents' examples."

Nightingale nodded.

"Same thing here. You can apply it to fathers, CEOs of companies, or anyone in charge. The followers are like children," Garrick said. "They need a hero, and if that hero teaches them to lie, they'll see lying as okay. If he pushes aside a waiter or busboy because that worker is of another race, the child sees that as okay. It's not rocket science. People look up to their heroes and imitate them. I didn't learn that until late in life. Good night."

Nightingale muttered a good night and began to take off his clothes slowly. In the corner, Bandit circled several times, making his own bed, and finally Nightingale, too, laid down with a deep sigh, welcoming rest. Too bad that Post had corrupted Adam. He probably had corrupted Joshua, too.

But too bad seemed too simple.

40

As the day outside lightened, Nightingale counted tiles on the ceiling and wondered how many times in his career he'd been shot. There were enough that he had a ritual to get back into the rhythm of work when he felt up to it. When he was fully awake and had decided he probably was ready, he would look around the room, then move slowly out of bed, checking for sore muscles. He would take a few steps and stretch his arms. Then he'd walk around the room and try a few squats. If for some reason the legs rebelled, putting his balance off, he would stop the exercise. By then, his body would be warm for the day ahead —and he had probably made Bandit uneasy.

He took the ritual steps carefully this morning. At the end, his left shoulder was stiff and painful but not hot with infection. A small amount of blood had oozed through the dressing. He kept his arm bent and picked up the sling the doctor had given him at the hospital.

If things went as they had in the past, he'd be almost a hundred percent by the time they got to Post's house. Come hell or high water, he was taking the search warrant to Edgar Post's house today and looking into every crevice in the entire domain.

So he wanted no reason for the search to be delayed, not even to the afternoon.

He downed a pain pill and left the rest in his nightstand. The remainder of the day would be for acetaminophen and ibuprofen. He mixed those two in a bottle in his bathroom and then pulled out a clean pair of jeans from the closet. His shoulder rebelled when he pulled on the zipper, but he finally contorted enough to get it up. The shirt was a different matter. That had to wait for the dressing to be changed, so he took the shirt with him.

He walked into the kitchen as Garrick told Bandit, "I'll give you a piece of toast, but then you go outside." Garrick glanced around and pitched a crust of bread to Bandit, who grabbed it on his way to the back door. "Imogene called and offered to come get Bandit. I told her we'd appreciate it," Garrick said.

"That's a good idea. I'll need the extra time." Nightingale hung his shirt on a chairback. He relieved himself over the porch railing while he watched the dog relieve himself in the back yard and left the back door open when he returned to the kitchen. He grabbed an old flannel shirt off a hook next to the door to put over his shoulders to lessen the cold morning air. Garrick was measuring coffee for the second pot of coffee. A thermos on the counter held all of the first batch except for a cup he had poured for Nightingale.

"Why do you think that kid poisoned Bandit?" Nightingale asked, picking up the cup and taking a tentative sip.

"Nothing except he was scared of him, and you remember when he told us his father said the dog 'needed to be taught a lesson,' or some equally thoughtless phrase."

"Did you ask Imogene or Portia?"

"No. I didn't know how much you wanted to tell them, although I think Imogene suspected something."

"Did Cordelia Comet say anything about Danny Hartford besides he was Post's half-brother?"

Garrick slid the coffee pot into its perch and looked at Nightingale, raising his eyebrows in recall. "No. She threw it into the conversation after I said I needed to go. I wanted to get back before dark, so I didn't push."

"Glad you didn't. Guess a lot of my luck is due to you." He smiled and tapped Garrick's shoulder as he went toward his bedroom.

His remark had surprised the older man, and he enjoyed catching him off guard, but he hated to think he'd been such a grouse that a thank-you was a surprise. He came back into the kitchen carrying gauze and tape.

Garrick stirred the cooking eggs. "You want me to change that dressing?"

"Yeah, it's grubby-looking."

"Can you wait till after we eat?" Garrick asked.

"Sure. This shirt feels pretty good." Suddenly, he was hungry. "Breakfast smells great."

Garrick said nothing but his smile grew bigger.

Nightingale went into his office and brought back the search warrant. He placed it at the end of the table away from the food.

Garrick had a plate of eggs and sausage in each hand. He set the dishes down and nodded toward the papers. "What are we looking for?"

"Any vehicle resembling a motor scooter or motorcycle, chemicals that might be used in controlling disease in livestock, or any illegal drugs."

"Sounds like you made it broad," Garrick said.

"I threw in unlicensed firearms as a postscript. Figured if we're gonna piss him off we might as well do a good job of it." Nightingale sat in front of his plate and bit into the sausage before continuing. "I'm thinking he'll read it while we search."

"Any problems getting a judge to sign it?"

"Just had to convince Judge Tennison that a very rich

newcomer may be a felon. The very wealthy don't commit crimes." Nightingale knew he sounded bitchy, but he'd seen what the wealth of the oil fields could do to justice. When he had called Judge Tennison to present his case, he had told him about the woman seeing the red motorcycle in the alley in town. Then he had the chemicals from the autopsy and the rumor of a large number of unknown animals at the Post acreage, which would mean a need for the chemicals. The judge had told him to come by his house, where he signed the warrant.

That was before the grocery store and ambush.

Plates were soon empty, and Garrick started clearing the table. "We need to get over there early, right?" he asked.

Nightingale stood. "I asked Gilbert to stay handy."

"Who did he send out last night?"

"I didn't see them. Some men from Broken Rock came out with Robinson and Hall and when they saw that I was okay, they and the Rangers went into the field across the road where they thought the shooter had been," Nightingale said. "'Course, by then it was getting dark, and I bet they didn't find anything. You might call Gilbert and see what they reported. I appreciate him sending people to help."

"Yeah, he's like you and me. He wasn't surprised that someone went after you," Garrick said.

"It goes with the territory," Nightingale said, as he carefully lifted the shirt off, wincing in pain as it touched his shoulder and the bloody bandage.

Garrick was changing the dressing when Imogene knocked on the door. She came in and immediately went to stand beside Garrick and watch. "You need some in-service training on dressing a wound," she said.

"You can come over an hour earlier next time and fix it yourself." Garrick's remark carried no testiness, only a playful challenge. He snipped the last piece of tape.

Nightingale turned around and caught them exchanging smiles that he didn't want to interpret, so he tried a light tone. "You two can fuss over my wounds some other time. Imogene, thanks for picking up Bandit. You okay with him staying after what happened yesterday?"

Imogene reached down, petted the dog, and snapped the leash to his collar. "He's a comfort to have around. Everything is fine." Holding the leash, she walked to the door, waved, and was gone.

This was no time to ask questions and probe relationships, so he relegated his curiosity to a later date. Bandit was in the best place possible for the time, and that was a comfort.

With the bandage done, Nightingale stood and Garrick helped him put on his shirt.

"Meet you outside in fifteen minutes," Nightingale said. In the bedroom, the buttons on the shirt were still a challenge, and he was sweaty by the time he grabbed a jacket and started out to the vehicle. It seemed to be understood that Garrick would drive.

As in times past, neither man talked. Nightingale always went over "what-if" scenarios in his head. He had never asked Garrick what crossed his mind before a search. He really never had asked Garrick much about his thoughts because Garrick usually told him what he was thinking. The few times he'd tried to pry information out of the older man he'd been told to mind his own business.

So now he looked out the window at the fields of chopped brown stalks on one side of the road and a field of winter wheat on the other side. The warming winters had increased the winter grain crops, but still, farming was a crap shoot. He remembered his father and his difficult life. Nightingale admired farmers like his father but knew he could never be one.

His mind moved to Edgar Post, who was also a father. But there the resemblance between Post and his own father ended.

Fatherhood didn't take special talent. Post had blown it, had damaged his sons rather than protecting them. Of course, so had Cordelia Comet. How much damage had been dished out to either of the boys might never be known.

"You know," Nightingale said, "the only thing we haven't considered about Joshua's death is suicide."

Nightingale was encouraged that Garrick didn't immediately cut off the idea. Silence seemed tangible in the truck cab.

"I'm listening," Garrick said. "How could it be suicide?"

"The way I'm thinking is: Joshua took a hypodermic up to the roof. He had enough ketamine in the syringe to kill himself. He injected and tossed the syringe—that's the reflection I saw that day when I walked up. He didn't know he would break his neck during the fall, so that complicated the information we had."

Garrick slowed the truck, his brows knitted as he thought. "He left no note, nothing. Did he mention killing himself to anyone? Was he depressed?"

"Portia and Imogene might have some idea. Did his mother mention depression?"

The truck slowed almost to a stop as Post's mansion came into view through the gate. Garrick turned to look at Nightingale. "No. She said he had some debts. She also said he hated his father. But why would his suicide be the answer?"

"I think he hoped we'd do exactly what we have done—try to find a murderer, and the best choice is Post senior. If I'm right, we'll find something today, inside those walls, that will make Edgar Post look guilty." Nightingale pointed toward a parked vehicle. "Looks like we've got help."

A Ranger vehicle waited outside of the foreboding gate and wall.

"We're gonna need it," said Garrick, changing gears and

moving forward. "I don't know as I want to save Post's stuck-up hide, and if he didn't do it, we'll have to prove that, too."

"Yeah, I've already decided that I don't like the guy enough that I couldn't testify in court. I think he's dangerous, but verbal threats and innuendos don't prove a thing."

41

Nightingale glanced at his watch as they neared the Post house. It was close to 8:30 a.m. He couldn't tell who was in the other vehicle, so an abundance of caution made him wait for the men to reveal themselves. He sat up taller and squeezed his good arm against his weapon.

A young man opened the driver's door, got out, and saluted. When Nightingale saw Bob Gilbert exit the passenger side of the SUV, he followed suit.

"I wanted to be here but can't," Gilbert said. "Amos Rogers is new, but he's anxious to learn. I figured you could use his help."

Nightingale glanced over at the officer. The young man was so eager he almost glowed.

Gilbert continued, but his eyes constantly swept the horizon. "How are you? Anything new about the shooter? We've got the bullets at the lab. The men that came to help said it got dark on them, so they didn't find anything."

"I appreciate the concern," Nightingale said.

"We'll check around," Gilbert said. After a pause, he shook his head in disgust. "I hate it."

Nightingale had experienced the straining for words before.

He'd tried to talk to men who were shot and always came up with nothing. Everyone knew when they signed up that they might die in the line of duty, so there was never an appropriate statement.

Instead, he consoled Gilbert. "I've got enemies; we all do. Thanks for the new officer."

They shook hands as another vehicle pulled up next to them. Gilbert nodded to the other driver, gave a brief wave to Rogers, and walked toward the third vehicle.

As it backed away and left, Nightingale's eyes, too, swept the horizon, checking for a shine off gun metal or the slightest movement that might not be right. Satisfied for the moment, he spoke to the officer. "Glad to have you. Just drive in behind me."

Garrick gave his name and Nightingale's to a faceless voice in the intercom and explained that the second vehicle was another Ranger. They drove through. At the front door, the butler came out, and Nightingale met him, explaining the search warrant. The man turned on his heel and went back into the house. Nightingale didn't let the door close.

In the foyer, Edgar Post was coming down the stairs. "Mr. Nightingale, if you and your comrades don't leave my house immediately, I will call the governor, and if this harassment continues, I will sue this county and state for every penny it may possess, now or in the future."

Nightingale said nothing. He handed the warrant to Post. As he read the bold letters, "Search Warrant," his already crimson face flamed hotter.

Garrick and Rogers had drifted in, one on each side of Nightingale.

Post stood on the staircase, glancing through the pages of the warrant. He had an audience, and his voice was gritty with vitriol. "You don't need to look in this house for a motor scooter."

Nightingale looked at Garrick and nodded toward the door.

Garrick returned the nod and with a glance at Rogers, the two trooped back outside.

Post didn't miss the coordination of the retreat. "Very nice." He crumpled the warrant in his hands. "My lawyer will be here soon." He turned and walked up the stairs.

Nightingale did his own exit out the front door, while the butler watched impassively.

Garrick and Rogers stood at the vehicles. Nightingale climbed into the truck and they followed suit. "What we're going to do," Nightingale said, "is follow the pavement and cobblestones and examine every building here. We'll park down close to that first building"— he nodded toward a barn with a workshop and a couple of other outbuildings nearby—"then walk. If the doors are locked, we go get keys."

After they parked, Nightingale handed evidence bags to Amos Rogers and Garrick. "We're looking for motorcycles, especially small, red ones, and chemicals with any type of label. The specific chemical may be a Rompun/xylazine mix or it may be ketamine, which is real popular for all ages right now. Either one is like an anesthetic and muscle relaxer used for animals, not crops. It may not be very well-labeled."

He also handed plastic gloves to each man. "Bag anything that looks remotely suspicious. Be sure and label it. If it's something big, we'll put it in the truck and tag it."

"What about the house?" Garrick asked.

"We're starting with outbuildings," Nightingale said. "I'm taking a chance that what we're looking for is easier to hide in these buildings than in the house. If we come up blank, we have to go there."

"What about talking to people, if anyone else is here?" Garrick asked.

"If they want to volunteer that's fine, but it's probably better to not ask questions." Nightingale knew the question was for

Rogers's benefit; no one was in sight. But they also didn't want evidence thrown out because a witness said he was coerced.

They had passed by the barn and gravitated to the building that looked like a workshop, labeled "Repairs Here." Once they were inside, the organization of the building became apparent. It was smaller than it looked from the outside, so while Rogers and Garrick started the search there, Nightingale walked toward the dairy barn.

The structure was big and open on each end with stalls on each side. There were twelve stalls, but only four cows stood contentedly, chewing cuds and swishing their tails.

An odor floated around, too clean to be in a barn, but Nightingale couldn't decide what it was. Bleach, maybe, or the new wood odor of construction. His father would have laughed at such an idea. He was heading for the front of the barn when he saw Garrick and Rogers silhouetted in the open door. They came toward him, with Garrick holding out something.

"We found the makings of a motorbike," Garrick said, and Nightingale saw that he had what looked like the red fender of a small motorcycle.

Rogers held up a sack and rattled it, indicating more pieces inside.

For a minute the trio stood at the opening to the barn and adjusted their vision to the darkness inside.

"Why has he got Holstein cows?" Garrick asked.

"I'll bet he uses fresh milk in the house," Amos Rogers said. "I read somewhere that he's a health-food nut. That would explain having only four. That'd be more than enough for his household."

"Where did you read that?" Nightingale asked.

"Some fan magazine, I guess, probably online." Rogers was maybe thirty years old. He blushed as if he'd been caught in a crime.

Nightingale shook his head at his own online searches, which had yielded so little.

"Whatever the reason, let's go through here and then on to the next building. Since there are cows in here, maybe there are medicines for them. I walked straight through and found nothing. Maybe you guys will have better luck." They each went to a different area of the barn.

He thought they had hit pay dirt when Garrick found a small refrigerator. But the appliance was empty. It was not very cold, and nothing was inside.

From the barn, they went across the pavement to a concrete block building that reminded Nightingale of a pumphouse. Standing in the doorway, they saw large boxes piled in a corner, labeled as washers, dryers, steamers, and irons.

"We can't ignore it just because it looks like a laundry," Nightingale said.

Inside the room, the unboxed laundry equipment stood haphazardly, some still with bar codes. The equipment was clearly awaiting installation and had never been used.

They continued to the back door of the laundry building. Stretching in the distance was the runway, where Post's airplanes came and went. The hanger for the aviation equipment and planes was quite a distance away from them. Also in sight was the lofty fence that separated the Post land from the Miller property.

Past the cow barn and laundry was a second barn, this one for horses. It was a two-story building of traditional wood and stone with Dutch doors at the entrance. Stairs led up each side to an outside entrance at the second-story deck. Once through the Dutch doors, Nightingale saw that the ceiling soared and even the five horses in stalls seemed a little lost. None of them seemed small enough to fit the description that Arnoldo had shared with Nightingale.

A few feet into the barn, Nightingale paused a minute to

grasp what he was seeing. It looked like rooms upstairs had been built on the outer edge of the barn, under the eaves. Something like a catwalk ran around the space, looking over the horses in stalls below, much like a hotel. Rogers and Garrick split up and began looking into the stalls. Nightingale found an inside staircase and headed upstairs.

The roof of the building soared and huge fans kept the air moving. Walking along the catwalk gave him the eerie sense of floating in space, unprotected. Nightingale had a brief adrenaline rush. Why the extra rooms, if not for hiding something? He walked to the nearest door and opened it into a room that ran the length of the barn. The place must have been soundproofed because when he closed the door behind him, a hushed silence enveloped him.

Model planes, two or three dozen, sat on a workbench, much like a desk, that had been built along the entire wall. A picture of Adam and his father took honors on one corner of the desk. Another photo, this one of an unsmiling woman wearing huge sunglasses, sat at the far end, away from the one of Adam and his father. Someone spent a great deal of time here. A large bathroom occupied the end of the room, toward the front of the barn. Drawings of airplanes and spacecraft of every age and design hung on every wall. Windows occupied the wall above the workspace and looked out onto the side and back of the property. He could see the fence and the peak of a roof over on the Millers' property. He turned back to the desk and saw the piece that he wanted to see. In large, gold block letters, the nameplate proclaiming this "Adam's Desk" explained it all.

Nightingale moved closer to the desk to inspect the models. Heights of the desktop varied. One section was about thirty-two inches high. Another section, which was about thirty-six inches high, was home to the most elaborate models. One model had four propellers on a metal base of four legs, like a large aluminum spider. From the internet, he knew it was a drone, the first he'd ever seen up close enough to touch.

A small camera lay next to the drone, along with a plastic bag of syringes. He saw nothing to use with the syringes—no liquid, no chemical. He began to pull out drawers and found only instructions for putting the aircraft models together. He felt like he was close to something but had no idea what. He jerked out more drawers, and in the bottom one, the last one, he found an apparatus that he had seen in a few cattle operations, an automatic syringe that could be used to inject antibiotics or tranquilizers in horses and cows.

Garrick stood in the doorway. "You found something?"

Nightingale leaned against the desk. He held up the syringe. "Found this back in one of the drawers. Did y'all find any drugs?"

"No. What is that thing?" Garrick pointed to the winged apparatus.

"It's a drone, but it's not listed on our warrant so we can't take it with us. This must be where Adam Post hangs out. I'm keeping the syringes. They don't have needles, but I'm calling them drug paraphernalia."

Nightingale looked out the window toward the massive fence and airplane hangar. For some reason he couldn't explain, he didn't feel elated at his findings. The person that probably had tried to kill his dog, the boy who lived surrounded by wealth that Nightingale could only imagine... This was a young man whom Nightingale pitied.

42

Searching the buildings on Post's property took all morning. But time had gone quickly. It was one thirty in the afternoon, and Nightingale wanted to go back over a few buildings. It was also past lunchtime, and they needed a break.

He made a quick decision. This would be a good place to cut the young officer loose. "Amos, we're going to check that last building. You can get back to town and see if you can get prints off those parts. I'll call if I need anything else."

Rogers looked like he'd just been told he was fired. "Sir, I can help until you finish. I'd like to stay."

Nightingale absentmindedly rubbed his throbbing shoulder and arm while glancing at the fence and buildings. He allowed himself an inward smile. The kid was young and full of energy, while he was hurt and hoping for caffeine to pick him up. Even the stalwart Garrick seemed ready for a break.

He pulled his meds out of his pocket and dry-swallowed one as he reached for a bottle of water that Garrick handed him. "All right. Bag those things you found and put them in the back of the truck. As you come back, bring Garrick's thermos of coffee."

They watched the Ranger as he jogged to the truck. "You think the chemical is here, don't you?" Garrick said.

"Yes," Nightingale said. "We need to find it. You heard Post. If this doesn't work, he's so pissed he'll make the entire county hurt, and he'll make the judge so miserable we'll never get another warrant."

They watched as Rogers carefully placed the bagged and loose motorcycle parts in the truck bed and went to the front for the thermos. "He's going to be a good Ranger," Garrick said.

"Already is," Nightingale said.

Rogers quick-stepped back to them. He handed the thermos to Nightingale. "Did you all notice that the last building we were in was supposed to be for horses, but it didn't smell horsey?"

"He's right," Garrick said. "There was hay in the stalls, oats for eating. But it's still new."

"What does that mean, though?" Nightingale asked.

"Could it be," Rogers said, "that he's putting together a small city to distract from something else he's doing that he doesn't want anyone to notice?"

They had started walking as they talked. Nightingale looked sideways at Rogers with something like approval. "Maybe. Or maybe he just needed some way to spend some of his riches for tax write-offs and this is it. He has the building expense and then starts depreciating everything."

They went back to the building they'd just left but found nothing further. Finally, they walked to the airplane hangar. Inside the hangar a dozen men hugged the walls. They looked to have been at work a minute or two earlier on the single plane that stood in the center of the vast space. Engine parts and pieces lay on worktables around the outer walls of the building, although nothing about the plane made Nightingale think the parts came from it. The air smelled of oil and gasoline. When Nightingale asked them to leave while the building was searched, every man walked politely outside, away from the building and toward the house. No one said a word.

Nightingale closed the door after they left. "I wouldn't want any of those guys working on a plane I was going to fly. They don't look like engineers, but they sure are polite."

"They've been trained to be quiet. They're probably regular hands for all these buildings," Garrick said. "Somebody knew we were coming and told them to keep their mouths shut."

"Yep. But I don't want to give Post any reason to slip out of this, so let's look through here. I've got a couple of things to go over after we leave here. Check the bathroom and first aid stuff."

The hangar had so much open space, it seemed hard to imagine hiding anything in the emptiness. Nevertheless, he walked around, peeking into every nook and under any piece of paper or plastic that might be hiding something. Again, something nagged the back of his mind. Sometimes he didn't notice enough details, but this was more than simple lack of observation digging at him.

He'd almost finished the search of the airplane when Amos came out declaring he'd found nothing in lockers or cots. Garrick also came out empty-handed.

"The plane has small hidden holes and shelves, but I didn't find a thing," Nightingale said. "I've been inside and out."

The initial elation had worn off, so Nightingale fell back to procedure. When they were outside and walking the cobblestones to return to the truck, he said, "We've slighted the laundry, and I want to go back to the workspace over the stable." Soon they'd be out of options if nothing turned up. "You two check the laundry. There was new equipment, so maybe something is inside some of it. I'm going back to the boy's workroom. I've missed one possibility."

Nightingale returned to the bathroom next to Adam's workspace. He hoped to find something in the back of the toilet. The lid to the commode was crooked, which was strange, but he found no plastic bag of medicines for man or animals.

He left the place and walked toward the small laundry facility.

He opened the door as Garrick said, "This looks like Santa Claus just came by and unloaded everything and then just left." Garrick looked over at him and continued. "This set-up is so new, they may not have stocked laundry supplies yet."

"You don't really believe that, do you?" Nightingale asked.

Garrick threw up his hands in frustration. "No, but there's nothing here except washing machines and dryers, plus a steamer, and they all look new. We checked inside the packing boxes and there's nothing."

Amos nodded in agreement.

Nightingale said, "I hit a dead end, too."

Once they were outside again, Nightingale looked at his watch. The time had slipped away. It was close to three o'clock. Temperatures had warmed to what he guessed was high sixties. From this vantage point, it was clear that Post had indeed erected a small village along the cobblestone path from the mansion. The laundry building was bland but would probably get a personality later with awnings and shutters. The stables could have been plucked from an English television show. The workshop had a drawing of a Bentley on a sign, but it had been taken inside and propped against the wall.

The three men stood in the middle of the cobblestone path while Nightingale said, "Let's think about this a bit. Why would Post create such a village?" He was about to say more when he heard noise farther up the path toward the house.

"Wait, wait," Carolyn Post said. She was running from the house. Her voice sounded frightened. "Mr. Nightingale, please wait." She tripped and almost fell as she reached the men.

Rogers and Nightingale caught her.

"Calm down," Nightingale said. Her clothing clung to her, as if she'd run a marathon, not a sprint from the house.

Her breathing was ragged. She clutched Nightingale's arm with one hand. "My brother is gone."

"Gone? Are you sure?" Nightingale knew he sounded patronizing, but something in Carolyn's face made him wary.

Her hand on his arm was cold. "You've got to help me find him."

"Maybe he slipped out and met friends," Nightingale said.

She closed her eyes, speaking slowly, but unable to control the vibrato of panic. "You don't understand. He doesn't know anyone here. He's disappeared."

"Have you told your father?" Nightingale asked.

"I told him, but Adam has disappeared before." She glanced toward the house. "He's not concerned."

"How can you be sure he's really gone? Maybe he's just taken off for a few hours."

She shook her head. "No, there's a note. It says he's not coming back."

He looked toward the house. "Where is your father now?"

She blushed and looked at the ground. "He left about an hour ago. When I told him about Adam, he just said Adam would be back by the time he returned tonight."

"You said Adam disappeared before," Nightingale said. "Did he leave a note that time? And how many times has he done this?"

"Only once," she said. "And he didn't leave a note."

"Where is the note now?"

She pulled a crumpled piece of paper from her jeans and handed it to Nightingale, who read it and passed it to Garrick.

"It says he's done a terrible thing," Nightingale said. "What has he done?"

"I don't know." Carolyn's eyes glistened with tears.

"We'll come up there now. Don't move anything in his room," Nightingale said. "We'll be right there."

She walked a few steps backward, then turned as she said, "Thank you. Please, hurry."

Nightingale started toward the house, and Garrick and Amos walked on either side of him. He glanced at Garrick and said, "What do you think?"

"I don't understand the father. I'd be worried if it was my kid, especially since he hadn't left a note before. The girl sounds scared, but there's something missing."

Nightingale looked at the new Ranger.

"I'm just learning, but my mother would be frantic if my brother did something like that," Rogers said.

"Good answer," Nightingale said. "I've seen Carolyn weigh in on her father before, and she's the panicky type. Most females I know would be in a dither. She's in a mild panic and to me, that means she's lying about something." Seeing the confused look on Rogers's face, he continued. "You need to get used to the idea that beautiful women lie as easy as the plain ones, usually easier."

When they got to the house, Carolyn Post had the front door open before Garrick could knock. Reeves, the butler, stood in the background.

"Please, hurry," Carolyn said. She sounded frantic while holding onto hope.

"We'll do what we can, but we may not be able to find him," Nightingale said. Unease was creeping into Nightingale's thoughts. His palms were sweaty.

"Please search for the boy," Reeves said. "May I help in any way?" The tremor in the man's voice betrayed him. He cared for the boy.

Nightingale turned to the butler. "When did you last see Adam?"

"Early this morning, here at breakfast," the butler said. "He left the house then. He usually spends his time in his room over the stable and works on his airplanes out there. I assumed that's where he went."

Nightingale turned to Carolyn. "Show me where you found the note," he said. "Garrick, you and Amos go over the rooms at the stable, where I looked. See if I missed anything."

Nightingale followed the girl upstairs. Everything in Adam's room looked like it had been placed in a stage set. Not one wrinkle sullied the bed. When he opened the closet doors, all the clothes hung neatly according to type and color.

A desk had homework, and Nightingale walked to it. A page titled "What the Humanities Teach Us" had been written on notebook paper. Number four was highlighted. "They teach us to deal critically and logically with subjective, complex, and imperfect information." The word "Lies" had been put in parentheses after the sentence. Nightingale glanced over his shoulder to the girl. "Is this Adam's writing?"

She stared at it. "Yes, I think it's some homework from his English teacher."

After checking the bathroom, he said, "Where did Adam hang out, besides his room over the stables?"

Carolyn closed her eyes. "I've been trying to figure that out." Her voice sounded raw, and when she looked at him, her eyes were huge with fright. "He loved flying. He went to the hanger sometimes and got in the plane, but you've been there, right?"

"Yes," he said, "but we'll go check again. You stay here."

"No. I'm going with you."

Nightingale didn't argue. He hurried out of the room and the house and called to Garrick and Rogers, who had nearly reached the barn. "We're going back to the hanger." Garrick gave a slight nod, pointed a finger to Nightingale, and the two men abandoned their trip to the barn, heading instead to Nightingale and Carolyn.

Nightingale started a slow jog, and beside him, Garrick did the same. Behind them came the sound of Amos and Carolyn as their feet hit the cobblestones. "Amos, run up ahead of us and open the hangar. We're right behind you."

Amos ran ahead as instructed with the girl right behind him.

Nightingale stopped and, for a second, leaned to rest his hands on his knees. "Adam had a line written and highlighted that may have meaning," he said. "It could have meant that the line, which was about the humanities, was a lie, or that Adam had discovered that his father had lied. Either way is not good."

Nightingale began to run again, the pain in his shoulder suddenly kicking in along with a feeling of mounting dread. Garrick caught up with him. Both of them panted. "If he's not here," Nightingale said between breaths, "we'll call in more people."

He and Garrick ran through the door that Amos held open. Nightingale forgot his painful arm and headed toward the plane. He glanced through the windows and thought he saw the blond hair of Adam. The door was ajar. His heart jerked inside his chest. He climbed inside. Adam was in a seat in the back. An awful sick fear came over him.

The kid looked like a doll that had melted.

Nightingale clambered over the seats toward the boy, refusing to believe his eyes. "Adam, Adam, can you hear me?"

Adam had slid down in the seat, and his head rested against the side of the plane. Nightingale placed his fingers on the boy's neck to check for a pulse. Nothing. Garrick had stepped inside but stayed back so Nightingale could move.

"Call an ambulance," Nightingale said. "And keep the girl out there. I'm going to try CPR."

He was not a professional. Maybe the heartbeat was so shallow he couldn't find it. Sometimes a person could be saved with CPR. His mind raced to details of drug reactions he'd read about. Sometimes the person couldn't talk but was aware of what was going on around him.

The ambulance would have Narcan. The stuff was a nasal spray used to reverse the effects of opioid overdose, which might help to kick him out of a bad reaction. Damn it, he was a kid; he had to live.

Nightingale laid the limp body on the floor of the aircraft and cleared his throat. The blue eyes had dulled, half closed, and it was hard to look at them. In another world, he heard the girl screaming and Garrick's voice telling someone something, but he began to push on the young chest and to blow breath into the mouth, hoping for a miracle. A tear fell on his hand. He couldn't die. He was only a boy.

At his back Garrick said, "I've called."

Nightingale nodded as the older man climbed into the plane and came up behind where Nightingale was working.

"How long?" Nightingale asked. Pump, blow, count.

"Ten or fifteen minutes. I told them it was an accidental overdose. Carolyn is making sure the gate is open," Garrick said.

Pump. Blow. Pump. Blow. Count. He's too young to die.

Nightingale kept up the rhythm and finally heard a siren. Medics appeared and within a couple of minutes had placed their hands where his had been, pushing, counting. He moved aside.

"What did he take?"

"Ketamine, but I'm guessing." Nightingale heard his own voice waiver. He wanted to talk, maybe that would help Adam. But he knew he couldn't. Another medic came in with an oxygen mask and tank. Nightingale squeezed aside, trying to hear their words, but they didn't speak. They just moved and worked while he backed out of the plane, still straining to see if the boy moved.

When they came out with Adam on a stretcher, he walked beside one man, trying to explain.

"He's really under," he said, knowing that they were aware of what he was saying but unable to stop. "I've been doing resuscitation. I can go along if you need me."

"No, no need. We've got the antidote with us." They exchanged somber glances that Nightingale chose to ignore.

Soon they had the boy bundled into the ambulance. They drove away, siren screaming.

Nightingale felt numb. Inside he was shaking. He closed his eyes tight for a second, aware that Garrick was standing by him.

Amos Rogers stepped aside as the ambulance passed him. Rogers walked over to Nightingale.

"Sir." Rogers seemed nervous, antsy. He rocked forward and back on his feet. "I'd like to drive Miss Post in my truck to the hospital, to see how her brother is."

"Good idea," Nightingale said.

Rogers lit out, running hard toward his truck.

Nightingale raised his voice to make sure Rogers heard the last part of his sentence. "Call me or Garrick, and let us know what you find out."

Nightingale knew he was wasting time standing there uselessly regretting what had happened. The boy was not his, and the fact that his life was wasted was not his burden, but sadness weighed him down.

"I fell apart," Nightingale said. "Reminded me of that kid I shot."

"We all have some sort of hell we have to live through several times in our lives."

They turned and went back inside the hangar to the plane.

"He's dead, isn't he?"

Garrick shrugged. "Maybe not. Maybe the doctors can revive him." Garrick walked over to the plane and stared inside the door. "It looks like he came in here after we left."

"You're right. That door was open a bit when we came back

the second time. I made a point to shut it when we left. He must have been watching us," Nightingale said.

"I'll bet the boy knew this place backwards and forwards. When he saw us leave, he came around to the back of the building to the plane and got inside," Garrick said.

Nightingale wiped one hand down his face and took a deep breath. "We need to tell his father what's happened. We can go by the hospital, but we still don't know where Post is."

The two men walked side by side toward the huge house. "Why," Garrick said, "did he do something that risky? He was smart. Do you think he realized the risk involved?"

"You mean death? He was so young he probably thought he'd never die," Nightingale said. "I keep hoping the doctors can revive him, and his will to live will save him. Let's go talk to the butler. I'll bet he knows where his boss is. Then we head to the hospital."

When Garrick knocked, Reeves opened the door quickly. While he had seemed stoic and like an enemy earlier, he now seemed sad. "Is Adam dead?" he asked.

"We don't know for sure," Nightingale said. "We're going to the hospital to check on him. Do you have any idea where Edgar Post is?"

Reeves bowed his head slightly and took in a long breath. "He went to a gala for the governor, which was to take place near Amarillo, I believe."

"Thanks," Nightingale said.

He and Garrick turned to leave when he heard Reeves clear his throat.

"If you don't mind, when you find out for sure about the boy, will you please call me?" Reeves handed a card to Nightingale. On the card, he had written his cell phone number.

Nightingale felt a shiver. This big guy in a suit didn't seem like a person who would care, but this was an act of caring.

"Sure," he said. "Garrick or I will let you know."

As they walked to the truck, Nightingale heard a lone turtle dove in the distance. "Would you mind driving?" He went to the passenger side of the vehicle and poured two pills out of a bottle for the pain in his arm. "I could get really jaded after much of this," he said.

They sat in the truck for a moment, just thinking.

"The difference, I think," Garrick said, "is that Adam was a kid. To me, he was a child. The teenager you shot all those years ago was older than Adam. And when you shot him, you were in danger and I would have been shot—maybe killed. You saved my life. Today is a waste."

As Garrick reached for the ignition, Nightingale's phone rang. It was Amos Rogers.

"Sir, Adam Post is dead. There was nothing they could do. I'm bringing Miss Post back to her house."

"Okay, we're heading to Amarillo," Nightingale said. "And Amos, it's best if you don't stay too late with the girl."

"Yes, sir."

"I'll call Reeves," Nightingale said.

Somehow the phone seemed heavy. They'd traveled a few miles before he dialed.

43

Governor Patricia Daniels admired the handcrafted mahogany bedroom suite, then looked out the bedroom window toward the flatlands of West Texas. The state had the most incredible sunsets she had ever seen. Pinks and reds and golds mixed in striations with varied blues across the sky. She smiled, remembering that God could get away with things, especially colors that human beings would never put together.

She'd been in the back of the big SUV, trying to work, all the way from Austin to this ranch outside of Amarillo. Mike Haywood, her bodyguard, had driven the vehicle, with Tony, the second in command, beside him. It was the smallest complement of officers she'd ever traveled with; nevertheless, she felt safe. She had argued with Haywood about letting men take time off, and she won. She needed to think and found that her time alone, going to and from events in the state, was a good time for that.

She had decided to write down her considerations about Edgar Post. But instead of Post, she found herself considering her own needs and plans and trying to figure out why those needs had gotten her into this mess. For she was in a mess. Thank goodness she had never gone to bed with him. The meeting in

New York had been close. He had magnetism, and she had power. They had been attracted to each other since the first meeting, and they both knew it.

He had suggested the meeting in New York. He had dropped by the governor's mansion late at night and she had sent him away, but he had been there. And anyone who wanted to mention her "having a man visitor at night" could make a political firestorm for her in the next election. Any opponent who said a woman politician was less than chaste in the South knew how to tear a campaign apart. The double standard still existed.

However, there were other things that had bothered her from the beginning. First, Post liked himself far too much for her comfort. Another thing bothering her was her own loneliness, which she now realized was a vulnerability.

Oswald Nightingale had served her well to tell her to wait on a decision about Post. Her intuition told her to stop the entire process. She sighed at her gullibility. Post had asked her to create a job for him. He wanted no pay. But he wanted access to the state's retirement fund. He promised he could manage it and create unimagined profits. She could have pushed the idea; she had yes people on her staff. But she refused to be manipulated. It had been several weeks since he made his proposal, and she knew he was getting impatient.

If she had gone to bed with him, he could have resorted to blackmail. Now, she shivered at the thought. He could be dangerous because he was accustomed to getting his way. Someone had told her, "If you tell a lie as the truth enough times, people will believe it." She looked again at the sunset and sighed.

She had not heard from Nightingale.

She'd arrived early at the ranch and met with her host and his wife, Charles and Eva Pentecost. They'd exchanged anecdotes and hopes for the state and the party. No one said flat out that this was an important fundraiser, but she knew this could make a huge difference in the coming years.

She had gone to her room to freshen up and change clothes. She looked at her notes and picked up her phone. Then she decided against it. She'd call Nightingale—and then Post—tomorrow, after she was back in Austin.

She was angry at Nightingale, feeling he'd put her request way down on his to-do list. But she was also feeling generous. She liked and respected him. No one on her staff told her the truth like he did. No one else was ready to admit mistakes when they'd made them. The truth was: she needed him, and he didn't need her. She wished she could get him as a full-time adviser, but that was pure fantasy.

Now, she turned away from the window and the brilliant sunset (which was already fading), determined to forget Nightingale and to stay on course. She pulled out the notes for her speech, figuring ten minutes should do the trick. Short speeches left more time for what she really wanted with this crowd: to mingle. One-on-one contact with contributors.

The bell rang. That was her cue to join the group. She checked lipstick, hair, and put her phone in her purse. As she pulled the door open, the phone rang. She hesitated briefly, but curiosity won. She opened her purse and saw Edgar Post's name.

She had not called him and now was no time to talk. He was on the guest list, so he would be in the audience. She snapped the purse closed, like it was the lid on a coffin. He would have to wait. She took a deep breath. The call made her remember her wrap, a light, silky scarf that could be handy if she became nervous. As she turned back to retrieve it, she thought with a tight grin that sometimes clenching silk was better than wringing a constituent's neck. She put her shoulders back.

Stepping into the wide hall, she smiled at Mike Haywood, who fell into line behind her. Her heels clicked on the hardwood floors, and she reminded herself not to get tangled when she reached the expensive oriental rugs. In another part of the house, she heard the clink of glasses, music of a string quartet, and laughter in the midst of mumbled voices.

One person caught sight of her, and the applause began. She let her host guide her to a space in front of a fireplace in the den which had been divested of furniture except for a few pieces pushed against the wall.

The applause stopped, and she told her modest joke. In the middle of the laughter, she saw Edgar Post. Their eyes met, and she knew what she feared. This man had no emotion, not love or hate, for anyone. He was an excellent actor, cold and as lethal as a knife. He was a charlatan and would just as soon strangle her as look at her.

He nodded and smiled. Her mouth went dry. Waiting for the applause to die, she took a sip of water, looked at Post, and did not smile. She glanced at her notes and called for renewed energy to make their lives wonderful, their children perfect, and everyone healthy.

Edgar Post stepped behind a man who was taller than him and disappeared in the crowd. The governor looked over her shoulder for Mike but saw Tony on the opposite side of the crowd. She finished the speech with, "Thank you for your help." She willed her knees to not buckle.

Applause broke out, and she raised her voice and one fist. "And thank God for Texas!" Glancing at her watch, she noted eight minutes and eased her way closer to Haywood. The bodyguard moved slightly to her back, so he was at her elbow.

A few people came toward her to speak, but these were sophisticated people who had more money than she, and most had expressed their desires to her at other times in closer circumstances. No one had the need to act like a groupie. Daniels heard her own heart pounding as she glanced around the crowd, looking for Post. She didn't see him and wondered if anyone could see her heart pounding against her dress.

She exchanged pleasantries for half an hour with familiar faces. However, one woman she didn't know came forward, her hand extended, her gaze straight on, as if they'd known each other for years.

"Governor, I had to meet you. My name is Portia Shoemaker. I'm a cousin of Oswald Nightingale, and I wanted to say you're doing a great job as governor, but I'm a teacher and our schools can always use more money."

Daniels shook the woman's hand, and out of the corner of her eye, she saw Edgar Post. Suddenly, Portia Shoemaker was a long-lost friend, and Daniels pulled her closer, using her as a shield to avoid Post. She would not talk to him now.

The governor swapped hands with Portia and deftly turned to be facing away from Post. "I am so glad to meet you. Mr. Nightingale has never mentioned his family. Are y'all a close family?"

Daniels half-listened to Portia, while her gaze moved through the crowd. Post had disappeared.

Portia continued to talk, and Daniels tried to listen to her. But her thoughts stayed on Post and the ice in his eyes. She dared not mention her uncertainty to any of her guards for fear they would confront him. And what would he say? He lied easily, and she would be the topic of the lie. Stupid, stupid. What had she been thinking?

Then out of her confused thoughts, she heard, "You look upset, Governor. Are you all right?" Portia Shoemaker was squinting, her face echoing the concern in her voice. Mike Haywood also stared.

Remembering that this was Nightingale's cousin, she tried to recover her poise. But, since she was taller than Portia, the governor continued to glance around the crowd. "I'm so sorry. I had a momentary thought about a letter I should have sent to a constituent. I'll try to be better company."

She made herself stare at Portia, trying to appear calm, though she could feel that her face had heated while her hands were clammy. She pulled the scarf from around her neck, letting it fall loosely in her grasp.

Portia was unfazed. "It's not a problem, Governor. May I help?"

"I want to get out of the crowd. Why don't you come with me to my room? I'd like to get to know you better."

The governor put one hand on Portia's arm and together they navigated through the crowd. Seeing the host and hostess, she said, "Thank you so much. This is a friend I haven't seen in ten years." She watched Edgar Post weave through the crowd to come up behind her host. She hesitated and then said, "We're going to my room to chat, and then I'll be leaving."

As she reached her room, Daniels was aware of Mike Haywood at her back and the other guard near the door. Pride surfaced. She was the governor, for God's sake. She'd would not let the menace of this man overpower her. She had two men trained to protect her. The host had hired off-duty officers to help with security and crowd control.

So why did the presence of Edgar Post get her in such a state? But she knew the answer. She was a leader, a woman of virtue, a woman of principals. What had she been thinking to have a flirtation with such a man?

∽

PORTIA DIDN'T KNOW EXACTLY WHAT WAS HAPPENING, BUT she was worried about Patricia Daniels. They were seated across from each other in a pair of white linen wingback chairs in front of the large windows of the bedroom suite, and the governor was flushed, as if she had a fever.

The governor had poured herself a drink and dropped ice into Portia's glass of ginger ale which sat untouched on a coaster. "I didn't hear everything while we were in the other room," Governor Daniels was saying. "You are related to—"

The door opened, and she stood abruptly.

The governor's bodyguard stood at the door, obviously frustrated, his face contorted in anger. Someone stood behind him. "Governor, there is a man here who insists he knows you and wants to talk with you."

Behind him, a man raised his voice, a hand waved. "Patricia, tell him how close we are. Did he come to New York with your group?"

Governor Daniels closed her eyes and shivered. "It's all right, Mike. He can come in."

The guard reluctantly stepped aside, and a man in a tuxedo barged in. When the guard asked if he should stay, the man smiled, a nasty little smirk, Portia thought, and walked over to the governor.

Governor Daniels shook her head at Haywood. "No, we'll be fine."

The intruder wore a tuxedo. Not quite six feet tall, he had black hair with a touch of gray at the temples. Goodness, he would be handsome if he didn't have such an unpleasant expression on his face. But the tension in the room went to lightning level the moment he stepped inside. The governor sounded calm, but she was not happy, and this man was the reason for her agitation.

The governor seemed to regain her composure. "Mr. Post, I have no news on what we discussed." She hesitated for an instant. "Oh, excuse my manners, Portia Shoemaker, this is Edgar Post. Mr. Post is interested in working for our state."

Portia stiffened at the name but tried to look normal. This was Adam's father. The boy had never said an ill word about his father, but Portia had been a teacher for over twenty years. Some things were just self-evident. Adam Post was scared of his father.

Portia smiled, held out her hand, which he kissed as he bent toward her with a smile. The man was charming, but his eyes were hard and cold.

He made small talk, walked around the room as he refreshed drinks, and asked Portia to excuse them for a moment. "You know, I've fallen under the spell of this lady, this governor. We're just going to the little lanai for a private moment."

However, the governor was not on board with his plan. "Edgar, it's too cold. You can speak in front of Ms. Shoemaker." The governor sat down, but now Post was not having it.

He walked over to her, picked up her hand, and pulled her to her feet. "But, my dear, some things are personal. This won't take a minute." His hard voice almost threatened as he smiled.

From her chair, Portia could see brutal strength as he squeezed the governor's hand. He probably bruised her, but she didn't protest.

He put his arm around her waist and Portia heard him say, "You have no idea how ... ruin ... continue this charade. Don't be a fool."

The governor gave Portia a lopsided smile and walked out with him. It didn't take a genius to see that the governor objected to going outside, but she seemed persuaded that this man would not harm her. Tension in the room was thick, as he bowed and playfully pulled her outside. Or was it playful? Portia thought not. She didn't like the man. Where were the guards?

Then she heard the governor's voice, "No—"

On the balcony, she saw Post pull the governor close. She couldn't hear what he said. Their shadows looked like they kissed. Then the man kept his arm around her.

Portia felt her heart pounding. She was scared for herself and for the woman outside. She wanted to leave but she couldn't desert the governor.

She looked for a clock. How long should she wait? What was the man saying? After what seemed to be a lifetime, she stood and started toward the outer door to get help when she heard the sliding door open.

Post and the governor came back inside. Daniels had changed. She was pale and would not look at Portia. Was she drugged? No, she was thinking, not looking at the man, thinking of something far away. She'd formed one hand into a fist that she held against her lips, and she stared into space, into the future, perhaps. But she had definitely changed, no longer the governor, now a woman controlled by a man. Portia tried to digest the transformation.

Portia couldn't be sure, but she drew on her time with children and adults. Edgar Post had threatened Governor Daniels with something; whether it was true or false, she didn't know, but it was something horrible. Whatever had happened had transpired quickly, but Portia kept her observation to herself. The change in the governor only underpinned Portia's lack of trust in men, especially this one.

"Mr. Post is going to drive me back to Austin," Governor Daniels said. "I'm not feeling well. Could you come with us?"

"Of course," Portia said. The woman was ill. That explained a lot. With Portia along, she would not be alone with that man. "But my car?" Her hand clutched her purse tighter. Breaths came faster. She stood and poured a splash of bourbon into a glass, which she gulped and then grabbed her ginger ale. The bourbon burned a quick shot of courage. She could do this.

"I'll have one of my men drive it back to your house," Post said. "You can give him your address outside. It will help Patricia to have you along. I have to speak to her driver, also. Everything is going to be fine." Post patted the governor's hand.

The governor bit her lip. "Sorry, Edgar. I'll try to stay awake on the drive."

"Do you need a doctor?" Portia asked. Now she was becoming convinced that this illness was fake.

"No." Governor Daniels brightened, almost alert. She shook her head as if to bring clarity and looked directly at Portia. "I will be fine. I need to talk to Haywood and tell him all is well."

The governor didn't look well. But Portia said nothing and clutched her purse.

44

In the car, heading towards Amarillo, Nightingale and Garrick didn't talk for a few minutes. Nightingale figured he could relive the death of Adam Post for hours and nothing would change. Finally, he broke the silence. "We've got a while before we get to Amarillo. We both know what this flat terrain is about, so let's go over what we know and don't know about the case."

"Good idea," Garrick said. "I've got some speculation to talk through. You go first."

"Okay, my first idea is a doozy. It's not fully formed yet. I think Adam may have killed his half-brother, Joshua, with a drone." He quickly glanced at Garrick before continuing. "In his room today, I saw the apparatus that vets use as a hypodermic on cattle and large animals. Maybe he put one of those on a drone and filled it with ketamine. He controlled the drone remotely, so he could have injected the man and then flew the device back home. Or ditched it in a cow pasture."

Garrick smiled. "Nothing I have can top that. However, you don't have motive and no definitive evidence. The boy was smart, but he'd have to have help."

"How do you feel about Post or Carolyn as a helper?" Nightingale asked.

"The sister, maybe. Did you notice the red tennis shoes today that match that ribbon we found behind the newspaper offices?"

"I noticed the shoes," Nightingale said. "But she acts like she loves both Adam and Joshua. She's pretty honest that her father is not her favorite person."

"And Post is not a favorite of either of us," Garrick said. "By the way, I know I don't like him, but do you have anything—I mean solid evidence—that makes you so worried about him?"

"He's got a terrible temper when he's crossed." Nightingale paused and shook his head. "I know what you're saying, but he's at this event tonight and the governor is, too. I'm worried about her because Post is a con. I've read enough articles on him to know he'd rather lie than tell the truth. He loves money. The temper is the unknown factor. I don't know what he's capable of when he gets angry and no one stops him."

"You're not telling me everything," Garrick said.

Nightingale didn't talk immediately. "What I'm about to say is purely from my observation. The governor is in a bad spot. Her family has sort of left her without a support system, and I think she's vulnerable. She's tough but trusting, if that makes sense."

Garrick cut to the heart of the matter. "You're saying she may have made a bad choice about this guy, and we may have to deal with the consequences."

Nightingale nodded as he watched I-27N ribbon in front of the vehicle with the sun setting to their left. "Yep, we'll have to see. I wish the governor had decided to fly, but I'm sure she came by car. Mike Haywood sent me a text earlier. The governor made part of her detail stay in Austin because this should be an easy evening. This is where we turn."

Garrick slowed the vehicle while Nightingale continued.

"I got some information last night about this fundraiser.

Charles and Eva Pentecost are the hosts. They've known the governor for several years. I didn't find out specifics, but he's done well with home security companies. At any rate, they now have this spread just south of Amarillo, and they are fans of Patricia Daniels."

A mile after the turn off the interstate, a massive double gate to their right had lights and two DPS officers. "Do we have an invitation?" Garrick asked.

"No, we'll have to show our credentials, but I think I know one of these men."

The trooper did know him, and they drove through the gates up a long road, toward a sprawling house with a few white tents stationed toward the rear of the house.

As they got closer to the event, Garrick said, "Do these gatherings last long?"

"I don't know. Let's hope Post is still there," Nightingale said.

Garrick drove slowly along the winding driveway. They finally reached what looked like the front door.

Nightingale rushed inside, leaving Garrick to take care of the valet parking attendant.

Nightingale entered a broad foyer and crossed it to a large ballroom filled with people. He found Charles Pentecost and introduced himself. "I hate to break up the event, but I need to find the governor and a guest, Edgar Post. I have some news for Mr. Post, which he should hear directly, rather than over the phone."

"I can take you to the governor's room," Pentecost said. "As for Mr. Post, I'll go look for him. I think he's still here. This way to the governor."

Pentecost led him away from the crowd to a hall off the foyer and an unnoticed door. The noise of the crowd waned in this new space. The host stopped several feet back when he saw the guard, pacing in front of the door. "This is the governor's room."

Mike Haywood quickly went to Nightingale. "Boy, am I glad to see you."

Pentecost excused himself to look for Post, while Haywood lowered his voice. "A man who the governor knows came by about twenty minutes ago and insisted on seeing her. When I opened the door, he said something about New York, and she agreed to see him."

"Was it Edgar Post? And was he armed?"

Haywood looked troubled. "He said he was Post. He didn't have a weapon. The governor said—"

"The governor thinks she knows him," Nightingale said. He stepped up to the door and knocked. "I'm going in. Haywood, stay out here."

45

Nightingale touched his arm against the weapon at his side and knocked on the door.

"Governor, this is Nightingale. I need to speak with you. May I come in?"

Immediately, the door flew open. Portia stood there, silent. She and Nightingale barely glanced at each other. Across the room, seated beside the governor, sat Edgar Post. He stood.

Behind Post's hate-filled eyes, the Ranger saw disbelief and then anger, but his voice gave away nothing. "Mr. Nightingale, I'm so glad you are here. The governor is not feeling well. She's asked me to drive her to Austin. I have a car, a driver, and a bodyguard. Ms. Shoemaker has consented to come with us to the governor's mansion. We only need your blessing to calm down the young man at the door."

Nightingale didn't speak. While Post talked, Nightingale looked at the governor and Portia. The governor looked angry and embarrassed. Portia was scared. She clenched her teeth, making her jawbone prominent. She'd die before she admitted fright.

Finally, Post finished. He glared.

The governor sat up straight; her hose rustled against her suit. The best way was to say it. Nothing got better with waiting.

"Mr. Post, your son, Adam, died this afternoon."

Behind Nightingale, Portia pulled in a quick, horrified breath and let it out in a moan of grief.

Edgar Post's eyes widened briefly, then he squinted in disbelief. "That is a lie. I left him well and happy. You sir, are a shame to the Ranger badge." Veins in his temples strained, and he took a step toward Nightingale, then paused and stepped back.

The man was Adam's father; he needed to know and understand.

A deep breath, heart hammering, Nightingale said, "Mr. Post, we have had cross words, but I came to tell you that your son took a drug this afternoon, after you left. We found him in your airplane in the hangar. He was given CPR and rushed to the hospital. One of my officers called to tell us that he had died on the way. I am sorry."

Rage took command, and Post trembled. "I don't believe you. This is the most cruel lie I have ever heard, and I expect the governor will agree. You need to be fired. Fired and punished."

The governor still looked horrified, like a knife was cutting her open. The eyes he often searched for readings of her mental state showed no clues except for cloudy anger of a trapped soul. "Nightingale, this deception is not worthy of you."

Post's hand grasped the governor's elbow. His flushed face began to lose color. "I'm taking the governor back to Austin. She's not feeling well and this good citizen"—he motioned to Portia—"has consented to go with us."

Portia shyly looked at each person from half-closed eyes. When others turned to her, she dropped her glance to the floor, clearly not enjoying the attention.

Nightingale knew his information was hard to accept, and he knew Post was probably a sociopath, but he was not prepared for total denial. Governor Daniels looked like all her blood had been drained.

Post's face remained livid. He did not weep. He showed no sorrow. His eyes did not settle into an exchange of thought with anyone. He seemed to simply not care.

A chill, cold air swept into the room through the lanai door, which stood open. Nightingale didn't speak, just looked at each face. No one believed him. This was slipping out of his control.

Governor Patricia Daniels stood and rested a hand on Edgar Post's arm. "Mr. Nightingale, I can't believe I have put my trust in you, and you have trampled my trust in the ground. "Mr. Post and his driver will take me back to Austin and, if Ms. Shoemaker still agrees, she will accompany me to the governor's mansion to stay for the night. I will speak with Mike Haywood and tell him I am ordering you and him to stand down."

The governor, now fully in charge, dropped her hands to her side and stepped toward Nightingale. Her hands drew into fists. He stared at her, absorbing her fury.

"Yes, ma'am, but you know we are legally bound to stay with you. Mike may—"

"That is enough," she said. "You will follow my orders." The last sentence was so firm and loud that he had no doubt about what would be done.

Nightingale stepped aside, his mouth dry, his hands sweaty, trying to see if Post had a weapon. Of course, he didn't need one here. He probably had several in that limousine.

The governor stepped past Nightingale to Portia. "I do appreciate this," she said. Her foot caught on the rug, and she jerked forward, but Post was at her elbow, supporting her, protecting her as if it was nothing.

Nightingale had been told in words and body language to step back. He watched them to the door, still not trusting Edgar Post and very worried about the governor and Portia.

Outside the door, Mike Haywood stopped short of arguing with the governor. "Ma'am, I have been told to never let you be without a guard. It's in the statute."

"I am telling you, as I did Mr. Nightingale"—she stepped closer to Haywood, and her voice went to a low, certain threat—"your services tonight are not required. If you disobey me, you will be fired. Is that clear?"

Haywood's lips pinched together. He swallowed hard, stepped aside, and closed his eyes. He nodded but said nothing.

Nightingale walked behind the trio, but he clenched his teeth and kept his hand ready to pull his gun at anything Post did to look intimidating. His heart pounded in his ears as his mind raced to scenarios of what to do.

He quit trying to hear what Post was muttering. They walked steadily toward the door, and his stomach knotted as he watched them. His boots clicked on the hardwood, then marble, floors and finally outside. His breath quickened. What could he do to abort this catastrophe? Why did Portia insist on going? Why did the governor believe this charlatan?

As Post helped Portia into the car, Garrick walked to Nightingale's side. Charles Pentecost was with him.

"Is that the governor and Portia getting in the car with Edgar Post?" Garrick asked.

"Post thinks we're lying about his son's death, and the governor believes him," Nightingale said. He sounded disgusted and didn't care. "We've got a major situation on our hands. I don't know what he'll do when he finds out his son really is dead."

46

Garrick and Nightingale stood a few feet back and watched the limousine leave. The night air had the smell of car exhaust and outdoor cookers.

Nightingale had a quiet conversation with Haywood and told him to follow the limo, despite what the governor had told him. "Stay back, we've got to protect her. Take your partner. I guarantee you won't be fired."

Mike Haywood gave a grim, "Yes, sir," He signaled his partner, and the two men ran to the car that had delivered the governor just hours earlier.

The host, Charles Pentecost, had loosened his tie and stepped onto the porch behind Nightingale. "You've certainly spiced up a rather boring political gathering," he said. "Is our governor all right?"

"No, and I need to get in front of them." Nightingale was irritated and didn't mind sharing his frustration. People with money usually had suggestions. He was in no mood to listen. He turned to Garrick. "Reckon Bob Gilbert can get us a plane? And a sniper?"

Garrick started to speak but Charles Pentecost interjected, "Would a helicopter do?"

"I reckon," Nightingale said. "We'd need a pilot."

"You're looking at him," Pentecost said.

"Where's the copter? And excuse my asking but are you licensed?"

Pentecost smiled. "Trained in Iraq. Now I chase feral hogs and count cows. The copter is in a building in the back." He had already started in that direction. "Let's go."

Nightingale didn't know how much Pentecost had gleaned from the exchange, but he had asked no questions. It seemed to be enough for him that they were Rangers. For himself, Nightingale was embarrassed that Post had been allowed to leave with the governor. Now, he knew the meaning of worried sick—he was sick his stomach. But he was even more worried because Post showed no feeling, no emotion.

Going over the scene in his head, he thought they had made the right decision. The governor was acting weird and there was Portia, not to mention the crowd. The damage in bodies alone made a gun battle out of the question here. But further down the road... He'd be willing to bet that Post had a hidden weapon.

Pentecost continued taking off his tie as they walked through the house to the pool area. The crowd parted as they went through. When he saw his wife he said, "We're going for a little ride in Ellie. Don't wait up for me. If anybody asks, I'll be back by early morning."

They exchanged a brief kiss, and his wife turned to look at Nightingale. Her tone was relaxed as she said, "I'll have breakfast ready for y'all. Don't let him do anything heroic."

Nightingale had the feeling that nighttime jaunts were not strange for her husband.

He and Garrick followed Pentecost along a lighted path

leading to a huge metal building from which a helicopter was being pulled on a flat board on wheels.

"I wondered how they got in and out," Garrick said.

"It's a dolly," Pentecost said. "I like keeping Ellie out of the weather."

"You've named your copter?" Nightingale asked.

"Women have to be pampered. And the first step is to recognize them by name. Your life may depend on it."

A worker jumped off the small tractor that had been used to pull the copter out and away from the building. The man handed a light coat to Pentecost who swapped it for his tuxedo jacket. They exchanged a few words, and the man walked away.

Pentecost turned to Nightingale. "I need some idea of where we're going. No one is going to know we're up there, at least not for a while, so we need to be direct and as straight as possible."

Nightingale nodded. "Follow the highway to Lubbock and continue south. Do you know where Broken Rock is?"

"Yes."

"We need to head south and a little east. We're a hundred and thirty miles from Lubbock. Broken Rock is forty more miles but we're not going quite that far. The Post house is roughly thirty miles from Lubbock, between Broken Rock and Lubbock. I think Post will go there first, not to Austin, when he hears that his son truly is dead. It's not that much of a detour."

As Nightingale talked, they all boarded the copter.

Pentecost directed Garrick to sit in the middle of the three side-by-side seats at the back of the passenger area. "It's easier for me to drive with a level load."

Garrick obliged, though Nightingale thought he looked a bit unsure about the whole business.

The lights in the drive, in the house, and everywhere else surrounding them went black as the rotors overhead started whirling. Pentecost glanced out at the man who'd met them. He got a thumbs up. The craft lifted and swayed in the darkened night, and when they could see the roof of the house in miniature, the lights there came back on. Pentecost hit the accelerator and they flew into the night.

Nightingale's arm was waking and burning. He dry swallowed two of the pain meds the doctor had prescribed.

Pentecost glanced at him, "There's water in the cooler if you don't want to choke."

Garrick pulled out a bottle for him and opened one for himself. Pentecost declined.

The lights on the panel in front of Pentecost looked complicated, so Nightingale concentrated on the traffic below. Soon, they passed over several cars with lights stabbing into the night.

"One guy is speeding and passing the others," Pentecost said. "He's the car we're looking for."

"You're probably right," Nightingale said. "Can you tell which one the guard is in?"

"No. A black Suburban, but there were several of those at the house tonight."

"I want us at the Post house before he gets there," Nightingale said. "I'm betting he'll go there because he has to check on his son, even after someone else tells him."

"Is his son really dead?"

"Yes." Nightingale nodded. "He is really dead."

47

The trip from the Pentecost ranch to the Post mansion was quicker than Nightingale had expected. He kept squinting toward the ground as the helicopter swooped south. Pentecost steered the craft primarily along the highway, and Nightingale tried to recognize landmarks in the darkened flatness. Sometimes a gas station or truck stop blared gleaming brightness into a circle in the night sky, but mainly there was only darkness and the pinpricks of light from cars below.

Pentecost didn't stay around the vehicle the governor was in. Nightingale called to confirm that Haywood was still a few car lengths behind. He also filled him in on the helicopter ride they were getting and Nightingale's guess that they would be going by the Post house before going to Austin.

Small beams flickered from the acreage, as if someone had left porch lights on at the various buildings they had explored just that day. The house itself was lit up to almost glow, with huge flood lights on each corner and illumination around the eaves. Nightingale could only guess that Post had called to his daughter or the butler to find out that his son was truly dead. He had no idea how he expected Post to react to such news, but if the lights were an indication, someone expected that he'd be fit to be tied.

Pentecost circled the copter over the house and acreage and said, "Where do you want me to park this rig?"

"On the runway," Nightingale said. "You hightail it as soon as we get out."

"I won't argue, but I'll pick a field near here to park, and if you need to get out of there, just call. My wife sent my cell number to your phone. If you need help, or just want to leave, call me and I'll be there in less than five minutes."

"If anyone tries to pick us off, we may jump back in."

Pentecost gave a thumbs up and set the craft down in front of the hangar. Both Nightingale and Garrick scanned their surroundings. They jumped from the copter and instinctively ducked under the rotor blades. Crouching with their backs to the copter, they waited a second to look and listen for snipers. Nightingale had his weapon ready but saw no one.

"I don't see a soul," Garrick said. He lit out and Nightingale turned, walking backwards, covering Garrick as best he could, but no shots rang out. When Garrick yelled, "run," Nightingale obeyed and ran after the older man, through an open door and into the relative safety of the hangar.

Crouched over, still scanning his surroundings for anything that shouldn't be there, Garrick said quietly, "So, what do you think has happened to all those men he had here working?" He covered his ears as the helicopter rose like a gigantic bug and disappeared into the night.

"Maybe they were only loyal to a paycheck, not the man. Or they could be ready to ambush us up toward the house. I'll see if we can get some clues." Nightingale pulled out his phone. He called Carolyn Post's number and was surprised when she answered.

"Miss Post, this is Ranger Nightingale. Are you all right? We're here to help you, if you'll let us."

"My father called. I told him about Adam, and he didn't believe me." Her voice was raspy and low. She sounded too calm. Nightingale visualized bottles of pills available for Carolyn because, if her brother could get ketamine, pills would be no problem.

"Is anyone with you? Where are you?"

"I'm in my room. Reeves is still here. He really liked Adam. He's very sad."

"Don't do anything. I'm coming to the house. I'll be there soon. Tell Reeves to open the door, okay?"

Nightingale pocketed the phone. "I think we can make it to the house. Let's try to stay out of sight as best we can."

"Maybe we can hit some breaker boxes," Garrick said.

"Maybe. But I don't want to take a lot of time. Post will be here soon."

"Okay," Garrick said. "We still better be careful of an ambush."

"You're right. I'm walking evidence." They cut the lights in the hanger and waited. Nightingale pushed open the door.

Both men stood listening for a minute. There was nothing, not even the sound of night critters. "I'll cover you from here to the horse barn, but I think those men we saw are gone."

"I like that idea," Garrick said, "but I'm not so sold that I'll walk out there with no gun."

"I agree," Nightingale said. "It could be a Trojan horse."

Garrick slipped out of the door and ran in a zig-zag pattern to the horse barn. He swung one of the doors open, turned, and motioned to Nightingale, who repeated Garrick's run.

Inside the barn where Nightingale had found the drone, they breathed hard. "I don't know who stinks worse," Garrick said, "you or those horses. What do you want to do now?" They stood at the back of the horse barn, weapons at the ready.

"I feel like I'm standing in the middle of a room with no clothes on," Nightingale said. "The animals are frightened, and I tend to worry about their senses of what's happening."

"I agree," Garrick said. "What's next?"

Nightingale wanted to look again upstairs, but the thought of the girl downing a handful of pills spurred him on.

Standing outside of the barn, the two men conferred again. From the barn to the hangar, the lights in the buildings were off. In the opposite direction, it was simply porch lights that glowed.

The next building was the garage. After the two men ran to it with no shots fired, Garrick told Nightingale, "I'll catch a few of these lights. You go on. I think they've all left."

Nightingale nodded and broke into a jog toward the mansion. Every building seemed empty. He continued to try to hide, but when no shot was fired, he looked closer, saw no movement. He felt like a fool. The workers were all gone.

At the door to the house, he knocked, then stood back. He heard rapid footsteps, stood back, and pushed open the door. Reeves, who'd been running down the hall, pulled up short, directly in front of Nightingale's weapon.

Reeves's eyes got big. He swung his hands up and said, "Don't shoot. I thought you might be Mr. Post."

"Where did everybody go?" Nightingale asked, lowering his gun.

"I don't know, sir," Reeves said. His words echoed against the marble-tiled floor and high ceiling. "They took off like rats on a sinking ship."

Garrick came in the still-open door. Nightingale went to him and lowered his voice. "Call Haywood and see if he still has the governor's car in sight and how far away they are. Then call Gilbert; where's our back up?"

Addressing Reeves again, he said, "Why did they go? Did they have orders to leave?"

Reeves shrugged. "I saw some trucks leaving, and they all had more than one man in them. Most of the workers saw the dead boy. A death is never good, and a youth is even worse. Even our kitchen help left. And Mr. Post is not the best boss..." His voice trailed off, his eyes on something behind Nightingale. "Carolyn?"

Nightingale followed Reeves glance to the top of the stairs, where the girl stood. She clutched a stuffed animal, a puppy, and came down the steps slowly, almost feeling her way like she was disoriented. She seemed to have regressed to her childhood, but Nightingale had a hard time deciding what to believe. When she had come to his house, she seemed to have a plan to get her father punished. She had seemed very mature, too.

Behind him, Garrick rushed in and pulled him aside to whisper, "Gilbert's inside the gate. They're out of sight. Post in ten minutes. Rangers will stay back so the governor won't get hurt, but they may rush him at some point. They've got a sniper."

His eyes never leaving Carolyn, Nightingale signaled that he understood and started walking to her. He got to her side as she reached the last step, but she was looking straight ahead, not at him, so he moved over to catch her eyes. When he felt she was truly seeing him, he asked, "Does your father have a gun? Has he called again?"

"A gun? Probably, but I haven't seen one. He called and said he'd be here soon," she said. She seemed to be in a daze. Drugged or in shock. She held the toy close, as if it gave her comfort. "I don't know what to do. Poor Adam. I think Father will want me dead next."

"Carolyn, you don't believe that. You're too smart, and I don't believe you." Nightingale took her by the shoulders. She had looked away again, so he turned her to face him and noted the dilated pupils of her eyes. "What have you taken?"

She jerked away from him, her face suddenly contorting with fury. Her strength surprised him. "I needed help," she said between gritted teeth. "My brother and I needed help, and you"—she bent over as if it hurt to try to find the words—"you didn't do a thing. You let my poor brother go like a lamb to the slaughter."

Nightingale stepped closer, but she let out a growl like an animal and slapped at him. "Get away from me."

They were still in the broad foyer and hall, with its stark black and white marble tiles. Garrick had pushed the heavy door shut.

Outside the windows, Nightingale saw Post's long black limousine pull up and stop. No one would shoot or attack until the governor was located. Nightingale turned back to the girl. "Go with Reeves and Garrick into the library until your father gets here."

She waved away the hand he offered her. "No. You've got to protect me."

There was no time for any action. The front door caromed open. Carolyn Post literally shrank, bending slightly and wrapping her arms around her body as she stepped behind Nightingale.

48

Portia stepped into the limousine, holding her arm across the knot in her gut. She was scared, as her weak legs would testify. No sound, soft velvet seats. Room for legs, even much longer ones than hers. A bar with champagne in an ice bucket. Outside was just dusky, but inside this noiseless machine, low lights hovered at strategic places. And the seats. Post bent slightly and went to one side, next to the door. That left her close to the other door, with the governor in the middle.

Before they reached the end of the drive, Portia knew what that knot in her gut was about. She had made a mistake. She felt like she was out of her body. Icy coldness crept up her back, making her hands tremble. Surely these were not her trembling hands. She fought a primitive need to run. After all, where would one run to in a limo?

He offered them bottled water and opened the bottle for the governor. Then he picked up a phone and began talking.

She wanted to whisper to the governor, "Don't drink that," but what could be wrong? It was sealed with a cap. But the governor drank as if she needed the water.

Somewhere, to the side, Post said into the telephone, "You are wrong. He can't be dead."

In the subdued light of the car, the governor's eyes went to the man and quickly to Portia. A few minutes ago she was so sure, but now Patricia Daniels looked frightened, her glance darting from the side window to the screen between her and the driver.

His voice grew louder, more agitated. "No, I refuse it. He is not dead. You have bought into this lie. They are all lying to get me." He slammed the phone down, angry but not sad.

"Carolyn says he is dead, and Reeves said so, too. We've got to go to my house before Austin to find out what has happened. Someone has the boy. I'll find him."

He poured three glasses of champagne. "We need a toast to my new job. Now, Patricia, I hope you know I don't need this position. It's just something I want, and as we discussed earlier, people do talk when they hear rumors."

The governor didn't speak immediately. She didn't seem interested in the conversation. She watched the champagne as if counting bubbles and set the glass carefully on the console. "Edgar, I am sorry if your son is dead, but you are not getting the job you wanted."

Post sat back in the deep seat and pulled slightly away from her in order to look at her. "What about the rumors? Do you not want a second term in office?"

Governor Daniels smiled and yawned. "Portia, this man is threatening to tell lies about me. He's"—her head drooped, and she seemed to fight to stay awake—He's going to say I went to bed with him. As if anyone cares. Edgar, my dear, most of the voters care only about the economy. They don't care if I'm bedding down with man, woman, or beast." Then she giggled, which was when Portia knew she'd been drugged. "Well, they might care about the beast part, but nothing else."

She had only drunk bottled water. Portia set her water bottle to the side.

Edgar Post did not seem to pay attention. He picked up the phone again, and this time he called the Lubbock hospital. He tried kindness; he tried begging for sympathy; he tried threatening. He said that he was a friend of the governor. His language became coarser, but nothing worked. His voice was so loud, the governor covered her ears with her hands.

Somehow the lights inside had gotten brighter, and in that light, Portia saw disdain for Edgar Post on the governor's face. The governor's voice became Southern syrup as she said, "Mr. Post, I feel sorry for you. Your son is dead, and you have so little power the doctor won't tell you about the poor child. And you have so few friends, you won't believe anyone—not even the man who told you the truth."

"Don't you say that."

He reached over and grabbed the governor's hand and squeezed it until she cried out, "Stop, stop." Tears ran down her cheek.

He flung her hand and shoved her. She fell against Portia and then struggled to right her body as she scooted away from him.

"They are all lying," Post said. "My boy is fine." He glowered at both of them and loosened his tie and collar. Sweat beaded on his forehead, and the smell of fear, acidic but mixed with burned cooking oil, came in small puffs as the car kept the air moving for the passengers' comfort.

She assumed the car continued down the highway. Maybe this was what a spaceship felt like. The ride was so smooth, but what about the end of the ride? The governor's head rested on Portia's shoulder. Her eyes were closed. Portia said nothing and kept her hands in her lap. She didn't look at him directly, afraid to meet his eyes. Her terror grew about what this man would do. He drank champagne and wiped sweat from his forehead.

Portia's knees trembled. Her pants, the ones she loved so much for the beautifully textured gray wool fabric, visibly jiggled because of her fright.

She reached toward the door handle, and Post said in that teasing, pushy voice, "The doors are locked, Shoemaker. You can't get out." He smiled, and his white teeth shone in the low lights. He laughed.

How could he be so cruel at such a time? Portia shrunk inside of herself. She wanted to get away, and there was no escape. Why had she agreed to be here?

Post slapped the governor's leg to wake her and pointed at Portia. "You said something earlier that made me wonder if she knows the Ranger. Does she?"

"She's a schoolteacher." Her words were too long, too syrupy. What was wrong with her? He had given her an unopened bottle of water. Nothing could have been in it, but the woman sounded odd, her words rounded and drowsy. Somehow, she'd been drugged.

Portia listened but didn't look at Post. She watched his actions, still not looking directly at him. She would have to do something when they arrived at the Post house. He opened another bottle of champagne while she tried to come to some conclusions.

Oswald had not lied. The man's son was dead. When he finally accepted that, he would do something, possibly kill the governor or her, or both of them, because he was not rational. She had not seen a gun, and without one the governor and she could overcome him—except right now the governor couldn't overcome a teddy bear.

Post picked up the phone again. He put it back down and knocked on the window behind the driver. When a space opened, he told the driver to stop. "I'm going to be on the phone." He looked from one woman to the other and frowned. "Don't try to escape."

The long car pulled to the side of the road. Post got out and got into the front seat by the driver. Portia couldn't hear the words, but she guessed he was on the phone. The governor seemed to watch through a fog, and the door locks flipped on and off too quickly for Portia to jump out. Besides, she thought, where would she go? Where would she hide in this flat land? How would she escape? When his door closed, Portia heard the thuds of the automatic locks on the doors. They rode for a few minutes.

She whispered to the governor, "Are you all right?"

Governor Daniels nodded.

Portia took the water bottle away from her and gave her a new bottle after she had discreetly poured the other bottle onto the carpeted floor.

"Sleepy," the governor said.

"Okay, but we are in a hell of a mess. Try to wake up." Portia couldn't stop her eyes from gazing at the screen that hid the driver and Post. She hoped the men couldn't hear her.

The governor opened her eyes briefly, only to immediately close them.

Portia's mind kept going in circles around the same subjects. This must be what happens to prisoners. They lose time. She heard nothing from the driver and Edgar Post. Then the car stopped quickly, almost throwing her onto the floor. Post reentered the back seat, shoved the governor to gain some space, and they sped away. Now, however, Post was different. He had his rage barely in check. His breath was ragged and loud. He sat with his arms crossed.

She had no idea of how long he had been in the front of the car, but she sensed that they were moving faster. The governor still leaned against her, asleep. Portia stared at the window, trying to imagine how to escape.

Suddenly, Post slammed a fist into the console beside him. "Why didn't you tell me that you were Adam's teacher, and that you knew Nightingale?"

She lurched backward at the noise, waited a moment, and swallowed. "I didn't think you would believe me." To her own ears she sounded timid. She cleared her throat, trying to put courage into her voice. "I only had him for four lessons. He was sweet." She felt the smile as she thought of Adam. Such a bright child. "He admired you."

"Don't. Say. Was." Post pounded his fist with each word. "He is still alive." He pulled at the collar of his shirt and breathed deep. "He's fine. How do you know Nightingale? The driver saw him at your house."

There it was. She drew in a long breath, looked straight at her executioner and decided. "He is my cousin."

At her right hand, Portia still had her purse and the Ruger.

The car had slowed, and over an intercom she heard, "We have arrived."

Portia pulled out the gun and pointed it at him. The governor moved, possibly waking up. "Governor, stay back," Portia said.

Post smiled and shoved the limp woman towards Portia, and when Portia tried to get out of the way, he grabbed the Ruger and pulled it away from her.

When she felt his hand over hers on the gun, she squeezed the trigger, but nothing happened.

He yanked Portia's arm, and she released the weapon. Then he squeezed her hand so tight she cried.

"Stop, stop," she said. She cursed her lack of practice with the gun as tears of pain ran down her face. "I'll go." Pain seared into her shoulder and hand. She'd do anything to stop it.

"Yes, you will," Post said. The driver opened the door, and

Post pulled her past the governor and out of the car. He barely waited for her to stand. He pulled her close and whispered, "I will kill you if you don't behave."

He had her arm twisted behind her, and he pushed her a few feet, but she could hardly walk. Post was furious. He quickly grabbed her other arm and pulled her along as he almost ran toward the house.

Portia tried to stay on her feet as he yanked her across the brick walkway.

He moved faster than she thought possible and pulled her to the front door, which he kicked open. Everything blurred. Inside the house, Post pushed the door shut, swung her in front of him, and tightly circled her neck with one arm while holding the gun at her head.

"Where is my son?" he yelled. The words echoed against the marble floor and tall ceiling, but no one answered.

Portia saw Nightingale and Garrick and a man and woman she didn't know as Post pushed and pulled her into a space in which his back was to a wall. She froze. Her teeth chattered. She couldn't stand, but she had to. Her feet scrambled and finally found purchase. Her hands and fingers held onto Edgar Post's arm around her neck, and she tried to breathe as she felt a tiny trickle of pee run down her leg. She could control nothing.

49

Edgar Post flung Portia around like a rag doll in front of him. His arm wrapped around her throat, and she became a shield.

He stared at Nightingale and slowly moved the gun in his hand up and down the side of Portia's neck to her temple. "Where is my son?" Post asked.

Portia's eyes were closed, tears tracked down her face, and she struggled to breathe.

Nightingale was paralyzed. His weapon was pointed at Post, but he couldn't use it. He couldn't hear much, and everyone was moving slowly. Garrick stood beside him with Reeves. Nightingale sensed the girl behind him. He glanced at the window, wanting to see Gilbert or other Rangers, but no one appeared. Hopefully that meant the Rangers were out of sight because there was still no sign of the governor. Otherwise, lawmen would have jumped Post the moment he stepped out of the car. He took a breath and thought about hostages.

"Mr. Ranger," Post said, "Why am I not surprised at your presence? Where is my son?"

His voice broke, and Nightingale heard a quick intake of breath.

"Dad, what…" Carolyn Post had moved out from behind Nightingale and stood barefooted, the stuffed dog on the floor. She had come to her senses or decided to quit acting; Nightingale couldn't tell which.

"Where is Adam?" Post repeated.

She took a step toward Post, but Nightingale stuck out one arm to stop her. "Mr. Post, we found your son this afternoon. I told you earlier, he was dead."

Nightingale wondered if Post was processing what he was being told. All he could do was to keep talking and hope to get through to him. He stared at Portia. Their eyes locked and her tears slowed. "Adam took an overdose of ketamine. Paramedics came to help him. I'm sorry. Please let this woman go. You're choking her."

"I found out this woman is your cousin," Post said in a singsong voice. "I figure an eye for an eye. Right, Mr. Ranger? You pushed my son, and he was scared of you and your dog."

Portia strangled back a sob.

Nightingale could see only fright in her eyes. He nodded to her, hoping that she would see it was a promise only for her.

"I didn't know your son, but I'm sure he was smart and loved you," Nightingale said. He talked slowly, trying to remember hostage training. What should he say? What should he not say? "Adam found out that he had a brother. Isn't that right?"

Post shook his head, raising his voice as if talking to someone who did not understand. "No, no. He did not have a brother."

"He had a half-brother." Nightingale kept his voice normal. Around him, at the top of the stairs, a rustle of movement, a glint of light, maybe a sharpshooter, but Post seemed oblivious.

Nightingale kept talking. "Joshua Tallman was really Joshua

Post, your son who ran away several years ago. He came here to work on this house, and he told you who he was, but you didn't want him around, or didn't believe him, or were frightened of him. Which was it?"

Post's eyes glazed; he looked away as he seemed to remember the scene with his older son. His grip around Portia's neck loosened.

Her eyes stayed on Nightingale, and tears ran down her cheeks.

He still hadn't decided what to do to get her loose. Again, he barely nodded.

"He said he needed a little money, and he'd stay out of my way and away from the family," Post said.

"Did you give him money?"

"No. He made his choice years ago when he left. I told him to get lost." Post's face blazed with anger. "I didn't know who he really was. So he had hair the color of mine? So what?" He flung his arm that held the gun upward but still kept a hold on Portia.

"Is that why you killed him? Because he wanted money?" Nightingale couldn't help asking. And was immediately sorry.

Post reacted like he'd been hit by lightning. He jerked Portia tighter, pushing the gun back against her head. She winced and coughed.

"I would *never*. Hurt. My. Child," Post said, the arm around her throat squeezing more tightly with each word. Portia's mouth flew open, and she began to gasp for air.

"She can't breathe," Nightingale said.

Post loosened his hold. Nightingale tasted desperation because he saw hope in Post's reaction.

But he'd pushed too hard. He looked around, saw the butler standing as if in shock, but Garrick was gone. When had he left? Gilbert's men were nowhere to be seen, either.

Suddenly, on his left, Carolyn Post took a step toward her

father. "Daddy, are you okay? It's all right if you hurt Joshua. I know he hurt you." Her voice was trembling, though her tone was conciliatory.

A look of confusion momentarily replaced the anger on Post's face, but he said nothing and loosened the arm encircling Portia. He barely glanced at the girl and then returned his gaze to Nightingale, his face tightening again.

"Where is Governor Daniels?" Nightingale asked. He worried about the answer and was trying to think of some way to get out of confrontation mode. A light flickered in the window at the top of the stairs. Trying hard to not glance at the window, he repeated the question to Post.

"She's in the car. Tell me about my son."

The plea in his voice seemed so genuine that Nightingale started talking, keeping his voice as normal as he could, telling what happened when he and Garrick went looking for the boy. "When we got to him, we thought we could help him, but I think he took pills and inhaled the drug. We called medics and started CPR but got no response."

Nightingale stopped talking and swallowed. He would never forget how small and innocent the boy looked, how he needed a father. The gun was against Portia's neck, but he continued. "I'm guessing Adam took the pills before he went to the hangar."

"Did he have dope with him?" Post asked.

"He had powder on a napkin he had squeezed in his hand. The powder was on his face and in his nose. He had a note."

"Do you have the note? Give it to me!" Post was back to yelling, swinging Portia around in a head lock as she tried to keep her feet on the floor to avoid choking. Portia had both hands on Post's arm despite the gun barrel pressing against her temple.

Nightingale pulled out a plastic evidence bag. He held it up so Post could see the paper in it. "Let the woman go."

"No," Post said. "Not now, not ever. That was my child, and you let him die. She's gonna die, too."

"Wait, wait," Nightingale said. Diversion, maybe that would work. "You can shoot me instead."

"Don't shoot. I'm getting my gun." He pulled the weapon from his back holster and slowly raised his hands, letting his gun dangle from one finger. "You like to make deals, I've been told. I will put my gun on the ground and come with you, but I need to know: how did you get the drone to inject Joshua with ketamine while he was on the roof? We can't figure it out."

Would appealing to Post's ego coax the man to explain the drone mechanism? It just might buy him enough time to get Portia out of his grasp.

Post squinted and shook his head, obviously confused. He was not particularly handsome, and his emotions twisted his face into ugliness.

Nightingale said nothing else, letting his words hang in the air.

"You are an idiot, Mr. Nightingale," Post said. "I've killed no one on any roof. My son played with drones, but they were toys."

The mockery in Post's voice made Nightingale think. Maybe he was wrong.

Beside him, Carolyn Post took a step backward.

"My son, my son," Post continued. "He was so smart, and he wanted to be like me. You knew he was smart, didn't you, old lady Nightingale?"

"She would agree, if you'd loosen your hold a little," Nightingale said. "Portia thought Adam was really smart. He memorized passages of Shakespeare and several poems without her asking. Did she tell you that?"

Post loosened his arm around her throat and said, "What did my boy say to you? Did he ever talk about me?"

The weapon drooped in his hand. Instead of answering, Portia slid her mouth onto Post's wrist and bit down hard.

Post screamed in pain. He pulled the trigger, and the gun dropped, sliding across the floor.

Portia stood for a few seconds, closed her eyes, and smiled.

The front door burst open, and Bob Gilbert shouted, "Post, drop the gun."

Nightingale ran toward Portia. He caught her as she crumpled and laid her on the floor. She was shot and blood ran onto the floor from a wound in her leg.

Garrick reached Post and with Gilbert pulled Post's hands behind him. Nightingale was vaguely aware of his words. "Call my lawyer."

Garrick raised his voice to Nightingale. "The governor was in the car. She's drugged but okay."

Nightingale cradled his cousin's head, trying to gauge the blood flow from her injury. A major blood supply ran through the leg. Portia could die from blood loss even from a small gunshot. "I've got to stop the bleeding," he said, laying her head gently on the floor and moving around to her feet. He ripped the bottom of her pant leg open.

"Don't, Oz," was all Portia managed before she passed out.

His hands were slippery with blood, and he couldn't find the wound. Someone, Reeves, pushed in beside him and ripped the pants higher. Nightingale found the pressure point in her thigh. He pushed his palm hard against her thigh. Blood still oozed, but not so much.

Garrick handed Reeves a strip of cloth to make a tourniquet and, finally, the blood slowed more.

Reeves worked with competence that made Nightingale say, "Thanks. Where'd you learn that?"

"Iraq."

The door opened again, and medics barreled through,

maneuvering a gurney over to where Portia lay. One of them bent to relieve Nightingale's hold on the tourniquet, and he moved aside so they could take over. Suddenly, Portia looked small and helpless.

Nightingale held her hand, and she opened her eyes.

"Thank you," she said.

50

Nightingale became aware of officers handcuffing Post, who continued his belligerence and promised to fire everyone. "I am friends with the governor, and you will regret this treatment of me. Is this the way you treat people new to the state?" As much as possible, everyone ignored him.

The medics exchanged information with Nightingale, and Portia was put into the ambulance. Carolyn had disappeared.

Nightingale's thoughts kept circling back to Carolyn, even as he looked at his cousin in the ambulance. Portia already had IVs attached, and her facial color had partially returned. He should feel uplifted at finding a killer, but he didn't think they had found the real killer Post's answer and his reaction about the drone question bothered Nightingale. He was left with sick apprehension. He would not leave Portia alone, so he stood at the ambulance and waved at Garrick.

Standing outside the open doors, he said, "You need to find that girl. Tell Gilbert. This is not over. I think she helped the boy kill Joshua. And what did you say about the governor?"

The EMT checking on Portia interrupted, "Sir, we need to go."

Garrick pointed toward two people heading slowly toward another ambulance before he hurried away to find Carolyn. It was Governor Daniels, leaning heavily on Mike Haywood's arm. She still looked pale, but happier than when he had last seen her.

Nightingale looked at the EMT and raised his eyebrows in question. He got a nod. "Thirty seconds."

Nightingale stepped out of the ambulance and went to her. "Governor, are you all right? I'm sorry."

"Mr. Nightingale, go with your cousin. I'll see you at the hospital."

Haywood nodded. "We'll follow. She needs a doctor, too."

BACK IN THE AMBULANCE, NIGHTINGALE LOOKED AT HIS cousin's pale face, regretting every mean thought and cross word he'd had with her. More than that, he regretted that he'd rebelled against her and Imogene, when all they were doing was trying to be his family. He touched the gurney that his cousin lay on and went over a mental list of regrets.

He'd resisted most of their invitations until he lost his job. He'd helped with money sometimes, but his time and his physical presence, those things that knit a family together, had been rare.

He tried to focus on how he would be a better cousin, but his thoughts kept going back to Carolyn Post. And there, in the ambulance, he was angry at his lack of resolve, but knowing that Portia would be okay made him feel relief. A murderer was still loose. And unless he was totally off base, the choices were Edgar Post, who seemed to know what a drone was but nothing else, and Carolyn, who must have known more than he ever suspected.

Nightingale stared at Portia and found his thoughts going into craters and gullies to answer the unsolved questions that still haunted him. He didn't think very highly of himself. He was a

Ranger and always would be. Probably he and Portia would forever be at odds about their roles as cousins. He would continue to try, and when Portia woke up, he would tell her how he admired her grit. But he was a lawman, first and always. It was his nature, and he might as well quit fighting his nature.

With that conclusion, answers began to fall into place. Carolyn Post had to be found.

The doctors whisked Portia away as soon as they got her inside the hospital, assuring Nightingale that she would be looked after. He went to Patricia Daniels's room while his cousin was in surgery. A trooper stood guard, and Nightingale had to show his ID before he could enter the room. The governor was on the phone.

She finished the call and put the phone aside before she looked at Nightingale. "I owe you an apology," she said.

Nightingale was not prepared for that. "Why? I'm the one who let you get in harm's way. That should not have happened. I can't tell you how sorry I am."

"I gave you an order. I was pigheaded, and I misjudged how low-down mean that man was, or is. He put something in my drink in the car, and after he knew his son was dead, he started railing on your cousin. He had caught my reference to her kinship in the conversation. I passed out, but part of what I heard still makes me shiver." She flicked one hand, showing her disdain. "He threatened to say we'd had sex. He will tell all sorts of lies. He threatened Portia and me in the car. Apparently, there is a larger story of which I am unaware."

"It's too long to tell you tonight, but we worried that he was capable of murder. You've got two guards on the door, one from your detail and one from the local sheriff's office. They won't let anyone in who shouldn't come in, and that means no news people. You heading back to Austin tomorrow?"

She nodded and closed her eyes.

Outside the door, Mike Haywood waited.

"Mike, she's going to be okay, but I don't feel good about this yet. I may see you tomorrow. Don't let anyone near the governor."

He hurried back to the waiting room, looking for something or someone familiar. His phone rang as Garrick walked in.

"Oswald, is Portia okay?" It was Imogene.

He handed the phone to Garrick and dropped into the nearest chair. Garrick walked outside.

A doctor walked up, and after making sure he had the right person, began talking to Nightingale.

"Your cousin's going to be fine," the doctor said. "She may have some initial issues with walking, but she was very lucky that someone knew how to stop the blood flow. I'll tell her that tomorrow. She'll need to stay here a couple of days, maybe more. You are her family?"

Garrick walked back in time to hear the last few sentences.

"Yes. Can I see her?" Nightingale asked.

"She won't be awake, but you can sit with her if you want."

"Will she know I'm there?" Nightingale wanted to stay with Portia, but he could not escape the urgency in his chest that said the girl needed to be found.

"Maybe. It's up to you." The doctor patted his shoulder and walked out.

Nightingale turned to Garrick. "Did you find the girl?"

"No," Garrick said. "None of the Rangers there saw her leave, but one of the men outside of the fence saw the taillights of a vehicle. We're guessing she parked outside the gate, farther down the road. I called Reeves. He said she has one of those little Mercedes sports cars but doesn't drive it much.

"I talked with Gilbert and got a bulletin out for a baby blue Mercedes. By the way, Imogene will be here any minute. She's leaving Bandit at their house. I'll go pick him up." Garrick looked at his watch. "She left about thirty minutes ago. Called from her car. She said she figured you had work to do, and she wanted to be with Portia."

"She's an angel, but I think I should stay with Portia." His stomach was knotted around the need to find the Post woman and the need to stay and be a decent family member to Portia. He couldn't help looking toward the hospital doors, hoping that his partner would leave and take his observations with him.

Garrick drew in a long breath and exhaled. "Look, everyone appreciates you trying, finally, to be a good member of the family, but Portia is safe now, and the governor is safe. Portia is asleep, and Imogene can call us the minute she gets here. Hell, we can stop and say hey when we pass each other, but you said we need to look for that girl."

Nightingale was saved by Imogene walking into the hospital. She headed toward him and gave him a full-on hug. Nightingale didn't expect the affection, but the embrace shored up his resolve. Imogene turned from him and gave Garrick a quick kiss.

She said, "I'm going to Portia now. Go by and get Bandit before you do anything else. The poor thing knows something is wrong. He needs to see you."

Nightingale didn't need more prodding. "Let's go," he said. "We need to talk."

"Sure," Garrick said. They headed to the truck, and Garrick drove since Nightingale's shoulder was stiffening up.

"I've had some new thoughts that I need your opinion about," Nightingale said. "If you agree with me, we'll call Gilbert."

Garrick glanced at him and nodded. "This is about Carolyn Post?"

"Yes. She's at the top of my list of likely killers of Joshua Post." He waited a bit, organizing his thoughts. "The weak part of my argument is motive. I don't know why she would kill her brother. However, I think she helped Adam rig up the hypodermic on the drone. Then she encouraged him to use it on Josh. Adam didn't know that Josh was his half-brother. I don't know how he found it out, but it crushed him. That may be the reason he took such risks with the drugs he used."

"You think he may have regretted killing Josh? Or are you looking to make excuses for the boy?" Garrick asked.

Nightingale heard the harsh appraisal of the boy and knew Garrick was right to question him. "I think the kid was desperate for a hero figure. When he was with his father, he felt he couldn't measure up to what the man said. But the girl has been a part of his world since he was a baby. That day that they served us coffee and tea, you could see that he followed her every direction."

"So, we're back to the girl. Do we go out and prowl around looking for her?"

"No. You know our odds are worse than any lottery that we'd find her tonight. But I need to call Gilbert and tell him how very dangerous she is. She may go back to her father's place. Probably need to call Reeves, too."

Nightingale called Reeves and told him to be aware that Carolyn could be dangerous. Then he called Bob Gilbert.

"Post is already out on bail," Gilbert said. "His lawyer, his money, whatever it was, he's out. I don't know where he went. The judge kept his passport and told him to stay in the state."

"After we get Bandit, you drive to your house. I'm sure I can get home from there. No offense, but we both need our own space tonight," Nightingale said.

"Anything else about the girl that you haven't told me?" Garrick asked.

"It's not just her. I can't put my finger on it, but the look on Post's face when I mentioned the drone was confused. I don't think he could operate one if his life depended on it."

"She has a temper," Garrick said. "I thought she was gonna lay into you before Post got there."

"She was on drugs of some sort, and she's like a chameleon. She changes her mood and her story to fit whatever situation she wants to go with at the moment. After I saw the drone and the hypodermic in Adam's work area, I thought that might have been the way Joshua got injected. That would also account for the reflection or shine that I saw right before I found his body. It was probably the reflection off of the drone."

Garrick picked up on Nightingale's train of thought. "That would fall in line with what I was thinking about Adam. He wasn't conniving enough to plan the method of Bandit's poisoning or Josh's death. The girl, now, that's different. She's got the smarts to figure this all out, *and* that little brother would have done whatever she told him."

At Portia and Imogene's house, Nightingale and Garrick found Bandit on Imogene's bed.

"Poor puppy." Nightingale rubbed and patted the shivering dog. "You get scared so easy. We won't leave you again for a while." They all got back in the truck with Bandit sitting between them.

"We both look like death eating a cookie," Garrick said. "I'm not cut out for these all-nighters anymore." He backed the truck out while continuing to talk. "What are you going to do with the girl if you find her? You have no evidence."

"We need the prints off of the drone in Adam's room," Nightingale said, "but I think Carolyn is responsible for the ketamine that caused Joshua's fall. The ribbon shoelace you found in the alley looks like it belonged in the tennis shoes that she had on when she came by my house. The bad thing about red shoes is they're memorable. I think you're right, Garrick: she and Adam worked together to lob the kerosene into the newspaper at Broken Rock and then to poison Bandit."

"Why? You still don't have a motive. Probably even less than with her daddy." Garrick pulled the truck into his driveway and got out so that Nightingale could get into the driver's seat.

"Are you sure you're okay to drive?" Garrick asked.

"Quit being so mother hen-ish. It's unbecoming. Gilbert has guys out looking for Carolyn and her car. We can't do anything else tonight. I'm going home to try and get some sleep. Talk in the morning."

As Garrick went into his house, Nightingale drove on into the darkness, heading slowly toward his house as his arm throbbed, wondering why he couldn't tie the pieces of this case together. He didn't like seeing Carolyn as the killer. But she was the one who fit. He remembered her eyes when she yelled at him earlier, before Portia was shot. He'd never seen pupils dilated so big. And she behaved as he had never seen in any other time he had talked with her, but maybe she was a great actress. He drove some backroads to get home, making the drive a little shorter than usual. He was glad to see the shape and shadows of his house as he neared it. He turned in the drive, feeling relief at being home.

He stopped the truck in his driveway and sat scratching Bandit's ears for a minute. When he looked at the overall time and actions of the last few days, the women were always what he couldn't figure out. Not Portia, not Carolyn Post, or Josephine Holly. What he wouldn't give for a plain old gunfight like cowboys used to have.

He felt a smile creep up on him because of his own foolishness. The night had gotten cooler, promising frost by the morning. The dog was a comfort.

He sat for some time, looking at the house, before unwinding his tall frame and putting his feet out of the truck. Bandit thudded onto the ground and headed for a shrub that seemed to interest him. Nightingale saw a light in the house, and as he peered around one side, a splinter of brightness came from between the kitchen curtains. Then he remembered that Garrick had cooked breakfast and probably left the light on over the stove.

He called to Bandit, and they went to the front porch where he opened the unlocked door. The stale smell of old breakfast mixed with a woman's perfume. The perfume was the same one he had just noticed at the Post mansion. Fatigue fell away.

He pointed at Bandit to sit and stay. His heart thudded against his ribs. He pulled his gun from the holster at his back and walked softly to the kitchen.

Carolyn Post was sitting at the table, her head resting on her hands, looking like she was asleep. Slowly, she raised her head off her hands. It occurred to Nightingale that she had her father's flair for the dramatic, only in her father it came off as bluster and egotism. In her, it was innocence bordering on animal attraction.

She had make-up on, dark and smudged around her eyes, making her look sleepy but twenty-five years older than the person she had pretended to be at her father's house.

Slowly, she stretched her hands above her head, acting like this was an everyday nap that she was waking from. She wore a t-shirt and no bra, and the shirt slid up as she stretched. "I had to leave."

Nightingale had lowered his weapon so that it hung by his side. But he did not trust her. She had used a slightly different personality each time she talked to him, each time finding out more about what he believed, what he would do as a Ranger, whether or not he could be persuaded as a human who would help someone in need, or if he was a man who might be bought. Apparently, she had still not settled on an answer because she began to talk after he remained silent.

Her arms came down slowly, tenderly touching her face, and finally she placed her hands on the table again. She had become serious but seemed uneasy. One finger found a spot of bacon grease that she rubbed in tiny circles on the oilcloth in front of her.

"Did my father confess?" She looked up at Nightingale, much like a snake would consider its prey before biting. "You know, he gave Joshua drugs to make him go away." Her eyes, still dilated too much, glistened with tears. She swiped at her cheek and smeared what was left of the eye liner. "I loved my brothers—both of them. Poor Adam." She put her hands to her face again, letting her tears fall. Taking a shuddering, long breath, she stood and grabbed a paper towel to wipe her nose and the grease off of her polished nails.

Nightingale flinched when she stood, and the weapon moved slightly but remained at his side.

Several things came to his mind as he listened. He still didn't like her as a villain. She was too young and had too much promise in her life to kill someone. But experience made him wary. "Why are you here?"

She sat back down and clasped her hands on the table in front of her. "I guess because being around you made me feel safe," she said.

She might have a gun hidden. A black leather purse lay on the table with the opening toward her. The bag had small gold letters at the top and looked like it was propped open, ready for some offering to fall out into her hands. His intuition told him to be careful. Her irises were still large, but they were flat and dull. Her hands had no tremor of fear. She was dangerous, although he had no evidence, only this crazy feeling. But the tell was that perfect left eyebrow that rose in sarcasm even as her words sounded sincere.

"How did you get in?" he asked.

"The door was unlocked." She smiled and grinned like she enjoyed teasing him. He wondered if he was more paranoid than usual because of the worry for Bandit. The dog couldn't be seen. He had stayed in the living room like Nightingale had told him, for the moment obeying the command. Nightingale didn't know how Carolyn would react when she saw the dog.

"I'm sorry I'm here," she said. She had a disgusted curl to her lips. "I came because I trust you. I guess that bothers you." She pulled the purse closer and laid her hands on the table as if to stand and then dropped back to her seat. "I should not have come. It was just so lonesome at the house before you came. Then all hell broke loose, and the lady got shot. I thought I kept hearing Adam. And I was scared to be alone with my father. I knew he would get out and come back. He is out, isn't he? Anyone with that much money always gets away."

"You're okay here, for the moment. Maybe your brother's death was an accident. They found a red ribbon behind the newspaper. Was that out of your tennis shoes?"

"I thought those red shoes might be a problem." She looked at him, her lips screwed up as if she'd tasted something sour. "Adam just had to get to your dog, so I went along but I stayed back, away from the dog. He flew the drone for me, but I pulled the trigger. He didn't know who Joshua was until later."

Nightingale heard what she was saying but was having a hard time believing her.

Slowly, but in a fluid motion, the girl stuck her hand in the purse and stood. She held a pistol-type syringe pointed at Nightingale. "This is what was on the drone. Adam was scared of needles, so I had to figure out how to make it work, but once I did, Adam pulled the trigger with a remote control. We had the vet back home order some for our horses. Compared to a bullet, the drug is slow, and that's a drawback. But a bullet is so crude. I knew it was risky, and I think a judge will understand that this is all I could find to protect myself."

Nightingale's arm twitched but she was quicker.

"No, no, don't move another inch. I don't mind shooting," she said. "But you, Mr. Nightingale, are not the type to shoot young women, even though they are armed. I can always say you attacked me, and this is all I had to defend myself with."

"I guess I'm slow about several things," Nightingale said. "Were you the rider I saw the day Joshua fell? I saw someone on a horse, but I couldn't tell who it was. And, why did Joshua have to die? I thought you loved him."

Carolyn's face twisted. The eyebrow raised. "I hated Joshua because he left me. My mother left first and then Joshua. He promised to come for me, and he didn't. He abandoned me. I was alone. And, yes, I watched from a distance on horseback. I saw you and your entourage. I couldn't ride up and check with all you people around." She moved a little way back from the table; she clearly wanted to pace as she spoke, but the kitchen was too small. "We had a blood pact. My father didn't care about me. He was busy making money and chasing beautiful women."

The heating unit kicked on and Nightingale thought he heard Bandit's paws on the hardwood floor. There might have been the soft thud of a car door closing. But Carolyn seemed unaware of any of that. She went on, "And you want to know the funny thing? Adam's mother is not beautiful, but he married her because she had fine blood lines, like a horse."

Carolyn suddenly ceased speaking, as the sound of the front door opening reached them. Garrick's voice came then: "Oz, why aren't you answering your phone?"

Garrick strode inside and stood at the kitchen door, Bandit at his side. Immediately, a low, menacing rumble, like a brewing thunderstorm came from the dog's throat.

Carolyn's eyes widened, shining with determination as she turned the syringe toward the dog.

Nightingale yelled, "Bandit, no."

The dog froze.

Nightingale pulled the trigger.

Blood splattered from the girl's arm. She screamed as the shot propelled her arm up and her entire body against the wall. The syringe flew into the door frame near Garrick's head.

Bandit started toward her, and Nightingale grabbed his collar, talking to him and Garrick in one breath. "Garrick, take Bandit. Both of you out."

Carolyn Post braced against the wall, cursing and crying all at once. Nightingale waited for Garrick to get Bandit in the other room and for her to quit yelling.

"Oh, oh, my God, this hurts so bad," she said. She had her back against the wall, literally. "My father will come down on you so hard, you'll wish you were dead."

"If you want my help, now would be a good time to be truthful. And quiet," he said.

"I'm dying," she screamed.

Nightingale shrugged. "Fine." He sat down at the kitchen table, keeping the Sig pointed at her. "You have the right to remain—"

"Wait a minute," she said. Blood ran through the fingers of her left hand where she held the wound. She looked gray. Her voice had lost some of the force as she slid down the wall. Nightingale thought she might pass out, but he didn't move.

"Call a doctor. I'm not feeling..." When her butt touched the floor, she toppled over.

Nightingale pulled out his phone and called the hospital to get an ambulance on the way.

Garrick stood in the doorway with Bandit on a leash.

"Good job," Nightingale said. "We need to stop the bleeding. Get me some clean dish cloths or towels."

"Belschner called me when he couldn't get you," Garrick said. "Her prints were all over the drone. Did she kill Joshua?"

"She just told me she helped Adam," Nightingale said. "Why did you come back?"

Garrick handed clean towels to Nightingale. "Because you didn't answer the phone, and I remembered why Post made me think of the past. He's like a modern version of my father, only worse. Never cared about anybody except himself."

"It's sad. He'll probably go free or have a short sentence. That girl had everything."

"Everything except love and guidance," Garrick said.

51

A few days after Nightingale last saw Carolyn Post he received a phone call from Portia. "We would like for you to come over for supper if you have the time. We've asked Sutton to be here also."

They settled on a time and about twenty minutes later Garrick called him. Garrick sounded worried. "Did Portia call you?"

Nightingale recounted the conversation and Garrick invited himself to stop by Nightingale's house so they could drive together to supper.

Garrick said he'd be at Nightingale's house at six. He arrived at five.

"You have any coffee?" He didn't wait for an answer. Touching the cold coffee urn, Garrick poured coffee and water into the coffee maker and began to pace.

"Garrick, what's bothering you?" Nightingale asked. "I'm feeling relaxed for the first time in two weeks. Maybe you're having too much caffeine."

Garrick stood beside the coffee maker and slid a cup in to get some early brew. "I think I need some advice. These are your cousins, so I need help."

Nightingale called Bandit inside. He got a cup out for himself and joined Garrick at the kitchen table.

"It's like this," Garrick said, "I went over and talked to Imogene the day before Portia got home from the hospital. You know, I'm crazy about Imogene and I told her I wanted us to spend some serious time together."

Nightingale stood and poured his coffee. "What's the problem?"

"She said she felt the same way, but we don't know what Portia thinks," Garrick said. "She's your cousin, what do you think that she thinks?"

Nightingale tried to keep a straight face. It sounded like the joke about "who's on third". He sipped his coffee.

"Let's just slowdown. Their new house will be done in a few months, and before that you'll have time to introduce Stanley Stockbridge to Portia. I'm not a matchmaker but that might help your cause."

Garrick's frown relaxed. He sighed and placed his arms on the table. "That's the answer I need. I didn't know Stanley might be available." He drew in another deep breath.

"I don't know if he is or isn't. But when the newspaper sale closes, he'll be at loose ends. Never hurt to ask and suggest."

Nightingale got up and fed Bandit.

"Since we're talking about answers," Garrick said. "I've still got a question about this last case. Did you ever find out who shot you that night?"

"No. I'm trying to forget it," Nightingale said. "I guess Carolyn hired somebody. We'll never know because now that she has a lawyer, she's not saying anything. Whatever she said here at the house that night is all we have."

"Too bad," Garrick said. He stood, again full of energy. "You about ready to go?"

"We'll be early, so I've got a question," Nightingale said. "Are you going to ask Imogene to marry you?"

Garrick looked seriously at Nightingale before he spoke. "I'm going to follow some of the advice I've been giving you, and if she'll have me, I'm gonna marry her. I love her and I told her so. I'll even tell Portia."

ACKNOWLEDGMENTS

This is my second book but I'm no less thrilled at seeing a story I've written come to fruition as a novel than I was the first time. My hope is that my readers, too, will get caught up in the fictive dream (thank you, John Gardner) and enjoy the story as if they were part of it.

Of course, many people helped me during the writing. The grandchildren and my brother who asked, "You getting any writing done?" or "How's the book going?" were encouraging. They actually cared. I was thrilled.

This book was a real pain—so I am grateful to Patsy Shepherd, my editor, for whipping it into shape. Thanks to Tosh McIntosh for superb help with the cover and doing the magic that makes a manuscript into a book. Also, thanks to Lolly Walter for proofreading precision.

Beyond that I had friends who have been beta readers and cheerleaders: Julia, Nancy, Linda, Lisa, Vonnie, and Leanna. They do more than read, they offer friendship to a really needy author.

Finally, to Maxx, thanks for being the inspiration for Bandit.

And to my girls, thanks for just being in my world.

ABOUT THE AUTHOR

Sharon Scarborough has been a mother, a teacher, a rural mail carrier, and media director for the Texas Senate. Her work has appeared in *18 Almanac*, *The Washington Star*, *The Nashville Banner*, *Paris Post-Intelligencer*, and *Country Music Magazine*. She lived and worked in Austin, Texas, for twenty-three years before returning to her native Kentucky, where she now lives.

Connect with the Author Online

Blog: sharonmscarborough.com
Facebook: Sharon Scarborough Author

Made in the USA
Coppell, TX
27 November 2019